Deadly Sins

Yanking the wheel hard around, Palmer aimed at the driver's door of the Mercedes and managed to butt-ram it into the face and arm of the other gunman. The sound was a chaotic mix, part monstrous twanging crash of many cymbals, part vicious stutter of Uzi bullets arching skyward into the starry night, triggered by an unconscious man. It choked off his scream. Finally.

Then came chilling silence. The stars glared down, passionless, unconcerned. Silence, a chill river thick with forming ice, trickled through Palmer's kiiler soul. They hadn't waited? They'd struck tonight? Then suffer, you bastards.

'You know what you just did?' Curtis asked, his voice shaking slightly with shock. 'You have put your name at the top of their hit list.'

Also by Leslie Waller
*available from Mandarin Paperbacks

Fiction

Three Day Pass
Show Me the Way
The Bed She Made
Phoenix Island
The Banker*
The 'K' Assignment
Will the Real Toulouse-Lautrec Please Stand Up?
Overdrive
The Family*
New Sound
A Change in the Wind
The American
Number One
The Coast of Fear
The Swiss Account
Trocadero
The Brave and the Free
Blood and Dreams
Gameplan
Embassy
Amazing Faith
Mafia Wars*

Non-Fiction

The Swiss Bank Connection
The Mob: The Story of Organized Crime
Dog Day Afternoon
Hide in Plain Sight

Deadly Sins

Leslie Waller

Mandarin

The characters, organisations and situations in this book
are entirely imaginary and bear no relation to any person,
organisation or actual happening.

A Mandarin Paperback

DEADLY SINS

First published in Great Britain 1992
by William Heinemann Ltd
This edition published 1993
by Mandarin Paperbacks
an imprint of Reed Consumer Books Ltd
Michelin House, 81 Fulham Road, London SW3 6RB
and Auckland, Melbourne, Singapore and Toronto

Reprinted 1993, 1995

Copyright © Leslie Waller 1992
The author has asserted his moral rights

'I've Been to a Marvellous Party' copyright © 1938
by the Estate of Noel Coward. 'I'll See You Again'
copyright © 1929 by the Estate of Noel Coward.
By permission of Michael Imison Playwrights Ltd,
28 Almeida Street, London N1 1TD

A CIP catalogue record for this title
is available from the British Library

ISBN 0 7493 0696 3

Printed and bound in Great Britain
by HarperCollins Manufacturing, Glasgow

For Ruth Elson Waller
In memoriam

The European Community should ask Italy for a
guarantee against the expansion of organized crime
into the single European market after 1993.

Nando della Chiesa,
son of General della Chiesa,
murdered by the mafia in Palermo

Prologue June 1992

Basel is the secret capital of the Earth. But that wasn't why Palmer felt uneasy.

It had taken him a bit more than an hour to get there from his home near Lugano. The night sky of June was choked with stars, as if camouflaging the grave, global importance of Basel, pretending under the innocent stars to be a rustic little college town.

Pretence was everywhere, even in Palmer's drive here, masquerading as an ordinary, commonplace motor trip. Perhaps he could blame his uneasiness on that. It was about to become, dangerously, much more.

Now he headed northwest from the sleeping city along a curiously erect finger of Swiss territory, shielded by high cyclone fencing, that rudely intrudes into France to touch the airport at Mulhouse. At this hour, under cover of darkness, his was the only auto in sight.

The night drive up from Lugano had tired him. He had kept careful watch for signs of being followed, but found none. Later, after tomorrow's work, everything would change. He found himself wondering why, at his age, he was still putting himself through this, still choosing to invite disaster into his life.

Curtis' plane from Paris would not arrive until midnight. As Palmer parked the tiny white Peugeot

205 GTI 1.9 near the airport bus, he reflected that once one became as senior as he was, well past retirement age, it should be the younger man, Curtis, who met him, not the other way around.

A man old enough to be a grandfather, Palmer thought, should no longer involve himself in a challenge that needed strong backup from younger associates. Damn it, Curtis wasn't even an associate, just a friend you could count on.

Palmer left his suitcase in the trunk but took the small attaché case Eleanora had packed 'to defeat boredom' into the terminal. For the last twenty years, since his divorce from Edith, Palmer had depended on Eleanora for everything that required the ability to anticipate trouble. She thought of him as her lover. To Palmer she was much more than that.

To take security precautions for his drive tonight she had stolen time from her translation bureau to call chauffeur-drive firms in Lugano and send up a false smokescreen. The reclusive Mr Palmer was travelling to Basel tomorrow afternoon to address the annual meeting of American bankers. The false signal hid the fact that he'd left tonight, alone, in Eleanora's car, reasonably sure no one was following him. But tomorrow, after he exploded his accusation before the annual bankers' seminar, he was a targeted quarry.

As he sat down in the empty terminal lounge Palmer glanced at the arrival/departures board and saw that Curtis' plane had been delayed another five minutes which, in airportese, meant half an hour.

Inside the case Eleanora had packed a diary/scrapbook and two clippings, one from the *New York Times* review of a memoir by a former one-star general, puffed up by a half-century of self-delusion into the man who had won the Second World War.

Palmer had been a major in Intelligence, heading the T-Force in Sicily that rescued top mafiosi from Mussolini's firing squad to set up Allied civilian governments. According to the book review, Lieutenant General Ed Kutz (Ret.) had won the very gunfights Palmer still reproached himself for, sacrificing American GIs to put the mafia back on its feet, a deal between the US and Lucky Luciano.

'See?' Eleanora had scribbled in the margin of the clipping. 'Sweet are the uses of a diary, even a faked one.' Her idea was that he should begin keeping one, if only to make a liar out of people like Ed Kutz.

The other clipping came from yesterday's pink *Financial Times* of London. As he read it, Palmer realised why he felt so uneasy. Letting them print this advance story had been a mistake. One must never let the enemy know one's plans.

PALMER TO ALERT BANKERS TO 1992 EURO-PROBLEMS

Basel, June 11, 1992. The twenty-first annual meeting of America's leading international bankers opens here tomorrow with former head of United Bank and Trust Com-

3

pany, stormy petrel Woods Palmer Jr, out
of retirement to highlight the dark side of
the European Community's unshackling
this year of financial frontiers.

Palmer will be remembered for standing
off an entire major mafia family in the
1970s when Manhattan dons made a bid to
infiltrate UBCO's gigantic . . .

This time Eleanora's scribbled message made him
grin: 'Stormy? Is this a misprint for snoozy?' No, he
thought, dopey was more like it. The first rule of
intelligence work was never to forecast one's itinerary accurately.

Old age was turning him stupid. He paid less
attention to things, especially Eleanora. She was
more than twenty years his junior and without her
he was finished. He grimaced at the way he had put
the thought. It didn't sound like love, did it? More
like self-interest. He glared down at the tips of his
black leather shoes. Is that what happens to love,
finally; it dwindles to convenience? God, how
passionate they'd been at first, like young honey-
mooners. It had lasted that way for years, never
dying but always diminishing.

Age had shifted all his priorities sideways. Retired
from banking, he still tried to keep his profession in
some sense clean, in some sense responsible. It was a
losing battle. And, in losing it, he was losing
Eleanora.

He could hear the faint approach of an aircraft.

There was literally no one else to be seen in the airport of the disguised capital of the planet. But that had always been Basel's basic camouflage: a rustic college town, indifferent to any mode of travel faster than a bicycle.

Never mind that the world got its tranquilizers and mood-enhancing drugs from Basler giants like Hoffman, Ciba-Geigy and Sandoz. Or that most of the secrecy protection of Switzerland was housed here. Or that nations settled their outstanding accounts in Basel's Bank for International Settlements.

One of the city's more formidable secrets – the Basel Accord of 1987 – had tried hard to stem world banking's suicide by greed. Palmer grimaced at the memory. The G-10 nations, the ten largest and sickest economies, had met secretly here to upgrade reserves before lurching into more lending.

Five years on, such desperate medicine had improved some patients, who now managed to hold 8 per cent of capital as reserve. But to do so they had all but sworn off lending. Oh, not mortgages or inventory factoring, but for them typical medium-to-high-risk lending was now like sugar to diabetics. In other words, Palmer thought, the Basel medicine was killing off all its patients.

Suddenly, from where the napping had been deep and good, a red-faced young guard in uniform began brushing his blond hair sideways to neaten it. He kept glancing at Palmer, as if apologising for such unseemly behaviour.

Palmer spotted Curtis before the younger man saw

him. He had worked for Palmer decades ago as a trouble-shooter for UBCO. Although Palmer had two grown sons and a daughter, he often thought of Curtis as his ideological son, the one with the shifty, brilliant mind, the courage of a demented lion and the experience that twenty years of chasing crooks had given him.

Curtis looked flustered. His sandy hair had gotten rumpled and he was busy doing exactly the same thing the customs guard had just done, trying to neaten himself. He looked apologetic, sleepy, but game. 'Lead on,' he called, a faint tinge of midwest American sarcasm in his voice.

Palmer was suddenly aware that men of Curtis' age might think of him as a father/authority surrogate, just as he thought of Curtis as a son. God knew, Palmer reflected as they left the terminal, his own sons couldn't be called on in an emergency.

Safely back home in the States, the oldest, Woody, with his gallumping size, was a high-earning attorney in Chicago, married to a brainy brunette Congresswoman. No grandchildren expected there. Tom, his youngest, slaved in advertising and was married to a freshman dancer at the New York City Ballet. No grandchild there, either. Only Gerri, Palmer's middle child, just thirty and working in television, remained single despite a long history of blighted love affairs.

So he was left with Curtis, intense, driven, resourceful but really only humouring him, as tonight. Following Palmer to the little white Peugeot he looked compact, half a head shorter, someone you had the curious idea was a tumbler or an acrobat in some secret life where that lithe, coiled body undertook great risks against the laws of gravity.

'This is her car,' he wisecracked, 'the woman I love, but where is she for whom I have made this idiotic trip?'

'Back in Lugano. She sends her undying love right back at you.' Palmer's voice had gone grumpy. 'Why idiotic? Don't you think I'll be targeted?'

'Why should the mafia care what you tell the bankers?'

Palmer put the overpowered car in gear and rocketed out of the terminal like a pellet from a blowgun to prove to Curtis he was wrong.

'In a few years it won't matter who knows. But what I reveal tomorrow is damaging to them *right now*, while they put all their pieces in place. By the end of '93 it'll all be over. All major lending will have to go to mafia fronts. Ask my old pal at the Vatican.'

'Archbishop Radziwill? He's your pal?'

'Enemy, pal, what matters is he's figured out the score lightyears ahead of the rest. Any financial institution that didn't sign the Basel Accord of 1987 picks up all the loot. If you could keep me from opening my mouth, wouldn't you?'

Glancing sideways, he caught Curtis in the act of suppressing a grin. 'I guess so,' the younger man said in a soothing tone. 'You know these goombars better'n I do. It just seems crazy to risk a takeout. Why wouldn't they set up their banker-patsies to stiff you? Why resort to capital punishment?'

'The best enemy is a dead enemy.'

Curtis' response was a nasal sound somewhere between a snort and a grunt, signifying less than total agreement. 'In that case you shouldn't've given that story to the *Financial Times*.'

'Mistake. I know it,' Palmer agreed. 'Just wasn't thinking.'

In pained silence the car roared along the road between high fencing. The other air passengers had taken the waiting bus. Palmer had the road and the fat stars overhead to himself. He opened the Peugeot to 160 kilometres, just under a hundred miles an hour, and the tough little car spurted forward.

He must be quite decrepit, Palmer thought, if all he inspired in younger men was disbelief and a compulsion to smooth down their cowlicks. Curtis had always been bright. Why this superior, suppressed smile, quite like Eleanora sometimes gave him, which translated as 'let-the-old-coot-think-he's-right'. Tomorrow, when he'd alert his esteemed colleagues that within a year they would all have become errand boys for, or victims of, the mafia, the old coot would truly need all the help Curtis could give him.

Further down the road Palmer's beams spotlighted a Vespa-like motorbike put-putting along. Reluctantly he let his speed drop, no sense passing at such a velocity that the backwash toppled the cyclist. Fifty yards ahead now, the motorbike swerved wildly. The driver spilled out like a rag doll slung across the pavement and on to the shoulder. Palmer hit the brakes.

In his rear mirror, he saw the oncoming high beams of another car. He could have sworn there had been no car behind him even a few seconds ago. Like the artistic spill, this event was choreographed.

'He's hurt,' Curtis said. 'Let me – '

Palmer grabbed his arm. 'Sit tight.'

The Peugeot crawled ahead warily, like a small stalking cat. In the grassy shoulder of the road the driver raised his head. His helmet, shiny black, encased his head and face with a knight's questing armour, the carapace of some deadly insect. In two hands, Palmer saw, he held the thirteen-round .9 Browning automatic NATO issued its troops, who sold them to the underworld for drugs.

His first shot went wide. The spill had unsettled his aim. Behind him the oncoming car squealed into a sideslip pass. It loomed as a black Mercedes braking hard into a rear-end twist, curling about-face. A man opened the driver's door and crouched behind it, aiming a longer gun at the Peugeot, something dripping knobs like an Uzi.

His first shot put a small hole in the Peugeot's windshield slightly above Palmer's head. His second would be on the money.

Palmer downshifted into second and tramped on the gas pedal. The tiny white car moaned and shuddered. It leapt forward so fast that it knocked the motorbike driver aside like a fly, one that had gorged on blood and was now spattering the road with it.

Yanking the wheel hard around, Palmer aimed at the driver's door of the Mercedes and managed to butt-ram it into the face and arm of the other gunman. The sound was a chaotic mix, part monstrous twanging crash of many cymbals, part vicious stutter of Uzi bullets arching skyward into the starry night, triggered by an unconscious man. It choked off his scream. Finally.

Then came chilling silence. The stars glared down, passionless, unconcerned. Silence, a chill river thick with forming ice, trickled through Palmer's killer soul. They hadn't waited? They'd struck tonight? Then suffer, you bastards.

'You know what you just did?' Curtis asked, his voice shaking slightly with shock. 'You have put your name at the top of their hit list.'

Palmer twisted the steering wheel again. Kicked the accelerator pedal. All the murderous impacts had been taken by the broad front bumper of the Peugeot, but so neatly. The lethal little car roared off daintily toward Basel and a quick scrubdown. Nothing, really, blood and bone-scrapes. And blood.

'What difference,' Palmer asked, trying not to show he was badly out of breath, 'targeted tonight or tomorrow night?'

'You elderly retirees are feisty old devils.'

Palmer's voice went low, as if choked with blood, his breathing still violent. 'Let the bastards know who they've tangled with.'

'They know,' Curtis mused aloud. 'Oh, God, yes, they know.'

Part One

August 1993

Chapter One

Around Rome sprawl rolling hills, patches of green threaded with broad high-speed national arteries and narrow two-lane country roads. The pace is rural except for bi-sex highway prostitutes soliciting trade. They, but more accurately their customers, sound the only hurried note.

The long, pewter-grey limousine proceeded at a majestic pace, nosing east along the ancient Roman road called the Via Prenestina toward one of the surrounding hill towns, Palestrina, where dry white Colli Romani wine is made.

These days it is better known as the village where the powerful Archbishop Radziwill has his villa. Since Villa Palestra was closed for the summer -- it had no air conditioning as yet -- the villagers rarely saw His Excellency. But a town must be famous for something. There had once been a Renaissance composer who bore the *da Palestrina* tag. While this does not make a suitable modern patron, Archbishop Radziwill certainly did, since he controlled an impressive part of the Vatican's earnings. Although not a lira of it was spent in Palestrina, fame is fame. Palestrinese walked proud.

Precisely at noon the limousine, a stretch Daimler, arrived at the entrance of Villa Palestra. The driver got out and scowled at the locked gates. His glare bit hard; the foreigners he was driving required macho displays of truculence.

Inside the limo, shielded by taupe-toned windows, sat three tall, elegant men. If one had called Central Casting for gangster types, these would be the first rejects. They conferred in muted tones, one in a soothing upper-class British murmur, the others in what they took to be Harvard accents but were the irremediably Boston-Irish nasals of the Kennedy family.

Suddenly a small helicopter jounced down inside the villa's grounds, spewing dry August dust. The pilot unlocked the gates for the Daimler. A slim man in a black leather jacket and large-lensed sunglasses got out of the helicopter. To his pilot he said: 'Divertiti per un mezz'ora.' His serious forehead slightly furrowed as he produced a rather chill smile. 'Gentlemen, follow me.'

He strode off toward the villa, over crisp gravel, until out of earshot of either helicopter or limo. Although it was hard to know his face behind such large sunglasses, one could see he was a handsome priest in his fifties, and so used to command that he didn't look back once to make sure he was followed.

The two New Englanders turned to the Brit. 'Brad,' one wheezed, a voice compounded of heavy smoking and late hours, 'you confirm his ID? He's Radziwill? In those monster shades he could be my own dear dead Zio Luigi.'

'It's our chap,' the other responded in British English. 'Mr God.'

'Follow me, he orders. As if we're stooges?'

'Well, there are three of us.'

They laughed, not sounds of amusement as much as the release of nervous energy. Starting off along the gravel path, their footsteps made sharp, menacing sounds, an advancing wedge of warrior lookouts moving with wary grace. One muttered: 'Coming here all the way from Providence I expect great things, Brad. So far it's a let-down.'

A bank of clouds obscured the August sun at that point and the temperature around them dropped alarmingly. 'You know how it is, cousin,' the British Brad explained, 'today we take orders, tomorrow we give them.'

The men from Providence chuckled gravely, again a tension-releasing sound almost devoid of laughter. 'This ineffable gent controls that much volume?' one New Englander wheezed.

'More,' Brad assured him. 'He has mega plans.'

'Cousin,' the other American muttered, 'if Brad checks it out, it's good enough for us. Otherwise we chainsaw his scrotum. And the Archbishop's, too.' This time there was a note of real humour in their laughter.

They joined the handsome man in the oversized sunglasses and, abruptly, the noon chill froze them into a statuary group. 'Eccelenza,' the Brit intoned mournfully, 'how greatly we appreciate this moment of your valuable time.'

'Eccelenza,' another said in the same sepulchral

plainsong, 'your fame grows everywhere, even in little backwoods Providence.'

'Eccelenza,' the other agreed, lost for specific words.

The huge eyeglasses regarded them. They stood like choirboys, which they had perhaps been in their youth. 'Oh, Men of Providence,' the archbishop said in a kidding tone. 'You are in on something truly . . . Providential.' He produced another sardonic smile.

'Sir, we are at your disposal,' Brad vowed. 'Pan-Eurasian Credit Trust basks in your sunshine.' He glanced nervously at the darkened sky.

'One black cloud is all defeat requires,' the man in the sunglasses reminded them. 'And there is one brooding over this enterprise: It's my old friend, Woods Palmer, the only banker who can still think.'

One American turned to the other. 'Basel? Eighteen months ago?' He turned back to the good-looking man and his reverent tone changed to that of one man conversing with his equal. 'Eccelenza, we have heard you. Your wish . . .?'

'I have wished for nothing.' Abruptly, the sun shone again. 'Leave your British colleague here with me. You gentlemen . . .' He produced that mingy live-or-die-I-care-not smile, '. . . can with my blessings return to Providence.'

An awkward moment. Did one ask for such a personage's hand to kiss? Did one back away as if leaving royalty? Did one bitch loudly at being fluffed off? Both Americans strode down the gravel toward their limo in the renewed heat.

'Cousin,' one muttered, shooting his cuff to adjust

a small gold-and-diamond link. 'Did you ever rip the balls off a priest?'

'Not yet.'

'Who does this hotshot nunfucker think he is? Our only source of supply?'

'His loans are always Class A profitmakers. And the old dons like dealing direct with Mother Church.'

'Forget the old dons. We stopped running a home for the elderly long ago. What does this Radziwill bastard represent, say 12 per cent of our outstanding? What gives him the balls to treat us like we had bad breath? Without our cash, even his most brilliant scam won't work. All those mega plans? Without cash, just ambitions, nothing more.'

'And such men are dangerous,' the other quoted.

'Brainy I give you. But nasty-brainy.' His colleague grunted as they got back in the limousine. 'Back to the hotel, Enzo.'

'I was really up for this,' he keened. 'An intelligent mind? A lunch? You notice he didn't even shake hands?' He grumbled wordlessly for a while. Then: 'A beautiful Rome day, a terrific business connection, and he makes me sorry we ever heard of him. I don't envy Brad, working him close up. Mega misery.'

'In our line of work,' his colleague responded, 'not all of it wins Nobel prizes, OK? But that doesn't mean we don't get treated with respect, *especially* by some candy-arsed archbishop we're netting millions for.' He paused and sighed unhappily. 'Did you hear him order us to update the Palmer takeout? Like *he* controls *us*? We have to reverse that, fast.'

For the first time a real smile lit up his colleague's face. 'Cousin, your memory's gone Alzheiming.' He reached his slim arm forward into the driver's compartment and picked up the Nikon N4004S camera.

'Ten shots,' the driver reported. 'All at 400 telephoto closeup.'

Broad satisfaction decorated both men's faces. 'Hey, Enzo, was I smiling?'

Palmer, in jogging clothes, ran steadily down the hill, a yard behind the small white Peugeot 205. His driver, Ziggy, kept the car moving slowly as they snaked downward toward the Lake of Lugano. Ahead lay a full hairpin right.

A thirty-feet cypress toppled forward. Its tight shape, like a dagger blade, moved more quickly as it began to smash into the back of the small white car. Ziggy gunned the motor. The cypress came crashing down on the asphalt road an inch behind the car and perhaps two feet in front of Palmer. He sprawled foward and broke his fall by banging his face into the tight-meshed, bruising needles. Their sharp scent choked his nostrils.

Ziggy braked and came running to him, automatic pistol swerving this way and that. 'We're alone,' Palmer told him. He spat out some needles and got to his feet. He smeared his hand across his face. His fingers came away dripping blood from a nosebleed.

Ziggy eyed the base of the tree, fully a foot across. It had been completely sawn through, quite neatly.

As he and Palmer examined it, splashes of dark blood spotted it as if, indeed, a killing had taken place.

When it began, Curtis had no idea it would be his responsibility. He was happy to have Palmer off his hands, behind his security barriers at his home near Lugano. The old tiger took poorly to living behind bars, but kept his claws sharp. Meanwhile, Curtis went about UBCO's business. Usually this meant chasing embezzlers and defaulting borrowers, sometimes equally dull business frauds. In the space of a year or two, excused from playing bodyguard to Palmer, he could enjoy a lot of old-fashioned brain-straining sleuthing with a minimum of auto chases and shootouts. But sometimes even the routine turned fascinating.

Issa Krykova, all on her own, defected from Czechoslovakia with exquisite bad timing in 1990, having chosen the week before the Velvet Revolution toppled the old regime. UBCO had nothing to do with it. Five-feet-two in her sneakers, Issa went a long way towards proving, as Goolagong once had, that in women's tennis, small could still be victorious. That was how she met UBCO executive VP T. Haven Phelps of the Philadelphia Phelpses in a pro-am mixed doubles for charity. She was twenty, the age of Haven's own daughters. Invited back in late 1993 to Czechoslovakia, Issa asked Haven along. But it was his own idea to bring a quarter of a million of UBCO cash with him. He estimated it would keep the two of them in style through the divorce.

Curtis got to Prague the next day, when the Charles Bridge stood hooded in conical white bishop's mitres of snow. The long, downdropping Wenceslaus Square, an oblong anvil of history on which the Czechs had forged their freedom once more, was littered with swept piles of the white stuff.

Curtis, who had a reputation for being in the right place at the right time, had crashed a reception in Hradcany Castle on the heights above town. The playwright-prime minister was welcoming celebrities like Issa. It seemed possible that T. Haven Phelps might be among the throng. A few moments of wrist-twisting might get him to cough up the quarter of a million. It often did in these cases. A man doesn't spend his entire adult life as a banker without getting the proper reverence for ownership of cold cash.

Curtis stood next to a slight, weedy young man with a high forehead, thick black curls and English good enough to encourage practice. '. . . I with great pleasure,' he translated, 'to welcome you.' He stopped himself with a yawn.

'Me too,' Curtis responded. 'Are you the local interpreter?'

'Czech I am not even,' the young man explained. 'I am of the guests. My native land adjoins this one, as do so many here in Central Europe.'

Curtis eyed him sideways. 'You're, um . . .?'

'Here my premier sends me for a loan. Here, where money is even more — you say hen's teeth? — scarce than my own land?'

Curtis produced a sympathetic chuckle. 'Any luck?'

'Psckraf!'

'I beg your pardon?'

'What is *he* doing here?'

A chunky young man edged sideways from a doorway. Curtis turned toward his interpreter-acquaintance. The young man had magically vanished. If he was as good at conjuring loans he was indeed worth knowing. None of the hangers-on resembled T. Haven Phelps. So much for being in the right place at the right time.

Palmer woke up from a dream, eased off the bed so as not to disturb Eleanora and made his way downstairs. In the dismal darkness he checked the perimeter proximity sensors. Two dozen sat outside on high poles or trees.

They were showing a pre-red alert. Palmer sat down at a microwave intruder-simulation transmitter which queried each sensor in turn. Boring, depressing, menace always was.

This kind of pressure had been maintained ever since the Basel shootout, the knowledge that they would come to him one more time and finish the job. Speaking of Adolf Eichman, someone had commented on the banality of evil. It applied to menace as well. Worse, there was no relief. The falling cypress was one of a dozen attempts. But they didn't need to be real to be disturbing. Tonight some tiny animal, a vole, a squirrel, had been sensor-spotted.

By checking the entire perimeter he would reset each sensor . . . for the next vole to waken him.

The price of blowing the whistle on organised crime, Palmer mused. It was not a new thought but it still made him angry. He had elected self-imprisonment. Biting back a curse he finished the long, careful security check. He started to rise but some heavy weight bore down on him, making it impossible to move or breathe or think.

Prague at night is a moody still life of low-voltage electric bulbs and vast walls needing bright paint. With Budapest, it was once the architectural showcase of the Austro-Hungarian empire. As he took a cab down the hill back to town, Curtis saw it could once again look elegant if it had money.

Imagine a neighbouring nation putting the touch on Czechoslovakia when the Czechs barely had a dime to their name. 'Driver! Where do people go at night?'

He found himself let off, freezing, at Number 11 on a cobblestoned street. A dark doorway suddenly opened and a great miasmic fart of human and cigarette smoke, intensely spiced by the bitter tang of hops, sloughed out on to the icy street. Curtis sniffed sharply and entered a joint called U Flekù.

Sweating, a fat waiter hefted a large tray of filled steins. He paused before Curtis long enough to let him grab a beer, half creamy head, half a broth as dark as Guinness stout. Then he pushed on past a huge wall clock and framed caricatures.

Three beers later, in accord with W C Fields' edict that no one owns beer, it must be returned, Curtis stepped up to a long zinc trough in the men's room. Its only other visitor was the weedy young man with the black curls. 'Get that loan yet?' Curtis inquired.

The young man's eyes lit up with recognition. 'First I must make here down payment deposit,' he explained. 'Then – ' His voice choked off.

A beefy arm encircled his neck like a hawser. The snout-like muzzle of a gun sniffed the ammoniacal air. Curtis recognised the chunky young man from the premier's reception party. 'Hey, you!' he shouted.

'Keep out of it, Yank!'

The two men, in forced lockstep, started past Curtis. The muzzle of the gun deflected sideways to indicate who would be shot if there was any interference. The tough one seemed able to control the weedy one's every movement. It made the matter no less grave that all three men's penises dramatised the grappling like those of ancient Greek wrestlers.

Curtis let fly a short, nasty kick that sent the automatic pistol clattering into the urine trough. 'Want to dive for it, fatso?' The chunky young man's grip tightened on the other man's neck and lifted his choking body up off the floor. 'Out of it, Yank!'

Curtis kicked him hard on his left kneecap. As the leg buckled, Curtis aimed a spade-like bunching of the fingers of his right hand like a javelin at the muscular man's throat or temple or ear or eye or anywhere weakly protected. It burrowed hard into the left eye. The chunky man screamed and lashed out with a click-lock blade at Curtis' gut. The knife flashed like a passing meteor.

Things were moving too quickly. The wiry young man was no help, too nice, too brainy. Curtis twisted sideways to take the stab cut on his hip. The slight young interpreter chopped down on the chunky man's wrist. He had shoved his knee up under the arm to heighten the impact, an evil little trick Curtis had once read about. There was a snap, as of wood breaking.

'It's time to leave,' the nice young man observed sadly. It was hard to imagine him knowing such a deadly chop. He stared down at the head in the trough. 'He will come to very quickly, this one.'

Outside, Curtis and his rescuer took a breath. 'You have saved me, sir. I am in your debt.'

'No,' Curtis corrected him, 'it's you who saved me. He was ready to slice a goodly chunk off my brisket, crown jewels and all.' He turned and stared up the street. 'Which way is St Wenceslaus?'

But the nice young man was gone, conjured off into the dark, twisting streets of the ancient city. Prague seemed made for disappearances and he seemed to have a map of it tattooed in his brain.

As Curtis turned toward where he imagined the city centre might be, the gaping hellmouth of U Flekù breathed hot sweat and hops on to the street as Issa and T. Haven Phelps emerged.

'Mr Phelps,' Curtis said, finally in the right place at the right time, 'you don't know me, but – '

Phelps looked dejected. 'Your fly's open, Curtis.'

24

Chapter Two

Spring on the Morcote hills above the Lake of Lugano made for ideal walking weather. Palmer and Curtis had wasted sunshine by examining proximity sensors. 'You sure know how to entertain guests,' Curtis murmured.

Palmer had the good grace to look guilty. 'I'm obsessed,' he admitted. 'Sometimes I walk out here at three or four a.m. with a flashlight. Does that sound paranoid to you?'

'Sound? It *is* paranoid.'

Palmer produced a sigh of aggravation. 'To hell with it. Tennis?'

'There is something so . . . so *hunky* about his thighs,' Gerri moaned. 'I want them locked around my skull.'

Eleanora burst out laughing. 'Curtis' thighs? You can't be serious.'

Gerri Palmer had blossomed since she'd turned thirty, with a boyishly handsome face. But like her father, Eleanora saw, she was still mostly ribcage, wary eyes, high cheekbones and the longest calves Eleanora had ever seen.

Spring had arrived early in 1994. The two women were relaxing within a warm verandah that formed the rear redoubt of Palmer's mountain, a designer eyrie high atop a Morcote peak near Lugano. It had always been a natural fortress but, since the attack at Basel, Palmer had vastly improved its security.

Around them the mountain dropped sharply away to puffing excursion steamers lacing the lake back and forth, windsurfer sails dotting the water with bright colour and, in the far distance, the Baron Thyssen-Bournemitza's Villa Favorita where culture tourists studiously filed past certifiably great art. Closer at hand, on a tennis court surrounded by the hedged garden, Palmer and Curtis tried to destroy each other. Palmer's hard serves had sweated the younger man, who scrambled back with junk lobs.

In the past two years, Eleanora noted, Palmer's impersonation of a curmudgeon had sharpened. His more frequent displays of bad temper signalled tension generated when a man knows himself to be under house arrest. Naturally, of course, his interest in sex had, as Palmer himself put it, been 'restructured', meaning diminished, but his killer slams were still lethal. At least against Curtis, his closest, perhaps only, friend. But there was a deeper dimension: Curtis coveted Eleanora.

One could see why. A German war orphan raised by Dutch foster parents, Eleanora had the symmetrical look so prized by a Europe imbued with ancient Greek ideals of beauty. In its movie stars, everything matched. Its Michele Morgans and Deneuves *balanced*, no strong chin, nothing off-centre. Eleanora's great pale-brown eyes hadn't a millimetre's difference in size and were placed over exactly identical high cheekbones and softly rounded lips. Nothing about her was exaggerated. Everything was in mystical balance, the classic golden mien, body slender, pale brown hair swept up into a tied-off knot, face animated whether talking or listening.

To be discussing sex and Curtis had for Eleanora a tang of danger. It didn't seem right that Gerri lusted for him, he craved Eleanora and nothing would ever come of any of it. Wasted heat.

'He's crazy about you,' Gerri pointed out with the same unnerving ability at mind-reading as her father. 'Maybe you could put in a good word for me?'

'Gerri, you have this dream job meeting all sorts of eligible men.'

'TV researching a dream? Next week they've got me in Rome talking to all those eligible bachelors who work in the Vatican under a vow of chastity.'

Both women smiled indulgently. 'Where is it written that priests can't – ' Eleanora mimed with her slender, powerful fingers, kneading dough. A silence ensued. 'Don't mention Rome to your father. A fax came in just now.'

Eleanora stopped. Palmer was never happy spreading word of his doings. Especially word that he was, still, on a hit list. There had been warnings. A car had rammed their driver, Ziggy, off the road. A cypress had nearly flattened Palmer. Reconnaissance helicopters hovered over them so often there had to be, as Palmer joked, a special mafia Homes-Of-The-Targets tour on offer. That sort of gallows humour was his dark side, a flippant familiarity with death. Whenever she was angry she pictured him as death's harbinger. Violence just happened to him, the way lightning just strikes a lightning rod. To a European this was so American.

If you analysed the meagre report he'd given her on the Basel affair it hadn't just happened. Palmer had the knack of initiating violence. When the hero of a Western came into town people stuck extra rounds in their cartridge belts. That he had spent most of his Basel visit trying to get the police to find evidence of an ambush when there was none – not even a spent Uzi cartridge – made the memory of two years ago especially enraging.

And the reception of this keynote warning:

> Soon after 1992, when the European
> Economic Community has abandoned
> financial barriers, the force that
> now controls some of the world will
> run the entire European land mass as
> the preferred and protected source
> of funding for business and government.
> With most banks belly up or dying,
> it will be Prime Lender Number One.
> I refer to the mafia.

The bankers had muttered, 'We need additional expert opinion,' and set up yet another committee.

What the ambush on the airport road had failed to do was now, as Curtis had forseen, safely accomplished by distinguished elders. But on the mafia's balance sheet it remained an uncollected debt. Some day, when the dons had nothing more pressing, they would try again.

His new diary habit *was* calming. He could now scribble diatribes in a book and paste in clippings describing how banks were being forced out of Europe. High on the list was his own, United Bank and Trust Company, NA, although he was no longer anything more than a major stockholder in it.

Someone in Palermo or Naples could buy from corrupt local authorities the necessary EC permits and licences to do business as any sort of financial institution anywhere in the EC. These financial entities licensed by mafia puppet-authorities were sopping up what cash flow there was throughout Europe. Non-EC institutions began to feel the bite of terminal anaemia.

'The bankers've waited till now, mid-May, to ask him to give their keynote address in June again.' Eleanora watched Gerri's face and saw that none of her words had gotten through. 'Only this time the meeting's in Rome.'

Gerri's small, narrow, cropped, pale brown head, nodded as if she had heard. 'Something subtle over the chilled pinot grigio.' She gestured airily. 'Dear Curtis, come to my room and I'll rub your tummy?'

Eleanora's eyes opened very wide, caramel-brown circles of desire, as she repeated that dough-kneading gesture with her long, take-charge fingers. Both women burst into laughter. For different reasons.

*

In Palmer's study the unlisted phone rang. He'd just finished showering off after tennis and, with his rudimentary grasp of German he had been reading an article in *Die Klarion*, a weekly news magazine. Eleanora's daughter, Tanya, worked on it as a photographer. It was a half-page item with the headline, UND WAS MACHT HERR PALMER? As far as he could make out, some dodo on the staff, nearly two years later, was wondering whether the controversial banker's forecast was proving true. And, if so, why was he still alive.

It was only in daylight that he was at ease in this study. At night, with its perimeter sensors glowing, it was as menacing as a submarine, stranded on the bottom while depth bombs slowly descended toward it.

Palmer picked up the telephone. 'Yes?'

'Wotcher mean yis, cobber?' a man with a thick Australian accent bellowed down the line. 'It's Corkery 'ere and it's flippin' Palmer theah.'

'Jimmy! Still pleasuring wallabies with your didgerydoo?'

Palmer sat back and lifted his legs to his desk for a nice long chat on someone else's expense account. He and Corkery had first met in Sicily, mid-1943, trying to set up the local mafiosi as Allied Military Government advisers, the operation for which Ed Kutz had taken credit fifty years later.

'How's little Nora?'

'Still putting up with me.'

'And the family?'

'Gerri's with us this week. So's Curtis. What's with you and Madge?'

'Flying rolling pins, the lot.' Corkery paused. 'Wot's this mean t'you, Blue? A merchant bank called Pan-Eurasian Credit Trust?'

Palmer's nose wrinkled. 'Never signed the 1987 Basel Accord. Offshore entity, incorporated first in the Moluccas but doing business in Japan, Singapore, the Caymans.'

'Ownership you know of?'

'You mean any ownership other than the old Patriarcha cosce from Providence, operating out of La Costa in California with Teamster funds? No.'

Corkery's laugh was so violent it choked in his throat. He coughed for a while. 'Damned ciggies. These Pan-Eurasian monkeys beat us on a seven-billion-dollar highway project in Perth.'

'Seven billion Aussie dollars.' Palmer whistled.

'Bleedin' roight. If we foight it, the cost is dreadful. If we let it happen they'll be back next week shoving something spinier up our bleedin' arse'oles.'

'Early retirement, Jimbo.'

'Wot?'

'The party's over. Put on your beach clogs and rub in the Coppertone.'

'Eff that. I thought you might 'ave some brilliant –'

'I did. Two years ago at Basel. There was still time then. We had a sort of window of opportunity. It's slammed shut now.'

'Is this the old Woods I'm hearing? Quitting?'

Palmer's face grew very grave. 'Never mind, Jim.' He glanced around the sunshine-filled office and shivered. The menace of life had conquered the sunshine. 'Never mind.'

This year the once hyperactive Palmer had started taking naps. Catnaps, he called them, and referred critics to the way Churchill had survived the Second World War. 'But I don't have his head for cognac,' Palmer usually added on a faked note of sorrow. Today he arrived at the luncheon table too quiet. He ate very little.

'Problems?' Gerri asked him.

'A call from Jimmy Corkery.' Silence. Nobody likes to relay the news that he's been called a quitter.

This time Palmer didn't bother with Churchillian excuses but started to slump at the lunch table shortly after his daughter and his protégé had agreed to work off lunch on the tennis court.

'I won't take it easy on you, the way Dad does,' she warned Curtis.

'Gerri, it's only a game, not foreplay.'

She lifted his arm and sniffed. 'You're not nearly rank enough for me.'

'Issa Krykova didn't complain.'

'I'm twice her size.'

'Half as sexy.'

'What nerve. You've had her?'

'Her runaway banker, not her.'

'Was that you? UBCO strikes again.'

Palmer's eyes had already closed as they left the

table. 'Woods!' Eleanora's voice, with its very slight German accent, was no-nonsense. 'To bed!'

''nsense,' he muttered.

'Oh? Then here's the morning mail.'

There was a longish pause. Slowly, his left eyelid raised and an iris of pale grey swivelled down to the papers in her hand. He read through the fax twice.

'Stupid lintheads.'

'Woods.'

A long, mournful groan followed. He opened both eyes and directed them in a bleak stare at his companion. 'Tell me something, my treasure, my own? You're so smart and good looking and neatly in charge of your life and mine.' He smiled slightly and tried for a bit of warmth. 'Tell me why it is that as the world ages it grows more ghastly?'

'Aren't you the one who explained entropy to me?'

'Why do I let Jimmy get to me, desperately trying to prod some life into a poor old quitter? Why do I even bother to get upset? Why can't I rise above this deteriorating pustule we call Earth and tell everybody to go to hell and – '

Her stare finally silenced him. 'Woods.' She was truly upset now and her accent deepened the word to 'Voots'. Her soft, easy, kissable mouth tightened in a horizontal line. 'The man I fell in love with – ' She stopped for a moment but tumbled on, 'Was not a sour man. Not a dour man.' She made both words rhyme with hour.

Palmer started to correct her but decided it wasn't

an appropriate moment. 'OK, sour. Maybe that's wisdom.' He shoved the fax at her. 'Got a pencil?'

'Just tell me your message.'

'Eleanora, two years ago there was still time. Today it's already happened. If I thought there was a way of reversing it, believe me, I'd try.'

She was silent for a long moment. Then: 'I know how you feel. That you're a prisoner here because you told the world the truth.'

He nodded somberly. 'And if I'm going to have to be that careful, it should be for something worthwhile. Not another cry of wolf when no one cares.'

They gazed at each other, his light grey eyes against her warm brown ones. Suddenly her face lit up. 'Look. Suppose they're giving themselves a second chance to get a little of your wisdom?' She patted his hand. 'The life you've led these past two years will have had a higher purpose after all.'

'Higher than keeping mafia hit squads off the premises?'

'The highest, revenge. And to let the bankers correct their mistake.'

'I love you. You're terrific, imputing decent motives to bankers.'

'The life you lead is making you a curmudgeon.'

He took her hand in his. 'That would've happened anyway. It goes with the age category.' He paused and grinned demonically. 'Please send them this message.' He turned the bankers' request blank side up as if urging her to write on it. 'It will test a very sour pH on your litmus. It'll sound to Corkery like quitting.' He cleared his throat with fake melodrama. 'Quote. Won't speak. My advice: close eyes, pull bedclothes over head and prepare to die. Unquote.'

Chapter Three

For an immense collection of buildings through which, each day, hordes of the curious and the devout pass, the Vatican is also a place of close-guarded privacy. Its more than six thousand staff must often feel akin to prison inmates.

On the north wall of St Peter's Square, behind the window where the Pope gives his Sunday blessing to waiting throngs, lie a congeries of sixteenth century buildings surrounding the inner cortile or court of Sixtus V. It houses the Pope's sixteenth-century office suite with its twenty-first century radiophones, computers, scramblers and fax machines.

The day after Palmer had so rudely turned down an invitation to address the bankers again, another fax originated in St Patrick's Cathedral between New York City's Fifth and Madison Avenues, head-quarters of the Archdiocese. When the fax was placed on the Pope's desk, he frowned. In his experience American cardinals and bishops played the tail that tried to wag the dog.

His Holiness was relieved to see that His Eminence, Cardinal Hogan, was asking a favour that made sense. The largely Protestant group of US bankers meeting this year in Rome craved the favour of a keynote address from one of the Vatican's top financial officers, the archbishop who headed the Vatican's extremely busy IUD, the Internazionale Uffizi Devozione. That Archbishop Tadeusz Radziwill was also an American, well-known but rarely a public speaker, made it a salubrious teaching moment. Himself a master of the trappings of charisma, the Pope appreciated another stamped in his mould, as long as he kept his place.

Radziwill bore his six decades handsomely. In a geriatric enclave like the Vatican, the archbishop's gift of looking fresh while thinking with the experience of an elder, made him a favourite with the Pope.

Since both came originally from north-European Slavic strains, there was a further link. The Pope's plain, farmer's face creased in a slightly crooked grin. He prided himself on being one with the great world, aware of its torments and tribulations, forever eager to go forth and celebrate communion with it. He had no idea how shuttered his knowledge of the world really was, how little focused on the teeming billions mashed together, a fleshy stew that procreated disastrously in the narrowing space between their rulers' murderous greed and the steady death of the environment around them.

Would it be better if they were rushed to God's judgement? But not before he personally brought Christ to each of them. In any event, letting his archbishop from Chicago, who raised the funds for so much travel, preach to the heathen was a good idea. He scribbled a 'si' on the fax and sent it on its way.

*

La Prefetura per l'Affari Economici used to meet once a month. It never took more than that to examine the Holy See's earnings and consider any new plans. Then two things happened: the new Pope indicated an expensive taste for carrying Christ to the great world outside. At the same time, a money-making rival for the scandal-ridden IOR was formed, under Archbishop Radziwill. No one needed to explain that the high-spending Pope required a high-earning money man. But the Prefetura, which supervised all funding, began meeting once a week.

Today the revolving chairmanship fell to Cardinal Huf, a small, white-haired Swiss from the French-speaking part of his country. Dressed in working clothes of black short-sleeved summer shirt with clerical collar, he had let it be known that the rest of the prefects should dress in similar work-day garb.

The committee room was vast, with a ceiling twenty feet high and, along one wall, leaded windows looking through Venetian-arched fenestration to the rich new green of late spring. Each of the dozen cardinals sat in an armchair of seventeenth century provenance. Beside them their monsignor aides crouched on high stools.

They came from every level, the Curia cardinals of the Holy See, from peasant stock, from the aristocracy, but mostly from the lawyers, accountants and petty bureaucrats who ran Italy, if not the world. Thus, to end up as prefects in charge of economic affairs was, clearly, an act of Darwinian selection.

Sitting half-way along a twenty-feet refectory

table, Huf clipped small spectacles on to his little nose as he read the agenda. He glanced around him and rapped his knuckles on the huge, leather-bound ledger book. 'Called to order at zero nine hundred, this fifteenth day of May, the year of our Lord nineteen hundred and ninety-four,' he began.

Some cardinals picked up earphones for the simultaneous translation. Others made do with Huf's Swiss-accented French. He took them through item one, a catastrophe of an African cacao project in which the IUD had taken a 51 per cent interest and corrupt local politicos the rest. After the first harvest came disturbing reports of overseer brutality and worker resistance.

'. . . Seven men dead,' a younger monsignor down at the far end of the table was reporting, 'and some fifty other casualties. The manager has been sacked.'

Amid general rumbling, Huf spoke out: 'Are we to take it this action puts an end to brutality?'

The young monsignor's cardinal, whose massive wrestling shoulders went directly into his ears, rumbled: 'That is correct. I have Radziwill's promise.'

Huf scribbled a few words on the open ledger in front of him. 'Tabled for two weeks. Item two. Your Eminence Cardinal Scarfacci, please?'

A thin old man, bones and tanned leather, nodded several times and continued nodding. 'The Vatican cannot be seen to invest in waste disposal. Our mission is to save, not waste, but – ' He seemed to lose the thread.

'Eminence,' Huf prompted, although he was perhaps the same age as Scarfacci, 'it is the profitability with which we are concerned.'

'Radziwill is quite pleased.'

Huf nodded and again scribbled in his ledger. 'Before we take up item three . . .' He murmured to a young priest standing behind him. As the aide left the table, Huf went on: 'I have asked His Excellency Archbishop Radziwill, to attend us this morning. So many of these projects require his explanation.'

Huf pushed his eyeglasses up on his small nose. 'Item three is the highway project near Perth, in Australia. I have put a copy at each of your seats. It is in English. The profitability relies on low labour costs, in this case Aborigine manual workers. Capitalisation is projected at seven billion Australian dollars.' He took off his spectacles and glanced at his colleagues. 'May I add that His Holiness has asked that his long-delayed visit to Australia be arranged to coincide with announcement of this project . . . if we agree to it,' he added hastily.

It wasn't until an hour and four items later that Huf's aide returned to the long table. He bent over the cardinal's short-cropped white hair and murmured something behind his palm. Huf's plain old face went through several shades of colour, ending in dead white.

'Eminences,' he said then. 'It appears we will have to continue without the participation of Archbishop Radziwill this week. He is locked in conference with His Holiness about a speech to American bankers. He is not expected to be free until much later.'

'Which is as clever an excuse,' he muttered to no one in particular, 'as any in this vast precinct of Christ.'

By the time His Excellency was free to join the Prefetura its weekly session had ended. Cardinal Huf, when it was his turn to serve as chairman, liked to keep his colleagues at the conference table until one in the afternoon. This was because more than a few of them never actually returned for the afternoon session. Most found it impossible after lunch and wine without a nap.

As for Huf, who lived in a small villa on the outskirts of town, each morning his housekeeper gave him a small brown paper bag with two apples, a stalk of celery and a slice of Appenzeller or Emmenthaler. He would eat alone at the long eighteenth century table where he and his colleagues discussed the management of billions of lire. Sometimes an aide helped him finish the business at hand, getting the benefit of the second apple.

A curious old ascetic, Huf, whom none of the other cardinals actually liked. By three or four o'clock, he would have either disposed of the rest of the agenda, passed it along with comments to other agencies of the Vatican, or tabled it for next week's meeting and a different chairing cardinal. That was why, at four, entirely alone as he scribbled minutes and notes in the huge leather-bound ledger before him, he witnessed the arrival of Archbishop Radziwill. 'Dear me, Eminence! Don't tell me I'm that late?'

Huf removed his tiny spectacles and examined the

handsome face of the man who seemed to commit so much Vatican money to so many projects. 'On the contrary, Excellency. You are a week early for the next Prefetura.'

Radziwill stood in the doorway. 'His Holiness had work for me.'

'Between the two of you . . .' Huf's pale blue eyes seemed to give off a curious frost-like chill, 'you keep each other busy.' He snapped his ledger shut with a sharp gunshot bang and got to his feet. Huf's icy gaze went suddenly warm with feeling. 'What a great gift lies in your power, you and His Holiness, if the funds for your vast projects could be diverted to produce medicine and food for the church's poor.'

'Yes,' Radziwill agreed smoothly. His great, dark eyes regarded the little cardinal dispassionately. 'How true,' he smiled, 'and how hopelessly impossible.'

These early mornings the first ray of sun lights up my cage. It's helped by a dawn wind off the lake that comes roaring in, filled with terrific negative ions. For a caged man it clears the brain, especially after a bad night.

Twice after midnight the circle of proximity sensors shifted to pre-red alert. Is it any wonder my nights loom so menacingly? I sit in the position a bad chess player lets his king get into. He's not in checkmate, but it's only a few moves away. His mobility is clamped tight *by his own circle of protection*.

How I hate this goddamned electronic jail!

Our social life has disappeared. I know Eleanora

hates this prison routine as much as I do. But just now! Suddenly! My telephone rings at five a.m.! It's my man in Rome! To a roll of drums and a flourish of trumpets, the entrance of Teddy Radziwill. Ra-ta-ta! His first public attendance in years!

Can't keep a good man down. I refuse the bankers so they come up with yet another Chicagoan. Why does the paranoid node in my left hemisphere start tickling? Why do I see a chance that didn't exist before?

Old Paranode, be with me in my dawn hour of doubt. Comfort me with plots, with enemies worthy of my steel in a battle already lost.

Should I care? Bankers corrupted banking from a useful service to another way of cheating money out of society. If the Federal government can turn a blind eye to the savings and loan scam, then bankrupt itself to pay hush money, you obviously own the nation and every sap in it.

What hurts is that the incompetents at UBCO are going down the drain with the rest. Hurts! When your estate is bundles of UBCO A-Preferred, you hate to die and leave Eleanora and the kids with fancy bits of paper.

But by putting Teddy up front, do they know what a target they've handed me? Me, mafia target numero uno, turned sniper once again! Out of left field, a way to beat them at their own game!

'Who the hell is this?' Curtis complained in a sleep-sodden voice.

'Did I wake you up?'

'At five a.m.? What makes you ask that? Just because Paris is in the same time zone as Lugano?'

'It occured to me that we don't have a second to waste.'

'On sleep?'

'I know I said we'd lost. But that was before some news I got today. They have made a mistake. We have the perfect way of exposing the mafia through the most prestigious venue in the world. In short Teddy Radziwill will do the keynote speech next month in Rome.'

'The one you turned down?'

'Ah, you're awake at last. This gives us a month to blow my old classmate apart. To prove that for the last decade or more he's been the intermediary bagman between the Vatican, the Christian Democrats and the mafia.'

'We'd even have time left over to develop an improved general field theory of relativity. All those gaps poor old Einstein left!'

'With a perfect showcase to call down so much worldwide publicity the mafia will never try this trick again.'

'What trick is that?'

'Setting up a Pasta Curtain around the EC. Keeping everybody out of Europe's business opportunities but their own trained seals. Getting away with the worst kind of murder in the name of religiosity. Slamming the door on banks who don't have the wit to bribe their way in. Stealing – '

'Enough.' Curtis' voice still sounded sleepy. 'Sounds like UBCO's largest single stockholder woke up mad this morning.'

'I haven't been to sleep yet. Curtis, as busted as most bankers are, and manacled by the Basel Accord, they still thirst for profitable European action, government loans, big construction, mergers, take-overs. They never get a sniff.'

'I can't stand all that sad violin music,' Curtis said in an irritated tone. 'These are the same bandits who raped Europe for the full twentieth century.'

'How well you put things,' Palmer admitted. 'On its own, the mob couldn't handle such rich pickings. But between Basel 1987's mistake and 1993's dropping of financial borders, the leverage is in place to make every bank channel its big lending through the mafia.' A worried silence overtook them both. Then Palmer added: 'The moment I heard Teddy was making the running, I knew we had one last chance.'

Curtis yawned. 'Why do you hate him so much? What'd he ever do to you?'

'I love him. He's an intellectual giant in an organisation more tilted toward faith than intellect. Besides, I suspect he's the reason his mafia associates haven't brought my name back to the top of their hit list.'

'He's begged them for your life? What are you smoking?'

'Something's staying their hand.'

'Your own vigilance. And what if you're right and

he's your personal saviour? Is this how you want to reward him?'

Palmer fell silent. Then he said in a lower voice, 'Curtis, I know you're sick of me calling on you for backup. But win, lose or draw, it seems right and proper that I do this one last thing.'

'And then you'll stop playing Lone Ranger? What's the deadline?'

'We have to bring it off by the Rome meeting. Or forget it.'

'Time to make over my life insurance in favour of Nora.'

Palmer made a noise like a cracking bough of oak. 'She'll already be the best looking heiress in Switzerland. Coming in with me? You can cut a fine figure for her. She'll bury us both under one modest stone. Here lies . . .'

'Two guys with barely one brain between them.' This time Curtis' pause seemed endless. Then: 'I have to think it's an invitation to a funeral.'

'For somebody my age, death's a viable priority. And mine's two years overdue.'

'I prefer to see you cop it on the tennis court.'

Palmer guffawed. 'I just bet you would. Can you be here tonight?'

'No. My first stop has to be Rome.'

Chapter Four

Where the River Tiber turns sharply south the vast Papal holdings begin, nearly 109 acres that extend west from the Castel Sant' Angelo past the great basilica of St Peter with its immense square. Beyond lie the Vatican gardens, insulated by high walls from the fumes and noise of Rome's murderous traffic. Finally, the Papal enclave draws to a broadly pointed prow, like a barge of state sailing towards the setting sun, with the masts and antennae of Radio Vaticano. At the very westernmost point, figurehead on a clipper ship, sits the helicopter pad by which important visitors arrive and depart. Or it used to, Gerri Palmer reminded herself.

She had wandered for some time through the blessed green leafiness of the gardens. This day in late May had turned quite hot. Even the birds had stopped their song. She had arrived early for her appointment and was slowly approaching by cool paths and luxurious leafy bowers the target of her work today.

Her crew would be shooting here in less than a week. Nothing in American television ever required anything like in-depth research. But her producer did need to know about permits, places to park generator trucks, sun angles, background distractions and must-shoot statuary, architecture and decor.

All through late 1989 and 1990, Gerri recalled, Italy had been on a construction spree, tarting up for World Cup soccer matches it eventually lost. Perhaps the Vatican's neighbours assumed that this new excrescence was a way in for soccer teams who needed a quick Papal fix. In place of the helipad had risen an attractive modern building, clad by four storeys of peach-coloured travertine. Atop this the new helicopter pad could be reached by an outside elevator.

The flesh-hued offices presented a sheltering curve, something like two hands reaching out. In the central loggia a truly unusual piece of art welcomed those with business to transact here. Only someone who had done their homework would have known that she was looking at one of the most heavily praised, celebrated and awarded pieces of sculpture ever unveiled in modern Europe. Not really unveiled, since access to this area was limited to those who had an appointment. Some came by helicopter or arrived outside the Vatican wall by car and entered the IUD enclave on foot.

Gerri's mother, Edith, who had married and buried two more husbands since her divorce from Palmer, was now one of the richest widows in the United States. Edith had been an early patron of the sculptor Hannah Kurd. In fact, a rendering by the feminist Kurd of the three Palmer children as naked imps was permanently on the display in the forecourt of the Basel Kunstmuseum, making Woody and Tom look like apes while Gerri seemed demure and powerful.

It was Edith, no Catholic, who had donated the half million dollars for the statue. This work at the western point of Vatican City was Kurd's last, in a technique called bolt-on bronze. Chunks of metal machined to a tight fit were bolted down with lock nuts, all bronze.

Here, in the forecourt of the Internazionale Uffizi delle Devozione, world headquarters of the Vatican's financial arm, Kurd, and the former Edith Palmer, had placed a human-sized Christ, under six feet in height, dwarfed and menaced by the cross he was carrying. The bronze had been in place for four years now. Rome's acid air had streaked it nicely with green and black strands of patina. Two things made Kurd's Christ unusual: how skilfully the bolt-on bits mimicked human flesh in agony, the pure bronze hues closely miming the several skin colours of Earth's races of mankind. The second was Kurd's inclusion of a bronze-tubing system that fed water to Christ's eyes.

He wept. Slowly, disconsolately, perhaps knowing he was now at the end of his human experience, he wept. A strange, almost furtive cult had sprung up around those tears. Civilian employees of the Vatican, the occasional outside courier or visitor waiting for an appointment, a devout pilgrim who had applied for permission to visit the gardens, all manner of people would somehow happen to have a small flask which they would surreptitiously fill with Christ's tears. Furtive because the Vatican frowned on such superstitions. But outside, in the superstitious real world, cousins and neighbours and friends in faraway places pleaded for those drops, all the more effective because not approved. Lucky was the Vatican staff person who could slip a tiny bottle out of a purse or pocket and fill it. In his or her cynical familiarity with Mother Church, the tears might seem powerless. But the rest of the world knew better.

Sitting to one side on a shaded bench, Gerri watched the odd passage now and then of someone with a vial to fill. In the shadowed coolness, birds had begun to sing again. Gerri found herself wondering to what use those bottled tears would be put, what withered arms to be made whole, what blind eyes restored to sight, what disordered brains set right. Gerri watched the tears fall for a very long time.

'Miraculoso, no?' A young man stood at the end of her bench in a terrible topcoat made of some hideous fibre. He looked about her age but needed his thick black curls cut. The newcomer's small face resembled Gerri's, narrow and discreet, but with a tall, worried forehead and lively eyes that kept darting from her to the Christ.

'Sorry. I don't speak Italian.'

'Ah! Nor I,' he confessed, smiling. 'But my English is rotting.'

She giggled. 'Rotten.'

'Even worse,' he admitted. Ceremoniously he ran his hand through his curls, to re-order them more neatly. 'Permit me to introduce myself,' he began afresh. 'My name is Boluslav Krevic.'

'It is not.'

'I assure you,' he said with deadpan sincerity, 'no one would ever such an alias invent.' He bowed again and his smile grew into a slightly goofy grin. He sat down suddenly, closer to her than before. 'Have now we met properly? Tell me your name, please?'

'Gerri Palmer.' She extended her hand and instead of shaking it, he lifted it to his lips and paused, his dark eyes on her. Something odd sparked between the two of them, a kind of tension created by the delay of the kiss. Then his lips brushed her knuckles lingeringly.

'Is that the custom in your country?'

'Only if the hand is as clean as yours.'

This started them both giggling. 'Do you visit here often?' Krevic asked in memory of some long-ago English phrasebook. 'Are you devout?'

'I am here to see Archbishop Radziwill.'

'I, too. I have inside an appointment in – ' He glanced at his watch. 'At this moment.'

'Please. Don't let me delay you.'

He sat back on the bench, placing on his lap a battered leatherette briefcase, its skin much crazed with age and hard use. He seemed to crackle with sudden portent, as if debating the formal issuance of a major policy statement.

'Miss Palmer.' He cleared his throat. 'The appointment can wait. I have fallen in love. With you, Miss

Palmer. Please? Is this possible? Do you believe me, Miss Palmer? It is Miss, not Mrs?'

'You have *not* fallen in love with me.'

'Let me to judge of that.'

Their glances, interlocked, had not faltered for an instant. A thin ray of sunshine got through the leafy cover overhead and ignited Gerri's face. She could feel his silly grin infecting her. 'Do you have much success with this line?'

He frowned. Then his rather high scholar's forehead cleared. 'But never have I told this to anyone before.' He thought for a moment. 'Not since I was of age six years, that is, so to speak.'

'You're . . . uh, Hungarian? Those big black-olive eyes. Czech?'

'Can we simply be two people?'

Gerri wished for a New York nifty, brittle and funny, that established superiority. 'Well . . . of course,' she said finally. 'What do your friends call you?'

'Slavko. Then we are friends, yes?'

'Slavko.' Her sunlit face broke into a great imitation of his grin. 'There was once another Slavko, very famous in his day.'

'Yes? Please to tell.'

'In the 1920s, in Hollywood, a very creative film editor gave his name to a certain kind of montage. Slavko Vorkapich. I did my master's in film cutting.'

'You are in films? An actress, of course. With those eyes, with those cheekbones. A romantic actress. The new Fonda. The new Hepburn.'

For another long moment Gerri tried to find something sharp and smart to reply. All that came out was: 'Which Hepburn, Audrey or Katharine?'

Slavko stared at the Kurd Christ. 'Mine is a very Catholic nation. We look for help from the Holy See now that we have returned to Mother Church. Not long ago I was a starving lawyer, in jail twice under the old regime. Today finance minister, here to beg a loan from the most powerful Archbishop Radziwill.'

'Not from the IMF?'

'My specific instructions are to avoid IMF. Too political.'

'You're too young to be a finance minister.'

'The qualifications were simple: never to have joined the Party.' He took her hand and fondled it. 'Please to be here when I return?'

'But I have an appointment inside, too.' She got to her feet without letting his hand drop. 'I'm to see His Excellency now at four. You take my appointment.' Gerri suggested. 'He'll fit me in later. He knows my mother quite well.'

'Is that not presumptive of me?'

Then an amazing thing happened. From her viewpoint, Gerri saw him with Christ just over his right shoulder. Christ wept, and Gerri felt a tear emerge on her lower lid, like a small bird when the hot sun abates. His face blurred for a moment and grew sad, as if accusing himself of bringing her to tears. But it was something else, some hypnotic magic about this place and their meeting, something mysterious about the spark between them when he kissed her hand. Something . . .

'Presumptive?' she blustered, dabbing at her eyes. 'Presumptive is picking up strange women when you should be waiting in his ante-chamber like other poor schnooks. Slavko, let's face it: you have just lucked in. Let's go.'

Chapter Five

It's true: scratch an itch and it gets itchier. All the new intelligence I'm collecting only supports the old. Teddy Radziwill is the perfect way to expose the mafia's takeover. More than a bagman, he's a brilliant strategist.

For instance, his past links to the EC parliamentarians and bureaucrats in Brussels and Strasbourg. Did he first suggest the destruction of financial boundaries? Or let them think it was their own idea?

Either way he can be blamed for fronting the mafia takeover of Europe.

'Sorry to disturb you, Woods.' Eleanora sounded out of breath as she appeared on the south-facing verandah, baking in the morning sun but still cool in the great inky shadow cast by its roof. Palmer had been doodling in his diary at a woven rattan table, a true hot-weather artefact designed out of air and reed to let any vagrant breeze pass through.

'At the TV checkpoint there's Ziggy with an enormous crate.'

Palmer replaced the top on his pen and folded the diary shut on the pen to mark his place. 'Crate?'

'From the improbable town of Watervliet, Wisconsin. Is there such a place?'

'Also a lake and, on it, an enclave of three frame

mansions from the McKinley era, all cedar shingles and pointed slate roofs. My father built one for himself, one for my brother, Hanley, and one for me.' He got to his feet. 'Edith got it in the divorce settlement but conveyed it to the two boys. There may have been some of my personal stuff there.'

Eleanora's tanned, soft features went blank, as they usually did when Palmer's former wife came up in conversation. It was one of their long-running low-level arguments, that Palmer had proved not to be good husband material and, therefore, according to Eleanora, they would be foolish to marry. Palmer's defence, typically, was an attack. He would suggest that it was Eleanora's obsessive need to control her own life that kept them from becoming man and wife. Married to a domineering German, now dead, she was ferocious in protecting her free single status.

The need for her own life made Palmer cherish her and want marriage all the more. As the world counted riches, he was rich enough for any life style she desired. But she chose, instead, to have her own small translation bureau in Lugano, earn her own money and keep her own bank account. In past years, before he had to immure himself on this peak, she would occasionally 'treat' him to some unexpected luxury, a trip to the French vineyards, seats for the Monte Carlo Open. She had been threatening to buy him his own Peugeot 205 so she could use hers when she liked. But this was before the Basel attack. Before he stopped driving anywhere himself, relying on Ziggy and sometimes an armed co-driver, a rotten way to live. It was testing the bonds of their relationship, her and Palmer's, and she often thought of his earlier life with Edith.

There had, she knew, been a time when he loved Edith as newlyweds did, starting off a family. Then another woman won his love and another man won Edith's. But that was not his history with Eleanora. From the beginning there had been something independent about Eleanora that locked deep inside him, something Americans called spunk or grit, the kind of independence so precious it was worth any sacrifice to keep.

Palmer had gone into the kitchen where the various TV receivers for security outposts were mounted. Titina, the massive housekeeper, dark and broody, stood by the TV monitor in a way that blamed her employer not only for this interruption, but for the invention of TV and the cathode-ray tube as well.

On its screen Palmer could see his white VW combi van and its bored driver. 'Grüss Gott, Ziggy.' Palmer zoomed in on a wooden crate and examined it for a while. Then he clicked open the gate. Ziggy drove out of camera range. Whereupon Palmer pressed the switch that closed and re-locked the gate. It was a security routine that none of the staff had the right to override. If neither Palmer nor Eleanora were there deliveries simply didn't get made. Together with the proximity sensors around the enclave, this was the old tiger's first line of cage-bars. He tried not to think about it.

An hour later, all the crate timber and wrapping

disposed of, the arrival sat in lone splendour on the verandah. Even the rattan table had been moved offstage. Palmer had poked and prodded its innards for explosives. Now he was satisfied.

'Oh, my,' he sighed with satisfaction.

Manufactured in Grand Rapids, Michigan, around the time William Jennings Bryan was exhorting Americans not to crucify mankind on a cross of gold, it was what was once known as a porch glider.

'Glider?' Eleanora asked. 'It's a couch. A swinging or rocking couch.'

Palmer sighed happily again as he lowered himself on to the dark green upholstery, a faint yellowish fleur-de-lis pattern discernable. The metal slats of the glider had been painted a pale Eau-de-Nil green originally. Twice repainted in his lifetime, the slats were still a pale colour but now verging on chartreuse. He did something automatic with his foot and the glider began to . . . well, glide. That is, it oscillated in very stately rhythm, from front to back, its hidden metal interior making the most of the original shove Palmer had given it.

A faint moaning sound came from within, not a protest but more of an orgasmic sobbing, as of Paradise gained and regained but not without pleasurable pain. He stared out at the bright blue sky. Two hang gliders circled overhead like unaggressive hawks, helped by updrafts from these Morcote hills.

'God, Eleanora. This thing is older than I am.'

'Nothing is older than you.' She sat down beside

him and gave a small kick to restore the glider's movement. 'Yes. Yes, that is lovely. To what do we owe Edith's magnificent generosity?'

He laughed. 'I doubt she even knows. She operates at a level far above most humans. Probably Woody or Tom sent it to me.' He glanced sideways at the woman whom a guest had recently referred to as 'your charming life companion'.

How much he cherished her, unable to voice it properly. Did other men have this problem with the woman they loved? One night, after too much wine, Gerri had complained about the inarticulateness of men. But those were the dumbbells she palled around with. He and Eleanora were on another plane entirely.

'You have to remember,' Palmer said as they sat on the glider, 'that years go by without my thinking of poor, dear Edith. And she's been so busy marrying and having the poor slobs die on her that she probably can't even remember who her first was.'

'That is rich people's philosophy.'

At the heart of her, like a true European intellectual, Eleanora considered herself of the left, defending the poor, those without rights or hope. 'There is a caste, to which you and Edith belong, that is so encased in creature comfort it has lost touch with jealousy or rage, with despair or revenge. It is as if you and Edith were former roommates who have simply moved on to other roommates.'

'But that's non − '

'You are cocooned by money. And so am I!' she

burst out suddenly. 'I seem to have elected myself a hanger-on of this caste.' Angrily, she rocked the glider harder. Its motion began to sink into her bones. 'What am I making such a fuss about?' she asked then. 'You love this old thing, don't you?'

'Memories. The kids as babies, then growing up.'

'Would Gerri remember this glider?'

'She broke it once, jumping on it.'

A long silence followed. Eleanora took tiny, covert sideways glances at him. Finally she spoke again: 'It is only fitting that it have an honourable retirement, with all the attention it requires and deserves. Peace at last.'

'If you think, like the glider, I'm now going to relax into the terminal catatonia of the ancient . . .'

'Did I say that?' She laughed somewhat bitterly. 'But these days, Woods, it is our sub-text. This juvenile obsession of yours with continuing to throw your weight around in the great world.'

'I told Curtis th – '

'And Curtis doesn't help, falling in with your schemes.'

'I told Curtis this was my last outing.'

'And he believed you.' She was silent for a long while. Then: 'Perhaps this glider will . . . will wean you away from violence, towards contemplation.'

Mid-morning quiet green radiated outward from the glider as they rocked and swung. In the near-noon sun the tennis courts blazed terracotta red, nets drooping. Beyond lay the gardens Eleanora had created, boxwood hedges, tanbark paths and beds of intense reds and yellows, blooming fiercely in the sunshine.

Overhead three of the cloth-winged hang gliders swooped with slow dignity. These hills were noted for their thermals, which kept one aloft sometimes for an hour or more. Here below, Eleanora realised, Woods was flying his own glider.

She glanced sideways again and saw that he was fast asleep.

Chapter Six

'Non,' Isabella, the Italian secretary, said in her own drawled, disdainful English. 'E is not 'ere, Il Signore Ems. Is massage?'

'No massage,' Curtis murmured, hanging up.

The secretary's great eyelashes, topped by masses of dark, wavy hair, vibrated for a moment as she glanced up at the elegant, patrician man who paid her salary. 'S'OK?'

Isabella had mastered the trick – quite common among Italians unsure of their English – of sounding like a superior hotel clerk announcing that there were no rooms and hinting that there never would be for such an inferior applicant of such high body odour.

Bradford Ames, listening on an extension phone, frowned at her. Then he smiled to cover the gesture. As he smiled his pointed canines gave him a faintly sharklike look. Tonight he would openly establish his high-entry level into Roman finance. The cousins from Providence would be proud of him.

When he had hired Isabella for his new Rome office – the gala opening party was this evening – she had come highly recommended for her mastery of English, to say nothing of legs so shapely and long that he often wondered if she were really Italian. But when she assumed the role of princess forced to earn her living among cretins with dirty fingernails, he questioned his decision. Too much ego. Bradford Ames preferred pliable girls with a masochistic streak.

He spent time on matters of appearance. The superior put-down was a dead giveaway of unsure origins and even more unsure command of English. He would be sorry to let Isabella, and her legs, go.

He, for instance, was well over six feet in height, slim, with close-cropped dark brown hair, a triangular face with wide-set eyes and sharp chin. His own English pronunciation – one of many dialects he had mastered – was superbly upper-class, with a very faint aristocratic tinge of Scottish burr. Although he had just reached the age of thirty, Bradford Ames already headed his own powerful merchant-banking group, best known for taking the risks others refused. It was barely yesterday that he'd graduated from Oxford with honours, breezed through his Harvard MBA in eighteen months and set up headquarters in London's Docklands near the financial heart of the city as part of the Pan-Eurasian Credit Trust group.

The glossy property-and-gossip magazines that flooded well-to-do London neighbourhoods never failed to include the very British Bradford Ames, bachelor, sterling millionaire and not noticeably gay. 'Mystery financier' was the usual tabloid label. 'Laird o'th'Munny' referred to his tantalising Scottish background.

Watching Isabella's common but pretty face, he thought: too bad. But this was not the right girl for his image. Tonight he was staging a very social opening of his Rome office. Everyone important would be there. The hotel would be equal to the occasion. This girl would not. For the future he would have to find a British girl with some grasp of Italian, one of a good family with throwaway Honourables and Sirs sprinkled about. A pliable girl, used to the casual sadism of British upper-class life.

Watching the secretary he had just doomed to unemployment, Bradford Ames asked himself why Curtis had called him yesterday and twice today. Curtis was bad news. As roving troubleshooter for the largest of US commercial banks, UBCO, he might at any moment swoop down on a Euro-banker. Not that anyone was required to answer his questions. But, somehow, Curtis already had the answers.

Curtis' long-time loyalty to Woods Palmer made him even more objectionable. But that was virtually a dead issue. His cousins from Providence had promised so. Palmer, who still believed that banks had to remain honourable institutions, should have been removed from life two years ago. His Excellency Archbishop Radziwill wanted it to happen again, and this time succeed.

Palmer was as close to non-existence as the soon-to-be-sacked Isabella, still at her desk disdainfully answering RSVP calls. Bradford Ames returned to his desk in the other room and stared out at Rome. The fees for the new office were hideous but the view . . . !

The Hotel Eden's top floor had always had this magnificent westward 180-degree angle on the Eternal City. The hotel was situated on the bluff-like hill that overlooked the tourist heart of Rome gazing toward St Peter's dome, the Spanish Steps, the Piazza Colonna, the Fontana di Trevi, the Pantheon, the Piazza Navona, the Colosseum and a dozen other sites that lay towards the Tiber and the Janiculum Hill beyond the river. Normally this view from Eden was the property of a few dedicated drinkers who each evening repaired to the Eden's penthouse bar for perfectly chilled dry martinis and fat crunchy almonds under a cascading arbour of flowers and vines. At nearly prohibitive expense Bradford Ames had talked the Eden into freeing two penthouse rooms normally devoted to private dining. These were his Rome office, at least until the men from Providence howled with pain when the first quarterly bill was tendered.

Bradford Ames dialled the number of a British employment agency in Rome that handled nannies, au pairs and clerical help. As he conversed with the director there, he propped up his long legs on his desk top and stared out his windows at Rome.

With his pale complexion, his small nose, his light-coloured hazel eyes and his athlete's build, Bradford Ames easily passed his own private tests of origin. It was impossible, as well he knew, to believe even for a moment that Bradford Ames had been born Amadeo Brazzi in the rank slums of Glasgow's Gorbals.

'Yes,' he told the employment person, carefully tailoring his vowels to a refined, Laird of the Manor burr. 'Someone wi' class . . . and brrreedin'.'

Chapter Seven

At the bottom of the Morcote hill the lakeside highway curved around a point of land on which stood a very modest snack bar. Palmer sat at a white metal table and slowly sipped a bubbly glass of mineral water. Ziggy, who had run downhill a few paces ahead of him, was still quite out of breath as he sipped his water and watched the surrounding guests for signs of mafia aggression.

The jog was a bit less than a kilometre, invigorating on such a warm, lovely day, the exercise run the zoo allowed an old tiger. But the run back up tired Palmer even more than thirty-year-old Ziggy, unless they rested at the bottom.

Originally, Ziggy had preceded Palmer in the small Peugeot or the VW combi van. But it was too easy to target a vehicle, much simpler for the two of them to melt into the surrounding forest. After the cypress incident they agreed they were safer on foot.

A small steamer chugged past, carrying tourists across the lake to the Italian enclave, Campione, where legal gambling casinos stayed open around the clock. Palmer got to his feet and immediately the proprietor of the snack bar hurried over to him. 'A lovely day, Herr Palmer.'

'Lovely.' He placed coins in the man's hand. He had been stopping here for some years now. It was only in the past two, with Ziggy as bodyguard, that he realised Herr Bartki, the owner, was Ziggy's great-uncle. Bartki was shaping up for seventy, but where Palmer was still tall and reasonably free of grey hair, the proprietor was short, slight and white-thatched. His wrinkled face seemed permanently worried. Standing beside him, Palmer felt the guilt of coming from an affluent family to a secure old age. If being on the mob's list could be called secure. 'You are looking well, Herr Bartki.'

Nearby, a woman screamed horribly.

Ziggy's hand dived inside his ski jacket, reaching for his gun. Palmer and Bartki ran to the railing that overlooked the Lake of Lugano. A yard or two below them lay a long, narrow wooden rowboat. The man's oars stood dripping, arrested by the scream. The woman, crouched in the bow, pointed at the water dead ahead.

Slowly, peacefully, a corpse with a bloated face surged upward through the water, its battered nose cleaving the waves like the prow of a ship. As it did, an orange peel lodged in its mouth. It looked as if it were on fire from within.

'Süss Gott,' Herr Bartki exclaimed. 'Another.'

'Grosser Gott,' Ziggy muttered, removing his hand from inside his jacket. He crossed himself.

'Do they float over from Campione?' Palmer's question seemed innocent. But he knew this passage between Italy and Switzerland, between closely controlled financial life and the secret, maverick freedom of Switzerland, had been a favourite killing ground for most of the century. Illegally exported money produced a kind of Styx through which unlucky souls entered eternal hell. But since 1993 the EC had decreed no financial borders. Therefore entry to non-EC Switzerland was unnecessary, wasn't it? Why were souls still being damned?

A vagrant wave from the steamer swept over the body and, in leisurely fashion, rolled the body over. Everyone saw the cruel bonds that tied together the corpse's hands. A professional kill, not a crime of passion.

Only one civil authority still had the right to exact the death penalty, the kind Palmer had been protecting himself against. The corpse could have been his. It stank of mafia justice. It took its place, anonymously, as a figure in a kind of bas-relief frieze, the sort ancient Greeks sculpted horizontally around the eaves of their temples.

Nothing personal, Palmer reminded himself. Just a small detail in the greater scheme of life.

'. . . And tell him I've found the go-between,' Curtis told Eleanora. He had placed his call from one of the international phone booths inside the Piazza San Stefano Post Office, insulated from the noise and clangour of the square outside.

Eleanora paused for a long moment. 'He'll be sorry he missed you. It normally doesn't take him this long. He may have stopped along the way to – '

' – To let Ziggy suffer a cardiac infarction,' Curtis finished for her. 'Nora, when the fitness freak passes on to the great gymnasium in the sky will you marry me?'

'Lust doesn't require heroic responses like marriage.'

'So you're suggesting a ménage à trois?'

This time Eleanora's silence lasted much longer. 'The ménage à trois requires that all three people are aware of it. In Woods' case, we'd never score more than a ménage à deux-et-demi.'

'Why is it my luck to fall for such a competent linguist?'

There was a silence and then she asked: 'Did I hear you rightly? Cunnilinguist? I have it on the brain. In my translation bureau I employ one of these modern lesbians. She dresses like a glamour girl and keeps coming on to all of us. Such a clown.' She laughed. 'Elfi says fornication creates a sexually transmitted disease with 100 per cent mortality. Called life.'

Neither of them spoke for a while, absorbing the sudden escalation towards franker talk. 'Nora, you're a worse clown than Elfi.'

'Au 'voir, Curtis. Where can Woods telephone you later?'

'La Residenza. Room 303. It has a bed wider than king size. One could stage a cunnilingual steeplechase on it.'

'Come back to Morcote and we can keep talking about it.'

Curtis stepped out into the dust and noise of San Stefano, wondering if he'd got the undertone right. Come back to Morcote and we'll do more than talk.

In the square ancient orange-yellow streetcars and buses started their noisy journeys outward to other parts of Rome. People rushing to board in the unseasonable heat might have seen his sudden grin. More likely they were too rushed to notice.

For some months now he had been grateful for this little lay-by along the winding road back up to the top of the hill on which his enclave was built.

Some kind person, around the turn of the nineteenth into the twentieth century, had placed a sturdy bench in this shady place. Palmer sat here now, having recovered his breath but not his peace of mind. Ziggy, a few yards down the road from him and more than thirty years younger, lurked behind a large birch and caught up on his own breathing.

It was not the corpse, casually surfacing, that had so disturbed Palmer, illustrating graphically the kind of fate against which he had shielded himself these past two years. This part of the world . . . ah, well, nothing personal, these corpses. Just business, pay no attention, turisti, just enjoy. No, it was his life that bothered him. A corpse did that, made you take stock. Why was he still so discontented? Why embark on this lunatic crusade? Wasn't it enough that he was already marked for execution? He groaned with frustration at his own behaviour.

At sixty, some years back, he had retired to this eagle's nest, fed up with the mendacious cheat the banking profession had become, sickened by the credit glut the banks had created. They had first hooked dissatisfied middle classes and then ambitious corporations and greedy governments, luring them irreversibly into total debt like a suicide walking out to sea until his hat floats. Then, as the pendulum swung back, shutting down the glut. it turned into what was now called a credit crunch. Sorry, no money.

Europe had been kind to him, a wandering American with no need to live in his homeland. This part of Switzerland, with a beneficent micro-climate and a varied offering of cultural events, had been an ideal retirement site. Why had he spoiled it at Basel two years ago? Turned it from an eyrie to a cage? Why hadn't he let evil have its way? It would, anyway. Someone would always tie the hands and push the victim into the lake.

He knew the menace around him was his own obsession. Eleanora had told him: 'You were not placed on earth, Woods, to frustrate evil men. No one has knighted you with Excalibur. Please relax. Please settle down.' And pay more attention to her, Palmer finished the thought.

Eleanora had just turned forty. Dear God, so had his oldest son, Woody. Eleanora, with her slim but ripe body and her welcoming face, set now in a smile that, Palmer recognised, could easily seem a come-on to a smitten male; Curtis, notably. Because Eleanora was pleasant and kind to him, poor Curtis was sure to read more meaning into her hospitality. Well, maybe he was right.

Curtis had also recently turned forty. He'd had two

blasted marriages but no children. Eleanora's husband had been murdered years ago and her one child, Tanya, nearly Gerri's age, came and went restlessly like a will o'the wisp. This hilltop fortress seemed to collect unsettled lives.

Protected as best he could from the mafia's hit squads, he'd also blanked it off from any beneficial form of life. It was like a forest gone to lichen and moss, twisted dead branches menacing the inhabitants. Neither Eleanora nor Curtis could be said to have fulfilled their lives. Perhaps there was no stopping either of them if they finally found each other.

Palmer groaned as he got to his feet. Bartki had said another. The bad old days continue. Nothing personal, of course, just business. Were the corpses sent to remind him? Mute menaces of mafia evil that never rested, even though it now controlled the whole European community?

He started walking. Upward strode Parsifal in his quest for the Grail. Put everything second, Parsifal. Put your relations with Eleanora second. Never mind that you love her most of anyone in the world and, odd as it seems, she must still love you. God knows why. Put all that second.

His pace increased to a leisurely jog. He could hear Ziggy's panting behind him. His own breath was coming strongly now. Never mind real life, Parsifal. Slay the dragon first.

The jog accelerated to a run. No puff, just steady

inhale-exhale, good. Onward, Parsifal, glory awaits and perhaps two things more: a place in that Greek frieze of corpses that surrounds the structure of this area; and a three-inch obit in the *Herald-Tribune*.

Chapter Eight

'Listen,' Palmer told Eleanora. He was seated in his office. 'What would you say to inviting some friends for an open house?'

Her eyes widened. 'But the security ... .'

'To hell with it. I have a pal in Swiss intelligence, you remember Staeli? Between the perimeter stuff that protects us and a few of Staeli's men as guests ... why not?' His glance fell on the circle of proximity-sensor alarm lights.

'Woods.' Her voice broke. He hadn't seen tears in her eyes for so long. 'Woods, you're not joking?'

'Look at that face!' he said. 'Look at that grin!'

Off the Piazza di Spagna, with its ornate fountain and wedding-cake tiers of stairways, at the point where it abruptly becomes the Via del Babuino, runs a sidestreet filled with mini-hotels dedicated to afternoon fornication. From it an archway leads into a leafy glen of ancient Roman cobblestones. Not knowing how much money Slavko was carrying, Gerri had picked one of the few inexpensive restaurants left in Rome. Her companion looked lower than the cobblestones. 'Tell me,' she began.

'What you have not already from my face guessed?'

'Tell me anyway. Let's kill a bottle reminiscing.'

They touched glasses and sipped the straw-coloured dry white wine produced all over the hills around Rome and thus testing excitingly high in tetraethyl lead. 'Did you have a witness for your interview with the archbishop?' Gerri began by way of encouraging him. 'A young priest, Father Bernardin, who sat at his computer.' She refilled their glasses. 'I found Radziwill's paperless office grand in terms of space. Lacking in ordinary human feeling.'

Slavko shrugged. 'He is a money priest, not a people priest.'

Gerri nodded, seeing again the modern Christ hung on the far wall, a study in smooth anguish when anguish was the one thing nothing could ever smooth. She had met the archbishop before, usually in situations related to art or philanthropy. He had thousands of dear, close friends like her mother, also from Chicago. But this afternoon there had been at first an odd, bored hauteur, with a mocking overkill to his manner, parodying himself being cool. Then the pounce.

'Tell me something,' Radziwill finally interrupted her. 'How did an ugly bozo like Woods sire such a gorgeous daughter?'

His lovely eyes went wide with shock at his own question and his mouth turned into a clown's O. This had the effect of reducing Gerri to giggles. She could feel his power creep over her almost stealthily. 'In the old days, he had a terrible time getting a date,' he went on. 'Thank God your dear mother decided to give in or this world would be bereft of your beauty.'

'This is my day,' Gerri countered, all Manhattan snap. 'Some other masher tried to put the moves on me a while ago.' She opened her purse and gazed into her compact mirror. 'It's the new freckle cream.'

'Drives archbishops nuts,' Radziwill agreed. 'But any golfer will tell you that's not a drive, it's a short putt.'

Perhaps this Radziwill, the laughing Radziwill who got on so well with her Episcopalian mother, perhaps he had saved some fun for his next interview, an impecunious beggar of dubious post-Marxist needs.

'So we left each other laughing,' Gerri finished. 'I gather he wasn't half as funny with you?' She signalled for a fresh carafe of wine.

'I produced for him the full range of my data.'

Gerri had always avoided knowing too much about what her father did for a living, but blood tells. 'You mean collateral?' From the look on his face she realised that finance minister Boluslav Krevic had no idea of how to present a loan request.

'Collateral? I pledged our national honour.'

'No. Product, industrial output, projected harvests.'

His small, unhappy face distorted. He puffed to make a busted-paper-bag noise. His lively eyes went dead for an awful moment. 'They are dreams.'

'No charts, no architect's renderings, no visuals at all?'

He fell silent, staring into the pale heart of the new

carafe. 'Dreams or lies,' he said then in a tragic voice. 'Charts would be cartoons of despair.'

'Oh, dear.'

She filled his glass again and waved off the waiter. Otello is a quick turnover place. If lovers want to linger, they have to find a discreet corner table. Lovers, Gerri asked herself. Lovers?

He was sweet. She felt sure that with the archbishop, as with her, he had been straight, speaking in his correct English but now and then, accidently, using a word in the same language the archbishop's parents had brought with them to Chicago at the start of the twentieth century.

'Only one time did I manage his heart to soften.' Slavko's eyes narrowed as he remembered the scene. '"I do take your meaning," he told me, "about the, um, splendid steadfastness of faith in your people."'

Gerri nodded encouragingly. 'And you zapped right back, hard and fast?'

'I said, very strong: "such faith moves mountains."'

'Bravo!'

'Ye-es, both the archbishop and his assistant smiled.' Slavko filled their glasses again. '"Very resourceful, young man." His Excellency says. "You must find other resourceful young men, not hidebound, slow-moving tortoises like IUD."'

'And . . .?' Gerri urged.

'That was nearly all. Oh, one small thing.'

*

Father Bernardin, the plump-faced young assistant, had been transferred to this post only a few months ago because he was fluent in English, like his Excellency and most computer buffs. His attitude towards the archbishop was a mixture of awe, fear and something else that had no name as yet.

He saw his superior key something on to his computer screen. 'Bernardin? Copy and print!' The data popped up on the young priest's green-glowing screen. At the top was the Hotel Eden's name and address and tonight's date, followed by the name Bradford Ames. 'At the suggestion of IUD,' the legend concluded in English. Below this, at the far right margin, in a different typeface and size was the access code, E154-KRV/004/OB-31-AMD. Bernardin frowned. Something left unnoticed?

'Ah. Your Excellency?'

'Print it.'

'But – ' The plump young priest tried to look properly businesslike and unfazed. Even a newcomer to this office knew that access codes were never made public. And especially so for an 004 file, which indicated some special status Archbishop Radziwill kept to himself.

Why OB-31, Oscar Bravo 31, was assigned the 004 level of secrecy Bernardin could guess, since his training in computers was easily above his superior's level. The 004 designation was a red flag. It might signal a 'ghost' subtext encoded between the lines of another document. It might indicate a switch in computer language. It could, as well, point out a change in software from a current DOS to an earlier C/PM operating system.

'Bernardin, are you deaf? Print it on one of my cards. Now.'

The young priest inserted a thickish piece of paper in his printer and obeyed.

Sitting with Gerri at Otello, Slavko began feeling in his pockets. 'I shall the young priest's face never forget. To be ordered to commit to paper was far beyond his physical, or spiritual, mandate.' Remembering the incident for Gerri, Slavko closed his eyes. 'You say in English? To blank out?'

'Say it? We invented it.'

'It reminded me,' Slavko remembered, 'that elsewhere in Vatican City with quill pens people are writing and with sand dusting the ink.'

Slavko's questing fingers had finally located in the breast pocket of his regrettable topcoat what he'd been trying to find. He withdrew the note and placed it on the table beside the decanter of dry white Castelli Romani.

'His Excellency was very precise. "Get there after the freeloaders have left and ask for Ames."' Slavko tapped the bit of paper. It was an exact square of almost parchment-like thickness, fat with the laid pattern of watermarking and an inkless engraved seal that one could sense with one's fingertips more readily than with the eye. Slavko wrinkled his nose at the note and its neat italic typing. 'What do you think? Alphanumeric gibberish?'

'What's this stuff? E154,' Gerri read aloud. 'KRV/ 004/OB-31-AMD.'

'The first part,' Slavko mused, 'is common. E is the fifth letter; May is the fifth month. So E154 is May 15, 1994, today's date. Is part of an access code. But is impossible, the rest of it. Well, except that KRV could be Krevic.'

Gerri frowned at the note. 'Whatever it means, you must see this Ames.' She stopped and looked worried. 'But if you love me, please do one thing first?'

'One thing? A thousand things.'

'Take off that topcoat. Do not wear it again. Ever.'

He looked shocked, fingering the scraggly fabric. 'Do you think . . .?'

She nodded without speaking.

Eleanora sat by the telephone, paging through her address book. Her long fingers delicately combed occasional strands of hair upward and rejoined them to her loose, but disciplined, top knot. She tucked them inside the black velour band that held them.

'Just a few close friends,' she promised. 'But such short notice for a party this Sunday.'

'That's just fine,' Palmer assured her. 'The shorter the notice, the less chance of unwanted visitors having time to work out a plan.'

'Woods.' She stopped and stared helplessly at him. 'Have I told you lately what a nice man you are?'

'Even tigers need visitors now and then.' He kissed the top of her knot and returned to his office. He stared at the circle of proximity lights. A king surrounded on a chessboard by his own pieces. If there were only a way to bring an enemy piece *inside* the circle. Some seamless move, as effortless and natural as the way Eleanora kept her hair in captivity, making it look like she had been born looking that elegant, balanced way. If he could, with such smoothness, lure an enemy piece inside.

The whole strategy would change.

By nine o'clock, as the archbishop had hinted, all the snacks were eaten, the bits of melon wrapped in prosciutto, the stuffed eggplant slices, the rounds of peppery salami, the dessert canneloni oozing creamy sweet ricotta. Guests had dwindled from over a hundred to fifteen nursing white wine. The Church of Santa Maria della Concezione chimed nine times, the magic make-out hour.

All such parties descend at last to make-out. Men and women eye each other, plotting assignations. Those with goods to sell move in closer to those with money. The air grows itchy with friction and undischarged static. No wonder Radziwill wouldn't appear in such a place, flaunting his venality. But directing needy applicants to this flesh-rack, nevertheless.

Gerri surveyed the tall, good-looking young man, back to the wall, whom the bartender had identified as Bradford Ames. He held an untouched half-glass of pro secco in his hand as he fended off an absolute circle of barking jackals.

'. . . Turnover of eighty mil a year, guaranteed,' one jackal was insisting.

'Total turnkey installation,' another barked, 'fully COCOM approved.'

'Mr Ames?'

'. . . Printed circuits from Taiwan, with chassis from Singapore.'

'Mr Ames?'

His tall, spare, Scottish laird's body, not beaky but somehow birdlike in form, twitched sideways. No one, neither a seasoned police detective nor a fanciful producer of crime films, would ever cast him as a mafia specialist.

Fifty years ago, his career in organised crime would have been limited. Today, with his elegant appearance and his knack of making money make money, there was no stopping him. He was new mafia. The sky was his limit.

His hazel eyes under heavy eyebrows flicked over Gerri and Slavko. He smiled, showing small teeth, the canines quite pointed.

Gerri held up the thick square note with the embossed, uninked seal. 'It's ri' over here,' Ames said suddenly in a loud voice, taking her arm. They found themselves in the smaller of his office rooms. 'Did His Excellency send you to me?' Bradford Ames asked, closing the door. 'We must be discreet.'

'I guess he sends quite a few people,' Gerri hazarded.

'Almost never. But now that we've opened here

in Rome, I hope there'll be more. So you're my guid-
luck charm, then? And you are . . .?'

'It's this gentleman the archbishop sent. Mr Ames,
may I present the Honourable Boluslav Krevic,
finance minister of the – '

The highland laird trapped Slavko's right hand
with both of his. 'No one told me y'wurrr in Rome,
sir.'

The honorific 'sir' had an odd sound being
addressed by one thirty-year-old to another, but
Slavko responded by nodding enthusiastically. He
lifted his leatherette briefcase with his free hand and
said: 'In here are what data I have. The archbishop, I
must be frank with you, did n – '

'The archbishop,' Gerri cut in, 'was so impressed
he sent Mr Krevic direct to you.' She tugged the
briefcase out of Slavko's hand.

'Ten a.m. in my office?' Bradford Ames suggested.

'Yes, agreed, certainly, why not, of course,' Slavko
went on. 'I shall bring my fiancée with me,' he
added. 'Her command of English is far better than
mine.' With that same doting grin, he bathed Gerri
in love, seeing her as quintessentially American, a
Hepburn, a Jane Fonda, serious and wise. Without
her beside him, he would have said all the wrong
things. With her they could scale any peak together.
Something behind her eyes, guileless but deep . . .
that said she had high standards and measured
everyone to them? Was that the reason for the faint
hurt behind her eyes when someone failed to meas-
ure up? Slavko felt himself drawn even deeper into

83

her being. She reminded him of the Fonda they knew in his country, not the fitness magnate of later years but the political-spiritual one, angel of honesty and protest.

'I luik forward to seeing you at ten, sir.'

'And I, to you, look forward as well . . . as well as to . . .' Slavko gave up tangling with English prepositions.

At the bar, Gerri ordered each of them a Bellini, the sweet drink in the tall glass that combines peach liqueur with bubbly. 'Geraldine,' Slavko said slowly. He drew a long, deep breath and reached for her hand. 'This morning I was alone, ignorant, unknowing, unknown. Rome had engulfed me. I was all but drowned. Then I met you, finally. After years of waiting. And now my life begins.'

They clinked glasses. 'For a finance minister,' she said, smiling softly, 'you are terribly impulsive. You hardly know me.'

They sipped. Gerri tried to think of some way of cautioning him about everything, about the archbishop, about cocktail-party smiles from Scottish killer sharks, about herself and her uneven record with men which, if expressed in baseball terms, had produced a lifetime batting average under .100. About how dashing and attractive he was, with his dark eyes and curly hair and scholar's brow, now that he had gotten rid of that horrible topcoat. About how much she wanted his mission here in Rome to succeed. About how something dark and steely, like a knife sinking in flowing water, had flashed through her soul as she watched Bradford Ames in action.

She wasn't accustomed to sudden romantic encounters with such admiring supplicants. New York men – at least the straight ones she met in television – had a very accurate idea of their value in the Manhattan scene. Compared to them, Slavko was a Labrador puppy licking your face with instant devotion.

What was she doing, shepherding him through this minefield, putting him in among the very people who would swallow him whole? People too flagrant for the archbishop to be seen with? A vagrant tear oozed out of her lower lid and she could no longer blame it on Hannah Kurd's Christ. She reached in her bag for a wadded-up tissue and cautiously blotted her eyes, smiling tentatively at Slavko's concern.

Never mind, Gerri thought. Having led him into this, I must stand by him. Bemused, she tucked the tissue and the thick paper note from Archbishop Radziwill in her handbag. Over the next few days it would settle slowly through the usual layers of Kleenex, lipstick, compact and comb to rest on the bottom, untouched, but surely not forgotten.

'. . . He's just gone to bed but I'm sure he's not asleep,' Eleanora said.

'Don't wake him. This can wait,' Curtis said.

Not knowing if Bradford Ames knew what he looked like, Curtis had monitored the launch party from a distance. Now, back in his room, he was creating another opportunity to speak with Eleanora under the guise of reporting to Palmer. He should have found a telephone booth but it was midnight and he was tired.

'No, I'm sure he'd want to talk,' she responded.

'And you don't.'

Curtis counted the faint bells of the nearby chapel inside the gardens of the Casino d'Aurora, decorated by Guercino on the commission of Cardinal Ludovisi. Not really meant to be heard by profane ears, twelve velvety chimes sounded as faintly as dream bells, luring sleepers further into fantasy.

Curtis found himself wondering what a heathen like himself, and the millions of other godless Romans and visitors, made of this immense city of faith, cradling its Vatican with more than three hundred churches and chapels. Three hundred, he thought, and not one for us atheists.

But most people solved their problems of faith the easy way. They simply walked on by. And here was Curtis, girding himself for battle against God's own warriors. Did he need such a turn to his life? Did Palmer, at his age?

'No, I'm wide awake,' Palmer said when he picked up his phone, 'I was just reading some printout I managed to get from a . . . a man in Rome.'

'On the IUD?'

'This source has, um, limited access to the IUD mainframe.'

Curtis whistled. 'You're an aggressive s-o-b.'

'I've just started. What's up?'

'Surprises. The lavish launch party for Bradford Ames' merchant bank. So posh he hasn't even given the firm a name. Just "Bradford Ames invites you". No Radziwill, of course. Hustlers, shysters, fraudsters, even legit financial types and . . . are you sitting down?'

'Lying down. Shock me.'

'And Geraldine Palmer.'

'What's surprising about that? Gerri's a very social girl.'

'On the arm of Boluslav Krevic?'

'What? Gerri can do better than that.'

'Not much better. He once saved my life, young Mr Krevic. Very mild-mannered but I want him on my side. They have an appointment with Ames tomorrow morning.' Curtis glanced at his watch. 'This morning.'

'How did she end up on Krevic's arm?'

'No idea.' He knew Palmer hated responses like that. Curtis hesitated. He'd read the body language between the two of them as they left the Hotel Eden. The vibrations were quite heated.

'You think Krevic is looking for a loan?' Palmer wondered.

'No idea.' Another offence in Palmer's nostrils.

'Lending money to Krevic's country, at this stage, is Las Vegas East,' Palmer mused, his banker's brain on automatic overdrive. 'Disastrous harvest last year. Disastrous underpro – .Oh, wait. It's coming back. Confidential CIA industrial espionage report. I saw it a year ago when the communist regime there gave up.'

'What are you doing, peeking at CIA esp – ?'

'What else do we pay them for? It's bituminous oil-shale deposits. Never exploited, never mapped, unknown capacity, unknown quality. What?' He spoke to someone in his room. 'Eleanora wants to invite you to a big at-home Sunday. After two years. Don't worry, I've got backup from Colonel Staeli.'

'You need more than that.'

'I'm working on a secret weapon.'

'What?'

'If I tell you, it's not secret. Say you can make it. Eleanora wants to gaze upon your gormless physiognomy. The woman is hopeless. Can you?'

'Depends on what happens here in Rome.'

'Sunday in the Holy City? Nothing.'

'Should I invite Gerri?'

An exasperated noise from Palmer. 'Will you tell me what Gerri is doing in the middle of this stew? With that Transylvanian nitwit?'

'No idea,' Curtis admitted.

'Full of no ideas tonight. That's your third strike. It retires the side. Good night. See you Sunday.'

His body looked pinched as he lay curled up, facing away from her. 'This always happens the first time,' Gerri assured him. What she meant, of course, was that it always happened to her, this failure of a first-time lover's erection. Were her breasts too small? Someone had once told her she had a luxuriant muff. Was it too heavy, all that gold brown pubic hair? Someone else had told her that men adored lush muffs.

There had been a time when she came on in bed with the same puppydog enthusiasm as Slavko had brought to their first encounter. But not since Gerri had finished her analysis, a short, sharp non-Freudian kick in the teeth by an angry male therapist on East 63rd Street. He'd explained that Gerri had, from two parents, too much money for her own good; break the rich-bitch image, or keep on enduring impotent lovers.

The first result of this deep psychiatric insight was that Gerri went to work full time in TV and took a tiny walk-up flat near the East River. The second was that she stopped all the puppydog enthusiasm.

Tonight Slavko hadn't needed any seductive moves from her. They were undressed and in bed and deeply into foreplay before they realised he wasn't responding. 'Nothing to worry about,' Gerri murmured, trying a few arousal manoeuvres that friends swore by.

It was the stricken look on his face, more than the non-performance, that got to her. 'My all,' he kept saying. 'I want my all to give you.'

Finally, the church bells nearby had tolled once but neither of them registered the fact. They fell asleep like two iced prawns, curved away from each other, buttocks touching, worn out by emotional failure.

Gerri's dreams were brief acrid snapshots by chill

blue flash: hand kissed; Christ weeps; here; there: and, finally, the smile of Bradford Ames, with those two sharp upper canines, triangular, like an actor playing a vampire.

Later Slavko awakened with a wild sense of pride and rolled over so that he was half on and half off her. She completed the manoeuvre, half asleep, by rolling back under him so that they fitted perfectly.

'Slavko. Oh, my God.'

Once started he seemed impossible to stop, until the church chimed five times and a faint pearly light enhanced the eastern sky.

Gerri got up from the bed and padded to the window. By leaning out, she could see a lone star overhead, fading as the sky went from black to indigo. She took a deep breath, smelling herself and Slavko. Someone else made the same sighing sound. She glanced across the airshaft and saw an older woman with larger breasts leaning out her window and examining the sky overhead. They nodded politely to each other with deadpan formality and each retreated back into her hotel room.

Gerri stood at the foot of the narrow double bed. Slavko was asleep and had, she thought, every right to be. But in sleep, he was aroused yet again to the role nature had assigned him. It looked huge, swollen from use, obviously so far over the top it would need a bucket of ice water ever to shrink again.

She smiled as she sat on top of him and very gently fitted him into her. He did not waken. Slowly, she began to move forth and back. Slowly his eyes opened. 'My all,' he whispered. 'You have it now, yes?'

'Oh, yes.'

'I hoped it would be thus,' he said, thrusting up against her opposing movement. 'When I saw you, in the garden, with the tears of Christ falling, I hoped it would be thus. And now it is thus.'

She watched his rather solemn, scholarly face with its high forehead begin to ignite as the luscious pain of yet another orgasm stirred inside him. 'Hold on,' she said.

He nodded, grinning suddenly. 'For ever, if need be.'

'That's the boy.'

'Or maybe thirty seconds?' They whooped with laughter.

Chapter Nine

The 'stern' or Castel Sant'Angelo end of the Vatican's mighty ship was already bright with dawn sun. Its west-plowing beak, figureheaded by the IUD's heliport, still lay in pre-dawn mist. Only its top floor caught the early light.

Christ wept alone, no flasks clandestinely catching his tears, alone and unseen except by Archbishop Tadeusz Radziwill at the window of the bedroom suite he occasionally used. The sun swept in from the east, blinding him for a moment.

Since this was Friday, and he had a full weekend of social and business engagements, His Excellency used this spartan accommodation to sleep and re-dress. His own villa, outside Rome, had never been air-conditioned; it was in the process of being closed against the summer heat. More and more he would be relying on these few cool rooms under the helipad.

He stared, half-blinded, down at Kurd's Christ. A faint shiver ran across his shoulders under the plain brown Franciscan's robe he used as a dressing gown. He tightened the rope-belt, wondering why the sight of all that agonized flesh-coloured bronze attacked him as a view not merely of a man being tortured and killed, but forever betrayed.

He knew the true and faithful thought of the IUD

as a prime betrayer of Christ. Hate letters over the years left him in little doubt. A man in his position focused the hate of others, gathered enemies. But these were the same pious souls who looked to the Church for every manner of service, from casting out the faithless to suborning the poor with subsistence-level bribes. Such proselytising, such protection, cost money. Under this Pope, it was bankrupting the Holy See.

The Sunday collection, even in a wealthy place like New York or Paris, barely covered the mainten-ance costs of the church in which it was collected. But this was mere pennies to a Pope who used cash by the millions. And when one amassed millions, these faithful critics meant nothing. His true enemies were those who understood amassing millions. One powerful thinker like Woods Palmer outweighed thousands of petty critics. One enemy who knew exactly how the trick must be done . . . he rated removal.

On a weekend IUD was manned by a small shift handling incoming problems from other time zones around the world. Radziwill considered himself a member of all shifts but was usually away on week-ends. There wasn't a lot to do, except for the regular Sunday afternoon preparation of a weekly forecast on a master disc. Then it was downloaded all over the world to client computers where it would be accessed Monday morning by top executives who depended on IUD for an unbiased insider view.

A faintly cruel smile disturbed the archbishop's thin, nicely cut lips. This Sunday summary was his propaganda organ. It was amazing how many companies and governments subscribed; major banks, brokerage houses, fiscal institutions everywhere.

The smile grew more genuine. He had always been considered a handsome man, in his youth and his prime, features firm. Now, in his late sixties, something of a further refining was taking place. He was growing yet more handsome. His cheekbones had begun to show. The flesh around his large, seal-brown eyes, instead of ageing into a network of wrinkles, had smoothed away closer to the skull, emphasising those bold eyes that saw into everything. His body, it was true, had lost an inch in height over the decades, gravity at work. But instead of making him stand smaller, he looked even more elegantly compact, distinguished, an angel used to traversing thin air who had deigned to park his wings for a lifetime and try the Earth.

Early in life, as a novice, he had already excited the angelic comparison among elderly monsignors who could find no other way to express what they felt for the almost girlishly beautiful young man. His voice in those days, descending from a boy's soprano to a strong tenor, had been raised in plainsong of school choirs. Once a priest, he had regretfully given up music, but still, especially at Christmas, enjoyed leading a round or two of carols. Having done his college work in one of Rome's best seminaries, he was happy as a young man to remain for a while in the Eternal City, even though it was hack clerical work as an English-speaking editor for the Vatican newspaper's weekly edition in that language. The more he learned of Vatican politics, the more he lost that angelic look.

Back in Chicago, as a monsignor, he began to come into the full reach of those awesome powers which Mother Church entrusts to its favourites. In an almost miraculous way he began to return to the appearance of a bright angel for whom everything would succeed. Assigned to head up the IUD a decade ago, he had returned to Rome once again. Perhaps permanently? Why not. He loved Rome, loved being at the centre of church power and of his own electronic network that dealt with the entire world of finance.

He turned away from the window and looked about his bed-sitting room. He prided himself on having converted the IUD from a fusty old Dickensian counting-house to an entirely paperless office where everything resided magnetically in boxed discs and tapes, not ledgers and dust-catching folders.

So, too, his living quarters, no notepads by the telephone, no spiral-bound diary book. Only a small monochrome VDU sat on a corner desk, glowing green. He strode up to its keyboard and tapped in today's date. The screen blinked and produced an alphabetized list of items:

> Bahrein debentures
> Bauxite

Deauville meeting
Ivory Coast drilling
Krevic

He frowned at Krevic, his gaze boring into the inanimate glass soul of the cathode-ray tube. Over the years, since it was he who had first programmed this souless machine, he had come to think of it as the one child Mother Church had granted him. As such, it often needed discipline, correction, even punishment. Impatiently he tapped the keyboard to settle a cursor mark in front of Krevic. Immediately the screen cleared and a new list appeared headed by: TRFR OB-31 TO AMADEO.

His Excellency dressed and walked down one flight to his office on the third floor. He sat at Bernardin's mainframe workstation, accessed the document he wanted and, using two passwords and an escape clause, copied it to his own PC's memory without showing that this had happened. He had accessed the same document yesterday, before his appointment with finance minister Krevic. But he hadn't copied it then. Or had he?

The archbishop maintained a very strict security watch on data. If anyone copied anything the software was programmed to show: a. that this had happened; b. who had done it and; c. when. But like all software, there was a way to slip around the safeguards which only Radziwill knew.

The software showed that he had accessed Oscar Bravo 31, not its text but its password. Yes! That damned note he'd given Krevic to introduce him to the man codenamed Amadeo! The note had to be destroyed.

He scrolled through document Oscar Bravo 31 slowly. A man high up in the CIA had leaked it to him a few years ago. The man had not been born into the faith but, as a prospective convert, was buying himself advance Brownie points.

Oscar Bravo 31 was headlined EYES ONLY UTMOST SECRET and reported the results of a fact-finding mission by Czech petrologists some years back. They had been invited by Krevic's nation to evaluate the bituminous shale in the Arpad Valley and the wilderness-desert region known as the Kneb. Nothing useful grew in these haunts of hardpan and tumbleweed. The Czechs had located underground domelike structures often associated with oil deposits. Their half-hearted test drilling, limited by a small budget, had proven little except that in the unlikely event oil prices went up, it might be worth some more ambitious, and costly, test bores.

In the interim, of course, crude had doubled in price.

So Oscar Bravo 31 had great profit potential. But its real secrets lay between the lines of the CIA-leaked report. Nothing less than His Excellency's deepest strategy, the one that would make him perhaps the first true modern hero of the Catholic Church. It was a plan so tainted with profit that its inventor could never hope for sainthood.

Hiding beneath Oscar Bravo 31 was a special

encoding in a separate computer language of what seemed a rather ordinary but quite long and detailed list of names, addresses, sums of money and compressed snippets of blackmail information, who had stolen what, killed whom, betrayed how many . . . a devilish list indeed for such a holy cause. It had no title, this master plan for, first, hi-jacking the fat mafia cosce doing business as Pan-Eurasian Credit Trust and, second, using its boundless cash to conquer all of Eastern Europe: all, from Budapest to Port Arthur.

Every fledgling government, every remnant of a faded old one, desperately needed funding. No bank could lend without fatally damaging its capital reserves below the Basel 1987 limits. But IUD, using mafia cash as its own capital, could leapfrog-multiply that sum by eighty-two fold. It could soon *own* Eastern Europe, once pious, then godless, but finally returned to the bosom of Mother Church.

This strategy lay, line by line, as a subtext only the archbishop could summon up from the depths of Oscar Bravo 31. He frowned, thinking about possibilities.

A computer fiend like Bernardin could probably safecrack his way into the subtext, given time and motivation. Any competent hacker could, given time and motivation. But Radziwill was not about to give anyone that kind of time, nor drop any hint at motivation.

Unable to contain himself, clearly committing an act of pride, he downshifted into a Cobol text and summoned up the hidden document for the sheer selfish satisfaction of paging through the names, the generals, the colonels, the politicians, the ministers of state, the lobbyists, the intelligence chiefs, the industrialists, the academics, the criminal syndicate managers, the technocrats, even popular journalists and TV figures, all of whom provided keys to bringing their country under the Vatican heel. Quickly now, he copied the CIA text on a separate disc, deleted every trace of CIA attribution and the entire Cobol list and shifted it into a fax mode. He transmitted it to an untended fax machine in Ames' Hotel Eden office.

As he did, something backshifted his memory. Just yesterday, that note. Any departure from the electronic to the paper-based was always fraught with dangers. The access code Bernardin had moronically included. What if . . .? In the hands of a truly gifted enemy like Palmer, what if . . .? How stupid of Bernardin, the archbishop thought, shifting blame, as any truly self-absorbed person must, from the fact that it had originally been his oversight, acted out by Bernardin.

A yard below him Christ's face dripped tears as the morning sun finally reached him. The drops glistened.

Father Bernardin in a black track suit and sneakers, with a white towel wrapped around his reddened face, jogged into the loggia of the IUD building. His glance, cast upward to Christ, caught sight of his superior. When he got upstairs, the archbishop saw that he was winded.

'Does that help with the weight?' he asked.

Bernardin couldn't answer at first. Then, puffing: 'A consummation devoutly to be wished.' Behind small, gold-rimmed granny glasses, his eyes darted this way and that around the office. 'Hard at work, sir?'

'I leave the hard work to you.' Radziwill looked stony. 'Such as printing out forbidden access codes.'

The sight of the young priest had triggered a deluge of furious images: first, the mainframe and its software as Radziwill's only son; the sharing of this child with a stranger who in age stood as a son; then suspicion that the two sons were in collusion; finally, a high, stinging shriek of pure paranoia at the mental picture of Palmer finding a forbidden subtext because Bernardin had mindlessly printed out its access code.

'Sir? I beg your pardon?'

Radziwill studied this confidential assistant, who had been wished on him without his request. Wasn't Bernardin at all responsible for correcting the mistakes of his superior? Could he not be depended on for any protection at all? How close were these two sons of his, the mainframe software and this hapless young priest? How near to killing their father?

Not for the first time, Radziwill wished he had elevated the other fellow to become his assistant, the elderly hack with the big family, Covici. He only needed a body to cover his mail and phone and fax when he was away. And he certainly didn't need a spy sent here by the Prefetura.

At seven o'clock, His Excellency tapped another Hotel Eden number into his telephone. It rang three times. 'Be sure you're the first one in this morning,' he began without identifying himself.

'A fax?'

He turned to the plump young priest. 'Bring us coffee, will you, Bernardin?' He watched his assistant leave. 'Be sure to destroy it, once read,' he told the telephone. 'And that note I gave Krevic. You have it?'

'No. But this morning I can – '

'It's the minor detail typical of a paper-oriented society. You know my sentiments about paper book-keeping. Burn it.'

'Consider it burned, Eccelenza.'

He hung up and sat for a while, replaying that meeting yesterday with Boluslav Krevic. It had not, of course, been unexpected. The obvious strategy was a straight, unequivocal 'no'. And then the referral. Not that the man code-named Amadeo was the only entity through which the IUD channelled loan prospects. Nor were the men from Providence, known as Pan-Eurasian Credit Trust, the only ones favoured to borrow from the IUD at low rates and re-lend it at exhorbitant ones. Amadeo was this year's favourite. It was not a permanent designation. It could easily be rescinded, a disciplinary act that kept such people keen to serve.

It was this willingness that presented the archbishop with such an ethical, delicious, tempting problem. When one signed a pact with Satan, the first thing to happen was the philosopher's famed paradox, the interpenetration of opposites. As when Adam's seed fertilized Eve's egg, the original sin was not curiosity or knowledge, it was the duality of opposites, a love-hate contract for power-sharing through guilt. Satan abided by the contract he'd just signed, *and so did you, the signer.*

One letter short of sinner was signer. Radziwill blinked at the way his mind wandered so in advancing old age. No, it hadn't actually wandered at all. When one commanded a limb of Satan as charred as Bradford Ames, one entered a zone of complicity. His sins became yours. Even worse, your sins were his commands.

Remove Palmer, hint, not command. Sinful but necessary, necessary, therefore commanded. How lovely did Satan make commanding this evil man. But he had an escape clause. After all, he worked with Ames simply to put Pan-Eurasian's cash in the service of the Holy See.

His Excellency made a disgusted face. Did anyone tell you in pure youth the compromises that made old age dirty? This business with Krevic, using Ames as the hook to land the fish, nothing shameful there. Not until the angler began the business of hooking, netting, and bagging.

The order to remove Palmer. To what lengths would Providence not go, in the name of Radziwill? The archbishop almost sighed, reacting to the other problem when one operated an evil man as one's agent. Evil was contagious. It made any course of action possible, a malign virus that anyone, holy or not, could catch. But, instead of sighing, perhaps in exasperation or chagrin, Radziwill smiled. He liked testing himself, pulling the unholy sharply into line.

His telephone rang. 'Eccelenza,' a man began in an American version of Italian. 'Sono un amico vecchio da New York.'

'Paul?'

'It's me, kiddo, Paul Doyle. Two a.m. here in Gotham but I wanted to nail your sought-after ear before the day began in Rome.'

'Paul, dear God, it's been how long?'

'Since we last saw each other? Couple of years. But since we first met? You were a kid in the seminary. I was a kid in the American Embassy. Rome was our apple, eh? La dolce vita.'

The archbishop sat back, grinning. 'Still playing nanny for the bankers?'

'Please. Chief of Protocol is the title. That's why I'm calling. To thank you for accepting on short notice. I know how seldom you speak in public. I do appreciate it. Take it easy on the poor dears, will you? They have been scared out of their laundry ever since Woods Palmer.'

'That's Woods. I'm more soporific.'

'Oh, you know the gentleman?'

'Even longer than I know you. I guess you could call him my oldest . . .' His voice died away. Oldest what, he asked himself silently.

'Coffee, sir?'

His Excellency blinked; he hadn't noted the return of Bernardin. 'Paul,' he said, 'if you're coming to Rome what about dinner at Grasso's.'

'The old pirate's still open?'

'Still asks about Il Signore Paul Doyle.'

Radziwill hung up and stared almost without seeing at the plump young mystic-savant his superiors at the Prefetura per l'Affari Economici had put in as a computer expert. But Radziwill needed no such help.

If only life had remained as simple as when he and Paul Doyle had gorged themselves in the old post-war Rome, prices at an all-time low. But still too dear for a seminarian. Good old Paul and his Embassy expense account. Today life was no longer simple. Life handed him anxiety like Bernardin.

The young priest had been lodged on him as a thorn in the side to be sent for coffee as often as possible. And, yes, this unwished-for son could have formed an unholy alliance with his own electronically created child.

Possible? No, probable, that the two were in some pre-Oedipal manner, working out a way to slay the father.

Chapter Ten

'Woods!'

Palmer looked up from his diary. He had taken to lounging on the pale green glider. He had sketched in a chessboard. A king stood in the centre, surrounded by an army of pawns. If only there were a way of introducing an enemy piece of the rank of bishop or knight.

He saw that Eleanora was quite disturbed. She was brandishing some battered plant. He snapped the diary shut. 'Is that the hedge?'

'It was.' She sat down beside him and gave the floor a vicious kick to set the glider in rapid sway. 'Woods, eight years ago I planted all that boxwood. I mixed the lime and peat and bone meal and vermiculite and – '

'Yes, I re – '

'And the watering. The spraying against insects. Year after year, until we had that glorious, full, thick hedge.' Her immense eyes filled with pain.

'Is that withered branch from the box?'

'It's what they've left of it. Chewed away by some sort of leaf-miner. But then look down here at the ground-line. A different insect, some kind of borer or beetle. The larvae eat their host.'

'Would you call them the lesser of two weevils?'

Her beautiful face went absolutely blank. 'I hate you.'

He put his arms around her. 'You look so godawful serious. That's why I love you, if you must know. Because for a gorgeous woman you sure are serious.'

'I want to get some serious insecticide that will kill. Kill!'

'You know my grandfather founded the family bank after the Civil War. You remember I showed you the head office on Randolph Street near the Illinois Central station? One of the first Louis Sullivan skyscrapers in Chicago?'

'Woods, are you listening to me?'

'Hanley was supposed to succeed Dad, but died in the war. After I got back to civilian life, Dad laid it on me.'

'I am talking about bugs, you idiot!'

'Me, too. When Dad died I found he'd merged several small banks into his and they'd eaten the host. They were mafia banks. The shock killed him.'

She watched him thoughtfully. 'Didn't the same thing almost happen to UBCO?'

'For your bugs what works best is so strong it's outlawed in the US, malathion. But Switzerland being the world centre of strong drugs, they may sell malathion over the counter to six-year-olds who can hardly pronounce it.'

'Good. We've got guests on Sunday and our beautiful hedges look like they've been scorched by flame.'

'Only one problem with malathion. It kills everything. Breathe enough and it'll kill you. It's a violent remedy.'

'Good. But don't think I approve of violent remedies.'

'Sometimes they are all we have.'

'You really are . . .' she paused and kissed him full on the mouth, 'hateful.'

As she left, he opened the diary and stared at his chessboard sketch. An enemy piece of any power, trapped with the king, could be as lethal as malathion. But wasn't that the whole idea of potent poison: to take chances with it?

Chapter Eleven

The electric toothbrush buzzed noisily inside Bradford Ames' mouth. It was powered by a rechargeable battery he was always forgetting to keep charged. Or perhaps Isabella had been using it instead of her own manual toothbrush.

In the vast bathroom of his Hotel Eden suite, Bradford Ames removed what he hoped was plaque from his sharp, even teeth with their sinister canines. Isabella, and other women as well, had often complained about his love-bites.

Submitting to him was part of any female employee's official duties. In a small office it was master and slave. The right to abuse was a key perquisite for the man on top. And biting was only good clean fun. 'Lo squale vicioso,' Isabella had called him only last night. 'Vicious shark. In your zleep I will file down those teeths.'

He finished dressing and returned to the bedroom. Isabella was fast asleep. No fear of such a spoiled Italian princess getting to the office before her boss.

Bradford Ames' smile was a bit frightening as he remembered that this morning, the moment she went to the office, the hotel staff was instructed to pack all of Isabella's things, her clothes, her makeup, and send it back to the tiny Trastevere flat she shared with a cousin.

Exit slave one. Enter, at least for an interview this morning, a replacement victim, Fiona Campbell. Fellow Scot! Of course, the Campbells were ever traitors to the other clans. But of what importance would that be to Amadeo Brazzi? Firing Isabella without notice was a fitting end to this supercilious imbecile. But firing her in this ignominious way wasn't enough. She needed real personal punishment, the kind that hurt. Only then would he be revenged.

Her long legs sprawled outside the sheets in the dawn of what would be another hot day, her small, tight black pubic muff parted to reveal all. Ah. Bradford Ames got the electric toothbrush and began tormenting her clitoris, the brush snarling in hair, then whirring on relentlessly. The action was not painful at first. Only later, he had cause to know, did such treatment draw blood.

She awoke with a scream and a desperate brushing-away gesture, as if attacked by scorpions. Eyes wide, she stared up at him, sensing the sexual power of the torture instrument. Her mood changed. 'Umm. Yes.' Then pain began to eat into her. With a convulsive twist of her legs, she sprang off the bed, feeling herself, checking her fingers for blood but finding none. 'Lo squale vicioso!' she spat.

He left her, long legs spreadeagled, as she searched herself for wounds. The Hotel Eden's elevator took him to his office, where he removed the fax text in his machine and sat down to study it.

Truly, he thought, he had never had such a good

relationship with a client. After working by phone and fax while Ames was in London, His Excellency and he had been physically together since last August, when the men from Providence had arrived. It had been His Excellency's idea to open a Rome office. 'We are seeing, but losing, a growing number of opportunities in ex-communist lands to the east,' he had said. 'You can deal with them much more easily in Italy than Britain. They will always distrust the Brits. But Italians are their kind of people.'

'Candy from a baby.'

'Unfortunately, I am sure someone besides myself has worked out this strategy. The man I mentioned to the delegation from Providence. And so far, I understand, he still lives in surprising good health.'

'Eccelenza, let me remind them of their responsibilities in this matter.'

Bradford Ames finished reading the oil shale report and made a series of small, scribbled computations on the margins of the fax paper. It was a very iffy equation, no more than a half-wild guess, but it convinced him that His Excellency's instincts, as always, had been correct: Krevic was a find. He was a victim wandering in search of a tormentor, existing in a pre-slave state, trained to obey no matter how deeply the whip cut. Bradford Ames looked forward to lashing the hapless finance minister into his web.

He was sorry the poor chump would be bringing his fiancée, who seemed a lot smarter than he was, with her American accent. Bradford Ames harboured no traditional British sniffiness about America. His cousins had even provided him with a US passport. The amazing thing was that it wasn't fake. Somewhere up in Providence, Rhode Island, territory of the Patriarcha cosce, someone named Bradford Ames, with a faked baptismal certificate supplied by a friendly Boston priest, applied to the US Department of Customs and Immigration. A legitimate passport was sent forthwith to Ames' Rhode Island address. How could you have anything but admiration for such cousins?

By the time the bells of Santa Maria della Concezione had rung nine times, Bradford Ames had memorized the oil report and shredded it. At nine-o-one a.m. there was a discreet knock at his door. 'Avanti!'

In his mind's eye, measuring the as yet unseen Fiona Campbell for Isabella's unofficial duties, he had envisioned her as tall and tawny, with a wide, reckless mouth and side-slanting grey eyes, daring him on. The woman who now entered was of average height, with bright, direct eyes, hair as dark as Isabella's and a tremendous bust on a slim body. 'Guid mornin',' she began. Her cheeks bore that highland swathe of red, as if satisfyingly slapped hard with a leather belt. Her glance was so direct, Bradford Ames felt she was measuring him for bed in that frank way a crofter lassie has. Bed and a wee cuddle between those brave breasties.

Despite himself, he smiled. He kept the smile distant and, he believed, cool. But it was hard to keep from grinning lasciviously, so neatly had Fate rewarded him. Grinning revealed the elegant cruelty of his canines.

'Sit ye doon,' he said in a joke brogue. 'Dinna tell me. Inverness, is it?'

'Maister, y'ken the Nessies have no accent but Sassenach.'

He sat back as he looked over her references. Reassuring that she knew at once he was to be her master, saved time. All that remained was to see how much punishment she could actually take. A lot more than Isabella, anyway.

Hungry or not, sharks seem unable to suppress their grin. It is perhaps the species' only failing.

It was just as well Boluslav Krevic hadn't brought his fiancée. The atmosphere in Bradford Ames' office was already tense with female stress. Intuitively egocentric, Isabella seemed to understand without being told that in showing the busty newcomer how the office operated she was not training an assistant but a replacement.

Krevic showed up five minutes early and said yes to a morning espresso and one of those croissant-like cornettos whose pastry is flaky-sweet and contains, like an elusive prize, a tiny dollop of fruit jam . . . or doesn't.

Bradford Ames asked both women to repair to the other office, closed the intervening door and sat back down. 'Now, then, ministair.'

'Now then,' Slavko mimicked out of sheer nervousness.

'Just for the record,' Ames said, 'you're not seeing IMF?'

'My government feels its loans carry too many strings.'

At the Ariston Hotel he had listened to a thoroughly American pep talk from Gerri Palmer, filled with those athletics phrases like 'go for it' and 'take your best shot' that had always puzzled him in American movies. Essentially, pep talk or not, he now gave Bradford Ames the same presentation he had given the archbishop. Neither mentioned oil; to his honest mind it represented faint hope.

'You're a terrible liar,' Gerri had explained to him. 'What possessed them to make you finance minister? You might as well stick to the truth. But please, Slavko, edit it a little?'

'Edit? A woman's name?'

'The British call it "being economical with the truth".'

It was she who had removed herself from the delegation. 'I've got a heavy morning. And, sooner or later,' she'd pointed out, 'Mr Ames will wonder if some US bank is involved in this. Now he doesn't even know my name, which is perfect. And Radziwill hasn't connected me to you. Even better.'

'Why must you remain invisible? I am so *proud* to know you.'

Gerri's small head, with its silky cap of pale brown hair, shook slowly, thoughtfully, from side to side. 'No, my instinct tells me you are about to be swallowed whole. I mean, those teeth! You need someone on the outside to help you escape. So, whatever you do, don't sign anything. I should finish by one o'clock. Let's compare notes then.'

'At Otello, yes?'

'No.' Her smile went softer. 'In Room 412, Hotel Ariston. I'll bring some sandwiches.'

A finance minister can never be impulsive. Nevertheless, he had lifted her off her feet with a giant kiss.

'By the way,' Bradford Ames was saying to him now, 'dinna forgi' that note the archbishop gave you. He may have written something more on it.'

'The note?'

'The one your fiancée showed me last night.'

'Ah, I – . She – ' Krevic paused, not remembering what had happened to the note. 'Is it important for you?'

'Not at all. By no means. Dinna gi' it a second thought.'

'I beg your pardon?'

'However.'

'Please?'

'Twuid be a tremendous help, there's no denying.'

'Then I will – '

'Dinna trouble yoursel'. We'll limp along without it.'

'On the contr – '

'Oh, well,' Bradford Ames said. 'In that case, many thanks if y'kin recovair it. Now. To business.'

Chapter Twelve

What do I remember of Teddy? Other than the good looks and the quick mind?

All façade. But that was true of a lot of kids, myself included, at Armour School, modelled on the great Francis Parker High School which saved the sons and daughters of the rich from public school alongside the offspring of Polacks, Hunyaks, Bohunks, Harps and Dinges, to say nothing of Wops and Kikes.

But a reverse twist applied by Chicago reformers like Jane Addams got Armour to give scholarships to precisely the 'elements' it had originally been founded to exclude. Teddy was such a scholarship boy and with charm enough to outpace the most social of the WASP, royal scions of the Armours and Palmers and Cudahys. Teddy dazzled them. He looked *so* good. Nothing else mattered.

Over the past decades, running into Teddy at parties and meetings, having the odd lunch with him, he still looks *so* good. But ruthless.

Now, if you run IUD, how do you look good? By ruthlessly making your competition, IOR, the Vatican's Istituto per l'Opere delle Religione, look lousy. Your bosses, the Prefetura per l'Affari Economici of the Holy See, those august cardinals of the Curia responsible for receipts and disbursements, then sing hosannahs to IUD and consider excommunicating the disgraced IOR, up to its armpits in banking scandals.

The European Community having razed its financial borders, Teddy's use of private lenders locks them into IUD funding. These private fronts look *so* good. They are decorated with fools'-gold titles like Providential, Offshore, Trust, Benevolent, Prudential, Mutual, Growth, Beneficial, Insured, International, Equitable, Guaranteed, Global and the other promised goodies of financial hype.

Even accounting for the inflated value of money, IUD had grown far larger than IOR with its malodorous, murdered go-betweens like Calvi and Sindona.

Teddy's façade silences any critic, muffles any scandal, rebuffs all but the most irreligious of journalists. One needn't be an old-line banker, son of a banker, grandson of a banker, to know how he does it.

The key is cash flow. People deposit cash in an account. The bank invests their cash, making a profit it shares with the original depositors, plus inflated service charges. Teddy's cash flow comes from – multiple choice – : a. poorboxes across the face of the Earth; b. massive contributions from wealthy communicants; c. sale of indulgences; d. none of the above.

Correct, none of the above. At the levels where IUD operates, the only way to raise such gigantic sums of cash is by marketing debentures, bonds, shares of stock or promissory notes, all honourable wheezes beloved of governments the world over. But IUD is flogging none of these.

Is there a source with a terrifying cash excess which normal investment techniques cannot safely sop up? Now that most legitimate banking systems of the West have gone sickly anaemic under 1987 Basel rules, only one lender has the cash flow. This entity has ruthlessly swiped first place. It has become the only game in town for even highly respectable borrowers. By giving society what it wants – drugs, girls, business and political clout – it generates the greatest cash flow in the history of mankind.

Having the cash is not yet everything one needs to become prime lender to western civilisation. One must also shield one's cash from the locust-like ravages of the tax man. So mafia cash is loaned to the IUD in gross untraceable chunks. IUD then invests it, benefiting from the fact that nowhere do governments tax religious institutions. But Teddy has added a wrinkle that freezes me with technological jealousy. He *loans the mafia's money back to it*. This is double-laundering, doubly shielded. But every façade has a weak point where it can be ripped apart.

In Teddy's case, ego. How it must *squirm* doing business with mafia scum, especially polished types like this new Ames shark. How it must gall to be only a participant in the world's greatest kidnap of lending leadership.

But surely, by now, Teddy must have devised a new strategy. With the Pope's own ego behind him, why not a financial crusade to convert the heathen who inhabit that gigantic landmass from the Elbe to Kamchatka? Oh, how satisfying to force billions of people to vomit up Marx and reswallow Christ, wine and host, body and soul. And to pay any interest you care to charge to replace one yoke with another.

One has to laugh, dreaming the dreams he must be dreaming, going down in history books, architect of a cutthroat Vatican Marshall Plan. The great fiscal crusade of the twenty-first century; St Tadeusz. Of course, only if he manages to stay out of jail. And ices his associates before they ice him. The moment they realise he's turned from patsy to competitor . . .

Palmer tapped a number into his telephone. As he waited, he doodled across his diary-page sketch of a chessboard with a king trapped by his own pawns. The phone began ringing in his ear. He pencilled in a chess piece with a mitred top, right next to the endangered king.

'Pronto?'

'Buona sera. Sono Woods Palmer. L'Arcepiscopo Radziwill, c'é?'

'Woods! Your Italian accent stinks.'

'Ciao, bello! We're having a rarity, our first open house in years. Sunday, after Mass, of course. We'd love to see you again, Teddy.'

Chapter Thirteen

'Well, I gather it is expensive,' Slavko mused.

'Tesoro? It's the most killer expense-account joint in Europe. More costly than a three-star restaurant, than any of Venice's most notoriously heartless tourist traps. Tesoro is utterly without mercy. My producer took me there for a glass of mineral water each and he signed a tab for a hundred clams.'

Slavko, lying beside her in a bed meant for one at the Hotel Ariston's Room 412, frowned. 'But that many clams might cost easily so much.'

Gerri nodded, deadpan. There were so many corners on Slavko that needed smoothing but for now all she wanted was the original, right where she had him. 'And he definitely invited me?'

'Invited? He demanded that my charming fiancée do him the – I have no head for Western, um, bullshit – extreme honour of his table at dinner gracing. Nine o'clock.' He rolled over against her and stroked her long, smooth flank. 'Perhaps he, too, has fallen in love with you.'

She had brought two panini for their lunch, long rolls stuffed with mortadella and salami. They lay crushed and untouched under her buttocks. 'Did you tell him my name?'

He thought for a while, his high forehead crinkled. 'Gerrishka?'

She stared for a long moment at the plain ceiling and chandelier. Slowly, nerve endings being scarce in that area, it dawned on her that she had been crushing the panini for more than an hour in an overly intimate way.

'He ask that from the archbishop you bring the note. He has never read it and wants its message. So I promised also you would bring with you the note.'

'What note?'

'Gerrishka! You showed him a note.' His forehead screwed up with the effort of recollection. 'Printed out by the young priest who assists the archbishop? A name,' he clenched his eyes shut to visualise the card more accurately. 'The name of Ames, the hotel. Another line? Something alphanumeric.'

She was silent for a moment, trying to remember if she still had the bit of paper and, if so, where it might be. 'Tell me, how close are you to a deal?'

'He is with him to the dinner bringing a draft contract.' He glanced at the only piece of clothing he was wearing in such unseasonable May heat, a wristwatch. 'We have many hours before dinner. Perhaps . . .' His hand moved up her flank and hip to caress her breasts.

'But you're *not* wearing that beat-up suit to a hotshot spot like Tesoro.'

'It is my only suit.'

'I'd give it in for pressing here but they don't need to have your presence flaunted. My TV company's paying a single occupancy rate. What about your hotel?'

'The Astor-Waldorf? Simple place. No valet service.'

'The Astor-Waldorf!' she screamed. 'That fleabag? For druggie backpackers? Can't your country afford something a bit more impressive?'

His hand dropped away from her. 'Too plain?' he asked, worried. 'But I can afford anywhere. I have a letter of credit. It has no limit. I issued it myself.'

Half an hour later they checked into Room 302 of La Residenza and gave in the suit for pressing. This had the effect of marooning them in their large, air-conditioned room. They had thoughtfully remembered to bring along the panini, which gave them something to do.

At about six, Curtis returned to Room 303 of La Residenza, showered and changed. He had put in a good, solid day but his compact, acrobat's body showed no sign of fatigue. In his experience, while hard work often led to success, a stroke of luck never hurt. Being in the right place at the right time?

Curtis had spent the late afternoon making the acquaintance of one Isabella Commodo whom he found in the lobby of the Hotel Eden, surrounded by her luggage, a churning welter of immense hairdo, long legs and cursewords directed against someone she called 'quel squale Ems'. Although his command of Italian was sketchy, Curtis instantly understood Ems-Ames. By handing him this attractive ex-associate of Ames, Providence had smiled on him. It was White Knight time.

The White Knight loaded her luggage in a cab and escorted Isabella across the river to her Trastevere apartment littered with female underthings. Her cousin, Rosanna, a more roly-poly carbon copy of Isabella, had the same big, big blue-black hairdo that seemed to have been administered by a carwash.

Promising to take both girls to dinner, Curtis was now returning to Trastevere, where he didn't actually care which of the cousins favoured him. He only knew that with both at dinner, Isabella would gossip freely and frequently about her ex-employer.

Slavko and Gerri had started by taking a shower together. After half an hour or so, this much cleanliness proved too wearing to their leg muscles. The valet's knock found them dozing together in the filled tub.

Temporarily without even his wristwatch, Slavko opened the door. 'Can you tell me the time?'

The valet hung the suit in a closet. 'Nine o'clock, sir.'

'Gerrishka! We are late!'

Naked, Slavko wondered why the valet was still waiting. 'Give him a thousand-lire note from my bag,' Gerri called. 'Give him two thousand.'

'But for what?'

'For leaving.'

Once the man had gone, Slavko picked up the telephone and dialed the Astor-Waldorf. 'Here is Signore Krevic. Are there messages?'

The desk clerk instantly began shouting. 'The

carabinieri are screaming! Your room is a wreck! The two friends of yours have frightened my chambermaid into quitting. Where are you?' In the shocked pause that followed he added: 'Sir.'

'My friends?'

'Two men. Americani? They have wrecked the armadio, the cupboard. For what were they searching?'

'They . . . wrecked . . .?'

Slowly, politely, Slavko hung up the phone. When he explained the call, Gerri called the Hotel Ariston. 'Miss Palmer calling. Any messages?'

'Miss Palmer?' the clerk asked in an unnaturally loud tone. 'Room 412?' She could hear him put his hand over the phone, but not so firmly as to mask an excited outburst of Italian and another, gruffer voice.

'Rimani nella linea.'

'Si, Capitano,' the clerk quavered. 'Allo?'

Gently, Gerri hung up. She stared at Slavko for a long moment. 'Your hotel he could easily learn from your embassy. But mine?'

'Someone has followed us?' Slavko wondered.

'It's that note,' she blurted out suddenly. 'They're trying to get their hands on that note Radziwill gave you.' She sat down in an upholstered chair and thoughtfully pulled on a pair of dark pantyhose over her legs.

Isabella pulled on a pair of sheer pantyhose over her legs. In the tiny bathroom her cousin, Rosanna, was finishing her shower. When Curtis knocked at the door, Isabella stepped into high-heeled black pumps and opened it.

'You must be wondering about me,' Curtis began. 'But a beautiful girl is used to men falling at her feet.'

'Yes,' Isabella agreed. 'And toni' you have four feet to fall for. Mr Ems, was how you call? Feet fetisher? You?'

'Did he tell you he was, or was it obvious?'

She bent over slightly to smooth her pantyhose. 'Some tings he told me. Some tings they were obvious. Which interest you?'

'Both. Everything.'

'Really?' For the first time that day she smiled. 'Then I must to remember whatever will get Mr Ems in the most trouble.'

The bathroom door swung open and Rosanna stood there absolutely naked, drying her breasts. She squealed 'Mannaggia! Mi scusi,' turned and bent over to finish drying her toes.

The sight of her rear end, so broadly displayed, gave her cousin an attack of giggles. 'Stupidoggine! Close de door!'

Father Bernardin sat before his mainframe work station and closed IUD down but left data on line for the weekend staff. They still had to prepare the Sunday afternoon round up summary and download it worldwide. Overhead he heard footsteps, His Excellency's chauffeur, taking the archbishop's baggage.

The plump young priest hit a keyboard stroke that displayed the time on his screen as precisely nine p.m. So prompt, His Excellency. Almost like a Swiss. Bernardin was a Swiss from the French part of his country. He counted himself lucky to get the IUD assignment with one of the Holy See's most talented men. But so reluctant to delegate work, let alone authority. So . . . well, suspicious.

Bernardin had been here four months. There were still access codes the archbishop hadn't given him. Bernardin easily hacked into them. But he was reluctant to call this to His Excellency's attention. It was as if his superior distrusted him or, worse, thought him unworthy of confidence or, perhaps worst, too uneducated to be trusted.

That, too, was silly. Father Bernardin had a degree from MIT in AI, Artificial Intelligence, something of a computer savant. He had done his dissertation on fractal geometry and mechanics. He adored fractals, not just for their graphic beauty but because they were today's link with pre-Christian concepts of controlling chaos. Fractals came down to the present day directly from the philosopher-mages of the Hebrew Kaballah and, before them, from the Phoenician star navigators who gave their people mastery of the sea, of the universe if only they knew it. The Frenchman, Poincaré, had guessed fractals were there back at the turn into the twentieth century. But he lacked the speed of the modern computer to do the mathematical work.

Bernardin worshipped fractals everywhere he

found them, in the branching of trees, the birth of crystals, the interplay of ripples, the flow of streams, the shifting of sand, the paths of our own blood vessels. Fractals were the language in which God revealed Himself to those whose faith was unsullied.

Oh, Bernardin reminded himself, he had the usual stains, mostly self doubt and ambition. Perhaps it was a particular facet of the archbishop's personality; he had the ability to open up a person to such self doubt.

The gift of showing everyone their worst. Was that possible in anyone, let alone a man of God? To bring to the surface one's latent or dormant – or at the very least carefully repressed – evil?

But if that was his gift, from what deity had it come? He felt sure it was this deadly gift that had caused him yesterday to forget to warn His Excellency about an access code printed out. The archbishop had the power to confuse him that much!

Bernardin was much more used to dealing with software. People were impulsive, sudden. They had their own motives for disinforming one. What had got into him yesterday? What circuit had shorted in his head and allowed his superior's mistake to stand?

Bernardin heard the expensive sound of a limousine door lightly swung shut. It clicked into place like gold coins caressing each other. He went to the window. At this hour the crepuscular light gave a bluish, shimmering quality to the tears of Christ. Below, the seven-passenger black Rolls stretched on

the cobblestones, the chauffeur in his uniform opening a rear door.

Tall, vivid in plain charcoal trousers and shirt with
its priest's collar, a pale white linen jacket over his
shoulders like a cloak, His Excellency strode down
the steps and entered the car.

Bernardin would have enjoyed using a key to
'erase' certain people like software. Surely an evil
thought to be confessed.

At nine-fifteen, Gerri and Slavko alighted from a cab
at the top of the Via Veneto where the Porta Pinciana
leads to the Borghese Gardens. The western sky had
dulled to a sullen bruise. Up here it reminded Gerri
of the Vatican gardens where they had first met. 'I
wish Tesoro wasn't so posh.'

'Posh? Like bosh, a derogatory term?'

'If a sauce requires one truffle for the right savour,
Tesoro gives it ten.'

Ahead stood Tesoro's small villa, near the eques-
trian Galoppatoio. The older doorman stood in the
uniform of the Third Austrian Light Cavalry, the
17th Regiment that ignominiously turned tail and
ran in 1917 on the alpine meadows of the Val
D'Aosta. He wore the high-crowned grey beaver hat,
flared top sliced rakishly, beak bright patent leather,
chin straps of rolled ochre cobra skin, epaulets solid
sterling with lapiz inserts. 'Walk this way, please,'
the doorman said, about-facing with a click of heels
and marching off, stiff-kneed and duck-spread.

'Walk this way, please,' Gerri repeated the vaudeville gag-line to Slavko, and started forward with a swooping glide and a discreet Bea Lillie hop.

As they disappeared inside, two eyes regarded the scene unblinkingly from a bench in the shadows of tall, funereal cypresses. A squat young man in hiking shorts displayed hairy legs. His backpack straps seemed to exaggerate his barrel-chested brawn. His right wrist bore a tight tape, split and dirty from long use. If badly set, a wrist fracture can take months to heal.

Bradford Ames had brought a dangerously pretty brunette with a Highlands accent and a cleavage like the Great Glen. The two of them rose from their table beside the small dance orchestra. To Gerri they made a startling contrast, not just in height, but in the exaggerated state of their secondary sexual traits.

'Such a grand plaisure to see you again,' Ames held her chair for her.

The moment Gerri sat, he was all over her, dominating her space as if sketching out in advance his plans to rape and eat her, in no particular order. She didn't mind this over-attention but hoped the woman, called Fiona, would not feel she had to encircle and ingest poor Slavko. Whores of Mammon, Gerri thought. To a New Yorker this was not unkindly nomenclature. She saw that whatever Fiona did – not a lot beyond erotic eye work – she couldn't really break through Slavko's certainty that there was only one woman and he had found her yesterday in the Vatican gardens.

'Ministair!' Ames exclaimed. 'They're playing ourrr song.'

Gerri recognised, mainly because her father had often sung it to her in her extreme youth, a song called 'We're in the Money', part of a Golden Oldies medley at which the five-piece band was pecking away.

Slavko's high forehead wrinkled. 'Ourrr song,' he mimicked faithfully.

'Niver mind,' Fiona said, getting to her feet.

She led him on to the tiny dance floor and embarrassed him by dancing too close. Gerri wondered if there were any other way for someone built like Fiona to dance. '. . . Pleased you could make it, Miss Gerrishka, since there may be clauses in the draft that need fine-tuning for the ministair. Och, his command of English is fair dazzlin' but yours is native?'

'Went to school in the States,' she said, truthfully. 'Can we finish the draft before we eat? I can't tell you how much my tummy would love that.'

He laughed appreciatively. She had put on a short-skirted, bias-cut number in pale rose that gapped sexily, or would have if worn by Fiona. His glance probed slits, caressing an underarm here, what could have been cleavage there, and fetching knees and ankles, if you favoured low joints. Bradford Ames maintained an eye-contact so heavy and so steady that Gerri wondered if he had a way of putting the eyeballs away afterwards for a long, long rest. 'Do you think the ministair will go for it?' he asked.

'Why not?'

The small orchestra had segued into 'When the Red, Red Robin Comes Bob, Bob, Bobbin' Along', followed by yet another perky little avian foxtrot none of them had ever heard of called 'Bye, Bye, Blackbird'. 'Down mammary lane,' Gerri murmured as Fiona led Slavko back to the table.

Being her father's daughter, Gerri never quailed before fine print. The six pages of single-spaced typing seemed to contain the earth, or that part which had entrusted its economic future to the financial cunning of Boluslav Krevic.

He and Gerri paged slowly, each waiting politely for the other before turning to a new page. Bradford Ames was bright enough to escort Fiona to the dance floor for a Latin medley.

'Jesus,' Gerri said as she turned the fourth page to the beat of a rhumba.

'No good?' Slavko asked.

'Too good. They're offering straight ten year amortization with prepayment privilege. It's as friendly as a mortgage. Let's see how much blood they want.'

They turned and read the fifth and sixth pages. Their eyes met. 'If I agree to this,' Slavko said, 'they will hang me from a lamppost in Duvku Square.'

She nodded. 'This stuff about mineral rights and leases? Are they talking oil? Because if they are, you sign nothing, Slavko. Nothing.'

She paused as the music changed to a tango. Bradford Ames bent his partner over so far backward Gerri could see a spasm of pain cross her face. Ah, that kind of bastard, was he? But was the Earth Mother of a mind to submit?

'Gerrishka, we are desperate for hard currency.'

She looked back at the simple face beside her. A lucky break, finding such an uncomplicated man. 'They demand exclusives, Slavko. That's a shutout bid. For that they shouldn't lend money. They should *give* it to you. In perpetuity.'

Once more Fiona was forced over backwards. As he hurt her again, Bradford Ames smiled down at her, his canines showing as small white points. She grinned back at him and moistened her lips, as if to enjoy the taste of pain more fully.

Gerri, whose imagination tended to the morbid, thought she saw in him a resemblance to the infamous smile of Dr Joseph Mengele. She winced as he tried to break Fiona's back a third time. The look on her face was ecstatic.

In glum silence she and Slavko reread the last two pages to the rhythm of the tango. 'This weekend,' she said in a very quiet tone, 'I must take you to my father. He's the only one I know who can save your poor, endangered arse.'

When the telephone rang at midnight, Eleanora was still in the kitchen. No one called this late except Curtis. She had stayed up late to fit together a gigantic bowl filled with water in which she floated a smaller bowl. This she had put into the freezer. In the morning she would shuck free an immense thick-walled bowl of ice.

'Elly, did I wake you?' Gerri asked.

Immediately Eleanora felt cheated. The truth of it was crude: she enjoyed sexually teasing Curtis over the telephone. Since she was anything but crude this side of her psyche worried her. 'Not at all, Gerri. But your Dad's asleep.'

'Can I bring a guest up on Sunday?'

'Naturally. It's our first open house in years.'

'Oh! Good. I want Dad to give my friend some advice. Elly, we'll take that Rome-Lugano overnight. Be there in the morning.'

Eleanora suppressed a smile. 'A wagon-lit friend, is it? Not Curtis?'

'Who? Oh, no.' The small joke had the effect of fuzzing the conversation to a halt. Finally, as if roused from deep thought, Gerri picked up the conversation again. 'No. Somebody else.'

'We look forward to meeting him.'

Eleanora returned to the freezer. She opened the hinged top and stared down at the two bowls, cradling a curve of water that would soon be solid. A strange lightness seemed to rise inside her. Gerri no longer interested in Curtis. It meant little, as insubstantial as water. Until it became ice. She closed the lid of the freezer. She understood how the world went, in sudden leaps, not boringly like a clock but rockets lit by a madman.

'. . . Yes, here at the Excelsior,' Gerri said. 'It's terribly thoughtful of you to take us home.' The grey Daimler limousine had negotiated the Via Veneto down from the Borghese Gardens in something under thirty seconds, pulling into the glitz-encrusted turnaround of the Excelsior Hotel.

'Not at all,' Bradford Ames said. 'Are you sure we can't have a night cap? No? Then about His Excellency's note? You've remembered?'

Gerri's brows contracted in thought. 'As I told you, I'm sure I threw it away, Mr Ames. But I promise to search for it.'

Slavko frowned. 'Gerrishka, this hotel . . .'

'Goodnight, Brad. Goodnight, Fiona. I just loved it as much as you did and so did Slavko.' She pulled the finance minister out of the limo and they stood on the sidewalk making small waving gestures until the big Daimler drove off.

'This is not La Residenza,' Slavko pointed out. 'This is the wrong hotel.'

'Wasn't tonight a thoroughly yuck experience?'

'That means?'

'Nauseating. Vomit-producing. Regurgitative.'

They entered the Excelsior lobby and found two richly upholstered seats out of sight of the street. His small face with its big forehead looked remarkably sad. 'To you alone I confess. To me most financial matters are . . . regurgitative.'

'When they find that out back home, they will revoke your entire existence. I wouldn't like that. I've never met anybody who . . . who . . .'

'Who you love as I love you?'

'Whom,' she corrected. They kissed and fell silent.

'But how obscene,' he went on. 'To demand of a

small country in great trouble that it give up the only future it may have. Moreover, to charge interest for raping it. Yuck!'

'I'd better tell you before it's too late. My father is a retired banker. A loan is not obscene to him.'

'No. An honest loan is not obscene.' He mouthed several words silently. 'This draft contract is not an honest loan. Does it anywhere oil shale deposits mention? Does it anywhere by being specific limit its greed?'

She glanced out through the doors. 'When a contract isn't specific as to time or tonnage or barrels, they own all of you.'

'What a terrible failure I am.' His voice had such a hollow tone that it gave her a strange turn under the heart. 'Can we run away? I am in disgrace.'

'As a matter of fact you are leaving Rome tomorrow. You and I are – ' She paused. 'Are your visas good for Switzerland?'

'I suppose. Would it matter? A failure is in any country a failure.'

'I have a funny feeling we shouldn't go back to la Residenza.'

'Funny?'

'Funny-peculiar. I'm not sure why. But we're only a fifteen-minute walk to the Stazione Termini. It's a bus station for coaches to Fiumicino Airport. It's an underground stop for trains that go to Ciampino Airport. It even has a diurno where you can get a wash and a nap.'

'Gerrishka, I am in your hands.'

'Um, how nice.'
'In all this something bright can be seen.'
'Yes?'
'Can I really be a failure if I have won your love?'

Chapter Fourteen

It amazed Bradford Ames to realise how much he didn't want to drop Fiona off at her apartment on the Via Sistina. How much he wanted, instead, to go upstairs with her to his place and, as he put it to himself, finish her off. She had that big-breasted Head Girl look that he loved to trample on till it crawled.

So it surprised him when Fiona said: 'Won't you come upstairs for another session of, um, discipline?'

'Then we'll be seeing a lot of each other. But not tonight.'

'My father's away all this month.'

Bradford Ames vaguely remembered, from her job resumé, that she shared lodgings with a Dr Campbell who had a lot of letters after his name.

He took her hand, turned it over and bit into the palm, hard. 'Dinner tomorrow. My place. Eight o'clock sharp.'

She turned his hand over and licked his palm. 'Aye, maister.'

He directed the limousine to the crowded Cavalieri Hilton high above Rome, far from everything but expense accounts. The two Americans were waiting at the bar, toying with a Friuli beer called Moretti. One was older and huskier than the other. The three men found a table at the far end of the room where an eavesdropper would have hardly any chance at all.

'No note,' the older one told Bradford Ames. 'Neither his fleabag nor hers.'

'She tells me she threw it away.' Bradford Ames attracted a waiter and ordered three double Scotches.

'How urgent is this?' the smaller American asked.

'Very. One of them may be carrying it around in a pocket or bag.'

The American made a blowing face as if cooling off something quite hot. 'You're talking mugging or purse-snatch. Maybe with weapon. Burglary's one thing, armed robbery's another.'

'Since when did you become a lawyer?'

Neither of them spoke as the waiter put down their drinks. Bradford Ames stared into the amber heart of his. 'This is not my action. I just know my client calls it urgent. And whatever he wants, I want even harder.'

Both of the Americans nodded in unison. Still synchronised, they lifted their drinks and waited politely till Bradford Ames lifted his. 'A personal question?' the husky one said. 'What happened to that brogue of yours? You Scot, or wot?'

'Scotcilian, as we say in the Gorbals.'

'Say who?'

'The Glasgow slum where I grew up with other Sicilians. They've cleared it all away now. There is nae accent I canna dui, from Laird o'th'Glen to posh English twit. I even know how to paak a caa in a Baast'n caa-paak.'

Both Americans took a while to digest this, the way people do when confronted by regional accents of their own country which they mulishly fail to identify. They chose to respond at last with non-commital nods. 'Nothing personal,' the husky one said, somewhat defensively. 'About the, uh, subjects,' he continued. 'They've blown their original fleabags. They're shacked up at La Residenza, third floor. Next move?'

Bradford Ames sighed unhappily,. 'I want these people sweet. I don't want them abused and connecting me with it.'

'You don't make things easy, do you?'

'A carabinieri raid?' Bradford Ames made a churning gesture, as in a pestilence of insects. 'Drugs? Pretext of the week. A raid and a search?'

'You want to spend that kind of money?'

Bradford Ames looked suddenly more attentive. 'What kind of money?'

'A fake search is a million lire.'

'Hey,' Bradford Ames reminded him. 'All my client wants is a slip of paper this size.' He made a square with his two hands. 'Give me a better idea.'

'Without all the cavalry, huh?' The husky, older man was silent for a while. 'Use the old bean? What do the subjects know about this piece of paper?'

'That I'm asking for it.'

'So, if we scare them into copping a sneak, they'd be sure to take the note with them?'

Bradford Ames smiled for the first time. 'My cousins in Providence said you chaps were real pros.'

He was too young to remember the old ways among the families, except as some elder's reminiscence. In most of the twentieth century mafia work had been handled by family members, not contractors like these. You wanted someone's hotel searched, Cousin Luigi did it. You wanted a scare chucked into somebody you called on Nephew Angelo. But by the late decades, and especially the 1990s, jobs got more tricky. So you contracted out. It cost more and you had less disciplinary clout over the contract-specialist, but it also gave you a layer of insulation from whatever deed he did. Only one drawback. You always knew Cousin Luigi's brain power; after all, you'd grown up with him. But specialists came to you on recommendation from others, really unknown to any depth at all.

'Chuck a little fright into 'em,' the husky American was bragging. 'Let 'em slip through our fingers. See how they run. The rest is kindergarten stuff.'

He finished his drink and sat there, waiting politely for his partner to finish his. 'We'll check out the Residenza. This late the lovebirds will be fast asleep. Shouldn't be too hard to spook 'em.'

'They suspect something already,' Bradford Ames said then. 'They went to some trouble to make me think they were at the Excelsior.'

'Keep tuned. Let's have breakfast at eight a.m.?'

'Where?'

'Where else? Where every fugitive heads for. The Stazione Termini.'

*

Ménage à trois affairs were never a favourite with Curtis. He suspected them of being lesbian events. He had no objection but balked at playing the human dildo. In any event, Isabella and Rosanna had no experience at all with such complex art forms. Their simple idea, after a lovely dinner featuring a bottle of Corvo apiece, was taking turns with Curtis until he died in their loving arms.

On his second round with roly-poly Rosanna, it occurred to Curtis that he served them as a mouse served a cat. The moment he showed signs of departing this life, they would cast him aside, bored, for a mouse that worked. Isabella had told him all about Bradford Ames and his business activities; she'd even sold him some useful xerox copies. Curtis was ready to call it a night.

That was why, after truly fond promises of more dinners lying ahead, Curtis left. At three in the morning there were no cabs in Trastevere. He reached La Residenza on foot at half past the hour, got his key and ascended to Room 303.

When one has spent half a night with two well-perfumed women, one's sense of smell diminishes. Otherwise, Curtis felt sure, he would have sniffed the intruders instantly. As it was they had locked the door and switched on the lights before he knew what was happening.

They wore the kind of fedayeen/mujahadeen head scarves much favoured by brave Muslim terrorists intent on hiding their faces. But no Arab had such chest development, such light skin, such pale body hair. These were weight-lifters, these two, although the only weights they held at the moment were two .45 Colts, army issue of Second World War vintage.

'Yes?' Curtis asked. 'You called?'

The huskier one gestured with his automatic. 'Siddown, schmuck.' Then an awkward pause. They were as surprised as he at this encounter. They were obviously in the wrong room.

'Pittsburg,' Curtis said. 'North? Altoona? You're some Arab, sonny.'

'And you're some Polack finance minister.'

Curtis' brain absorbed this second shock. It took a while. Apparently Gerri Palmer's Graustarckian boy-friend was staying here at La Residenza and these two clowns had patiently staked out the wrong room.

'This is me,' Curtis said, reaching for his wallet.

'Easy!' The husky one's Colt showed its nasty little mouth, hungry for Curtis' abdomen.

'Here,' Curtis said, producing a calling card.

'United Bank and Trust Company? What the hell?'

'I believe we may even have a branch in Altoona. And now, your card?'

'Stop shitting me, Curtis.' The husky one was on his feet, moving to the door. 'Listen up, dumdum: we own the night desk clerk. You touch that phone for the next half hour and we open a new bellybutton for you. Capeesh?'

The moment they left, Curtis opened the window to the front area three floors below. The false feday-een had to exit by the front door, down a flight of steps directly under Curtis' window where cars were parked. He held the TV set's heavy bulk poised on the window sill, ready to drop three floors. The implosion of the tube alone would wake the neighbourhood.

As he crouched there, tensely awaiting the two hoods, he scanned the street below, empty of traffic at this hour. But not of people. Across the street, standing in a narrow setback, stood a pair of chunky, hairy, muscular legs in walking boots and a sort of Ur-Teutonic pair of leather shorts. Who he was the shadows didn't reveal. One hirsute arm hung in view of the low-wattage street lamp. The wrist bore a filthy splint that looked stiff, much-abused and, to Curtis, somehow familiar.

So, Curtis thought, there'll be a witness to this. Couldn't be helped. He hefted the TV set and waited for the precise split-second to send it crashing down. He would have preferred to be back with the ladies, ménage à trois or not.

Chapter Fifteen

Stazione Termini is both an ancient and a modern place. Its north walls are built on those that guarded Rome from the Gauls in 4 BC. But its huge length, open vistas, halls and stretches of track, are sheltered by an undulating, pre-stressed, ferro-concrete roof finished for Holy Year in 1960 and still unrivalled as a good-looking way of sheltering so vast a space.

There is only one direct train to Lugano, the diretto, an overnight sleeper, leaving a bit before ten p.m. All the rest are Rome-Milan, both non-stop and those that stop at every possible village along the way. Once in Milan trains leave for Lugano regularly. The only way for a stranger to know all this is by mastering the arcane footnote symbols of the FS, Italy's national railroad.

Few tourists do. Nor do they have Gerri and Slavko's need for invisibility. Consequently, when they tipped the diurno clerk to buy them two tickets to Lugano, he of course bought two to Milan. It would be up to some clerk in Milan to explain the next step.

After a night's sleep Gerri and Slavko planned to separate and be reunited in the dining car. Not even an FS footnote would have warned them that the diner was shut down. Trains this slow served no food. Panini salesmen at the stations along the way would have to keep the passengers alive.

Although it cost as much as a fast train, a local was elderly, filthy and permanently late, in accordance with the Italian rule that those who do not demand the flashy hustle and bustle of the express train must be rustics who have no need of clean seats, aisles or toilets, or food and drink, or prompt arrivals.

The great hall of the Stazione Termini extends, like a cavern of the winds, from Via Giolitti to Via Marsala. At eight a.m. Bradford Ames found his American goods there, looking quite damaged. The slighter one's temple was covered with adhesive tape. The huskier one's right arm rested in a light-weight black sling. He shoved Curtis' business card forward. 'Mean anything to you?'

Bradford Ames' face paled as his elegant body collapsed in a white pressed-metal chair. Only a few days ago, Curtis had been on his trail, trying to phone him. 'Where does he come into it?'

'We figured you for the answer. This bastard . . .' The husky one spun a highly fanciful tale of woe in which nothing that happened was their fault, not even being booked on suspicion by the Vigili Urbani, nor their injuries.

'And what hospital is Curtis in?' Bradford Ames fell silent, trying to separate facts from lies. These two contractors had come highly recommended by his American cousins. They had radiated that typi-cally Yank aura of can-do-no-problems expertise. So much for specialists. Oh, for blood relations.

As they sat there, fabricating excuses, great morning hordes of Romans shoved past, suburban commuters with their attaché cases, locals reading the morning newspapers as they erupted from the underground Metropolitana, tourist arrivals hauling heavy luggage, back street merchants setting up displays of counterfeit trademarked goods, pedestrians taking a shortcut through the station. Noise rose by the second. Heat and smell escalated accordingly.

'And Krevic? The girl? The note?' Bradford Ames fell silent. It wasn't just doubt about their physical abilities now that Curtis had, seemingly without any great effort, converted them into walking wounded. It was their mental ability to extract from Krevic or his fiancée a bit of paper without either murdering them or alarming them against doing business with Bradford Ames.

Then necessity produced a better invention. Another strategy began to form in his mind, its outline still unfocused. Hadn't the archbishop already issued the proper sanction for this? Hadn't he, back last August, escalated this thing into a takeout mode? OK, maybe Krevic would have to remain alive. But everyone else, the girl especially, was expendable because Palmer was expendable. The logic of it had to be back-formed, but it was still powerful.

So the tactics went like this: kidnap Krevic and the girl. Pocket the note. Keep the girl hostage while releasing Krevic to fulfil his part of the loan. It kept him in line, no matter what. A hostage, of course, was a loose end. But only if allowed to live.

'If I were smart,' he said, more to himself than to either of them, 'I'd take you off the case. Give me one good reason not to. Your goddamned Curtis links into an entirely different scenario.'

'Yeah? Then what was he doing last night in their room?'

The shock was everything the husky man desired. It stopped Bradford Ames cold for a long thinking moment. 'Why did you wait till now to tell me that?'

'Didn't I say so before?'

'It makes all the difference.' The tall, handsome young financial genius paused for a moment, his faith in contract-experts partially restored. 'OK. Now listen. Get yourselves to Lugano. Then, here's what you do.'

Part Two

Chapter Sixteen

Noon, Saturday. The preparation of koulibac or coulbiac is probably as varied as its spelling. Eleanora's recipe had come from her mother, one of those nineteenth-century productions calling for many servants. With forty or more guests, several large koulibacs were indicated. This called for, say, three medium salmon.

'These are too small,' Eleanora pointed out to Titina, the housekeeper, a large Yugoslav woman, dark, not endearing, but very, very efficient. 'Telephone for three more.'

Titina's vast body, not fat but large, made the telephone into a toy scaled for baby's play. As she picked it up, it rang. Without paying any notice she began tapping in a number. Nothing happened and she started again.

'I think someone was trying to call us,' Eleanora observed.

Titina's brooding dark eyes signified a superior understanding and tolerance of the ways of the world, or at least this Swiss-Italian corner of it. 'They will call again.' She got through this time to the fishmonger's and terrorised him into sending three more fish within the hour. Doing business with Titina always carried an implicit 'or else' to it.

The moment she hung up and thudded off to

another part of the kitchen, the telephone rang again. Eleanora answered it. 'Hullo?'

'Elly? We're at the – ' Gerri's voice was cut off.

'Hullo? Gerri? Gerri?'

Eleanora waited by the phone to be called again. Only Gerri called her Elly. After five minutes she punched in a three-digit number that rang in the garage where Ziggy would now be having his sandwich and beer.

'Ziggy, I believe Miss Gerri is at the train station in Lugano. Will you pick her up? Oh, and – ' She flagged Titina. 'He can bring the fish?'

The housekeeper's massive head shook slowly. 'Let them deliver. It is . . . their duty.' The words had the weight of a hanging judge's guilty verdict.

Eleanora pulled a small notepad to her and began sketching in a menu, to be served buffet style and not requiring any knife-and-forkwork from guests in a stand-up position. The very act of sketching such a meal had become foreign to her. Before the business at Basel, they had had open house several times a year and small dinners almost every weekend. To return to such social events was a weight lifted from her heart.

Therefore: koulibac, plates of buttered dark bread, Titina's sweet-sour slaw, Eleanora's own warm potato salad with bacon bits, several large platters of air-dried, rosy-hued viande de Grisons beef, sliced almost transparently thin, more platters of bundner-fleisch, this time ham, bowls of ripe olives and tiny cornichons, Eleanora's mother's gurkensalat, but with a yoghurt/garlic dressing, three wines, coffee and tea and, from Posteriori's in Lugano, great wheels of sweet pastry, choked with ricotta and other aberrant cholesterols.

Palmer's study, large, broad-windowed, was flooded with noonday light. Later in the day, to accommodate a proprietor given to naps, the sun would dutifully swing around so that a wall intervened and the study grew ideal for snoozing.

'. . . Not so sure of Tanya's brilliant idea,' he was scribbling in his diary. 'When I was still in the business world, any publicity was good publicity. But now I'm not sure I need to give some muffin-brained German investigative reporter my time. Just because she's Eleanora's only child doesn't – '

The fax machine made a small noise like a shudder. It produced some fast-paced clicks and a sheet of paper began inching forward out of the belly of the machine. From a distance – that was what you put between yourself and trouble – Palmer could see on the paper a faithful reproduction of the UBCO letterhead, the larger one the home office on Fifth Avenue used. His heart sank. He had no further connection with United Bank and Trust Company, NA, except to own a lot of its preferred stock, part a golden handshake when he retired, part his own investments and part a hefty chunk Bill Elston's lawyers found in his will after Bill was murdered.

Palmer's mind slipped sideways, thinking of Bill and of the other people close to him who had died by violence. When she was really angry, Eleanora taxed him with being a bird of ill omen around whom death reaped its victims. He usually joshed her out of it by pointing out that, after two decades by his side, she was prettier, healthier and younger-looking than ever.

Retired, carefully distanced from UBCO, Palmer made it almost a religion never to do business with R Musgrave Vanderpoole, president and chief operating officer since Elston's death. He found Vanderpoole annoyingly smooth and inexperienced to head up the largest commercial bank in the United States, with its correspondent relations to hundreds of smaller banks coast to coast.

At the Basel meeting two years ago Palmer had counted on him for support. It had been Vanderpoole who moved the formation of a committee, tantamount to drowning the baby in the bathwater and dumping both down the drain.

'Dear Woody,' the fax read, 'can you telephone me on receipt of this facsimile message? I'll be at my club, the following number from two to five p.m. Lugano time. Please reverse the charges. Hopefully.'

'Dear Hopefully,' Palmer composed a mental letter. 'Starved by two years of non-social living, we are less than twenty-four hours away from an open house featuring attractive and intelligent people I look forward to seeing again. Does the fact that you are not among those invited give you the idea that if I never see you again it will be too soon? Faithfully.'

Palmer glanced at his watch. Annoying little nerd,

with his gratuitous urging to reverse the charges. At his own expense, Palmer tapped in the telephone number and waited. It rang at nine a.m. in Connecticut.

'This is Mr Palmer calling Mr Vanderpoole.'

'Woody? God, thanks a million, Woody.'

Only people who didn't know him well called him by his eldest son's nickname. His close friends called him Woods, his grandmother's surname grafted on to his father and him and Woody at christening. 'What's the beef, Bob?'

R Musgrave Vanderpoole liked to be called Muzz. 'It's Muzz,' he said, as if Palmer didn't know whom he'd called.

'Can we proceed?'

'It's . . . let me put you in the picture. You know how badly Europe had dried up for us. And we're not alone in – '

'Get to the point, Bob. What is the name of the bank that has offered to intervene for UBCO and get it back into Europe?'

'Wait a second. You know this gimmick?'

'I knew in Basel. Two years ago. But did that goose you into action?'

'My God, Woody, they've got some very prestigious stuff on their books. They've just underwritten a seven-billion-dollar highway sequence in western – '

'Pan-Eurasian Credit Trust?' There was a long pause at the Connecticut end. 'This is my nickel, Bob. Keep talking.'

'But you already know. How the hell di – '

'Two years ago in Basel, what did you think? Here's old Palmer, whacking off again? Why should UBCO worry about old wives' tales?'

'But there is not a sniff of maf – '

'Listen closely,' Palmer went on. 'Make notes. Implicit in every mafia shutdown is the opportunity to have the gate reopened for a price. What is Pan-Eurasian asking? Anything more than a 5 per cent finder's fee is blackmail.'

'Twenty per cent.' Vanderpoole sounded dazed. 'What have I done to get on your shit list, Woody? We're supposed to be friends.'

'No. You're supposed to run UBCO so my preferred makes money.' Palmer paused. 'String Pan-Eurasian along. Seem interested. Do nothing yet.'

'Till when?'

'Till – ' Palmer stopped. He could have told Vanderpoole to wait three weeks until the Rome meeting of the bankers, when with any luck he would use Archbishop Radziwill's keynote address to blow wide open the inroads made by the mafia since 1992. He could share with him the menace he was living under and his do-or-die strategy of putting the enemy bishop in with his king . . . if nothing else, a way of safeguarding his open house from attack. But even if he told Vanderpoole to wait for mid-June, this would be giving away his timing to someone too inept to be entrusted with a date.

'Till you hear from me,' he finished lamely, well

aware that he was breaking his promise to himself
not to get entangled in UBCO affairs again.

'That's great, Woody. That's – '

'Bye,' Palmer said and hung up.

His Excellency was in his limousine when the call
came. 'Eccelenza, I am sorry to bother you.' Bradford
Ames' voice. 'Would it be an imposition, sir, if I
asked you to, um, modify your position and call me?'
He gave a telephone number Radziwill knew was
not the one in his office or suite at the Eden.

His Excellency hung up. 'Carlo, find a telephone
kiosk.'

In a caffé-and-gelato bar, Radziwill dialled the new
number. 'Ames, this is a silly waste of my time,' he
began.

'I beg your pardon, sir. I must use convincing
pressure. Which may alienate me unless – '

'Dear God, what psychobabble!' the archbishop
interrupted brusquely. He could feel sudden, thrilling
voids opening up around him. Satan has always been
the aviator angel: dizzying heights, titanic depths,
thrilling power on leash.

'Sir. I deeply apologise. But I need your help.'

'Prayer? You have it. Concrete instructions? What
do you take me for, Ames? One of these corrupt
police chiefs who chomps down on his cigar butt and
mutters, "OK, you guys, shoot to kill." Could I give
such an order?'

There was a long pause at Ames' end of the
conversation. 'In other words . . .?'

Radziwill remained silent, letting the younger man nurse his grievances and worries. 'Nothing remains static,' he said then. 'We have moved forward, even as you waste my time. I believe I mentioned that to begin the Krevic relationship we would soon start assembling the funding? This phone call comes opportunely. The time is now.'

'Eccelenza, there is a lot on my plate at the moment.'

'Always give important work to a busy man.' The archbishop's voice grew steely. 'The time is now and the form . . . is cash.'

'Cash?'

'I would counsel that you begin at once to pass that famous plate of yours. Time runs short.'

Ames was silent for a long moment. It is not always possible for sadists to shift into reverse and without warning take strong punishment. Then, meekly: 'A su disposizione, Eccelenza.'

Radziwill hung up and turned on his heel to see if anyone in the bar had been listening. No one seemed concerned with anything but buying cones of ice cream. He felt strangely alone. Consorting with evil had that effect, giddy-making at such heights.

The archbishop strode out into the May sunshine. His driver stood with the limousine door open. Radziwill glanced around him at the light on the chestnut trees, the narrow cypress, the deep green pine. It was a glorious day for those with power. He smiled at Carlo. He smiled at his own reflection in the limousine window. He had never looked more handsome.

Chapter Seventeen

Father Bernardin had weekend duty thrust upon him as part of IUD's skeleton staff. When he'd arrived in Rome a few months before, he'd resented being so low on the totem pole that he had no choice. But that was when the intense proximity of the Holy City had excited his curiosity almost to the point of idolatry.

Then his commonsense prevailed, as almost any Swiss can rely upon it to do. Bernardin's interest in statues and monuments, in colourful crowds and swirls of human activity, even in the scenes inside Vatican City, seemed juvenile to him now. He had found one friend with whom spending a weekend was far more exciting than wandering wide-eyed around Rome.

That friend was the software. Its graphic capacity was endless. It could draw any fractal design. On being given the generator shape – a triangle, a square, a parallelogram – it could then iterate a command until, thousands of iterations later, it yielded its mysterious, mystical new shape and meaning. This, after all, lay at the heart of fractals, the tireless repetition, like a thousand Hail Marys, of the generator formula until, suddenly, with a leap of one's heart, the VDU revealed its miraculous design.

He could quite understand and empathise with

Benoit Mandelbrot, perhaps pondering on the Kaballah's sacred six-pointed Mogen David star, as he elaborated Helge von Koch's Curve. Since the fractal's Hausdorf dimension was always greater than its topological dimension, what lay ahead was always hidden at first. But Mandelbrot, unlike Poincaré before him, stood on the threshold of the computer age. With processing power of the order now available to Bernardin, what miracles could not be revealed!

When it became obvious that Bernardin *liked* weekend duty, those lay people who worked beside him in effect nominated him to be in charge. Bernardin was the only ordained priest among them. There was no designated second-in-command because His Excellency could not conceive of such a person. But Nature, if not God, abhored a vacuum. Silently, the weekend staff, who prepared the Sunday afternoon forecast downloaded to banks all over the world, chose Number Two by deferring all decisions to him.

It suited the plump young Swiss, although he knew if word of it got back to His Excellency, he would be sent to shrive lepers in Malaysia. Meanwhile weekends also gave him the chance to explore and learn his superior's security and access codes. Any weekend call or fax addressed to him inevitably ended up on the young priest's desk.

'Is His Excellency there?'

'Not until Monday. Can I be of assistance?'

'It's Bradford Ames.'

Bernardin felt the stirrings of deep guilt. This was

a part of the software's secrets he already knew, the man codenamed Amadeo, included in the incredible error of not warning the archbishop before printing out document codes on the note of Ames' address and telephone.

'A weekend telephone number for the archbishop?'

'I have none, sir.'

'But surely he cannot be out of touch.'

'There are several social engagements, I believe. Today, Saturday, he is in Milan, I seem to recall. But where I cannot say.'

'And tomorrow?'

'Milan and in the afternoon Lugano.'

At Bradford Ames' end of the conversation there was a long pause. Then: 'Lugano? What mysteries you high priests hold. No wonder someone so young is entrusted with such weighty matters.'

'Yes, Lugano.' Bernardin started to warm to his unoffical Number Two-dom. His software often asked him questions but it seldom enhanced his ego the way a human could. He was now being flattered into the role of archbishop confidante. Very well. He blossomed with information.

'On Friday the daughter of an old school friend visited him. I believe he, in turn, is visiting her father on Sunday.'

'Oh, marvellous.' Bradford Ames voice perked up. 'His name, please?'

'I have no idea.'

'You surely have in His Excellency's diary the name of the daughter.'

Bernardin swung over to his terminal. The office diary for today appeared on his screen, the usual Saturday near-blank. He keyed it back one day. 'Of course, daughters marry,' he said, scanning the crowded screen. 'The name may be different. Here, a Miss Geraldine Palmer, so the father's name may be the same. Minister Krevic was late and she volunteered to let him use her appointment time. You recall Boluslav Krevic?' The silence at Bradford Ames' end was profound. 'Hullo?' the young priest asked. 'Hullo?'

He could hear the line go dead. Hung up on. Not a word of thanks. In a world of ill-mannered, self-seeking human beings without even the rudimentary breeding to show appreciation, his software beckoned enticingly. Every time some flattering human being demanded attention it ended nastily.

In those many moments when Eleanora examined her own behaviour, she could never accuse herself of being shy about joining in conversations, even those arcane kinds Palmer's banking friends loved.

The truth was that by now she knew as much about banking as he did. He'd always been honest enough to demystify what other bankers tried to hide. Now the two of them saw the world with the kind of stark clarity that hurt the eyeball. The only difference between them, and it grew more sharp with each passing year, was that Eleanora accepted the world while Palmer still burned to change it.

The knot of young people around Palmer on the verandah, the companionable creak of the glider, the tinkle as one of Titina's girl cousins brought iced tea in tall glasses, all was for a silent audience of one, Eleanora. Tanya had gone off to find a tennis partner. Nearer at hand, Udo Raspe sat at one end of the glider, listening to Palmer's low voice.

Eleanora played audience at the rear of the verandah in an immense woven raffia armchair. She felt strangely unfulfilled. Perhaps it was all the young people. These two years had deprived her of being with young people. And this open house: why were most of their guests Palmer's age? Why not Tanya's and Gerri's age? As someone perilously balanced between the two groups, Eleanora longed to be surrounded by youth.

Across from the glider sat a good-looking man called Bert. He held a Nagra tape recorder in his lap, fiddling with the controls and the phallic microphone. The terms of the agreement with Udo Raspe had been that if an interview was granted it had to be recorded and Palmer had to be given a copy tape.

'I hear lawsuits rumbling in the wings,' young Raspe said. He was an impish, jokey redhead in shorts, a T-shirt and tennis shoes. There was an fresh quality to his gnome's face with its strawberry blond eyebrows. His whole body seemed frosted with hairs of the same colour that bristled with animal vigour as if a groom were constantly brushing them against their natural grain.

Bert's longer body wasn't as hairy. He kept tilting the microphone down and up, like a rising penis. His shapely legs and arched bare feet could have belonged to a girl.

Between them, Eleanora felt, the brunette and the redhead, they stirred intense sexual feelings. Curtis could still do that to her, but it had become a kind of formal quadrille. These two males sent echoing signals of impromptu collision and explosion like contact mines waiting to be stepped on. She yearned to step all over them.

Eleanora frowned at the feelings these two roused in her. It didn't matter that she could have been their mother. Nor that one of them was her own daughter's lover. She recognised the sensation. It was the same one that had gripped her so long ago when she'd first met Palmer in Paris. It had nothing to do with her mind but it did have a name: out of control. That delicious lust in which one's own blood seemed to heat the insides of veins and arteries almost beyond quenching. Eleanora took a practical view of this. A large ingredient of lust was novelty, she often reminded herself, and after two decades novelty was an artefact, not a found object.

'. . . Classic collusion,' Udo Raspe was saying, 'between institutions who benefit from the status quo and have everything to lose from a reform, an overturning of the status quo.'

'Meaning the Church and the mafia,' Palmer mused out loud.

Bert put the Nagra on the floor and flourished his erect microphone. 'Do we have a deal, Herr Palmer?'

Palmer glanced at his watch and turned to Eleanora. 'These two have bypassed my nap for me.' He smiled at her. 'What's your verdict? Kosher?'

'Mine?' She got up and took a pace or two towards the men, holding in her stomach. She was wearing a sort of tennis skirt that could be called mini in length but with a bright chartreuse halter top that emphasized her breasts. She watched Bert studying her as she moved. He pointed his microphone at her and followed her movements with its engorged tip, as if the thing's sensory powers had been aroused. All this with one of Bert's impish smiles.

'If Tanya trusts him, who am I to – ?' She pirouetted before Palmer so that the brief skirt flared out. What am I doing, she asked herself. What would Palmer think of her, behaving in such a demented way? But she saw that he had noted that foolish gesture with satisfaction, as if being granted a view of her legs up to her thighs was a rare boon. Men were insane, weren't they? At any rate, she thought with a sense of relief, Palmer was. Still.

Embarrassed, she sat down between him and Udo Raspe. 'I suppose,' she said in a much calmer, lower voice, 'it depends on when *Die Klarion* would run this article.' She began tucking a drooping lock of hair into her knot.

Palmer turned to Raspe. 'How soon?'

'Fifteenth of June. It breaks the day the bankers meet in Rome.'

Palmer glanced sideways at Eleanora. 'Your daughter has terrific taste in journalists.' He reached across to Raspe and shook his hand. 'Deal.'

Chapter Eighteen

On a Saturday the battalions of tourists in places like the Piazza di Spagna are augmented by squadrons of young Romans looking for action. As the day progresses and the mixture is enriched by cash remittances the tourists have gotten at the nearby offices of American Express, the situation grows more and more meat-rack.

Although only recently established in Rome, Bradford Ames tended to stay away from the area, with its bad sidewalk art, its frequent mobilisations of carabinieri sniffing for drugs and its general look of open-air flophouse.

Tourists are never elegant, not in the age of package tours. But in hot weather they shuck down to near-underwear, bathroom clogs and bottles of designer water. Their rabbit-warren hotel rooms, booked for double occupancy, are ovens. With hollow, heat-stunned eyes they gaze mindlessly at the passing parade.

Fiona's flat on the Via Sistina was too close to where Roman boys and girls auctioned their charms. He suspected what went on in really exclusive girls' schools involved a good deal of fagging and birching, so she'd have developed a taste for it. He telephoned to establish hegemony.

'Be here at once, slave.'

It was a tribute to his abilities that his voice quavered not at all, while his mind reeled with dire anxieties. When he'd learned who Gerrishka was all risks escalated. He regretted having sent the US Cavalry on to Lugano. They had already proved creampuffs in the hands of Curtis. That those two, targeted on Lugano, could produce results, was a crackbrained dream.

He hadn't been in Basel two years ago – and he could prove it – when that takeout of Palmer had failed. Now that Archbishop Radziwill had clearly provided the proper sanction to reactivate the takeout there was no margin for any further mistakes. To cap Ames' misgivings, he had no way of making contact with the two creampuffs.

His telephone rang. For one bright moment he felt a pang of hope. Surely the Americans calling. Thank God!

'A young lady visitor, sir.'

When he opened the door to Fiona he saw that she was playing a different role from the subservient one. The tight black-leather miniskirt, brutally tight leather bra and long black-leather torturer's gauntlets announced her purpose. The iced champagne under one arm signified her chosen method of conquest.

As they kissed she slid away to the nearest sofa and crossed her legs in their dark taupe stockings. Moody pools shifted and glowed in the curves and crevices of her knees and ankles. Removing one stilleto-heeled black leather pump, she held it out to him with the champagne.

'Fill it and drink it,' she commanded. 'I can't tell you how I've longed to dominate someone as dishy as you.' She smiled prettily at him.

The slap caught her completely off guard. The imprint of his fingers on her cheek looked for a moment like a brand. Slowly she slid off the couch and on to her knees. Hugging his leg, she pleaded: 'Forgive me, maister.'

'Banks,' Palmer said, 'are never choosy about the enterprises they finance.'

The reels of the Nagra recorder spun slowly. Bert lounged seductively, his eyes half closed but glinting with attention, his microphone erect and listening. Udo Raspe, on the glider, kept it in soothing motion, its faint cries of pleasure a kind of counterpoint to Palmer's voice.

In the distance, where the sun shone brightly, a lone hang glider with red-tipped wings darted through a low-lying cloud. The older man, Raspe saw, had the knack of speaking in complete sentences, no ums and ers. English's simple grammar made it easier than if he'd spoken in German. Whether the sentences added up to the kind of cover story he hoped to write was still to be proved.

Even under the best auspices, being Palmer's future foster son-in-law, so to speak, didn't build a common cause between journalist and source. The source had a point of view to publicize. But the journalist's motives? First, a sensational story; second, an exclusive; third, the freedom to slant it as needed to titillate the great public whose preference, in any case, was for bare-arsed adultery. Being a pre-step-son-in-law only bound him more closely to honourable behaviour, filing stories that ran in back with the impotence ads.

'Clearly, Europe isn't Europe without Eastern Europe, cringing into capitalism,' Palmer went on. 'They desperately seek financing on normal terms. But legitimate lenders hardly exist. If there's any big money to be found it's, surprise, with the mafia, suitably laundered to avoid being traced.

'But never forget one of the mafia's nicknames is Il Piovra, the Octopus. Its other tentacles encircle even legitimate lenders, especially those it has frozen out of Europe. Nearly all high-risk lending is now mafia controlled and brokered. The only high-risk money being offered is the laundered stuff.'

Raspe's bright brown eyes narrowed. 'Most of these lands were heavily Catholic. Is that how the Vatican becomes implicated in high-risk money?'

'Parts of the Vatican are meant to produce income. They do. How they get involved in mafia dealings I hope to prove.'

The words hung teasingly. Up 'till now, Raspe realised, he had boring business-news. Now Palmer was hinting cover story scandal.

'How would you go about it?' the redhead asked.

The glider creaked as Palmer sat up. 'I don't need much. Some sort of link. Just financial fingerprints will do.' He paused and watched Udo Raspe's sud-denly intent face. 'To identify a particular office within the Vatican as the working interface by which the mafia launders money and then invests it.'

Bert coughed nervously, which reminded him to light up a cigarette. He studied its tip. 'High-explosive stuff. You might not sink the Vatican but you would surely plaster Europe with anti-mafia danger signs.'

'I'm working on it. An associate of mine is working on it. You two might also work on it. That's all I can say.'

Bert returned to his half-somnolent pose, but Udo Raspe got to his feet and stretched his arms and legs. 'Oof. Too long in one place.' He indicated the Nagra. 'Switch it off for now.'

'We don't have a story yet,' Bert complained. 'Herr Palmer is a tease. Where's the part that smells bad?' He pinched his nose derisively.

Palmer stretched, too. 'Tanya told me *Die Klarion* is not that kind of weekly.'

'There isn't any other kind,' Raspe told him. 'We're competing for readers with every scandal mag in Germany. Just because we try to include quality reporting doesn't mean we don't have to keep giving them a whiff of shit.'

It was obvious to him that Palmer was on the brink of telling him more . . . and the Nagra was still running. Then the older man's glance went to the recording machine and his face went bland. 'Either of you up for tennis?'

'Not I,' Bert murmured lazily. 'If you're expecting us to do your investigating for you, Herr Palmer, I have to conserve my energy.' He smiled saucily and blew a plume of smoke. 'You're one of those old-time activists, eh?'

Palmer looked even blander. 'Retired activist.'

'One of those like my father who think individuals can change history.'

'I am more your grandfather's age,' Palmer remarked. 'We dinosaurs don't believe in excuses like, "Well, I did the best I could."' He turned to smile at Raspe. 'We don't see the point of underestimating our readers. Not everyone who buys *Die Klarion* is a moron.'

Not wanting to reply, Raspe shifted his attention to the red-tipped hang glider now circling above them. 'You see?' Bert crowed. 'The air is filled with activists, risking their lives. And history won't remember one of them.'

'I don't give a rat's arse for history,' Palmer said, being careful to smile. 'I just want to comb the mafia out of the EC.' He held up his hand as if one of them had said something. 'I know. The minute the well's clean it silts up again.'

'Not just an activist,' Bert murmured. 'But also an idealist. And . . .' He grinned maliciously. 'I know a tennis shark when I see one. In any event, I – ' He broke up laughing.

'In any event?' Palmer repeated.

'In any event, I couldn't trust myself with you in the shower room.'

'Please don't bugger up the story this soon,' the redhead said, deadpan. 'As for tennis, killer pre-step-father-in-law, you're on.'

Chapter Nineteen

The dark, good-looking one, Bert, removed all her clothes and slowly dropped to his knees before her. His powerful hands, dark with hair, clutched her buttocks as he . . . The telephone rang.

Eleanora awoke at once with a terrifying feeling of loss. Gone for ever. She slid out of bed without waking Palmer and tiptoed down the hall to the upstairs phone. There was no way in her heated state that she could talk to Curtis here in the long, listening corridor of bedroom doors.

'Please hold the line.' She switched the call to hold, hung up and tiptoed downstairs. It was only then that she realised she had no clothes on. In her randy middle years, she chided herself, she was becoming hopeless about sex. Bert, in an attack of sleeplessness, might wander these downstairs rooms and . . .

She picked up the kitchen extension. 'Ach, Curtis, go to sleep.'

'You sound miffed.'

'You destroyed a beautiful dream in which a handsome young man – ' She sighed. 'What is it?'

'Nora, I'm not handsome or young, but – '

'Making fun of the old girl's wet dreams.' She laughed, a tight, rueful sound, as she caught sight of her naked body in a glass cupboard front. 'Why did you call? To torment me?'

'To ask if Gerri has arrived yet.'

'She's due in tomorrow with a new friend.' Eleanora smiled to herself as she lifted her breasts, one by one. Still riding high. Her depressed state disappeared. 'It must be serious. They're taking the overnight sleeper from Rome. You seem to have lost the girl,' she added mischievously.

That tummy, situps. She turned sideways and frowned, otherwise, not bad. 'Curtis? Around noon today she called. She's the only one who calls me Elly. But the call was broken off. I sent Ziggy to the train station in case she'd come a day early but she wasn't there.'

'Mm.' He let out a pent-up breath, as if in exasperation. 'Her hotel room and Krevic's were busted up by two rent-a-thugs. Gerri and Krevic checked in at my hotel but I didn't know it. Later the same two clowns staked out my room and I had to stick the cops on them. But Gerri and Krevic have vanished.'

'Who is Krevic?'

'Actually, a young man who once saved my life. The two of them are like a bob-sled off the rails on fresh glacier ice.'

'Is this serious, Curtis? Be honest with me.'

'The romance is very hot. They may be shacked up somewhere. Do not under any circumstances – '

' – Tell Woods. I understand.' She turned sideways to gauge the look of her buttocks in the cupboard window. Pendulous? Too full? Where was Curtis when you really needed an answer to an important question?

Mounting the stairs she felt the low-pressure heat of Rome soughing northwards. Even on this mountain the night had grown humid and warm. Everyone's bedroom door was open. Tanya's bed was empty. Frowning, Eleanora padded softly along the upstairs corridor and looked inside Raspe's room. The bed was a tangle of legs. Her own tousleheaded daughter had claimed the high centre. Her fleecy blonde pubis glowed phosphorescently in the dark, although the redhead's hand was cupped over half of it. Tanya's hand had his penis gripped firmly. The two of them, thin, muscled, babyish, reminded her of cast-out angels who had plummeted down on to the bed from a great height and, exhausted, were sleeping until Hell's special side gate for fallen angels opened up.

The nerve of the little cat, with the door wide open! Angry and in the same moment amused, Eleanora tiptoed down the corridor and into the big bed she had shared for so many years with – what was that sickening term? – her 'life companion'.

Palmer, sheets off, had that same fallen-from-Heaven look. Eleanora snuggled in against his bony chest and grasped his penis. The direct approach worked for daughter? Perhaps mother too? Palmer grumbled. She began stroking him. Underneath her fingers, his penis stiffened in small, hectic jumps, not smoothly but with an erratic popping motion keyed to his pulse. The moment it was full its head began to swell.

'Mm?' His voice sounded low, still half unconscious. He turned slowly on top of her, his eyes opening gradually. 'Mein Gott!' he murmured, thrusting slowly up into her. 'You promise you'll still respect me?'

She started to laugh. He was recalling an old movie favourite of his called *Dr Strangelove*.

'Honey,' she quoted George C Scott. 'I'll respect the hell out of you.'

'Whooee.'

'Sh.'

She grabbed a pillow and muffled his cries. Together now, more calmly, they both worked at slowing everything to a long, comfortable, leisurely build-up. Mustn't upset the children.

Titina had coffee ready on the electric warming tray. Even this early on the morning of the party her young female cousins had arrived. The men were due soon even though the sun had barely risen. Next to the coffee she had installed a covered basket of dark bread and rolls. On the sideboard waited pots of jam and honey and a brick of butter. It was set up in the dining room, with its long plate glass refectory table that seated twenty people. Through an immense picture window lay the lake below.

At this hour, eight of a Sunday morning, the Lake of Lugano was almost devoid of life. A small steamer conveyed early risers back and forth across still waters. On the Italian shores to the southeast, contrasted with the slow-moving steamer, a carabinieri speedboat laid down a roostertail of foam as it skittered here and there.

Having spent a quarter of an hour checking his proximity-sensor system, Palmer now stood watching the lake as he sipped black coffee. The carabinieri boat seemed intent on a display of activity. At such speeds the men aboard it would be hard put to notice anything but their own spume and engine scream. Palmer picked up the 7 × 50 binoculars that sat on the window ledge and tried to focus down on the twisting speedboat. He was unaware that anyone else was in the room until he felt a breath on his neck.

'Anything?' Bert asked. Silently, Palmer turned and handed the binoculars to his guest.

'This is a very strategic Adlerhorst,' Bert said, sweeping the horizon with the powerful glasses. 'Eagle's eyrie, yes? Yet it gives the sense of still being *in* the world.'

Palmer nodded. 'Very important for elderly adlers.' His smile was slightly crooked. 'Did you sleep well?'

To his amazement Bert's face reddened slightly. Palmer knew he had the knack of sounding intimidating, even when he had no idea what he was saying except the usual breakfast chatter. Bert busied himself at the coffee trays. 'Did we – ?' His voice cut out as he seemed to restore himself to his usual slightly cynical, sardonic self. 'Mountain honey, lovely.'

Palmer's smile hung on at a disbelieving angle. 'Is today the day?' he asked, hearing the faint note of intimidation again. 'When we get to the smelly parts?'

Bert's blush deepened. He stirred his coffee and sipped some. 'You – ' He stopped and regrouped his thoughts. 'Our sales motto is "*Die Klarion* ist Klarheit", clarity, which creates an image of, well, crusading fervour.'

'But it ain't necessarily so?'

'Have you any idea of the national schizophrenia we Germans live with?'

'So a magazine that promises clarity should be a winner.'

Bert favoured him with one of his pouting, don't-be-naughty looks. 'Like my father you take personal responsibility for the universe. We are not like you. We take a more Eastern, a more Islamic view of life. You are the adler swooping down, killing the lamb at a stroke. We are the ants who, in our tens of thousands, transport the lamb, liver and lights, back to our nest-cities.'

Palmer tried for a neutral, non-intimidating tone. 'The industrial giant of the West, the financial leader. And you compare yourselves to ants.'

Bert turned away to stare out the picture window. 'When you don't take responsibility for anything, life can be quite peaceful.'

'Anything? Hitler?'

'We're too young to have to carry guilt for him.'

Palmer picked up the binoculars and watched the carabinieri pull two bodies up from the depths, hands manacled behind them. They had been submerged a week or more along the money trail and wore gowns of long green-brown weed. He thought: no point in disturbing Bert. With others protecting his delicate sensibilities, he could remain perfectly peaceful. A marvellous strategy.

'We never forget,' Bert murmured in an almost conspiratorial voice, close to his ear, 'that everything, and especially the eagle, is in the lap of normal chaos. You win. You lose. Despite your best effort, chaos can defeat you. Am I wrong?'

Palmer put the binoculars in a desk drawer. With its long sight, the busy eagle lived a life of constant alarums and excursions, attending to matters for which he assumed responsibility but which were often merely up to chance and normal probability. The ant, minimally instructed, only responded when required.

'Then you take a dim view of the story Udo is getting from me.'

'I?' That same mocking, don't-be-naughty look raked across Palmer's face. 'Udo's already decided to help you hobble the mafia. If he asked me I'd give him a warning about chaos structure. You two can plot your plots but something you don't even know about, a bit of fluff from an unknown nowhere, can bury you.'

Palmer stared at him for a long time, at close range, wondering if there were more to his message. He thought of today's party and all its risks, its places where everything could go lethally wrong. Then he lifted his coffee cup. 'To the peaceful life.'

Chapter Twenty

Striding briskly, eagerly, Father Bernardin returned to his office at seven-thirty Sunday morning. He came from an early Mass in a nearby small chapel for Vatican City weekend staff.

The young Swiss priest had set aside most of the morning to find a way through a maze, via fractals. He was giving battle, religious as well as mathematical, to the new researchers, called chaologists. They first devised equations, then illustrated them with computer-drawn fractals. But, being lay people and often non-believers, they had turned truth upside-down, Bernardin felt. *First* came fractals, the prime proofs direct from the Supreme Being, the vanguard probes. Anything manmade came second.

Today's experiment was secret. He was spending mainframe overhead costs on a problem quicker solved by a young and energetic rat. So-called social animals like ants, lemmings, bees, displayed the kind of minimal-instruction-maximal-success intelligence necessary to solve a maze problem. The maze was the core of life. If only, Bernardin often wished, mankind could realise how simple it was to pin one's faith in God's minimal instructions.

Every whole was an infinite variety of parts, as a circle was an assembly of arcs. So each ache of the heart, each twist of the political world, was an arrangement of tiny mazes. Each social animal got the simplest gene-instruction solution. For an ant: find food; bring it inside the nest. Multiplied by thousands, this produced complex results beyond the intellect of the individual ant.

The almost mystical ability of fractals to grow into unlimited form-designs rested on the same minimum-instruction concept. For any regular polygon, an equilateral triangle for instance, the first instruction might be to divide each side in three. The second instruction might be to add two lines to the central third, creating a smaller triangle. Instantly the Kaballah's Mogen David, no longer lurking in limbo, bursts into view. But repeat the 'generator' form again and again and the design grows dense, startling, revealing . . . all with two simple instructions.

Chaos *could* be encompassed that simply, Bernardin knew. So could life. Fractals disproved the atheist concept of chaos. What seemed like chaos in this infinite multitude of discrete objects – sand crystals, electron paths, snowflake formation, wildflowers, lightning discharges, Brownian motion, galaxy distribution, even urban growth! – was God's word made form. In the flutter of a moth's wing, the upward curl of smoke, the branching of a tree or our own arterial system, the scattered points of brilliance reflected in the ocean's curving rush of wave, in everything seemingly unprogrammable was God's *design* for chaos.

The telephone rang. 'Where were you half an hour ago?'

'At Mass, Excellency.'

'Mf. Give me a quick report.'

'It's been quiet. Our correspondent in Hong Kong downloaded some weekly averages. They seemed quite normal.'

'Fascinating.'

'There was a query from Johannesburg about a municipal debenture we refused to buy. The fax is accessed into your diary disc.'

'How exciting.'

'The night man discovered a leak in the basement. Someone left a valve half open. It's been mopped up and the valve tightened shut.' A yawn, barely muffled. 'And a Mr Bradford Ames called for you.'

This time, instead of a sarcasm, Archbishop Radziwill spoke in a suddenly sharp, hard voice of interrogation. 'And you told him what?'

'I?' Bernardin's voice wavered slightly. 'He wanted a telephone number for Your Excellency over the weekend.'

'And?'

Not everybody can get that much menace into a single syllable, the young priest realised. 'And, of course, I had no number.'

'Re-al-ly?' Three syllables, bristling with dread.

'Sir, even if I knew a number, I am n-not authorised to give it out, am I?' Bernardin loathed the sound of his voice and himself for being so readily cowed.

'Is that a fact.' Radziwill's voice had strange pulsation in it now, as if ripples of derision swept across its seemingly bland surface. He often sounded as if in jest. As if . . . as if mocking the work they did, the office in which they served, the Holy See that oversaw them. 'My, my. Tell me, Father Bernardin, with that precise mathematical mind of yours, exactly – ' He stopped dead.

The young priest's throat closed down as if clamped. He had started to sweat. This unholy gift of the archbishop's! This knack of bring out one's worst!

'Enough,' His Excellency snapped. 'Calling you precipitates the most incredible ennui. Till Monday.'

The plump young Swiss sat back in his workstool and watched the greenish numbers and letters on his VDU smear and blur as tears welled up in his eyes. He understood how old Giuseppe Peano had felt when here in Rome – God's Holy City! – Mussolini's blackshirt OVRA thugs had arranged his death in 1932 for 'tampering with nature' by using fractals to study nature's irregular and fragmentary patterns.

Now he, Bernardin, had made sure Authority would single him out for punishment. He had just told His Excellency a lie. Why? How? In a mysterious way only His Excellency had mastered, Bernardin had been inspired – was that the right word? – poisoned? Betrayed? He had been induced to lie.

It was possible, if Bradford Ames called him at Mr Palmer's residence, that His Excellency would see Bernardin's lie of omission revealed. Not possible, probable, highly probable.

What power His Excellency had, the gift of suborning one's own honesty. It had always frightened

Bernardin. Now, as he sat back and viewed the ruins of his Sunday experiment, he realised how deep into his soul, his bones, every fibre of him, that fear had crept. The archbishop had the power to make him a bad priest.

By eleven o'clock Palmer had already beaten Bert 6−1 at tennis and was prudently delaying his shower. That was why, after the telephone had rung a dozen times without being picked up, he answered the call himself.

'Is this Mr Palmer?' An American voice, male and harassed. 'I'm Gerri's producer. Can I speak to her?'

'I always assumed it was her mother and I who produced her.'

'Ha. Listen, we're all set up, crew, sound men, on-camera commentator. A zillion unpaid extras milling around St Peter's Square waiting. And the fuzz is telling us we have no permit. I have paid them off one by one. They take the money and disappear. Gerri is supposed to have − '

'If she calls or shows up here, I'll tell her.'

'That isn't good enough. I need her this second.'

'Tough shit.' Palmer hung up and instantly the telephone rang again.

He snatched it up. 'Don't you know when you've been hung up on?'

'I . . . I beg your pardon,' Bradford Ames' best British voice said. 'Is this the Palmer residence?'

'And if it is?'

'I beg your pardon. If it isn't too much trouble, may I speak to His Excellency Archbishop Radziwill?'

'No, you may not.'

'I beg your pardon?'

'Try him Monday at – ' Palmer quoted IUD's telephone number from memory and hung up wondering when he'd been promoted in this establishment to chief telephone answerer.

He found Eleanora in the kitchen with Titina and the three serving girls who formed a Radio City Rockette background to the tableau vivant. He also solved the problem of why telephone calls hadn't been picked up. The girls looked like graven images, frozen in time, as the two older women coaxed frozen blackberry sorbet to slide, glacier-like, into a great bowl made of ice. They wore rubber gloves against the cold. Once the bowl was filled, Titina placed mint leaves across its surface and returned it to the freezer.

'That was a call for Gerri.'

Eleanora took Palmer by the arm and led him out of the kitchen. Her touch was gelid, even through the rubber glove. 'Woods, Ziggy met the overnight from Rome. She wasn't on it. I assume she'll make a later train. Curtis called to explain that this, ah, liaison with the finance minister has, ah, hotted up somewhat and perhaps we shouldn't, ah, expect her to be as prompt as she usually is. He should be here this afternoon in case we, ah, need him.'

'With all those ah's, you sound as if something grim has happened.'

'Not at all. But she seems to have gone gaga over this man.'

'May I remind you Gerri's been up to her chin in torrid romances before. It's not as if we're being asked to countenance a deflowering.'

'I'm, ah, yes.'

'I can't stand too many of those ah's. Beating Bert 6–1 has made me real feisty. Level with me, will – '

The cricket-like chirp of the checkpoint TV camera interrupted them. They buzzed in two sets of friends who, because they came from faraway London, had arrived much too early. 'Christ, I have to shower and shave,' Palmer yelped. He stopped and thought for a moment. 'What can we do about Gerri?'

'I'll cope with the arrivals. But hurry your shower, please?'

'Maybe she's still in Rome,' Palmer mused, not listening.

'Maybe the British guests will be at the door in forty seconds.'

'She's too smart to be in trouble. But this Krevic thing sounds serious. Who is he, anyway? Jesus. That girl . . . I mean, you know.'

'She's your favourite. Mine, too.'

'Why do kids have to grow up?'

She gave him a sympathetic look, touched his chest with her forefinger, and returned to the kitchen.

He stood motionless for a moment, thinking of Gerri and then of Teddy Radziwill. He had hoped, by inviting the archbishop, to put him inside the circle of defence where the two of them were face to face. It might disarm him before the kill, pry open the current state of his handsomely evil brain and in a thousand smaller ways update Palmer's Know Your Enemy chart as they prepared for battle.

Teddy, in turn, would show up for equally warlike reasons: see how old Palmer was deteriorating into second childhood, help him wither thither, open a few new wounds and, if there were moneyed women about, score big for IUD.

He glanced down at his tennis shirt. Eleanora had left a small red-violet spot of sorbet stain there about the diameter of a .9 mm bullet entry wound. It lay directly over his heart.

And the battle hadn't even started!

Chapter Twenty-One

Palmer had insisted on three bartenders. Most of the guests wandered widely, swung on the verandah glider, chatted in corners or strolled among the box hedges. They had brought uninvited guests, Colonel Staeli, for one, had brought three husky young men with him, pushing the total past sixty with about half on the verandah and the rest everywhere else.

Almost everyone took a turn in the May sun, not too hot at this altitude. The sound of conversation grew louder. It being a European group, young and old chatted with each other, or got off in twos and threes to argue.

Bert and Raspe trolled these waters for sardines next to Big Tuna Palmer. What a lawyer might call entrapment, modern journalists call in-depth research. It was possible to create a scandalous headline: 'Friend calls Palmer obsessed.'

It was hard to tell those whose opinion might matter to readers of *Die Klarion*. There were elder male specimens who were convinced they looked like fools in sports attire rather than three-piece suits. Which they did. On the whole their wives or mistresses managed the Sunday-informal look better. Tanya had assumed short-shorts and a shoestring halter top as she gave a good imitation of someone merely taking snapshots for Mommy's album. The two British women had agreed in advance to display more bright blue eyeshadow than is necessary to well-being. Somewhere in their late forties, they had the saucy look of pre-teenagers who'd raided Mum's dressing table for anything bright and smeary. It was a tribute to their under-the-make-up good looks that men, with the exception of their husbands, flocked around them.

Palmer kept making eye contact across crowded rooms with Eleanora. He would mouth the word 'Gerri?' and she would shake her head unhappily.

A French couple arrived by motorcycle, strapped into enough leather to upholster an Alp. As the afternoon grew warmer they shed significant chunks of their rig until the woman – larger and more powerful than the man and sporting a bristling platinum hairdo – was down to bright red brassiere and panties. Her partner, short and nervous, was a Socialist cabinet minister whose day would have been complete if only he could get Tanya to notice him. She had managed to cast a spell over the youngish Colonel Staeli and the paunchy Herr Wentkos, private banker for the oil sheiks' personal investments.

If *Die Klarion* had run a contest for Most Handsome Man, it might have been won by Staeli, high up in Swiss intelligence and enjoying a phenomenal run of luck as a randy heterosexual bachelor. His natural prey would be someone like Fraulein Wentkos, a year or two older than Tanya but with more clothes on. But she had taken the occasion to back into a corner of the verandah a young Italian tennis player named Paolo. He had arrived with one of the Agnelli sisters or cousins, an attractive woman his mother's age. She stood with Palmer on the terrace, watching several hang gliders darting here and there overhead.

'How lovely! They play with each other,' she mused, 'like your guests.'

'Ours is a game of passionate chairs,' Palmer explained to her.

'Passionate what?'

'You've played musical chairs?' he asked.

'Ah,' the Agnelli woman responded in her British-accented English. 'Quite so, except that Paolo would never be crude enough actually to bed Fraulein Wentkos.'

'The ladies quite admire Colonel Staeli.'

'Too military. Too independent. To sure of himself.'

'You're awfully sure of Paolo.'

'He's a very well-brought-up young man. His decorum is impeccable. His bank account is non-existent.'

One of the British women was showing a Swiss a dance that had arrived from South America. It seemed no different from others except that it mimed sexual movements more explicitly. The Swiss blushed but did not stop the lesson.

In the distance, unheard by most guests, a deep-throated twin-toned auto horn sounded three imperious blasts. In that instant, a cloud covered the sun and a faint chill sprang up. Palmer saw Ziggy motion to him and pantomime a telephone call. At last, Gerri!

But it was the checkpoint monitor Ziggy meant. A high-sided black Rolls limousine had drawn up to the camera. A rear window rolled down electrically and Archbishop Tadeusz Radziwill leaned forward so that the light, dimmed by cloud, caught his face. As of that moment, the Most Handsome Man contest ceased to be a contest.

'Benvenuto, Eccelenza,' Palmer called. He clicked the gate open.

The railway station in Milan is not far from the centre of town, so grown from a small one at the end of the last century to a Manhattan-style enclave of finance, pollution and the arts. A Vespa with two young women dashed up to the station, their faces covered by tight-fitting filter-masks.

Gerri Palmer peered into daylight like an animal emerging from a den. She had the oddest feeling: the two Vespa riders were a pair; two carabinieri patrolled together. Where was her other self? Were pairs the rule?

She turned to find Slavko, lurking in the shadows. His eyes had gone wide. Hiding the gesture from everyone but her, he indicated the side entrance. Through it Gerri could see the bulky man with the sling and his thin, bandaged companion. *Pairs*!

She watched the thin one turn to face his partner, hiding his hands as he screwed a four-inch-long silencer into the muzzle of an automatic even shorter. Gerri grabbed Slavko's hand and pulled them both into a telephone booth. They were a pair again. But would it help?

The coast road that leads up from the town of Morcote, via hairpin curves through the village of Vico and around Palmer's fenced-in peak, then leads on to a second peak, Agra Carona, beneath which the autobahn tunnel speeds traffic north to Lugano. On Agra clouds now gathered fast.

Any atmospheric movement was rapid around these peaks. With the arrival of the archbishop the day darkened, the air grew heavy, his usual familiars. A short jagged stiletto of lightning cracked down and, a moment later, thunder rolled across to Palmer and the rest of the party.

The Agnelli sister or cousin shuddered. Palmer took her arm. 'Come with me. There's a new arrival especially designed to make you forget Paolo.'

'Dio mio. I don't want to forget Paolo till he earns back his deposit.'

'. . . No, no, a thousand times no,' His Excellency's tone was mocking. He seemed to be giving a tongue-in-cheek version of himself, as if rewritten and performed by Noël Coward. 'I'd rather die than say yes.'

He and Palmer stood on the verandah, the enemy bishop inside the ring of pawns. Every conceivable piece of the chessboard was also inside his proximity circle now. One couldn't kill a bishop with this many witnesses. Nor could the bishop strike down the king. Stalemate.

Whatever Palmer had hoped to find out remained hidden; whatever Radziwill expected to accomplish was veiled. But the game had just begun. Rain had come and gone without lightening the air. Beyond the cloud layer overhead the western sky shone still bright with mauves and pinks.

Night was coming fast, as it does on mountaintops. Pawns, rooks, queens and knights were inside, milling around the koulibac for seconds. Herr Wentkos began to annoy Eleanora by the way he had closed the gap between them.

Palmer smiled at the archbishop. 'You do utter refusal very well, Teddy. I almost believe you.' In his all-charcoal ensembled, his white jacket still draped over his shoulders, Radziwill looked ten years younger and twice as well dressed.

'If an old friend can be frank, Woods, that has always been your problem. You only hardly believe. No wonder your life is so . . . so up on in the air.'

Palmer listened happily to the Chicago accent, the hard, hard r's, the flat, flat a's, the muffled head notes. It was twinned with his own accent and rare indeed to find in this part of the world, like a long-lost relative.

Seeing that his point had been totally ignored, the archbishop produced an arch-frown, meant to pardon ecclesiastical advice-giving. 'Semi-atheists are an abomination in God's nostrils.' In the half light his cheekbones gleamed like ivory under huge, dark eyes. 'God wants you committed, if not to Him then to Anti-Him.'

'There are no believers in banks,' Palmer murmured with mock solemnity, placing his hands in an attitude of prayer. 'I must say, Teddy, apart from this weakness you have for pithy aphorisms, you keep getting better looking.'

'Worrying about old friends does it. Old friends who keep on fighting dragons. The trouble with being Mr Infallible,' he went on with another aphorism, 'is that the only man who can get away with it is the Pope.'

Palmer felt the key message click into place; he was being asked to lay off. 'I've got it now. Oscar Wilde, right?' Palmer punched Radziwell's shoulder lightly. 'Stick to the ladies, Teddy. I think you can count on La Agnelli. If I had never seen a prize hen and a cobra before, I have now.'

The archbishop's face went dead-pan but the eyes looked mischievous. 'You calling your old pal a snake?'

'You have mesmerised that lady. The way you mesmerised Edith into footing the bill for that weeping Jesus. Signora Agnelli can't wait to fall at your feet.'

'About time, too.'

'There is an old Latin phrase for you, Teddy: chutzpah?'

'Woods, Mother Church is haemorrhaging like a sieve. Charity has always been a bottomless pit. But this Pope . . . the more I make the faster it's spent.'

'Is that what you're going to tell the bankers at their meeting?'

Radziwill's face seemed to retreat, as if the light no longer reached it. 'I'm not going to scare them out of their tiny minds, Palmer style. We're the same age, kiddo. Seven-oh is our next major streetcar stop. Retirement time.'

'Retire? You? Breadwinners aren't allowed to retire.'

Radziwill's face emerged slightly, the nose and chin, as if testing the air. 'That can't be *your* excuse, Woods. Why do you hang on so tenaciously?'

'But I'm not in the public eye.'

'Oh, yes. It's a very small public, the banking fraternity, but you're stuck in it like a piece of grit. Why?'

The archbishop drew himself together, seeking to stand taller in a stand-off. 'Let's get inside and fill our plates.' Then, in a lower voice: 'That's my point, Woods. What's left on our plates at this age? It never hurts to fast.'

'Hang back. Cool out. And die.'

'Die? You're not leaving till you figure a way to take all that A-Preferred UBCO with you.' The archbishop moved inside, then turned back for a last word. 'You're the father of grown children. Any day you'll be a grandfather. Life's only a stage, amico mio. Start rehearsing the next role.'

Palmer nodded in the same deliberately misleading way as Radziwill had. Why let him see any of his darts had bullseyed? Why did everyone wish him mellow? Plenty of time to mellow after they screwed down the coffin lid. Mellow, he thought, was the preliminary state to putrefaction. Of course, this was still opening game. There were other pieces on the board for the archbishop to menace and take.

Unconsciously, he touched his chest on the left side where Eleanora had placed that bright blot of red this morning. Nothing like a heart-to-heart with his old Chicago pal to bring cheer to his waning years. Like an expert hang glider pilot sensing invisible thermals on which to float, Teddy swooped in on the assumption that to be holy meant you didn't have to watch your mouth.

Palmer had never before sensed this special power of . . . of . . . of bringing out the worst. But then, he'd never before let the archbishop get this close to him. How else could he find a weak spot in his armour?

Bert expected the tall, powerful platinum blonde to speak French but it turned out she was Dutch with a good command of English. Taking her time to do it right, one at a time she resettled her breasts inside their bright red brassiere. 'You go boths ways, do you not?'

'I beg y – '

'So do I,' she cut in. 'And you and I are exactly the same height. One hundred and eighty centimetres, yes?'

'More or less.'

'And M'sieur Le Ministre is . . . Well, he sometimes

gets lost in bed. I have to go looking for him between my toes or up my butt.'

Bert burst out laughing. 'You're coming on to me, you mad thing.'

The two British couples, who had brought their own gin from London, were rooting about the bartender's bailiwick for lemons. 'Small,' one of the blondes said in a loud, clear voice, showing him an egg formed between her two hands.

'Nein, entschuldigen Sie mir.'

'No,' she responded. 'Not nine. One only. Only one. Compris?'

The Swiss she had taught the Latin-American sexual dance was demonstrating it to a petite Italian actress. 'You see, how it mimes fellatio? Watch closely.'

In the kitchen, carefully placing a third koulibac on a great fish-shaped porcelain dish, both hands fully occupied, Eleanora felt Herr Wentkos caressing her rear, his slightly smashed nose twitching. 'Glorious! I die of hunger.'

'Herr Wentkos? Stop it at once.'

'It's my metier,' he explained in a very grave voice. 'I am the Nijinsky of the derriere. It is my food and drink. I pine to bite it, chew it.'

'Please leave the kitchen.'

'Ask me rather to commit suicide.'

'Please commit suicide.' When he left she began rearranging the third koulibac. Someone patted her rear. She whirled, furious, and found herself staring at Curtis. 'Didn't your mother ever explain that you can't make a pass at a woman feeding sixty people?'

'I got no sexual instruction from Mom whatsoever.'

'Will you accept some from me?' The minute she said it she blushed.

'Can you lend me a map?'

'Not even a compass.'

'There is only one direction on my map,' he explained. 'You are my north.'

'Am I that chilly?'

'Feverish, I'd say,' Archbishop Radziwill lifted the third koulibac high over his head and carried it out to the dining room.

Neither Eleanora nor Curtis spoke for a moment. 'Queer uniform for a waiter,' he finally said.

'Ah, His Eminence!' Herr Wentkos crowed. 'With a practical parable of the loaves and fishes.'

'I'm not a cardinal yet, Herr Wentkos,' His Excellency responded. 'And I never shall be if I keep consorting with low banker types.'

'He is the Vatican's miracle man,' Herr Wentkos confided in a braying tone to Tanya. The moment he cupped her buttocks she fired a flash shot, as if the camera's remote cable had been connected to that part of her anatomy. The tall Colonel Staeli came up behind her just then, his grave face alert, his eyes boring into Wentkos'. People nearby turned to watch. Radziwill's glance went from one to the other, obviously enjoying the tension.

Finally, to break the mood, Tanya picked up a

large bottle of mineral water and held it out to His Excellency. 'Archbishop, do your thing, please?'

'What's for salmon, white or rosé?' He let her continue to hold out the heavy two-litre bottle. 'How well today's young people remember only the material acts of Jesus.'

She let the bottle sink back to the table. 'I'm sorry.'

'As for making it wine . . .' He took her small hand and held it tightly. 'If you'll excuse me, I have a date to walk across the swimming pool.'

He turned and left, almost running head on into Curtis. 'You,' he said, taking the younger man's arm. 'Come outside a moment.' He led them on to the verandah. In the darkness, until his eyes adjusted, Curtis could only see the white jacket and the clerical collar.

'You're Curtis, aren't you? Palmer's dogsbody?'

'You do have a way with words. Good I don't know what a dogsbody is.'

'Sorry. Sorry. Sorry. It's just – ' Radziwill's sharp eyes glittered, 'I get angry when somebody's romancing my oldest friend's girl.'

Curtis produced a sound between a guffaw and a bark of anger. 'With your history you can't take a moral tone even with the lady who cleans your latrines,' he rasped, his voice getting a dangerous edge to it.

'She's not an adulterer.'

'Neither am I, but don't let that stop you.' Curtis turned to leave.

'I was standing right there,' Radziwill reminded

him. 'We seem to have gotten off on the wrong foot. Still, would an innocent man get as angry as you?'

Curtis turned in the doorway, the light coming from behind his compact, acrobat's body. 'Still,' he mimicked His Excellency's derisive tone, 'would you know an innocent man in a month of Sundays?' Curtis frowned at him. 'Let's not pretend this is our first dance, archbishop. I have been circling you since 1992.'

They watched each other. Then, just as Curtis started to turn away, His Excellency spoke in a low, urgent, tone, as if to a son or a younger brother. 'You've been too long at the ball, Curtis.' He shook his head in great sadness, his handsome face looking sombre and despairing. 'For twenty years you've fetched and carried. My God, Curtis, you're still a young man, but you've grown old helping him slay dragons. Eleanora has, too.' When he drew a breath it was a trembling one, as if almost overcome by the tragedy. 'He's not a bad man. I love him. But, like all bankers he's a taker. No wonder you and she try to console yourselves with each other. She's let only one partner fill in her dance card. Now she's left with a scrap of paper.'

'I'd better warn Palmer you're coining aphorisms again.'

'No danger. Nobody follows my advice, anyway.'

Curtis' small, prudent mouth quirked sideways in a crooked grin, almost of appreciation. 'Archbishop, they're waiting for you at the pool,' he said and left.

*

Palmer sat hunched over his desk, a drink beside him.

Beyond his office, his home echoed with excited chatter and laughter. By the small cone of light from his desk lamp he paged through address books. He picked up his telephone, dialled Italy and began with the number of Gerri's original hotel, the Ariston. Next he tried La Residenza. Then he dialled the embassy of Slavko Krevic's nation. Finally, he called a number in the headquarters of Guardia di Finanza, a high-ranking officer he'd known for decades. Nothing. Either telephones rang unanswered or, in the case of Coronello Minghetti, he'd retired last year and his home number was confidential.

Palmer sat back in the darkness, listening to the pleasure all around him. To minimise false alarms, he had switched off his private juju, the circle of scarlet neon sensor lamps. He felt, first, deprived of protection. Second, sudden, unreasoning anger at these people, having fun.

Gerri'd been late before. She was an intelligent young woman who could handle herself in foreign lands. But so many things could have happened. Was it impossible that she had been kidnapped? A hostage for her father? A time-honoured way to capture the king? Or the well-meaning imbecile with whom she'd cast her lot. He, too, had to be some sort of target. What did Curtis really know about Krevic? A resourceful young fellow, resistance hero, honourable jailbird. Schoolmate of the man now leading his just-freed land.

But the land itself, riddled with disgruntled secret police, out of power and thirsting again for nasty torture and murder. Agents, like land mines, planted in hatred, itching to explode. Who knew what fate dogged Krevic? And, standing beside him, Gerri?

He stared at what was left of his whisky, diluting to ice water. He stood up, emptied the glass in his wastebasket and squared his shoulders as he strode off to rejoin his happy guests.

The hired bartenders had gone home at ten, along with Titina's other family. As he listened to someone pecking out a rhumba rhythm on the piano in the library, Ziggy concentrated on producing a dry martini. So many years in Palmer's employ, Ziggy knew that even one fat drop of vermouth was too much. He looked up to find Palmer watching his work. 'Has my daughter called?'

'Not that I know of, sir.'

In the library, Bert and the tall, platinum-blonde Dutch woman were dancing the new South American dance of desire while one of the British women made rhumba noises on the piano. 'Faster,' the Dutch woman demanded.

'Randier,' the British woman called. 'Bite it.'

Ziggy brought the archbishop his fifth martini, setting it on a cork mat atop the small black Steinway grand. The British mock-pianist gave Radziwill a big, bold smile. 'Shall we dance?' But the archbishop deftly replaced her on the piano bench and produced a long arpeggio. 'A singing priest,' the British blonde enunciated with precise clarity. 'How utterly bizarre.'

The Socialist cabinet minister had had about as much to drink as His Excellency, but was a much smaller man. 'Song sov you ryouth?' he pleaded.

'Balls to that,' said the second British dollie. 'As the chorus girl said to the bishop.' She had come up on the other side of His Excellency so that he was now fully flanked by blondes. 'Give us the songs of *my* youth.'

'You are still in it,' he parried.

'Be a pal, padre? What Bea and Gertie and Noël used to sing?'

Radziwill ran a long arpeggio. 'Quite for no reason I'm here for the season,' he began in a sniffy voice devoid of any shred of Chicago accent.

> And high as a kite.
> Living in error with Maude at Cape Ferrat,
> Which couldn't be right.
> Ev'ryone's here and frightfully gay.
> Nobody cares what people may say.
> Though the Riveera seems really much queerer
> Than Rome at its height,
> Yesterday night . . .

People gathered around that kidding voice with which he handled life, a brilliant form of diguise.

> I've been to a mahvelous pahty.
> I must say the fun was intense.

> We all had to do what the people we knew
> Would be doing a hundred years hence.

He glanced up, smiling gamely. 'Haven't sung it for centuries. Hm-hm. Hm-hm.'

> Dear Cecil arrived wearing armour . . .
> Hm-hm and hm-hm-hm.
> And Freddie, who hates any kind of a fuss,
> Did half the Big Apple and busted his truss.
> I couldn't have liked it more.

⌐ne British woman on his right planted a great heavy kiss on his cheek. He dabbed nervously at her lipstick smear. Palmer came to the piano. 'I haven't heard those dulcet tones in, what? Forty years?'

'Fifty,' Radziwill said in a hollow voice. 'What's my right cheek look like?'

'Fetching,' Palmer said, dabbing off the rest of the heliotrope kiss with a paper napkin. 'Sing on.'

'Remember this? Circa 1934?' His schoolmate did a march-time vamp.

> Cheer for old Armour;
> Armour will win!
> Fight to the finish;
> Never give in!
> You do your best, boys;
> We'll do the rest, boys.
> Cheer for old Armour High!

'A very Depression-type fight song,' Palmer mused. 'Fight to the finish. Never give in. The way our generation was trained.'

'Only some of our generation. You, for instance, remind me of those ancient B-17's and Mustangs people get in flying condition. I always ask, because you can make it fly again, is that a reason to take it up in the air?'

Palmer gave him a pained look. 'And with what aphorism do you always reply?'

'Another song!' the Agnelli woman said, boldly sitting down next to Radziwill on the piano bench. 'Ancora, maestro!'

The archbishop stared down at her heavy upper lids. 'Signora,' he murmured. 'Life has not yet finished drawing the beauty of your face.'

'I'll see you again,' he sang in a straight, no-kidding
   Irish tenor.
Whenever spring breaks through again.
Time may lie heavy between,
But what has been
Is past forgetting.

As he played a slight arpeggio he murmured to Palmer: 'The potency of cheap music.'

Passengers for Swiss destinations board on Track 3 of Milan's station. Gerri and Slavko stood in the dark stairway. No one seemed interested in the Lugano train. Later the diretto would come through, bearing most intercity traffic.

Slavko's hair looked wildly awry as he took a step up to the level of the platform floor. Loudspeakers wheezed. 'Parte al binario tre il treno per Lugano.'

'Anybody watching?' Gerri muttered. She could feel her heart start to pound. Milan had been a sickening series of near-encounters. She nestled in behind Slavko, their eyes searching steadily, thoroughly. 'The baggage cart at the other end,' she whispered in his ear.

At that moment the thin man with the bandaged head emerged from behind the luggage. He had no time for careful aim, nor was the silenced automatic a weapon of accuracy. Nevertheless the slug snapped a white hole in the blue enamelled sign riveted over Gerri's head. Nasty razorblade chips of baked enamel showered over her.

She and Slavko backed down the stairs and out of sight. 'They have us bottled up,' he murmured.

'In a town this big? There must be some way.'

'Not if all ways end here on binario tre. And the airport would be even more conspicuous.' He was silent for a long moment. Then he patted his high forehead with a paper napkin. 'Perhaps . . . one way. A safe haven.'

Eleanora had sent Ziggy and the last of the serving girls home. Curtis had gone back down the hill to talk to the police about finding Gerri. The Dutch lady and the minister had retired. Bert and Raspe had, too. Eleanora saw that Tanya's door was open. Her daughter, sitting crosslegged on the bed, was scrawling something with a black crayon on rolls of film.

Tanya looked up. 'More than four hundred individual shots. If I'm lucky, *Die Klarion* will use three.'

She grinned but immediately her face lost its animation and she stared down blankly at the film cannister in her hand.

'What's wrong, liebchen?'

'Nothing.'

'An immense nothing, or a tiny one?'

'A marriage proposal,' Tanya snapped out, as if getting rid of something foreign in her mouth. 'That colonel.'

'Staeli?' Eleanora's voice shot up into the coloratura range.

Tanya gave her mother a withering look. ' "Can you imagine," he says in a low voice, "how barren one's life can be, emptying one's seed into endless condoms and diaphragms? And nowhere a single offspring of that seed?" I burst out laughing.'

'At a cry from the heart?'

'It's ludicrous. He's thirty years older than – ' She stopped, eyeing Eleanora sideways. 'Well.'

'Well, yes. A decision I myself seem to have made long ago.'

'This is different. He wants to sire a regiment of infants. I told him flat out: the world's a death pit, toxic, murderous. No babies.'

'Right!' Palmer stood there in his bathrobe, lurching slightly. 'No babies! Ungrateful imps. Well, at least we can account for one daughter.'

'We'll hear from Gerri soon,' Eleanora said. 'We have one guest left. I'll get his chauffeur to remove him.'

He straightened up appreciably. 'Poor old coot's

turned wino'n'is old age.' He raised his right hand and solemnnly made the sign of the cross. 'Nihil obstat. Amen.' He lurched into the bed₁oom and disappeared from sight. 'In nomine patri,' they could hear him intone, 'filius e spiritu sanctu. Yowsah!'

Eleanora lifted her eyebrows to Tanya. 'How did the colonel react? Does he think a weakness for older men runs in your family?'

The chauffeur was waiting in the kitchen with a nightcap mug of coffee. Eleanora moved through the downstairs – that melancholy air of noxious cigarette ends, wine dregs and the immortal peanuts that always come to rest under the chaise longue – into the darkness of the verandah.

The archbishop had removed his white jacket and was mostly invisible in his charcoal grey outfit. But the telltale squeal of the glider gave him away.

'Eleanora? This porch swing is hypnotic.' The glider creaked as he got to his feet, slowly but with no unsteadiness. If there were such a thing as the archbishop's queen's mate, he was about to execute it.

'Your chauffeur . . .'

'Yes, I know. It's a long drive for him.'

'Back to Milan?'

'Rome. The autostrade are empty this time of night.' He led her back into the house. 'Oh, I'm giving La Agnelli a lift. Please take care of Woods, my dear. We all love him but he's self-destructing.'

She was silent for a long moment. 'He doesn't listen to me.'

'He's the last of his race. Watching him tilt at windmills, people laugh behind his back. If he won't listen to you, or to me, then to whom?'

'Sometimes Curtis, but only rarely.'

'That young man . . .' He stopped for an instant. 'I like him immensely. He is perfect for you, my dear. I'm going to ask something quite unforgiveable in a priest. How long are you two going to play Sancho Panza for Don Quixote? You are both caught up in his impossible dream.'

'It hasn't been all dream. What gave you that idea?'

He smiled pleasantly, like a father or an old family friend. 'Just seeing the two of you in the kitchen. You're a widow, aren't you?'

She laughed helplessly. 'Such research.'

He paused and his handsome face grew terribly grave. 'It's never too late to go for your heart's desire. You have a powerful friend in me who can cut through red tape. There are some simple advantages to the Church. Take them.'

He gave her hand the same strong squeeze he had given Tanya's earlier in the evening. Eleanora wondered whether he meant more than that. Like an obsessive smoker who gives up the weed only by never smoking again, like the anonymous alcoholic who dares not take even a small sip, so perhaps His Excellency knew he mustn't kiss a woman, even on the cheek, just as their kiss on his cheek had to be eradicated. Eleanora frowned at the thought and at the array of temptations he had scattered before her.

Outside, at the long, high-standing limousine, Carlo installed the archbishop on the roomy back seat with the Agnelli woman and tucked a great travelling rug over their knees although the night was warm. The woman's great eyes searched like spotlights for Eleanora's, as if seeking forgiveness or, if not that, then understanding. It would never have crossed her mind, Eleanora thought, to ask for help. She was too rich for that.

'One must be tired, Eccelenza,' Carlo said. He had picked up speed on the southbound autostrada as they crossed the border into Italy. They were bypassing the outskirts of Milan. The wind tore his voice from his lips as he turned slightly toward his passenger, who always liked windows open, American style.

'A good evening's work, Carlo.'

He glanced down at the attractive Agnelli woman. Her lustrous dark eyes stared up at him, their great upper lids swollen with rapture. Her short, dark hair fluttered wildly in the breeze. Italians hate open windows, he remembered. Perhaps that accounted for the look in her eyes, half fascination, half dread.

'I'll see you again,' he sang softly. 'Ma, é la primavera ancora, no?'

Yes, Palmer, had been right. She *was* the prize hen, mesmerised by the cobra. Palmer's insights cut too deep for comfort. Not that it mattered. After tonight? After tonight he could be endowed with X-ray vision and still languish, powerless to act. His resolve would be leached away by a murderous acid bath to his psyche poured by his closest, most reliable dogsbodies.

Racing through the night, Radziwill almost regretted having passed a sentence of death on his old enemy. To destroy him, he needed no help. Still, it was always best to be safe.

'But doing good can be as tiring as any other work, Eccelenza.'

'Yes, indeed. But who said I was doing good?' He pulled down the blind between him and the driver. 'Just shut up and drive.'

When you have no idea where you are or what Milano looks like, everything fearful expands toward panic. The cab driver was no help. 'Ma, a dové?'

The cab was tearing around one of the circulars that makes Milano a concentric target for archers. With a black Mercedes sedan in hot pursuit, the cab was being driven closer toward the bulls-eye. What made it worse, Gerri knew, was that the whole evening had been like this, the two followers, meaner by the minute, closing the gap until now it barely measured a few yards.

With no other sound than a small snap, two holes opened up in the front side window near the driver. He ducked, eyes bulging, then slowly raised his head again.

'Che succede?'

'Faster,' Slavko shouted. 'Piu presto!'

'Ma il fucile?'

An instant later, hurtling around the circle, another hole opened in the rear side window. This time diamonds of safety glass rained down all over Gerri and Slavko. She brushed his hair free of them, then leaned forward and did the same for herself. Her lap sparkled. 'I'm afraid,' she said, 'their aim is getting better.'

'We can't keep this up,' he muttered. 'Next time one of us is sure to – '

'Stronzo!' the cab driver shouted, shaking his fist at the black Mercedes. 'Muso di culo!'

By way of answer, and still eerily silent in the rushing night, a fourth hole opened to the right of the windshield. It had miraculously passed through the shattered side pane without touching any of them. This peculiar trajectory gave the whole chase an almost supernatural quality, as if the cab was being pursued by gorgons or djinns.

'Vai fanculo!' the cabby screamed in rage. He stamped wildly on the gas pedal and the cab jerked forward hastily. The engine whined as if in extreme pain. The tyres yelped in horror.

'We cannot outrun them,' Slavko muttered. 'So, we must – '

Blue signs sprang into view with grotesque names like Gorgonzola and Monza. Off to one side a road led through a forest of tall, force-grown pines. 'Qui!' Slavko shouted. 'Torna, piu presto!'

With another sickening squeal of rubber, the cab slewed off at the last possible moment. The Mercedes failed to make it in time and sped on. 'Presto!' Slavko held the door handle against the force of the swerve. 'Quest'alberi li! In dietro!'

'You wamme to hide in dere?' the driver suddenly blossomed into English.

'Grazie! Grazie molto.'

'Is noddeen,' the driver assured them, tearing down the exit road at top speed but grinning back at them. The cab suddenly swerved right through a narrow slit in the curtain of pines. 'Dem bassers!'

The checkpoint monitor chirruped. Eleanora, gritty-eyed, watched Curtis's face under his sideways sweep of thinning blond hair. Like most men, she saw, in his middle years his face would widen, was widening, like a tomcat's. Palmer's hadn't. The skull lay too close to the surface. But Curtis was much younger than Palmer, as was she. Plenty of time to deteriorate.

She ran barefoot in the darkness to meet Curtis as he parked his car. They embraced, lightly at first, socially as friends would, then strongly, like lovers. She could feel every bone in his tight, tumbler's body.

Waiting for him she had undone her top knot and combed her toast-coloured hair down around her head like a longer version of Gerri's hair that radiated like petals from a central point.

'And Gerri?'

'My cop contact's moved to the a.m. shift. He comes on at seven.' He stared at her. 'You look – I've never – I mean, I've never seen you with your hair down before. You look like a little girl.'

She broke the embrace and stepped back. She sat on the stone porch steps, hugging her knees. 'This has been a hideous day. I'm not used to the social life.'

'I thought Radziwill enjoyed himself.'

'I didn't. You didn't. Woods didn't. He lurched off to bed, quite pickled.'

He stood over her, smoothing her hair softly, caressingly. 'Here we are, doing his worrying for him again.'

'Did you get that lecture, too? I never listened to any of my own priests' sermons. Why, the arch-bishop even gave me permission to sleep with you.'

'What nice friends Palmer has.'

Curtis sat down and caressed her legs with his cheek. 'Too bad I'm not a Catholic. With pre-absolution we'd be in the sack by now.'

'Too bad you can't keep doing that without talking.'

He kissed her knees. Her skirt had started to ride up her thighs. 'So soft,' he murmured. He buried his face between her thighs and she squeezed his head.

Gerri had wished to have her own head impris-oned between Curtis' thighs. The world turned, often upside-down. Wishes floated into the atmosphere and were granted in backwards fashion. 'This is not a good place,' she whispered. 'Titina's apartment is directly behind these steps.'

He gazed up at her peacefully balanced face, eyes

and cheekbones perfectly placed even now, even when fatigue or emotion might have distorted them. And always with that clear sense of otherness, of attending the other, hearing, talking with a firm sense that she was one of at least two.

'I know a better place,' she said.

They walked to the wine cave, hand in hand, smelling the dry, cool floor and walls. 'Someone's been smoking in here.' Curtis lit a match.

Racks of bottles on their sides seemed to retreat in peculiarly sinister perspective. He blew out the match. They lay down. 'Curtis, I've been thinking.'

'My curse is talking. Yours is thinking.'

'Radziwill. He wants Woods destroyed. By us.'

'Because we have the hots for each other.'

'How precise American slang can be.' She turned sideways towards him. 'The match was hot. When you blew it out, its "hots" ended.' When he didn't reply Eleanora said, 'I'm trying to understand why I can think of betraying Woods.' He struck another match. The sulphur stench almost choked her for an instant. He blew out the match and a moment later pressed it against her skin. '*Curtis!*'

The pain of its heat was shared between her palm and his thumb. 'The hots,' he said then, 'don't die as easily as you seem to think.'

In the blackness she heard him get to his feet. 'That bastard Radziwill,' he said, pacing back and forth.

'Please come back to me, Curtis. I can't see you.'

'He knows that if I didn't spend my life working

with Palmer and worshipping you I'd just make another unsuitable marriage.'

She laughed softly, despairingly. 'My problem exactly.'

As with sunset, sunrise comes quickly to mountain tops. At five a.m. the eastern sky showed a thin razor slash of orange-white like molten steel. Curtis lifted her to her feet and kissed her lightly on the lips, thinking that the hour they'd just spent in each other's arms, without moving on to the next level, reminded him most of his youngest, fumbling experiences with girls. But the two of them were forty. It was silly. It was noble. It was loyal. It was silly.

'I'm going back to town. My contact comes on duty soon.' He smiled and left.

Eleanora waited until she heard his engine start. She dashed back barefoot to the kitchen.

The wine cave fell silent. Its utter blackness began to be tempered by faint shadowless, featureless light from the east. The big, well-muscled Dutch woman emerged from the very rear of the cave, brushing dust from her naked body. She stood over the sleeping Bert, scratching at her platinum hair. Then she prodded his testicles with her toes. Gently.

He squinted up at her. 'Did you get *any* sleep? What do you call an hour of true confession that never gets to a fuck?' He flexed his slender legs and feet. Then he coughed for a while and lit a cigarette.

'I found it romantic,' she confessed. 'Touching. Even so, Herr Journalist, you were dying for a flashlight so you could scribble in your little notebook.'

'To report assignation without penetration?' As she pulled on a yellow dressing gown, he eyed her sideways with a look reserved for naughtiness only if it tested high in malice. 'Do you have any idea what this past hour is worth to me . . .' he leered, 'in sheer filthy scandal?'

She gave him a fake hurt look. 'For a moment I thought you were going to pay me a compliment.'

'You? But we're the same sex.'

'Then go fuck yourself,' she said, laughing as she left the cave.

Bert pulled on his clothes. The tiny spiralbound notebook was thin; he filled it quickly, chain-smoking as he did. Normally he loathed scandal culled from people not in the public eye. Only public figures had surrendered their right to a private life. But this was so apropos, this agonised goodness. This material Curtis and Eleanora agonised over would elevate the Palmer story from the lifeless financial exposé Udo would write to a steaming hot chestnut.

It had everything: controversial international banker, long-time German mistress, UBCO tie through Curtis, the matinee-idol face of the charismatic archbishop, the runaway daughter, the Slav-Balkan finance minister. It even had one of those things everyone was searching for. Something about a missing note from the archbishop? He scribbled away. Names he spelled phonetically, although he already knew how to spell Krevic.

It was nearly seven when Bert appeared in the dining room and found Titina serving coffee to Eleanora and Curtis. A small wood fire blazed in a stainless steel hearth, taking the morning chill off the room. As he entered, a knot of resin hissed and spat smoke.

He smiled broadly at the almost-lovers before he sat down with a grunt of pain. Cave floors made bad beds. Hyper-athletic Dutch blondes were even worse. Still, an amusing experience . . . and mammoth scoop.

He watched the faces of two people whose deepest secrets he already knew. They looked washed out, as if whoever had painted them had mixed much too much water with the colours. He longed now to strengthen the misty outlines of these near-lovers with India ink. Or erase them entirely with laundry bleach. Funny how much sex depended on fluids of one kind or another. 'Sleep well?'

'Be careful what you tell him,' Eleanora advised. 'He's one of those fearless investigative reporters. Nicht wahr, Bertl?'

'One of those gutter snoops,' Bert agreed. He smiled conspiratorially at both of them in turn. 'What do you two have to hide?'

'Whatever you want,' Curtis offered sleepily. 'Name it.'

'Name what?' Palmer asked, appearing in the same grey seersucker bathrobe he'd gone to bed in. 'G'morning.' He kissed Eleanora, then held out his cup. 'Morgen, Titina. Morgen, Bert. Morgen, Curtis. Where the hell is Gerri?'

'I was with the Lugano cops last night. She has definitely not yet arrived in our part of the world.'

Palmer pushed back his floppy sleeve and stared at his wristwatch. 'Train 384, overnight from Rome, via Milan, arrives in Lugano in half an hour.'

'You keep all that in your head?' Bert inquired.

'Numbers,' Palmer said in a fake tough-guy voice, 'are my business.'

'Amazing.'

'It's my daughter. That makes the numbers easier to remember.'

'I can hardly wait to meet her.'

Palmer laughed almost helplessly. 'Me, too.'

Bert watched him more closely. How could Palmer not feel the tension between the other two? How could he not sense what they had sacrificed on his behalf? Amazing how bright-shiny-morning arrogant he looked. A few hours ago, Bert thought, the two Palmer trusts most had nearly jettisoned their loyalty. But Palmer's mind is elsewhere, a missing daughter. How Victorian.

How degrading to be the one person at the table who knew all of it. Bert made a face, as if his coffee was cold. A seasoned reporter should long ago have come to terms with information overload. A hard carapace of scar tissue should have grown over any feeling that he was the lowest form of slime-life.

Palmer sipped his coffee. 'I'm going to drive down to the station. Anybody coming with me?' His glance, bright with future action, shifted from Eleanora to Curtis and back again, several times. 'Not a popular option? OK, go back to bed. All three of you look like you haven't been to bed at all. I mean to sleep. That's the trouble with you young people. No stamina.'

'Behold: the perfect example of middle-aged stamina,' Eleanora said.

'Who?' Curtis asked, somewhat confused.

'Back to bed,' Palmer ordered as he strode out of the room. 'Three different beds.' He left.

'Fight to the finish,' Bert quoted. 'Never give in.' He got slowly to his feet. No question, the elderly adler who marks the sparrow's fall and cherishes the missing daughter. Who takes responsibility for every-goddamned-thing in the whole goddamned world.

'Why does our generation not fight to the finish?' he asked Eleanora and Curtis. 'We have seen what fighting to the finish produces. Is that why winning is of so little importance to us? He knows history as well as we do,' Bert continued. 'But for him, life is still his responsibility. Mein Gott.' He went to the bright steel fireplace and held his hands out to the heat. 'A modern father that concerned about his child?' He cut off the words and glared at the burning embers.

'Fathers of his generation are that way,' Eleanora suggested.

'Not all of them.' Bert made a tuneless whistling sound like an Arab flute played by vagrant desert winds, quarter-tones whining and entwining. 'This mafia business,' he said then. 'It's his crusade, is it?'

'His last crusade,' Curtis explained. 'Win or lose, he's promised after this to take up knitting.'

'Is there such a thing as a retired eagle?'

Eleanora sniffed. 'That's the best question you ever asked, Bertl.'

The younger man stared into the embers. 'You know, it is comforting that somewhere someone takes responsibility for something. It . . .' he gestured helplessly. 'It's gone almost completely out of fashion. He's promised to change his ways, win or lose? But to win is better, nicht wahr?'

'With Palmer, need you ask?'

'If winning means that much to him.' Slowly, still staring at the flames, he felt in his jeans pocket and pulled out his notebook. 'So,' he said then. 'It's very simple. He wins.'

'Hey!' Curtis called.

Bert chucked the notebook on to the flames. The three of them watched it burn to pale grey flakes. After a moment only the spiral wire was left, blackened and writhing in agony. 'What was that all about?' Curtis asked.

Bert gave him one of his roguish sideways glances. 'Absolutely nothing.'

Chapter Twenty-Two

Evidently he wasn't the only one interested in train 384. Palmer stood on the platform of track two, watching a pair of uglies. The shorter of the two had yanked a dark blue beret over one corner of his ferret's forehead to cover the rather large bandage there. The other, beefier, wore his leather jacket draped over his shoulders. This was supposed to hide the thin sling on his arm, supporting a sprain rather than a fracture.

Palmer would have lost interest if they hadn't been so concerned about camouflaging their infirmities. It suggested that in their business infirmities were a drawback. Like the faint electrical charge that shimmers about an object before lightning strikes it, Palmer began to feel his skin crawl. Not unpleasantly.

The station clock click-jumped and, on schedule, the overnight diretto from Rome appeared in the distance. Palmer moved in behind the two men. He had no idea why, just skin sensation.

The massive railroad cars ground to a halt. Passengers inside wrestled baggage down on to the platform. Soon everyone had cleared off. That was when he saw Gerri staring at him, still inside, looking out. Someone her height stood behind her.

Palmer felt a great wave of sheer relief. He knew he'd been anxious about her, but only now did he realise how much. He moved forward past the two muscle men and boarded the train. Without a word he picked up Gerri's overnight bag and led the way off, marching straight through the two uglies and across the tracks — despite signs warning everyone not to — into the station. Across his shoulders and biceps, the horripilation felt like an iced needle shower.

Once inside he turned to watch the men. They had two moves: illegally across the tracks or legally down a flight of stairs, through a tunnel and up another stairway into the terminal. They did neither, ignoring the world.

Palmer switched his attention to his daughter, purposefully not examining her companion. 'You're a day late.'

'Dad, I can't tell you how happy — '

'What is that pinned on your jacket? A corsage?'

'Dad, give me a ch — '

'Wait a second!' Palmer's voice went very quiet. 'Don't tell me.'

'Dad, I'm trying to t — '

'You two are married!'

Slavko jumped forward and seized his hand. 'Sir! You are amazing! Psychic! We are married! Last night.'

Palmer still refrained from eye contact with him. He stared hard at Gerri and raised his eyebrows.

'In Milan,' she explained. 'At Slavko's embassy. By the assistant consul.'

'I'll be damned!'

People were beginning to watch the three of them. Palmer dragged them into the café. 'You're Krevic?' he asked. 'One has to make sure. So many young men fully as eligible as you have been seeking the hand of the fair Geraldine.'

'Dad.'

His light grey eyes, in their deep sockets, regarded the fledgling finance minister with the glare of a thermic lance. 'Say something.'

'Dad.'

'I am Boluslav Krevic, sir, your new son-in-law. Called Slavko.'

Palmer swung around to Gerri. 'This on the level? Is it legal? Binding? Were you tricked into it? Unduly pressured? Drugged? Can you get out of it?'

'I don't want to. I'm happy.'

'Oh.' A long pause. Then he felt his face creasing into an immense grin. He drew her to him and planted a kiss on each cheek. Her face went beet-red. 'I guess I'm happy, too,' he managed to say through something thick in his throat. A sudden, awkward silence fell over the three of them. Palmer glanced at the doorway and saw that the two uglies were coming in.

'Those two,' Gerri's eyes narrowed as she glared at them. 'You have no idea the anxieties we — ' Her blush had faded but she looked not quite pulled together, not the brisk young Manhattanite.

'That was why,' Slavko cut in eagerly, 'we took asylum in my embassy, sir. You must forgive us. It was a matter of safety. And while there . . .' He shrugged.

'It seemed a good idea,' Gerri added. 'And they gave us a guard to the station. Otherwise we'd still be there.'

'It shouldn't be a total waste of time,' Palmer finished off, 'you got hitched. I have heard weirder excuses for matrimony.' He ordered coffee and sweet buns for them. At the counter, the two uglies studied the menu at some length.

'I can hardly believe it,' Palmer told his daughter, the broad grin reappearing suddenly. 'You, married. Wow.'

This time she kissed him. 'Me, married.'

'OK,' Palmer said then. 'You're happy. I'm happy. Slavko's happy. I think it's time you let me in on the secret. What's it all about?'

When he got no answer he saw that his daughter and son-in-law were staring into each other's eyes. Age must be patient with impetuous youth. 'Not the marriage. The two clowns on your tail. Hullo?'

His question trickled into Gerri's head. 'It's a note,' she said then.

'Could you be a little more sp – ?' Palmer stopped until the waitress left them. 'What sort of note?'

Stirring her coffee, Gerri explained at some length. The three of them fell silent then. 'But you threw it away, finally,' her father concluded.

'That's what I told them. It's right here in my bag.'

Palmer watched her fingers reach involuntarily to snap open her handbag. 'Steady. In the world of thieves you were about to commit a "tell". You know what a tell is?'

'I have that film seen, sir,' Slavko volunteered. 'It is called *House of Games*, yes? A tell betrays to a thief where is something weluable hidden.'

Palmer glanced at him as if for the first time. Slavko's English pronunciation seemed to be wilting beneath his father-in-law's intimidating stare. His small scholar's face under dark curly hair looked as harassed as Gerri's.

'Before you became finance minister, you were an attorney?'

'I represented people who had into political trouble fallen with the government. My father is a lawyer. He has inherited my practice, poor man.'

'Oh? People still get in political trouble?'

'My nation has only imperfectly graduated from Marxism, sir. There are great remaining patches of entrenched resistance to new ways.'

'Your English is very good,' Palmer said almost grudgingly, code for something more vast. It was, Palmer knew, his way of truly accepting the marriage. Being an attorney, this kid probably knew the marriage was air tight.

'Dad wouldn't it be an excellent thing to get the hell out of here?'

'Soon.'

'I'm not adjusted too well,' Gerri said, 'to being the rabbit of those wolfhounds.'

'Just one thing,' Palmer turned to his new son-in-law and gave him his normal steely interrogator's look. 'Why are you fooling around with Teddy Radziwill?'

'I beg your pardon?'

'What about IMF?'

Slavko's eyes went up toward the ceiling. 'Everyone asks me that. My governm – '

'The Dutch banks might take a chance on you. They have a few guilders to spare. Even my old bank, UBCO, would take a flutter if I shoved hard.'

'Mr Palmer, sir.'

'You have to call me something else.'

'Father?'

'Try Woods.'

'Woods, sir, you must understand why to the Vatican I first applied.' Slavko watched his father-in-law for signs of more forbidden lenders. 'Woods, sir, ours was a very Christian coup. My premier, in his head, does not trust any source of funding but Mother Church. At least not until he hears of my adventures in Rome.'

'Ha. What then? Will he let you look elsewhere?'

'But first I must convince him that our saviour will not be the Vatican.'

'You've talked to him on the phone?'

'Woods, sir, he and I are creatures of our lifetime in the underground of my nation. Telephones we do not trust. Post we do not trust. Messengers we do not trust. Fax we especially do not trust. What we trust: sit eye to eye and speak.'

Palmer nodded. 'Smart.'

Gerri cleared her throat. 'Dad. These creeps have been shooting at us. Can we get out of here?'

He gave her a big, fake smile. 'Why the hell didn't you tell me that first? Get up, loudly ask the cashier where the ladies room is. Walk off in that direction.' Under the table, his left hand passed her car keys. 'Outside there's an escalator down to street level. Around the corner to the right, find the car and bring it as close to the escalator as possible. It's that little white Peugeot of Eleanora's,' he added, shielding his lips from being seen. 'I'll give you, say, five minutes to do that. OK?' He turned to Krevic.

'After five minutes, irritation. Where is that girl? How long does it take to pee? Et cetera. Then you say you're going to find her. Disappear down the escalator. I follow right behind with the bags. Into the car. Whoosh.'

Gerri's nose wrinkled. 'Slavko and I will get loose but you won't.'

'They don't want me. I don't have any magic notes from Teddy Radziwill.'

For a long moment none of them spoke. Then Gerri got to her feet and asked the cashier, in piercing Italian, where the ladies room was.

Palmer had no real alternatives. He counted on the two pursuers believing that their quarry had merely stepped out to take a leak. And they did. That is, they believed Gerri's absence. But when Slavko followed, Palmer could see that the ruse was wearing thin. He left money on the table, grabbed the two bags and fled.

The down escalator was empty of people. Good. Palmer craned his neck around and saw that five or six steps above him the burly man had jumped aboard, followed a step higher by his colleague. The thin one produced a silenced gun. No good.

Palmer started down the moving stairs two at a time. Someone started up the other escalator, Curtis.

Palmer's pursuers leaped from step to step. Curtis grabbed the upward rubber railing and vaulted to his left. Like an acrobat, he landed on the stainless steel midway strip, crouching as if on a tightrope. As the pursuers came jumping down the moving stairs, Curtis crouched lower and stiffarmed them forward, one at a time. The burly man teetered, lost his balance and began to tumble down the rest of the escalator. He landed hard but had started to get to his knees when his sidekick slammed onto his shoulders and they both went down.

Palmer swung Gerri's overnight case, the heavier of the two, and heard it connect with the burly man's chin. It produced one of those nasty clicks as a bone broke somewhere. The man's eyes rolled up into his head just as Curtis tumbled down the escalator. He landed hard on the smaller man, knocking the wind out of him. He snatched the silenced gun.

The tiny white Peugeot 205 rounded a corner, Gerri at the wheel. Slavko swung open both rear doors. Palmer and Curtis tumbled inside.

At the down escalator passengers were descending. They found their way blocked by two dazed men. They began to complain in several languages.

'I'm ashamed of you two,' Gerri remarked, yanking the lightweight car around a corner at a speed that shifted them all sideways. 'Attacking cripples.'

'What?' Slavko asked, eyes wide.

'Those are the only opponents I can handle these days,' Palmer explained.

'What?' Slavko pleaded.

'What brought you to the rescue?' Palmer asked Curtis.

'Just being in the right place at the right time. Anyway, Eleanora said if I didn't she'd never speak to me again.'

'Does she think I need a keeper?'

'Don't you?' Curtis turned to Slavko. 'You again! I thought you only operated in men's rooms?'

'Hah!' Slavko shouted, eyes shining now. 'Bread upon waters!'

'Slow down, Gerri. Bewildering, Mr Krevic?'

'Inwigorating, the American style. Woods, sir: I see I have married into the right family.'

Part Three

Chapter Twenty-Three

AMERICANS RECOVERED FROM LAKE

(Special to Corriere Luganese) Two male cadavers presumed of United States origin were recovered yesterday from the Lake of Lugano near the foot of Morcote, forcibly drowned. Campione carabinieri Maresciallo Ruggiero Rigori, reported both men had suffered injuries.

Capitano Urs Bruntschli, Lugano police, identified the men as having caused a disturbance last week at the railroad escalator. They had been booked but released on bail.

Bradford Ames reread the newspaper clipping. It had not been sent from Lugano but Providence, Rhode Island. A cousin, who'd recommended the two cadavers in their once live state, had faxed it. As for the double takeout, after a brief conference in Lugano last week Ames had hired the proper specialists.

If he'd been less preoccupied, he might have marvelled at his ability to contract for a whole series of specialist-specialists, each removing the previous specialist. Being a mafia specialist was not a sinecure. Being one himself, Bradford Ames understood that when things went awry even as highly-placed a specialist as he suffered pangs of anxiety. But receiving this clipping from his cousin made him understand that he was in trouble almost as deep as if he'd let the Americans live.

He reached for the telephone, then recalled it was still night in the States. He stared out the window at Rome and tried to relax. Later, in remembering this day, he thought of it as having three telephone calls, two unmade. This was the first he drew back from making.

He'd returned to his own apartment in the Eden. Fiona Campbell's father was expected from an archeological dig in far Calabria, at the toe of Italy. He mustn't find Ames' electric toothbrush in her bathroom. However, it was hers in a sense. She had the bruises to prove it.

Bradford Ames gazed bleakly at the morning view of Rome laid out before him. The urge to smooth-talk his cousins gnawed at him. He was sliding into deep melancholy. This fax in his hand signified his first important failure. That he couldn't immediately alibi it represented a second failure.

Of all the financial organisations for which he might have worked, Bradford Ames served the one that enforced its discipline with death. It was used as sparingly as possible, especially when it came to valuable profit-makers like himself. But the threat was easily as effective as the act. Perhaps more so.

In the few years he had fronted for his family's interests, he had never before had to cope with failure of any kind. He called his own shots. In a rising market at first, then a falling one adequately forecast, he had managed to show magnificent profits. This was not due to luck, as amateurs often supposed. Two factors bolster all professionals: adequate funding and inside information. The family's cash flow, channelled into the IUD, was certainly much more than adequate. As for inside information, between his own contacts and those of Archbishop Radziwill, Bradford Ames could anticipate any turn of events.

The archbishop was the cleverest financial man he had ever met. That Sunday forecast he downloaded into clients' computers, for instance. In return, don't think they didn't let him in on lucrative manoeuvreings. How could he fail? Yet he represented another failure Ames smarted under: he had still not activated His Excellency's takeout sanction on Palmer, nor had he recovered his note. 'Eccelenza,' he'd explained on Monday. He was using his regular Monday telephone booth in the foyer of a hotel near the Eden where Radziwill could call him at precisely nine in the morning. 'I believe the girl actually threw the note away.'

'Some girls might. Not this one.' The archbishop's voice developed a nasty rasp. 'From an associate with youthful energy you've become a problem. Must I keep following up orders I assumed had been executed? For example, the cash.'

'Eccelenza, it is being assembled.'

'You have great leeway. It can be any combination of currencies.'

'That much cash – '

'Pounds sterling, dollars, guilders, deutschmarks.'

'That much – '

'And you've started repeating yourself, too.' His Excellency pressed on cruelly. He had finally sorted out Ames' number: hard punishment. 'Do I start giving you deadlines?'

'Back in Providence, they're asking a lot of questions. They claim it's a record amount of cash to be – '

But Radziwill had hung up.

Holier-than-thou bastard. Did he have any idea how hard it was to pump up such oceans of cash? And it had to be of denominations not large enough that banks recorded serial numbers. Hundred-dollar bills. Fifty-pounds notes. Hundred-DM German currency. Did he understand how his demand had caused a cross-current of hyper-activity? Chicago numbers runners, Tucson smugglers, Philadelphia counterfeiters. Detroit crack dealers, New Orleans whoremasters, Los Angeles torch squads, St Louis extortion teams, Manhattan merchant bankers, every high-volume scam artist who wholesaled through Providence or its affiliated families was being milked and stripped of every crying dime. And the security involved! You moved that much cash into the IUD coffers in Rome and other mobs sat up and sniffed the air.

Melancholy settled down over Bradford Ames with the deadly weight of one of those heavy Aztec ceremonial cloaks the sacrifice wore as he mounted the pyramid to surrender his hot, smoking heart to the obsidian daggers of the high priests. Ames sighed and tried to cheer himself. All good strategic thinking begins with doing one's homework in advance, even before knowing it was necessary. In the past week, while contracting in Lugano for the removal of the two tough guys, Ames had done his Palmer research.

The Morcote eyrie was designed to be impregnable. Ames had established the parameters of Palmer's defences, using light aircraft and, once, a helicopter, to produce a detailed map of the top of his hill, the double fencing, the single entry gate and the sprawling, hunting-lodge edifice at the centre. The reconnaissance was well worth the time it took and the cost of suborning from an employee of the security firm that had installed it, full blueprint details of the warning systems.

Like all impregnable places, Palmer's security was firmly based on the technology of ten years ago. So much had happened in ten years! We understood so much more, now, about subverting video circuits. About surprise assault from the air. About the difference in motivation between a mercenary operating for money and a terrorist acting on political principles.

Ames began to cheer up. The cash was out of his hands, anyway. All his successes were based on finding weak points and exploiting them. Krevic was a walking weak point. Once Ames controlled the Morcote eyrie Krevic would sign the loan agreement. The cash would arrive. To convince Krevic's principals back home to honour the loan required another development of the past ten years: hostage-holding.

What was he waiting for? He had a kill-order from the client. It surely applied to the target's daughter as well. Hostage-holding always included killing the hostage. Understood.

Bradford Ames' eyes, focused on the city of Rome from his Hotel Eden viewpoint, switched sideways for the third time to his telephone. His nasty canines glinted as he smiled. The plan still had loose ends but Ames would clean it up later. Now he had to get moving, fast. He needed a small cohort, a few specialists under strict discipline. But they had to be political specialists. Fortunately a very active underground existed in Krevic's country of former security people, now stripped of power, but not of knowhow, and certainly not of the will to return to power.

This time Bradford Ames picked up his phone, his smile widening into a grin of scary proportions. In a city the size of Rome one can find anything, if one is patient and resourceful – and has a Vatican kill-order.

In Caserta the graves are endless, fields of pale stones with British and American names, Italian names, German names. But Caserta, just north of Naples, is only the beginning of the Second World War's graveyard trail. It blossoms more richly with fifty-year-old cadavers as it reaches Cassino to the north.

There is only logic, not irony, in the fact that here, where the Wehrmacht stubbornly dug in, the earth hides still-live artillery shells, undetonated land mines and aerial bombs. With such buried memories go a great many deliberately excavated ammo hides. These were never hastily dug foxholes. When the Wehrmacht buried, it did so in stone-lined caverns twenty feet under the earth. A lot of these mausoleums of death were taken over during the Cold War by an Allied 'stay-behind' army of secret soldiers. In Italy it was code-named after the short sharp sword-dagger of the Roman gladiators, Operation Gladio.

This NATO-directed terror network helped supply or engineer right-wing atrocity killings like the Bologna Massacre. Funds came mostly from America's bottomless coffers, particularly ISA, the much feared, ultra-secret Intelligence Support Activity which specialised in assassinations. But each Gladio depot was expected to earn its own keep. For this one a Colonel Campbell was the troglodyte left behind by British spooks under an archeological cover identity.

A short, roosterish martinet in his mid-sixties, the colonel kept a sharp eye on the freshness of ammo and weaponry to bomb civilians, kidnap political leaders and provide fresh opportunities for neo-fascist bloodshed. Those involved in right-wing terror used Gladio depots as a quartermaster's store. These three young supplicants had found the trail easy to pick up. Campbell held court in a farmhouse between Caserta and Maddaloni toward Naples.

'Which of you wankers spika Inglese?'

They had yet to reveal which was leader. Instead,

the two slighter, shorter young men played with Campbell's black cat. She looked half-starved both for food and attention. Affection seemed to have been erased from the menu.

A square, muscular young man smiled very slightly. 'Speak I, please.' He jerked his thumb to send his two colleagues off on a discreet walk. The gesture made his bandaged right wrist ache. He rubbed it thoughtfully. 'Sir, I bring you greetings from what is left of my nation, before reformers castrated it.'

'Your damned nation's bloody commie!' the colonel barked.

'No longer, please.'

The tough young man, broad through the shoulders, scooped up the cat and tickled the star-shaped white patch on her throat. 'Am sent here,' he told Campbell, 'to eliminate finance minister, lousy reformer called Krevic.'

The little rooster patted his holstered .9 Browning ominously. He frowned. 'This is a cash business, you know.'

The leader shifted the cat to his left arm and reached inside his jacket to bring out a wad of hundred-dollar bills the thickness of a normal wall brick. 'Finance minister is arranging cash loan with Vatican backing. With that money, reformers keep hold of our land. Unless we kill finance minister, please?' He sat there, easing his wrist, his eyes dead blank, the professional's stare, not the zealot's.

Colonel Campbell gave him one of those withering

glances sergeant majors use to detect brass that hasn't been entirely and completely polished. 'Gammy wrist?'

The young man, sensing the importance of his being physically whole and sound, dug his fingers into the grimy adhesive bandage. He stripped back the tape. It crackled, startling the cat and revealing two small flat wooden splints. Brusquely, as if brushing off insects, the young man ripped the bandage from his skin and flung it aside. 'Finished, please.'

Campbell produced a sound very close to 'hmppf' and pulled over a small notebook-sized computer terminal attached to a modem. Squinting at the hard-to-read LCD screen, he accessed a neo-fascist MSI member of parliament who held high rank in the Italian secret service. Once passworded through, Campbell looked up. 'Name?'

'Grodov, Alex.'

The colonel's stubby fingers slowly punched in this data. Almost immediately the databank produced a greenish scroll of entries. 'Says you were captain with the secret police. And SovInt. Lie! SovInt never hired anyone as young as you.'

'Not in Russia, please, where too many elderly relatives require employment. But in my land, yes.'

'Hmppf.' Campbell switched to another network transmitting English. 'Yanks never heard of you over at ISA. That's it, sunshine. On yer bike!'

'Not under Grodov. Try André, major.'

The colonel's frown looked ferocious as he entered the new name and read the screen. 'Hmppf.' He managed to get a certain new respect in the mono-syllable. 'All right, those Yank prats think highly of your miserable body. You're cleared.'

By midnight their battered beige van, stolen in Naples, was loaded with explosives, ammunition, automatic assault weapons and semiautomatic sidearms. The colonel was moved to view the pristine $100 bills with suspicion.

'How'd a young bloke like you get to make captain?'

'Talent,' Alex snapped. He rubbed his right wrist almost by habit as he sat thinking. It had occurred to him that Gladio was a prime listening post for clandestine activity. Campbell's probing created quite a sub rosa dossier. For instance, the $100 bills had been stolen in Germany from an American peace-keeping regiment. Campbell demanded to know which US officer had been in on the deal. That information could later be sold to others. So could the assassination of Krevic. How quickly this ancient Brit had settled his own hash.

Alex placed the cat on the blowsy front seat of the van. 'Here,' Campbell barked, 'Blackie's no great moggie, always grafting for tucker, but she's company.'

'Not,' Alex advised him, 'where you're going, please.'

Each of his compatriots took one of the colonel's arms and yanked them so wide, scarcrow fashion, that he only had time for a barked:

'Wot!' Agony choked off the howl in his throat as Alex showed him a long boning knife.

'For breath,' he murmured, inserting the seven-inch blade slowly into Campbell's right nipple. 'Um?' he asked, doctor-like. 'Yes?' He felt it scraping bone as it lanced open the right lung. The colonel's small eyes widened in shock. Gasping, he choked up instant blood. 'Now for digestion.'

Alex twisted the boning knife mercilessly as he withdrew it, letting in germs. He studied the area below Campbell's navel. It took him a long time to select the upstroke and sideways slash of a hara-kiri disembowelment. A thick stench of sour faeces gushed forth. One of the accomplices muttered some complaint. Alex wiped the knife clean across his companion's face. 'For your digestion?' He sheathed his knife and went about the looting of Campbell's cash hideout with studied expertise. Then he waved his two assistants into the van.

One of them stared down at Campbell's chunky, big-chested body leaking blood. He might take a day or so to die. Deadpan, the young man shoved one of the just-purchased Browning .9 automatics into the colonel's mouth. He fired a mercy round through the brain.

Alex gave him the withering look one gives a sissy. Then he switched on the van's engine and headed off toward Rome. Alex, at the wheel, heard mewing. He reached behind the front seat and lifted the small black cat on to his lap.

As he drove, he massaged the part of his wrist,

gleaming faint pink on his unwashed skin, that had been covered by a splint of long standing. He could have removed it some time ago, but it served to focus his attention more fiercely on his quarry, the man who had broken his wrist. Now, within hours, armed and informed, he would be ready at last to strike back.

Over the ragged engine he could hear the cat purring at having his companionship and warmth. Food would not be long in coming. Blackie? Stupid British name. 'Sacha,' he muttered, giving her the honour of one of his own nicknames.

One of his comrades coughed. 'What?'

'Shut up, softhearted coward.'

He gave up rubbing his wrist. Stroking the little cat's fur while his comrades slept, he drove the hundred miles through the night along the autostrada to the Eternal City.

Chapter Twenty-Four

Father Bernardin held the cashier's cheque in his hand as if it might catch fire at any moment. It was signed with an illegible scribble he knew to be the signature of Maria-Elena Grimaldi Partago Agnelli. But as redolent of power as her last name was – her departed husband had claimed a closer relationship to the 'other' Agnellis than he was entitled to – the amount on the cheque stank of lucre so rich it might combust spontaneously in its own outpouring of rank methane.

'Un milliardi di lire,' it read, spelled out. Not a million but a billion. 'Lit. 1,000,000,000.' To get a rough dollar equivalent one lopped off three zeroes. La Signora Agnelli had given IUD a million dollars.

The young Swiss priest realized how far ahead this placed IUD over its only rival in the Holy See, the disgraced IOR. The ancient cardinals who comprised their supervisory body, La Prefetura per l'Affari Economici would be pleased. Bernardin owed his appointment to one of those old men.

The moment he thought of old Cardinal Huf, the telephone rang. The man to whom he owed this prestigious job, weekend slavery and all, was on the line. Huf came from the same small village in the Swiss Valais as Bernardin. When the young priest had returned from America, filled with academic degrees and computer knowhow, his diocesan bishop had assigned him to teach small children arithmetic. It was His Eminence Cardinal Huf who had rescued him.

'A billion lire,' he chuckled. 'I congratulate you, Bernardin.'

'But I had nothing to d – '

'Ach, learn to take compliments.'

Bernardin realised his corruption had just advanced by a significant increment of mendacity. He was already lying to his archbishop. Now he had begun misleading his cardinal as well.

Bernardin accessed a form letter of transmittal and printed it. He signed it in the archbishop's name, sealed it with the Agnelli cheque and addressed it to the Vatican's internal bank. Then he picked up a phone to call for a messenger.

When he arrived it wasn't a proper messenger but one of the IUD's weekend staff, a middle-aged drudge called Covici who worked the worst hours and shifts for IUD. This strategy had not gained him promotion, only seniority. As a result, unlike the other lay workers, he rarely walked about with the subservient smile of a sinner allowed to earn points in the house of God.

Covici stood in the doorway, skinny where Bernardin was plump, already greying and showing the vertical furrows of dissatisfaction between his dark eyes. Bowed down by injustice, he now straightened himself to such a ridiculously erect posture that one could almost hear his bones creak. 'I have to take some other deposits to the bank anyway,' he explained.

As he watched Covici, the young priest realised that the other man was not really that much older than he was. What a physical deterioration. 'Thank you for handling the deposit.'

'A demon for widows, our archbishop, eh?'

The young priest looked unhappy. 'The bank closes at five o'clock.'

'They know me. I can get there as late as six. What does old Huf-n-Puf think of this? If I have him to thank for putting you here instead of me, I can at least speak frankly about your rabbi.' The term was one Christians reserved for acts, like using influence, that Christians never committed. Covici's smile grew less intimidating and more pleasing. He put a scrap of paper on the priest's work counter. 'Translate this Yiddish, maestro?'

Bernardin studied the line of alphanumeric characters. There was something hideously familiar about them. The moment he saw what it was, his face went grey. The Oscar Bravo 31 gave it away.

'Perhaps over the weekend,' he said hurriedly, 'if there's a free moment.'

Covici's dark eyes snapped with malice. 'If there's a free moment you haven't filled with fractal craziness.'

Bernardin's grey face broke into a hurt frown. Fear heightened like mist sweeping in from the sea. 'I had no idea you wasted time monitoring my work.'

'You and I have to stick together, Bernardin. Cover

for each other. It's our Christian duty. So,' he concluded the quasi-blackmailing procedure, 'untangle that 004 access code like a good fellow.'

'Never,' Bernardin blustered, suffering friction burn from such intimate contact with another.

'Oh, never say never.' Covici gave him a mock look of sternness. 'I have a friend who pays good money for copy discs. Money to feed my family. I ask you, Father, could there be a duty more Christian than that?'

Chapter Twenty-Five

Always a sticky wicket, meeting a parent of the woman with whom one is having an affair that produces welts all over her. Bradford Ames, his head full of the day's problems, hadn't been paying close attention when he'd accepted Fiona's invitation to dinner. 'Just the three of us and Da's always good fun.'

But Da was late arriving from wherever in southern Italy he plied his trade as an archeologist. 'The ancient site of Sybaris,' Fiona explained as she fixed her master a whisky. 'The ancient Crotonians didnae sack the place, as most armies might. For the ancient Greek world, Sybaris was hedonistic, orgiastic, pleasure-worshipping. They sacked it, raped it, buggered it, razed it, sowed it with salt and diverted a river across its bluidy ruins.' She took a deep, satisfying breath that made her nostrils flutter with bloodlust.

Ames' day had been choked with the caracasses of false leads. He'd made endless telephone calls. He'd met discreet people in parklike surroundings. He'd wasted influence trying to contract for the kind of specialists, quasi-political, semi-psychotic, to take the Morcote hilltop. All he got for his trouble was Italian versions of the two Americans he'd removed. One was violent enough, with eighteen murders to his name. The other was one of those self-preening Calabrese princelings, scion of a major crime family. He spent the interview disdainfully picking his large nose.

At ten p.m., after phoning several southern towns for 'Il Professore Campbell', Fiona served dinner. 'It's nae like Da,' she complained. 'He may have faxed me at the office. After we eat, can we . . .?'

The Hotel Eden seemed deserted as she and Ames crossed the lobby to the elevators and up to the top of the building. Bradford Ames inserted his keys in the door and found that it was open. He stepped back. He knew he'd locked it. Perhaps the cleaning womer. . . .? Wishing he was carrying something more lethal than keys he swung open the door. A small black cat jumped into Fiona's arms.

The office lights flared on. Across the room a stocky young man in hiker's clothing pointed a brand new .9 Browning automatic, standard NATO issue. 'Close the door, please. Lock it from the inside, please.'

Fiona Campbell did so, slowly. Then she cuddled the cat. 'Puss, puss. You're not all black are you?' She tickled a white bib under the cat's chin. Although the cat responded with a purr, its owner regarded Fiona stonily, as if she were not human.

'Hands up, please?' The young man patted them for weapons and then relieved Fiona of the not-entirely-black cat. He stroked its fur and tickled the star of white on its throat. 'Unruly Sacha.'

'Her name's Sacha?' Fiona inquired brightly, one cat lover to another.

'Alexandra.'

'But that's my mother's name. Sandy.'

Fiona, as sensitive to accents as her master, realized that the intruder's command of English and his pronunciation pattern resembled that of finance minister Krevic. Their native land, like Yugoslavia or Czechoslovakia, had been created by mashing warring tribes into intimate contact. Krevic's fine features were contrasted to this one's peasant stockiness.

'What did they send you to steal?' Ames asked in an insulting tone.

The broad face with its massive jaw and high cheekbones remained immobile. The front sight of the Browning raked across Bradford Ames' tight mouth. It snagged for a moment on one of the sharp vampire canines.

Fiona flinched, imagining the short stab of pain, the rich salt taste of blood tinged with the not unpleasant stench of gun oil. 'Does that establish the rules, please?' the intruder asked.

He zipped open his backpack. 'Sacha!' The cat jumped up into a small canvas cubbyhole at the top where she snuggled down for a much-needed rest from all the exertion. Her green eyes followed their movements for only a moment or two before the lids slowly shuttered.

'The text of the loan agreement, please,' the hiker

said then. He stood planted in the centre of the office floor on hairy bare legs.

Fiona wondered about the band of pink wrist that stood out from his hairy, sun-darkened arm. She glanced at Bradford Ames as he licked from his lower lip another drop of blood. He shook his head.

The oily muzzle, now carrying a bright spot of red, pushed into Ames' abdomen. 'I did say please,' the intruder explained.

She knew her master was trying to think his way out of this, save his own skin and still look masterful. But he seemed to feel that fate might have intervened at a brilliantly opportune moment. Bloody, the look he flashed her was anything but bowed. He resembled a gambler whose bet has just paid off. 'In your country,' he began slowly in the earnest tone of an insurance salesman, 'there is as yet no unanimity of political purpose. Am I right?'

'The loan agreement, please?'

'The man sent here to bring home hard currency will become overnight both beloved and politically powerful. Am I right?' A silence in the room grew more tense. 'Another man,' Bradford Ames added, 'a man who destroyed that hero of the people? Would he earn a great deal of money thereby? And his victory, would it not establish his name in his countrymen's hearts as their future saviour?'

The hiker's face had been quite immobile through all this. His only human expressions had been reserved for the cat. Now, abruptly, like a low-wattage electric bulb switched on at the farthest end of a damp tunnel swirling with mists, something showed in his eyes. 'How much money, please?'

Ames smiled bloodily. Fiona knew that look. Her father often took on that same thrillingly cruel look of conquest. It meant that, despite appearances, he had won. Something secret, but hurtful, had gone his way. He had put something over, something nasty to the other person but delicious to him. Ames' obvious feeling of triumph made her shiver with excitement. She had no idea, yet, of what was happening. Poor old Da. Too bad he was missing all the excitement.

Chapter Twenty-Six

Although they had started this stroll as a foursome, Tanya with Bert and Gerri with Slavko, they kept re-pairing as they hiked about the knob-like top of Palmer's eyrie. It was a farewell; all would be leaving later in the day.

Eleanora's many plantings had given the place a gardenlike look. 'She works so hard keeping this place green,' her daughter Tanya mused. 'It's touching,' she added on a patronising note. 'Not good for her, this isolated place. I made her promise to have open houses more often.'

They strolled along a path between boxwood hedges, enjoying the feeling of criticising one's elders. 'It's something to do with security,' Gerri suggested vaguely. 'But would it be wise? Elly looked absolutely washed out after the party. The next day she was like a ghost.'

Tanya laughed. 'That's the effect of too much Curtis.'

Gerri stopped in her tracks and brushed back her pale brown hair from her small face. 'You mean they . . .?'

'I mean they don't.' Tanya stooped to pick short-stemmed clover blossoms. She inhaled the clover's scent and then tossed the blooms away. 'And having young people around only emphasises her . . .' she paused to find a ladylike way of further diminishing her mother, '. . . problem.'

'Really?' Gerri demurred. 'She's always been very open and warm with me.'

'She's not *your* mother. To me, your father is wonderful, but he's an emblem of middle age. At the party I got a proposal from another charismatic elder. What makes them think I want to spend my prime of life nursemaiding an old man?'

'God, how depressing. Who was your suitor?'

'Some Swiss intelligence spook. Brags about spilling his seed. Wants to pump me full of kiddie-juice. Don't men see themselves as we see them?' Tanya thought for a moment. 'Mother needs a vacation. Doesn't your father need a visit to the States? Doesn't he have sons there?'

'And my mother.'

'They still see each other?'

'My mother breathes only in the upper reaches of the art world, morning till midnight. Nobody *drops in*, least of all me and even less her first husband. But shipping him to the States is brilliant. Without Elly, that is.'

'I'll invite her to Berlin for a month or two. I can get her a tiny flat. There are some very attractive people in Berlin.'

Gerri felt the uplift of exercising strong leadership. 'They'll thank us for this. A vacation away from each other.' Gerri scooped up a handful of fat clover buds and crushed them against her nose, inhaling deeply. Then she stuffed the decapitated flowers in the breast pocket of her blouse and strode on happily, the two of them with their strong personalities having solved everything.

'. . . . Not disputing you,' Bert assured Slavko, 'just finding that sort of thing hard to believe. I mean, love at first sight. Dear me, dear me.'

'But it was not love at first sight,' Slavko assured him. They had stopped at a part of the inner cyclone fencing where something had wriggled through so vigorously and so often that the links had been spread wide. Slavko had gone down on his knees and was trying to close the gap. This had, without them knowing it, triggered a proximity sensor. At the moment they were being observed by Palmer through his binoculars.

'Not at all,' Slavko assured him, getting up and dusting off his knees. 'I had in my mind always the picture of the woman I would love. I knew she resembled Jane Fonda, calm and purposeful.' He smiled guiltily. 'For socialist youth, she was once a true icon, believe me.'

'This tale grows less believable, my boy.'

Krevic shrugged helplessly. 'We were brought together by Christ.'

'I beg your pardon?' Bert's expression shifted between derision and shock.

'That Christ in the Vatican gardens where is the IUD office. He weeps, this Christ. A totally vulgar concept that appeals to the lowest common denominator of the faithful, miracles in Rome tap water.

And it is also a touching intellectual concept, given that the IUD's purpose is to help the deserving poor.'

'Dream on,' Bert said in a waspish tone. 'I don't meet people like you very often, people with dream girls, especially ones they actually find and marry.'

Slavko nodded somberly. 'You should try to meet more of them.' He knelt again and fingered a clump of clover blossoms. He removed some dead brown blades, fluffed up the flowers and went to other clumps nearby. 'You have a loved one of some kind,' he pointed out. 'We all have such a person.'

Bert hunkered down across from him and began sprucing up the clover near him. 'Not one. Two.'

Slavko looked up at him. 'You mistake my meaning. Two is not possible.'

'Udo Raspe and I have been together since kindergarten. Everything he feels, I feel. Right now he's fallen madly for your father-in-law. He is going to print an article designed to bring the mafia down on *Die Klarion*. I've told him he's wrong but he doesn't listen to me. I'm only the one who loves him.'

Slavko's mouth, open during this, snapped shut. Then: 'And Tanya?'

'Is my other love. Either I must love them both or give Udo up.'

'I do not understand.'

'It's called bisexuality. There's a lot of it around.'

Slavko started to smile. Then his face went grave. 'But this is a condition of the bourgeoisie, is it not? The poor can't afford such fancy styles of life.'

'Once a Marxist always a Marxist, eh?'

'Perhaps. Do they both know how you feel?'

'Of course. It's a ménage à trois, at least on the nights I get lucky.'

'You . . . you mean . . . you have congress with both of them?'

Bert's face broke in a huge grin. 'Have congress! Dear me, dear me.' He got to his feet and stared back at the low-lying house, with its tennis courts. 'I may work on a scandal sheet but I prize my privacy as much as you do.'

Slavko stood up. 'I apologise. But surely you, ah, have sought professional treatment for this problem.'

'Too expensive. And too invasive.'

Slavko returned the grin and with it gave Bert a friendly poke in the ribs. 'Poor man's wallet. Rich man's taste.'

To the astonishment of them both, Bert broke into tears.

'They have fallen far behind,' Tanya said, shading her eyes to see the two men. 'I despair of Bert, anyway. There's another obsessional, like your father. He's obsessed with Udo, childhood friends, closer than brothers.'

'Obsessed how?'

'Emotionally, physically, sexually.'

'Doesn't that get complicated?'

Tanya shook her head with its thick fleece of pale blonde kinks. 'Men constantly amaze me anyway. What they put in their mouths. Licking like dogs. There isn't anything sexual they won't do.'

Gerri, whose sexual experiences had been limited mostly to middle-class upwardly-mobile young Manhattanites, medically overeducated by *Sunday Times* magazine scares and, thus, frightened to death by AIDS, HIV-positive infections, thrush, mononucleosis, herpes, monillia albercans, cystitis, pyritis and the newer antibiotic-resistant strains of syphilis and gonorrhoea, to say nothing of salival strep infections, ME, dental plaque and the common cold, fell silent.

'And then they want you to crave it, too,' Tanya pointed out. 'They're delirious if you start demanding such things of them. As long as I live, I will never – '

She stopped short. A small black cat had approached the outer barrier of the inner cyclone fencing. What was very clearly the long tail of some recently dispatched vole or fieldmouse dangled from its dainty mouth. 'Here, kitty,' Gerri said, dropping to her knees and making enticing gestures. 'Here, kitty-cat. Yech, get rid of that thing. Where on earth do you think she dropped down from? Do you suppose she's bad luck?' The cat sat down and delicately removed the tail. With a curled paw she began to rub mouse from her face, lick the paw clean, and rub some more. It was hard to tell if she enjoyed the taste as a dessert or was merely being hygienic.

'No,' Tanya responded. 'See that nun's white bib? She is definitely good luck.'

Chapter Twenty-Seven

Palmer glanced at his watch. Across the desk from him in the afternoon darkness of his office Curtis also checked his watch. Three-thirty. 'The *Klarion* people are leaving in half an hour,' Curtis said, 'stuffed with Palmer gospel. And those papers Isabella sold me don't hurt.'

'Christ, I hope so. I keep asking myself . . .' He focused on Curtis' face. 'You only fight the maf by turning it against itself, like getting a rattler to bite its own rear end. If we've made Ames the culprit, incompetent, bungling, they must take him out. And never trust Radziwill again.'

'That note of Gerri's? What's happened to it?'

Palmer leaned back and linked his fingers behind his head. 'How's your long-term memory? The name Emil Corvo?'

'Emil Coburn, aka Emil Covici, Emil – '

'Ah, shut up.' Palmer grinned. 'Remember when you nailed him in our Vaduz office, skimming daily receipts?'

'And you refused to prosecute.'

'Then you must remember that I got him a job in Rome.'

Curtis' eyes almost bugged. 'At the IUD?'

'Emil Covici married a Roman girl and knocked off

five bambini in a row. He's nailed into IUD for life. I merely enhance his monthly take now and then.'

Curtis quickly smothered wonderment in his voice. 'So what's he tell you?'

'Covici says that Gerri's note exposes the Radziwill-Ames connection through a CIA document called Oscar Bravo 31. I'd seen it but never had my own copy.'

Curtis' small, discreet mouth produced a whistle. 'Mamma mia. Hand that document over to *Die Klarion* and you validate the entire article. It's not just Old Palmer vapouring off, it's the CIA explaining why Krevic's country is worth stealing. But can Covici – ?'

'I'm sitting here. In my mind's eye I see him looking for a payphone outside Vatican City.' Palmer closed his eyes tight. 'But a fat lady inside is giving a piece of her mind to her single daughter who's just announced she's pregnant.' Palmer's face clenched tightly, eyes shut. 'Now her daughter's hung up on her. Covici shuts himself inside the booth – '

'Which reeks of patchouli, BO and garl – '

'And stuffs gettoni into the slot. Bing. Bing. Bing. Now he's dialling my number to give me his number so I can phone him back.'

'Hello, senile dementia. Good bye, smarts.'

The telephone rang. Palmer snatched at it. 'Emil?' He listened, scribbling numbers on a pad. 'Hang up.'

Curtis' face went bland. 'Wrong number?'

'Oh, ye of little faith. Tell that *Klarion* bunch to stick around. As soon as I get Covici to a fax, the sexy stuff arrives.'

Chapter Twenty-Eight

Standing at the window of his Spartan quarters on the top floor of the IUD, His Excellency noted that after heat the first weekend in June had now turned rainy and cool. It made him wonder if it were not time for him to cool his own blood and reconsider his path.

Chief among his doubts: his standing order of last August, calling for Palmer's removal. He doubted not that it was wise; he only wondered now, after concentrated exposure to his old enemy, whether *it might work*. In a perfect world, a perfectly clear order would long ago have been filled. Yet Palmer lived, invited friends to parties, seemed able to coerce protection from Swiss intelligence.

Radziwill stared out at the sideslanting rain. The wage slaves of Rome had been expecting this weekend to drive to the tree-shaded yard of Nonno's house, wolf down great bowls of Nonna's pasta, a piglet grilled on a makeshift rotisserie and Nonno's strong vino rosso. Sorry. The archbishop smiled distortedly. His own plans, too, had been changed and he was feeling strangely off centre, of no fixed abode. Overexposure to a strong personality like Palmer, ensconced in what was evidently an invincible support system, could be quite off-putting. One's centre shifted.

Someone in His Excellency's position soon got used to being the sun around which everyone was planet or moon. Any shaking up of soul could be disastrous. Any archbishop without a fixed abode was a dangerously loose canon. He smiled recklessly at the pun. Ah, La Signora Agnelli's voice when he, so regretfully, had called just now to cancel the weekend at Porto San Stefano. But it had smelled too much of her own lascivious dreams.

He trifled with Satan, selling himself to her, even for a million. And there would be more rich, hungry women at San Stefano, more occasions of conscience-damage. Fortunately ended by bad weather and the telephone call from Amadeo pleading hard for a private meeting, 'Somewhere secure. Funds are arriving.'

As if there was any secure place. Archbishop Radziwill had been careful not to be seen with Amadeo since last August. But he had no idea who was watching the man who called himself Bradford Ames. Possibly London's Special Branch. The Serious Crimes Squad? FBI or SEC or IRS. Perhaps the British VAT people and whatever corrupt and inefficient effort the Italians were putting forth to regulate – i.e. grab a slice of – financial crime. And the EC itself? Did their watchdog commissions and Interpol watch Amadeo, floating aloft like a condor while prey shivered below, prey pointed out for kill, like Palmer? As Amadeo's falconer, controlling his swooping hawk-flight, Radziwill shared the emotions of the malign bird.

Dealing with the aptly named Amadeo, His Excellency's conscience told him, was dealing not with the original Satan, the angel who so loved God. But one had only to look at Amadeo's prey-sharpened canines to sense the breeding line.

Radziwill stared down at the bronze top of Christ's head. From this angle Christ's tears were hard to see as they fell. But when they splashed below, Radziwill could easily count them. They made absolutely no sense on a rain-drenched Saturday morning. But within a minute or two someone with an umbrella, a porter or cleaning man, came by surreptitiously to dip a tiny bottle. No way of knowing, was there, to what use people put those collected tears. Perhaps –

The lopsidedness of his grin became frightening. Lacrimae Christi, Vatican-bottled. Oh, the howls of disgust and anger! Oh, what bottom-line profit, tiny bottles and seals, a label, fifteen cents in raw material. And what could one charge for such a filled vial? Was five dollars too little? Fifty too much? He laughed as he turned his face away from Christ, feeling lightheaded. People who supposed his soul loaded down with numbers and percentages had no idea how often His Excellency grappled with the Devil.

He keyed a command into his terminal and heard it dial a telephone number. The confidential phone at the desk of General Sforza, Guardia di Finanza, was answered brusquely. 'Si?' A gruff, stop-bothering-me voice.

'Radziwill here, General.'

'Eccelenza. Illustrious friend of the poor. A problem?'

'Cash deliveries in the next week or so.'

'Say no more. For you my newest armoured truck. And for you, honest drivers!'

Both men chuckled. 'General, I ask only for help. Miracles are His Holiness' business.' Now both laughed freely. 'Ciao, General. A thousand blessings.'

'And one miracle.'

As they hung up the archbishop wondered if his time-lock vault was powerful enough to guard this much cash, so much it would bankrupt Pan-Eurasian Credit Trust; so much it would conquer all of Eastern Europe.

In the past he'd stored large amounts. But what he needed this time was a monstrous war chest big enough to create a central reserve for his operation upon which he could borrow, and thus multiply, his capital.

The archbishop pulled on a thin leather jacket with a short-haired fur collar. With sunglasses and the collar turned up, he looked like half the men in Rome this June. He mounted the stairs to the helicopter landing pad. They had sent a smallish craft of the Lynx type, and a pilot who had dressed in garb identical to His Excellency.

He switched on the engine's roar and gearbox chatter. The rotors began to chop the air. A moment later, tail high as if depositing eggs on the surface of a pond, the dragonfly craft lifted off and slewed sideways over the Vatican walls, heading toward Ciampino Airport. It tilted rakishly into the rain.

This was perhaps the archbishop's favourite moment, aloft and rootless in thin air as Satan had been, each with their own secrets. Below them the pentagonal redoubt of the Castel Sant' Angelo slipped by as they crossed the Tiber, its flow hammered into a matte silver by the light drops of rain. Ahead lay the Piazza Navona, its long oval dotted with morning tourist umbrellas and the stands of artists, fortune tellers, caricaturists. Directly below as they headed south lay a sharply-tiered wedding cake surrounded by jammed vehicular traffic, the white excrescences of the Vittorio Emanuele memorial, all furbelows and frills. Rome's toxic air was turning into Swiss cheese.

His Excellency took a cautious breath. This morning heathen Icarus could have been his patron saint. His crooked smile remembered a more recent icon: A helicopter, a big, industrial-strength machine. From its undercarriage, on long steel cables, swung a large Christ. So Fellini had begun his *La Dolce Vita*, Our Saviour being carried above Rome, just as His servant, the archbishop, was now being – progressed? – decades later.

In fact, he suddenly remembered, he had actually been a seminary student here in Rome when that scene had been filmed. Nowadays, the screen ate up everyone's life. Even in the IUD offices he overheard clerks discussing last night's TV variety show. Such an abdication of their own lives!

The Colosseum moved by on their right, another wedding cake, one that someone had sat on. Ahead of them silver railroad lines converged on the Stazione Termini. Ahead, through the thin rain, he could see the vast spread of buildings that made up the sanatorium, hospital, palace, basilica, baptistry and convent of San Giovanni in Laterano which the Vatican owned.

Despite the rain, it was good to see the tour buses, private limousines and cars clustered in the streets around the enclave. Aerial views suited him. Although his work dealt directly with the Almighty, he reflected, it also toyed with he whom the Almighty had cast out, the first aeronaut, Satan.

How often one saw that debt acknowledged. The names flyers gave themselves and their aircraft: Devil Divers. Satan's Squadron. It was clear: all flyers descended from the first aeronaut, cast out of heaven, powerdiving through loop-the-loops and lazy eights into the vastness of Hell below.

In those days, he recalled, when the Earth was still an intellectual construct in God's mind, Hell was a fixed abode. One descended to it, perhaps not in a screaming engine-stalling crash. If eternal torture embraced one, it was at least heartening to know that loved ones left behind were eons of miles above your torment and knew nothing of it. Nowadays, Hell was right here on Earth, on the living room screen, flickering, or in the streets. Its inhabitants, tired of waiting for death to issue their ticket to the hereafter, had chosen Hell while yet alive.

They were passing a section of the Grande Racconto Anulare, the ring road that circled Rome, past
scrubland, factories and warehouse-showrooms. Like
nature goddesses, prostitutes in short skirts smoked
and read gossip magazines until a passing motorist or
trucker pulled over for an act of worship and a drain
job. Scrotum tapped, he would be back on the
Racconto within minutes, having made proper obeis-
ance to the goddess. Surely these women, and
especially the transvestites passing as women, were
creatures from Satan's new ground level Hell who
had selected penis-conducted disease as their eternal
punishment.

That was why being aloft, a thousand feet above
Hell, gave the archbishop this special feeling, not at
all worrying, delicious in fact. The same suspended
sense of being, at one and the same time, in *both*
Their hands, God's and Satan's.

In the distance, at Ciampino, a colleague of Amadeo's ran charter airlines. On Saturdays the man's
office was both secluded and empty. The helicopter
settled down delicately near the detached, jerry-
built, tin-walled prefab described by Amadeo. 'Wait
here,' Radziwill ordered. Room 3's huge picture
window was obscured by a tightly drawn Venetian
blind.

The man who called himself Bradford Ames stood
at a small desk beside two glasses and a bottle of one
of those sweet whiskies like Chivas Regal the Italians
employ solely for ceremonial purposes. He bowed

and smiled. 'I see you so seldom, Eccelenza. Profound thanks for coming here.'

'A risk.' Radziwill sat down and poured a glass of spirits. He stared at Amadeo, wondering if, beneath his narrow English brogues he had cloven feet.

Bradford Ames looked tired, his lip bruised. His long, elegant frame drooped but his face still shone with whatever news he had to impart. 'I have been working very hard, sir, assembling forces, Eccelenza, and cash.' He sat down. 'Today is the fifth of June. In ten days you address the bankers?'

'Get to the point.'

'Starting tomorrow I will have four things to hand you, actually to put in the palm of your hand. The first, of course, is the cash.' Ames paused dramatically. His vampire's canines glistened whitely, turning his battered grin into a rather disturbing grimace. Archbishop Radziwill tested the air for brimstone, the smell created when that much money passes hands, implicating giver and taker in a dizzying web of complicity. 'That note you so want, if it still exists, I will hand to you. With it, a signed copy of the final loan agreement with Krevic's nation.'

Radziwill looked up. 'And the last?'

'Eccelenza's request of last August regarding Palmer. Fulfilled.'

Not saying something placed shattering emphasis on what was left out. The archbishop stared for a long time at his creature. 'Yes, this could not have been reported by telephone.' He filled a second glass and got to his feet. 'Cin-cin e buona fortuna,

Amadeo.' He managed a small, shaken smile, thinking: the order can still be rescinded. They touched glasses. Overhead a jet aircraft deafened them for a moment as it took off.

Palmer can be left alive, Radziwill thought, to continue opposing me. I can surely behave as humanely as he?

They sipped the sweet whisky. Ames brightened visibly. 'With any luck, no one can prove it's a zap. Just an acci – '

'No!' The archbishop slammed down the glass with such force that a drop of spirit splashed up on to his fingers. 'Tell me nothing.' He dried his moist fingers by jamming them in a pocket of his leather jacket. 'Not a word.'

'Ah, yes. Deniability. I understand, sir.'

'Deniability, hell, young man: conscience!' Radziwill thundered, turned on his heels and left. He was smiling, but keeping it from Satan's disciple.

This was the only way to manipulate evil, blindly, able to know nothing. What a fearful combination: his brains, Ames' ruthlessness. Too bad people like Palmer and his daughter got entangled in the mower blades. But as this limb of Satan had assured him, it wouldn't look like a zap.

The sky was clearing. He needed it. He needed a bit of self-indulgence to celebrate Amadeo's four promises. He would order the helicopter to Porto San Stefano after all. Senora Agnelli would be so pleased. Her extra dry martinis were preferable to ceremonial Scotch. True, he was handling sins again. What else

could one call the promises made to him just now –
not one of which had he rescinded. But, like murder,
no matter how many you committed, they could
only hang you once.

Chapter Twenty-Nine

'Restless,' Eleanora murmured.

In the darkness of their bedroom Eleanora and Palmer lay beside each other, knowing it was well past midnight. Neither of them could sleep.

'I'm trying to descend from a power high,' he confessed. 'Feeding poisoned sweetmeats to the press can be a Godlike ego trip.' Neither of them spoke for a long moment. 'What's *your* excuse?' he asked then in that abrupt way of his that was so disconcerting when first you met him. Eleanora was used to it now. But it still disconcerted her.

She hardly understood her own actions that night with Curtis. The event still demanded explanation. Nor was Curtis there to discuss it with her. He'd left for Berlin with the rest of the *Klarion* people, to help expedite the production of the article and tuck in any loose ends that showed up. She decided a sideways diversion. 'You think it will help vanquish the mafia?'

'Ruin Teddy Radziwill; alert the stupidest of bankers; plop the mafia in a log-jam. But to vanquish them is wishful thinking.'

'Then why waste your time this way?'

He paused for what seemed an endless moment. Then he set up his own diversion. 'Did I tell you I'm crazy about your daughter? She was nice enough to hand me *Die Klarion*. I owe her one. As for Gerri and her bridegroom, not so crazy.'

Eleanora accepted the diversion. 'She seems very happy.'

'I tell you this and only you,' he responded after a moment. 'He strikes me as a bright, brave, sincere kid. But against all the drawbacks of where he comes from and what he's trying to accomplish?'

'Late marriages are all the thing. And she's just turned thirty. It's no reason to panic. But at least,' Eleanora said, pausing for a breath, 'she didn't sign on for a ménage à trois.'

'Who did? Tanya? What're you saying?'

'Bert should not be allowed on the streets without a bell around his neck. He's a menace. If Tanya were ever foolish enough to marry the Raspe boy – who by himself is quite a catch – then she inherits a bisexual succubus. Raspe's always been the focus of Bert's adoration. To Raspe it's nothing unusual to be adored by two people. Simultaneously.'

'You mean . . . in the sack?'

'I don't want to know how it's managed – '

' – who does what to who?'

'Not funny,' she snapped, 'if one's your misguided daughter. At the party, your friend Staeli proposed marriage and, of course, she turned him down. Compared to her, Gerri is a blessing.' This observation seemed to damp down their talk to utter silence. He found her hand and squeezed it softly. She pushed her face in against his neck and they lay quietly for a long time.

Palmer sighed. 'In Slavko's native land, these days, political prominence is grounds for assassination. Who knows who's put a price on Slavko's head? Who knows what patriot is stalking him? And if he manages to stay alive, where am I going to find him a legitimate lender to take on the loan he needs?'

'UBCO?'

'UBCO is hurting, like the rest. Intellectual pygmies the magnitude of Bob Vanderpoole choking on bad debts.'

'Then stop taking responsibility for everything around you. Gerri is a grown woman. She's made her choice.' She laughed unhappily. 'Weddings and babies. As Elfi says, life is a sexually transmitted disease, invariably fatal.'

'Who's Elfi? I like her already.'

'You remem – ' She stopped, realising she had had this conversation with Curtis, not Woods. 'A lesbian girl in my office. Oral sex is her answer.'

'To what question?' When she didn't respond, Palmer turned over towards her. 'A sex chat with you, my dear, is downright educational.'

'Any time.' She yawned. 'Do you think . . .?'

'Sure,' he said, his hand opening the buttons on the front of her nightgown. 'Absolutely.' He stroked her body for a moment. 'Although, in view of what Elfi says, maybe . . .'

'Maybe what?'

'Maybe it might spoil you.'

'Take that chance.'

Chapter Thirty

The private telephone on His Excellency's desk rang. 'That you, Bernardin?'

'Excellency? I can hardly hear you for the noise.'

'Calling from the helicopter. A change of plans again. I'll be in Porto San Stefano, as planned. Over and out.'

When, finally, Bernardin realised he would have the weekend free, he gave a small leap as he crossed the room to his own mainframe terminal. His fingers danced over the keyboard, entering areas of the software only he had programmed.

His fractals were threading a complex maze like yeast bubbling to fill a tunnel. Because of their divine origins, one never knew a fractal's conclusion until it took place. He had set this one operating on what MIT graduate students referred to as B-FLURD Instructions. B-FLURD was an acrostic-mnemonic: back, forward, left, up, right, down, the six directions available in a cube. Upon hitting a maze wall the fractal would search backwards, to the left, upwards and so forth until it found a way open.

Bernardin stared at his screen. Trial and error was God's gift to every creature and He put no limit on the process. But, what if — ? 'Asleep at the screen?' Covici asked. 'Not too busy for your old comrade?'

'We are not comrades.'

'His Excellency would certainly think so.' Covici bent over him like an interrogator. 'How else access Oscar Bravo 31?'

Bernardin frowned. 'His Excellency knows nothing of last week's folly.'

'Folly? You did me a favour, Bernardin.' Covici's hand rested on the young priest's shoulder and gave it a reassuring pat. 'And I'm not ungrateful.'

'I am in the middle of a very del – '

'Ah! That's part of the favour.' Covici's dark eyes flashed rather wildly. 'Your fractals remain our secret,' he reminded the priest. 'Also Oscar Bravo 31.'

Bernardin's glance, intent on the screen, suddenly swerved towards his tormentor's face. 'You – '

'The original archive disc is doctored. None of what we did shows.' Covici smiled. 'And my friend has paid much gold for a copy disc.'

'You are an abomination.'

'No. I am an underpaid and overworked father of five small children who hopes, like any decent, devout family man, to better his position and salary.'

A hurt look shone in the young priest's eyes. He shifted on his stool so that he was turned half away from Covici. 'You get no more help.'

'We're in this together.' Covici's voice grew harder. 'My motive is the welfare of my family. For you it is giving aid to the poor. You have only to access and copy out a few more documents. The rest, the hard part, is up to me.'

The two men seemed frozen in place, Bernardin's

body turned away but craning back to stare at his tormentor's face, Covici smiling down at him, well aware he had already won this discussion. All the rest was detail.

Covici would match stolen secrets with potential buyers. These databanks, with their precise, specific notes of who, what and how much – and especially the bonus possibilities of hidden texts – were almost beyond price.

'My dear Saint Bernardin.' Covici's smile seemed etched for ever on his face. He glanced at his watch. 'Soon I'll have to start assembling the Sunday round up. Let's see what we can find.' Aggressively he shoved himself in front of Bernardin's keyboard and punched in a series of instructions. The screen flickered and another part of the mainframe software appeared.

'Covici, *in God's name!*' Bernardin's voice had risen high with fear. The note in his voice forced Covici's head to turn towards him.

'Calmly, young saint.'

'Did you exit my fractals befor y – '

Covici frowned uneasily. 'Did I exit first? I don't remember. Is it important?'

'Is it important?' Bernardin echoed, dumbfounded at his own fears. How could he explain that a fractal, programmed on B-FLURD, would seek and fill, seek and fill, until there was no space left. On its own, under control, it was of great use. 'You shorted over! We may have a disaster.'

'You're behaving like a child,' the older man said in a tone that wavered childishly itself.

'Covici.' Bernardin's plump mouth opened and closed twice, as if unable to frame his thoughts properly. 'Covici, you have read about computer viruses? I was running an instruction. If you have shorted it into the mainframe memory . . .'

Bernardin's eyes went wide. He was a gentle man, but he was younger and bigger than Covici. With one hand he knocked the older man's shoulder and shoved him out of the chair. The priest sat back down at the keyboard and tapped in some new instructions. He watched the screen display and flip through file headings until it came to an accounting spreadsheet where things like Signora Agnelli's recent contribution were noted, including date and the deposit-slip ID.

'You see?' Covici crowed. 'Nothing's changed, you young alarmist.'

Bernardin continued to watch the screen for a full minute, flipping through different memories and databank headings. 'You understand, B-FLURD is a slow programme even on a thirty-two-bit processor. Ten years ago, this was 1984 state-of-the-art, no RISC restricted instructions. Therefore, at each maze-turn, the fractal often takes the full run of moves before an obstacle is overcome.'

'You priests are shameless. You invent hobgoblins to frighten us poor laity. How long would it take such a virus to show up?'

'I – I'm not sure. It hides, often for months. Then reappears.'

'You're mad,' Covici snapped. His eyes strayed to the screen, where the young priest had returned to the accounting spreadsheet. Bernardin's glance followed his.

Glowing green, the words and numbers seemed to be expanding. Bernardin's sharp intake of breath was the only sound. He knew that the formatting of this spreadsheet produced spacing, punctuation, line advances. In addition to the actual binary coded ASCII letters and numbers there were signals that never appeared on the screen except as spacing. As the two men watched, the hidden formatting began to come alive. Between letters that spelled out Agnelli, for instance, random symbols appeared, some letters, some numbers, arrows, punctuation, a hideous example of every computer technician's GIGO nightmare, garbage in, garbage out. Before their eyes, the basic data was self-destructing.

Bernardin's fingers tapped furiously at the keyboard. 'I can't – !'

The destruction on the green-glowing screen was reducing the spreadsheet to something like turf, a sward of individual blades of grass signifying nothing.

'It has to run its course,' the priest muttered.

'How long?'

'I don't know: minutes, weeks.'

In desperate silence they watched as the entire accounting spreadsheet dissolved into green chaos. It was like watching an animal die, but silently. Finally, Bernardin sighed. 'It's over.'

'But you can't just – '

The young Swiss tapped in a series of new commands. 'I'm reversing the B-FLURD. Its own memory will take it back to the start again. I pray.'

For a long time the screen showed no sign of life, the turf of grass speaking only of chaos. Then, abruptly, a line was restored. Another dropped back into place. Soon the original spreadsheet had returned to the screen.

Covici breathed: 'Don't ever frighten me like that again, you alarmist.'

'Don't meddle with my software, Covici. You nearly brought down the whole mainframe structure. Even now it may still be infected.'

The older man, much calmer now, eyed the priest for a moment. 'Look at you. You're trembling.'

'You would, too, if you weren't such an ignoramus.'

Covici glanced at his watch again. 'All this gibberish! I've got to start working on the round up. I'll be back this afternoon, around five.'

When he left, Bernardin switched through more of the mainframe files. Of his own knowledge there were forty. Correspondence, for example, was stored under geographic headings with cross-referencing by date and alphabet. Income also used three accounting files, as did Lending. Bernardin felt sure there were other categories His Excellency had installed but, in the few months he'd been here, the young priest hadn't had time to uncover these apocrypha.

As he shifted through the known databanks, he was relieved to see that his fractal virus hadn't had time to lodge anywhere but the Accounting memory, apparently. Bernardin supposed this was a blessing since, following B-FLURD instructions, his fractal could easily freeze any electronic data, rendering it useless.

A narrow escape, if true. A warning that any traffic with Covici could explode into disaster. Gnawed by having been passed over so often, the older man was desperate, gambling all and sure to lose. But I would lose much more, Bernardin warned himself. This position, for one thing, and the support of His Eminence, Cardinal Huf. But even more, he thought, I would lose the support of the software. Where could a poor priest find this much computer power for his research?

To keep Covici at bay he must feign illness, a small enough lie to see him through the weekend. With His Excellency back in the office, Covici didn't dare harass him. Slowly, moving as if already ill, Father Bernardin switched incoming calls to the tiny bedroom he occupied on the floor above.

Before climbing upstairs he watched for a long moment the green screen of his terminal. He had returned it to the Accounting file, which shone unflickering and seemingly untainted by its close call with chaos. Bernardin's head shook slowly from side to side, remembering that horrible moment when the software had died. If anything illustrated faith in God, this did. Faith in the unseen, in simple instructions like B-FLURD, the invisible programme that could destroy as readily as it could create.

Where did fractals go? When he reversed them, did they die? As constructs of God, not man, could they be immortal? What was the geometry they inhabited? Cubic, yes. But once into a reverse mode, did they proceed backward to do the same thing they did forward? For ever? A cold, sick sweat broke out on his forehead. Because, if so, they were lethal in either direction. Forward or backward they would fill and wreck any software. The thought made him ill. He moved slowly towards the window that looked down on the patio below.

Although Christ's face was hidden, his tears could be seen to fall. As Bernardin watched, a pretty young woman in a pale pink raincoat, one of the secretaries, perhaps, paused and held out her hand, palm up. She touched Christ's tear to her forehead and then crossed herself before walking on. Simple faith, therefore strong. In her mind there would be no question. A construct of God was immortal. Ask her and the answer would be clear.

Once summoned, Bernardin thought, could fractals be recalled? Never. Once born, how could they die? Impossible. His forehead dripped chillingly, like Christ's tears. And once he had instructed the fractals, how on earth could he ever hope to make them ignorant once more? Or show themselves. Or do anything other than hide, hide, hide . . . and pounce.

Chapter Thirty-One

Decades before, just after Fellini films had made it famous, the Via Veneto was captured by tourists, the whole short, curving thoroughfare that drops from the Borghese Gardens, past the open-air cafés, the Excelsior Hotel and the American embassy, down to the Piazza Barberini.

Less than a kilometre in length, the street marks off eons in status. In the days of *La Dolce Vita*, Roman illuminati lounged here to see and be seen while papparazzi flashed endless snapshots. Now out-of-towners prowled it, glancing furiously about for celebrities, puzzled at what all the fuss was about.

But Alex stipulated the Via Veneto as the place for him to make contact with his group, so Fiona and Bradford Ames sat with him at a table up the street from the Excelsior, the more expensive side. Soon Alex had spotted one of his group, a skinny young man who didn't seem all that happy to be recognized.

'Grischka, sit down, please?' Alex commanded. 'We wait for Ivan.'

With his small black cat hidden in her nest atop his backpack, Alex had begun to shed the more clownish elements of his cover persona. His voice had assumed authority. He no longer displayed a grimy wrist splint, nor did he forgetfully massage the place it had been. That didn't mean he'd forgotten the compound fracture, or how he had gotten it.

Fiona knew these foreigners filled some secret slot in Ames' plans. It was part of being his slave that she be kept in the dark. This all seemed quite normal to her. For instance the first inkling she'd had that her father was leading a double life had come last night. Two uniformed Guardia di Finanza officers had appeared at her apartment.

They had asked meaningless questions in execrable English about a Colonel Campbell. He might, Fiona decided, also be Professor Campbell. He might not. The officers had left without shedding any light at all, showering her with the usual 'just routine' and 'do not leave town'.

Being poorly informed had the same classic effect on Fiona as it did down through the ages on other slaves: it made her curious and sly, knowing what your master was doing, but not telling him you knew, was the ultimate power. Right now she felt at ease in her bondage. The way Ames had handled the ravishing of his lip told her he was worthy to command. Pain hardly existed for him, except to inflict it. Something deep in her groin stirred.

Amid the early afternoon passaggiata up and down the Via Veneto the missing Ivan suddenly slipped into a chair without even nodding his head.

June's warm sun set the glasses sparkling on tables along both sides of the street. The three young men lounged in easy postures, as if plotting calcio bets for tomorrow's games. Only Bradford Ames looked out of place with his uptight three-piece dark grey bank-er's suit, broadly pinstriped. Only he glanced around them as if fearing eavesdroppers.

Alex looked entirely at ease and in control. The small black cat emerged daintily from her bed space and lay across his legs. Fiona began giving her in quick succession potato chips, two black olives and a salted almond. Now the cat looked up to mark the clatter of two amazingly tall, thin models in minis-kirts and four-inch heels. Her green eyes blinked and slowly, slowly hooded. Thus she missed the passage, behind the models, of someone so truly Italian that her like might never be found in any other capital city.

She was a Fellini-grotesque whore, overweight in a way that turned flab into a challenge to the eyes, ugly baby-face make-up and a musky reek that lingered long after she strolled past on the arm of her pimp, a tiny man in checked jacket, two-tone brogues, a hairline moustache and a long cigarette holder. Time seemed to have reeled back fifty years along the Via Veneto.

At the corner an elderly waif with a concertina keened a wavering version of 'Non Discordar di Me', the poison-sweet sobs reeking of self-pity. A cloth cap lay on the pavement turned upside-down to receive coins. Despite the posh ambience, only alu-minium coins lay in the hat; too many quick fingers about.

In the opposite direction, striding with great con-fidence, two male whores advanced, pelvises thrust forward, butts tucked in, eyes slanting this way and that. Dressed as males, one had very long, very clean platinum blonde hair combed back and down his see-through pale voile blouse while the other wore a grubby brunette crew cut, a riding crop he flourished across his own groin and unclean steel-studded black leather sweat-inducing garments.

'Kiss, kiss,' Grischka twittered.

'Please,' Alex said then. 'We are ready. The date?'

Ames frowned. 'Tenth of June. Actually the night before.'

'Night of ninth of June.' Alex consulted one of those fat digital wristwatches that tells you everything from tides to oestrus cycles. His broad face utterly blank, he turned his glance to Bradford Ames. Fiona couldn't help noting the extreme differences in the two men. Alex's muscular chunkiness, Ames' elongated elegance.

'Question of payment, please?' Alex said.

'Question of ability to do the job,' Ames countered.

'Question of payment, please?' Alex repeated then.

Ames felt the wound on his lip, touched it gingerly and examined the tip of his finger for blood. 'For doing a job you've already been sent here to do, what's your idea of a fair fee?'

The young hiker's heavy eyebrows went up. 'Three men, ammunition, considerable risk, expertise and, above all, will and dedication to destroy Krevic. Where do you find anywhere in Rome? Anywhere in Europe?'

'You're not unique, my friend.'

But Alex's head was already nodding. 'Yes, please. I am entirely unique. A million pounds sterling. In fifty pound notes, please.' He sipped his drink, a rum concoction in a tall glass decorated with paper umbrellas and tinsel-topped pompoms. Then, in the growing silence, he picked an orange slice out of his drink. With a great set of teeth he deftly bit the flesh from the rind and chewed thoughtfully.

'A million quid?' Ames echoed in disbelief. 'No, thanks. You're already being paid by someone else, remember. But I'll be fair. I'll share the price with your other sponsor. Half a million from him, half a million from me. Done!'

Alex's shrugged confidently. 'Is needed electronics expert.' His massive right hand indicated Grischka with a careless wave. 'Is needed weapons and demolition man. Ivan. And is needed infiltrator who arrive in the night, disarm all security devices, open gates to quick assault.'

Ames' smile disclosed his canines in a sharp, jagged flash of white. 'You've seen the plans. Are you the invisible man?' Ames' glance flicked past Fiona as if to say: must keep these lower orders in line.

Alex produced a gesture with both hands like a flower unfolding. 'No. Am expert hang glider pilot.'

A sudden silence enclosed them in that normally noisy place. 'Ah,' Ames said in a suddenly satisfied tone.

'Three men and a cat,' Alex said.

Fiona watched the two men jockeying over a price one might not be able to pay and the other be too dead to collect. Ames burst out laughing. 'For the cat alone, yes. But for all four of you, half a million.'

Alex frowned portentously. When he spoke at last it was with great authority, as if handing down a verdict that had been his all along. 'Three men and a cat: half a million sterling. Done!'

Chapter Thirty-Two

Northwest of Rome, that coast of the Mediterranean called the Tyrrhenian, offers the very rich a number of enclaves with only limited threat of being kidnapped for money or bombed for politics. If one's pleasures include yachting or, more properly, sunbathing aboard a yacht, there are harbours and islands where, by employing a loyal crew, private security guards and bribing the local carabinieri, peace of mind can be enjoyed.

This does not come cheap. Simple pleasures rarely do. Perhaps the dearest of these enclaves is Caspia Bay, north of the big airport complex at Fiumicino and backed by extremely high cliffs. There are two ways to reach the small rind of sandy beach and marina where fifty-feet yachts are considered rather small. Visitors can descend in a guarded elevator barely big enough for a couple and their luggage. Or, like His Excellency Archbishop Tadeusz Radziwill, they can arrive by helicopter.

He had actually landed aboard the yacht owned by Madame Agnelli's close friend, the Baronessa Barletta, known as Babette or elsewhere as la vedova felice, the merry widow.

The Barone Barletta's death, of cocaine overdose, was popularly attributed to his new wife, a slander without foundation. Babette, who claimed to be

French, had been born in Bournemouth, England, of
a couple named Eastcheap who worked the coconut
shy. Her husband, a great lone-wolf investor, had
been about to sink most of his funds in a near-
bankrupt Czechoslovak auto works. His death, in
that respect, was timely for Babette. The Czechs
eventually sold out to Fiat, conserving intact the
Barone's fortune. Children of an earlier marriage
sued but everything, including the yacht, was
Babette's.

Archbishop Radziwill knew Caspia Bay many years
before as a penniless seminarian. Now he had a
stateroom to himself, discreetly across the corridor
from Madame Agnelli. A slim young homosexual
valet called Pippo laid out his clothes, drew his bath
and would have been pleased to administer it.

At the moment, the improving weekend weather
had produced a superb sunny Sunday with sea
breezes to keep it from growing actually hot. Radziwill, in tennis whites, lay on the sundeck among
nearly naked women who occasionally fretted about
the propriety of wearing bikinis in the presence of an
archbishop.

The only other male was an Egidio Fascinante, a
young gigolo wearing a tiny pouch that nearly
covered his penis but not the odd testicular bulge.
He, not Pippo, waited on Babette, bringing her
drinks, caressing suntan lotion into her skin. He
would then grovel at her feet like her largish, hairless
dog.

His Excellency spoke rarely and then usually to

praise the dry martini, or the excellence of the small snacks. Back in Rome, Radziwill knew, IUD was mired in the routine labour of the weekly round up. Soon he would get a phone call from Bernardin giving him the high points of the five-page document. A few changes and the forecast would download simultaneously into select computers all over the face of the earth.

Major banks, even on Sunday, kept a line open for the transmission. Government agencies did, too. Smaller financial institutions eagerly awaited the IUD outlook for the week ahead as it related to currency exchange, securities market fluctuations, new issues, expected fiscal policy changes of the major powers, large corporate movements, new business ventures, in fact, a great host of financial insider-trivia cobbled together by that ageing hack, Covici.

It tested low in the kind of mendacious special pleading that flawed most market newsletters. Radziwill's insistence that it tell the truth, and his distribution limit of 100 recipients, gave a tremendous cachet to being a subscriber. The service was, of course, free, but it was common for subscribers to feed IUD confidential information in return.

Tomorrow morning, when corporate executives, bankers, financial civil servants and high-ranking politicians thumbed their way through their own printout of the IUD forecast, they easily believed the one or two special bits, the casual reference to a particular stock issue, the report of a new debenture, an oil-search consortium, an aerospace development. Would they suspect that IUD had first taken a concealed financial interest in such events? Never. And if it were proved that such tips served to fatten IUD's coffers, didn't the readers of the forecast also benefit? No one was hurt and the Church had a bit extra to spend on the Pope.

Pippo appeared. He would have loved to wear the scrap Egidio was clad in, but the Baronessa insisted on full livery. 'A thousand pardons, Eccelenza,' his sibilance tickled the archbishop's ear. 'Your office is on the radiophone.'

Aware that the naked ladies were watching his every movement, Radziwill strolled to the radio room, where the Captain himself stood holding the telephone out to him. The moment the archbishop picked it from his hand, the captain removed himself and closed the door behind him.

'Yes, Bernardin?'

'It's Covici, Excellency.'

'Why you? Oh, get on with it, then.'

Clearing his throat, the elderly employee read through the headlines. The archbishop, bored with the summary, was as bored with the prospect of returning to the sundeck to observe carefully massaged and lotioned nudity of sleek women in their early fifties, each of them hoping.

Some priests – he knew them – behaved like ordinary men, swilling in the velvet trough between these rich women's thighs. Some kept their vows. They were rarely invited back. And some, he, for example, kept the world guessing. He preferred it that way. La Agnelli could make up any story she wanted about the two of them. No one would believe it unless, with their own eyes, they saw concrete evidence. He made sure they didn't.

'Put that business about the drop in sterling in bold type, understand?'

'Yes, Excellency.'

'And the new Ciba-Geigy story must be boxed. Understand?'

'A box, sir?'

'Lines around it. Where's Bernardin? He knows what I mean.'

'Bernardin is — ' Covici put his hand over his phone. His Excellency could hear angry words.

'Excellency?' the voice of Bernardin interrupted. 'I must apologise. I had no idea he was telephoning you with — '

'Can't I leave you two alone?'

'It's . . . it's a technical problem, sir. The transmission, the download. A . . . um . . . a problem with the modem comms. Nothing for you to be concerned about.'

The archbishop found himself looking at his own face in a small wall mirror. The vertical frown between his big, clear eyes made him look older. He glanced at his watch. 'You start downloading in seven minutes,' he told Bernardin.

'Yes, absolutely. Certainly. Of course.'

'Make the changes I gave Covici and get going!' Radziwill slammed down the radiophone handpiece.

He glanced at his face again and painstakingly smoothed away every sign of annoyance. Why did he have to be subjected to the office squabbles of underlings? Covici he had always found tiresome with his five needy children and sly secrecy. With all his mystic mathematical mumbo-jumbo, Bernardin was, at least, competent. Too bad he had to be considered Cardinal Huf's private ear.

Suddenly the radio telephone rang. Startled, Radziwill picked it up. 'Pronto?'

'Is it you, Eccelenza, the saviour of the poor?' General Sforza asked. 'Have I interrupted your weekend devotions?' The archbishop listened to the faint note of irony that always infected Sforza's tone.

'Like the Guardia di Finanza, General. I never sleep.'

'Alone,' the officer added jokingly. 'Eccelenza, cash has begun to arrive. In all my days as a money-policeman I have seldom seen so much. But there are two problems.' The policeman cleared his throat. 'The gentleman who supervises the cash deliveries to me? Do you know him well?'

Radziwill frowned at himself in the mirror. Satan hands one tarnished goods. 'Hardly at all. Haynes?'

'Ames,' Sforza corrected him slowly. 'He is associated with a young woman already under investigation. Her father – It is a sordid story with national security problems. Involving the Gladio scandal?' The archbishop waited silently. Nothing nasty about Ames would surprise him. He had become a liability.

He had to be fed to the lions. 'That is my first problem, Eccelenza. The other is embarrassing.'

Watching himself in the mirror, Radziwill smiled. He had returned to familiar ground. 'Tonio, amico, how much?'

'Handling? Safeguarding? Is 1 per cent agreeable?'

'Agreed, old friend. And here is a bonus. Whatever trouble Haynes causes you, do not spare him because of a supposed connection with me. There is none.'

Sforza sighed happily. 'You make my job so much easier, Eccelenza.' When he hung up, the archbishop could not help but compare the simple world of police corruption with the complex problems his own staff gave him.

Too bad a sunny Sunday afternoon had to be tainted with such low-level power struggles between Bernardin and Covici. But a sixth sense told Radziwill it had to be suppressed at once. He returned to the sundeck in time to see Pippo remove his empty martini glass and replace it with a full, tempting one.

Technical problem? In all His Excellency's years of IUD software there had never been what the trade called a glitch. Especially not in the modem that facilitated the downloading across cable and satellite circuits.

He lowered himself into the canvas chaise longue, his handsome face turned up to the strong sunlight. He eyed the fresh martini, the conical cocktail glass frosted with beads of condensation. Nothing to be concerned about, Bernardin had said. But that would be precisely what Cardinal Huf's man might say.

The archbishop sat up straight, staring as it happened at the large firm breasts of La Baronessa Barletta, their nipples and areoles barely hidden. He saw nothing. Instead he found himself wondering which was worse, an incompetent who might be dishonest or a competent who was spying on him. He got to his feet.

'Ah, Eccellenza,' La Agnelli murmured. Her body with its tiny buttocks and breasts was encased in a one-piece bathing suit cut very high at the thighs to make her legs look longer. Her great, heavy-lidded eyes studied him with some worry. 'Is something – ?'

'Maria-Elena, I must go. I am desolated.'

'Now?' three women asked in unison.

His Excellency was already moving off the sun-deck. 'I shall have to find my pilot and leave. Believe me, only an emergency could tear me away.'

'We had hoped,' Babette murmured, 'you would be able to stay the night.' Her glance, saddened, fell on the Agnelli woman.

In under half an hour the helicopter settled on to the roof landing pad at IUD and the archbishop sped down the stairway to his office. Only Bernardin was there, not staring at his terminal screen but standing at the window watching the tears of Christ as they fell in the brilliant late afternoon sunshine.

'But Excellency, there was no need for you t – '

'Never lie to an archbishop,' his superior snapped. 'Especially one from Chicago. Even over the phone your voice reeked of trouble. Has Covici been acting up?' He was used to getting quick answers from this brainy young priest. When Bernardin failed to respond, alarm bells began to ring in the archbishop's mind.

'He – I – No, sir. Not . . . acting up.'

This time the silence went on unbearably long. Where he had been annoyed, Radziwill was now beginning to grow worried. 'Why did he call me, not you?'

'*Damn Covici*!' Bernardin blinked at his own fury.

His superior drew back a step. He had never seen the plump young man angry, only guilt-ridden. 'Is that the duty of a priest, to damn a co-worker?'

'I'm sorry. He gets . . . I'm sorry.'

'He gets?'

Bernardin's face had gone red down to his clerical collar. 'He gets on my nerves, sir. It's my fault. I should be more forbearing.'

'You haven't answered my question, Father.'

Bernardin made a visible effort to calm himself but his flushed face burned. Nothing came for a long time and Radziwill waited in silence, his great eyes glaring at the younger man like twin rocket launchers.

'I suppose,' Bernardin began, his voice beginning to shake, 'he wuh-wanted to ne-negotiate.'

This time the silence lasted much longer. The archbishop studied Bernardin who, when he expelled his breath, was sobbing. 'Good Lord! Calm yourself, Bernardin.'

The plump young man turned away and mastered

the convulsive movement. 'This is all my fault, sir. We were . . .' Bernardin's voice died out but he managed to turn back and face his superior. 'Accessing . . .' His throat seemed to close down so sharply it almost clicked.

'Speak!'

'Oscar Bravo 31,' the young Swiss managed to get out.

Oscar Bravo 31 was protected by ingenious codes. It was impossible accidentally to access it. 'For what purpose, Bernardin?' Radziwill's voice had gone dead, as if produced by an array of microchips behind the twin cannons of his eyes.

'Ss – ' the faint sibilance seemed to electrify the atmosphere. Bernardin gulped, his mouth working. 'Ss-sell it,' he managed to gasp. Immediately he sank back into the nearest chair, breathing as heavily as if he'd just finished his morning jog. His superior's face had grown entirely grave, cold, but still not panicked. 'To sell it?'

Bernardin moistened his dry lips. 'Sir, it *is* sold.'

Radziwill's face now went quite pale. The hollows under his cheeks seemed to darken. His dry voice had developed a crack, as if from foundation to roof-peak a house was tearing asunder. 'To whom?'

'To your friend, sir.'

'My f – ?' His Excellency's great eyes went wide with shock. 'Palmer?' Bernardin nodded. 'A print-out?' The young priest nodded again. 'But not a . . .' Radziwill found it hard to speak. 'Not a . . . copy disc?' Bernardin lied by shaking his head.

Radziwill sank into a chair, at last showing his vulnerability. Bernardin began to catch his breath. Having to confess a major catastrophe had been averted by reporting a smaller disaster. With any luck, if Bernardin had the time to patch it, His Excellency would never learn the real problem: a virus lying dormant in the software.

Outside, dusk gathered around a weeping Christ.

Chapter Thirty-Three

Sometimes, Curtis mused, the hand of Lady Luck moved so obviously that you had to admit we were pawns in a game whose rule book had yet to be published. If he hadn't telephoned Isabella from the *Klarion* office in Berlin to check a detail in the photostats she had sold him . . . If, hoping to lure him to Rome and sell more information, she hadn't told him of spotting Ames at the café on the Via Veneto with three troublemakers . . . If Curtis' work on the magazine article hadn't finished, giving him the time to check out what Isabella was telling him . . . And, finally, if Isabella's roly-poly cousin hadn't gone back to the Abruzzi for a week, making Isabella's double bed less life-threatening for Curtis . . .

But then, he reflected, lying quietly beside her in the middle of the night, his relationship with her had always been shot through with luck. This was something new in his affairs with women, a trouble-free interval between two exploded marriages and one long, honourable longing for Eleanora.

What a pleasure a simple, corrupt woman was who loved him only for his money and his ability to wreak vengeance on Bradford Ames. Isabella was Everyman's ideal, the honest whore. What made her far better was that she wasn't up for public sale. But of her many attributes, Isabella's greatest was that she had the Italian thirst for revenge. Curtis found it strangely reassuring, even peaceful, lying in the same bed with her while she fizzed with hatred of Bradford Ames.

Curtis knew there were Italians, mostly from the north, for whom revenge was not a necessity of life. After years of operating throughout Europe, he knew that only in Italy, and occasionally Greece, could one find the true, cut-off-one's-nose obsession with getting even that turned revenge into a toxic thirst.

Luckily, again, her enemy was his. Ames, she confessed hotly, sometimes suspending fornication to tell him this, had treated her like a slave, had introduced electrical instruments of torture to her intimate crevices, had sacked her because he had found an equally filthy-minded Britisher who enjoyed taking his abuse.

'Whoa!' Curtis would laugh. 'He sounds like a perfectly normal Brit. You have to be more tolerant of other people's perversions.'

'Curto, always men want women a slave, no? Have work in many offices. Have live with . . . a few . . . men. How not to know how they treat women? But not as he did.'

'Nasty?'

'He hurt me,' she breathed heavily, her pronunciation degenerating through rage into 'E urd mi.' Her nostrils flared alarmingly. 'I want is, ow you say? Is peeni, right ere.' She held out her hand, palm up. 'I want chop into polpettini. You unnerstan?'

'Please.' Curtis winced.

'Oh, you I adore.' She began kissing his penis as though it were the big toe of a saint. 'You I love. You will drown Ems in merda for Isabella, yes?'

It would have been tricky bugging Ames' office in the busy Hotel Eden. But Isabella's vendetta had led her to spy on her former employer enough to have spotted Fiona Campbell's apartment.

It proved quite easy for Curtis to short across some Italian government secret service lines already bugging the mistress of a left-wing deputy. Apparently one of Ames' group had a cat the Scotswoman had volunteered to take care of while the gang was engaged in training exercises.

According to Isabella, something big was under way. Ames had bought himself a hit squad of tough young men who seemed to have a grudge against Boluslav Krevic. More than once someone had referred to a mountain-top arena. Palmer was their target. It was also clear that they had the benefit of good reconnaissance and a level of expertise. Since Ames could no longer risk being seen with the group, Fiona would relay information to, and commands from.

This made Curtis the message centre's secret sharer, another clear instance of luck. Staring at Isabella's ceiling, Curtis shook his head slightly. Traffic at this hour in the Trastevere was sparse but now and then auto headlights below cast sweeping patterns across the much-painted pressed-tin panelling overhead.

Pawns in a game that Palmer had to win, or die,

both Curtis and Eleanora had invested too much loyalty in the man to allow for a defeat. So he had to win. How?

Curtis grunted and awakened Isabella. In the half dark, her eyes reflected the light from the ceiling. Her mass of dark curls in disarray, one eye hidden, she placed her hand on Curtis' chest. 'Tu sei molto preoccupato, no?'

'Preoccupato, si.'

'I take your mind off,' she promised. She began to massage his nipples until they grew hard. Then she began pinching them, gently at first. 'Mind off!'

'Your friend Ames.'

'One day I drink his blood.'

'This gang of his.'

'I boil his balls. Mind off.'

'They have a schedule. There is a deadline.'

'Curto, amore, stai calma.'

'I don't have time for calma.'

She pressed her hand down over his mouth. 'Is bad? Boring?'

She rolled over on top of him. Now she was nibbling at him, biting his lips, his neck, his nipples. Her huge mop of curls engulfed him, blotted out his vision of the ceiling and its hint that, outside this room, life went on without him.

Chapter Thirty-Four

Dusk changed the peach-coloured travertine to a pearly glow. His Excellency's office still looked bare, not a human ambience. He stared, unseeing, at the dying light. His private telephone rang.

'Sforza here.' No note of deference or even of ironic joking. 'Your young man? Who is mixed up in the Gladio murder?'

'Haynes? How bizarre.'

'Also in something else of which you have never heard. Pan-Eurasian Credit Trust, yes?'

Radziwill fell silent. Troubles never came singly. Fortunately, they had a solution. 'Tonio, shall we make it 2 per cent handling fee?'

Sforza sighed audibly. 'Eccelenza, shall we make it three?'

Afterwards the archbishop sat wondering how soon the Guardia could rid him of Ames; wondering how basically stupid Ames must be to get involved in the Gladio scandal; wondering if the IUD's plans were being torpedoed not by a clever enemy like Palmer but by greedy hirelings like Covici and Ames.

If Covici had sold Palmer a copy disc, of course, the game was up. Any talented hacker could sniff out the Cobol subtext and bring it alive. It might take a while, though . . .

Meanwhile, there was only one course of action. His eyes lighted. *Attack*!

Father Bernardin glanced about his bedroom. Like the larger one in His Excellency's suite, it came fully equipped with a computer terminal. After Bernardin's moment of confession that afternoon, the archbishop had been brooding alone. Then he telephoned for his helicopter to be refuelled and ready. At seven he had pounded on Bernardin's door.

In his bathrobe, Bernardin opened up. His superior's great eyes glanced in disgust at the tattered robe. 'You and Covici,' he said in a low, bitter voice, 'have destroyed me. Knowingly.'

'Excellency, we had no such — Where are you going at — ?'

His superior's ivory cheekbones flushed a darker olive hue, as if burned by some malignant flame. 'Your Cardinal has no need to know,' he snarled.

'But when will you return, Ex — ?'

'And you have no need, either.' He slammed Bernardin's door and strode angrily upstairs on to the helipad. A moment later, in a rising a clatter of rotor blades, he was gone.

It was true that the plump young priest wore an ancient wool robe. It had been new when his mother had given it to him on his ordination. Now his right elbow poked through a hole. Bernardin sat for a moment before the VDU and said a prayer. Selfish pleading, but, God knew, he needed help.

Archbishop Radziwill probably had an evening

engagement. He was never one to let office problems interfere with his social life. His absence gave Bernardin his chance to make everything right.

Bernardin remembered with shame how he had burst into tears, so frightened was he of what he might be unable to do. But now he could count on being alone for some hours. And he needed every minute of it.

He punched up the same Accounting file that had been attacked by the fractal operating under B-FLURD instructions. He ran the spreadsheet, searching for signs of the hideous, withering blight he had witnessed. But everything seemed in order.

Bernardin frowned. He was too experienced to believe he had undone the damage simply by reversing his fractal. It was analogous to putting an automobile in reverse while its engine was turning over. One could be at rest as long as the accelerator pedal wasn't pressed down. But one was *not* safe until gears had been shifted back into neutral and the engine switched off. This he had not done.

Reversed, the fractal had dropped off the screen once it restored the wrecked data. But until he located and removed it, it lived an unseen, unseeable life.

At midnight, after three hours of chasing it without finding it, he thought he heard His Excellency's limousine outside. He snapped off his lights. His room was illuminated now only by the green screen, mocking him with its clarity and his inability to locate the fractal.

He tiptoed to the window and saw Carlo, the driver, lock the limousine before walking away. No archbishop. The night was dark, no moon. Somewhere beyond a limousine's reach, where only the helicopter could take him, the archbishop pursued his social life. Throughout Vatican City the faithful slept. In this kind of night, Christ Himself stood unseen beneath His cross, even His tears invisible.

Bernardin stared hopelessly into the night for the reassuring figure of the Saviour. He failed to find Him. The thought he had been avoiding now returned to him. All this weekend, since the fractal had turned virus, he had held off thinking about the possibilities.

Since he wasn't sure he'd exorcised the fractal, downloading the weekly forecast to 100 subscribers now seemed catastrophic. If the fractal lived an outlaw existence, no longer appearing on screens or in printouts, it might easily now live in the software of a hundred subscribers.

Chapter Thirty-Five

The four of them sat around the fireplace, enjoying a drink before Sunday supper. Hidden loudspeakers in the great room produced a low sighing of Puccini strings, melancholy and without end.

Palmer had made the same drink for all of them: brandy, curacao and lemon. 'The original happy juice,' he said, serving Eleanora and Gerri. He handed them two deep-bellied red-wine glasses, each with a large cube of ice. Then, from a twenties-style chromium cocktail shaker, he poured a chill, cloudy amber liquid. He went on to fill two glasses for himself and Slavko. 'Do you have a special toast in your country?' he asked, raising his glass.

The young man's face grew worried. 'A dozen. But for a parting, none of them will do.'

'You'll be back,' Palmer said quickly, firmly, as if nailing the promise in place. 'Anyway, you don't leave till late tomorrow.'

'And we will be back, sooner than you think,' Gerri told him. She lifted her glass. 'Arrivederci, non addio.'

'Farewell but not goodbye,' Eleanora automatically translated.

Many yards away, in Palmer's office, the fax machine started printing. Palmer frowned. 'Cheers.'

Eleanora watched the two men, hoping her close

surveillance was discreet. For the past week this guarded mountain-top had been a cave with two he-bears. They were, as a matter of fact, behaving terribly well toward each other. But little things had begun to impinge on Palmer's hegemony of the cave, reminding him that another Alpha male was in residence.

Yesterday and today, Sunday, the phone had rung all afternoon. Most of the calls had been for the finance minister, not the retired banker. Twice the calls had been high-priority conversations with his prime minister. Once it had been a woman who, it turned out, was Slavko's mother.

'They very much hope to meet you, my parents,' he had told Palmer. 'Travel to and from my country is now no more easy than under the old regime.'

Both of them had fallen silent as the faint noise of the fax machine continued and Puccini's bittersweet lament, wordless, filled the air. 'I suppose it's for you,' Palmer said then.

'I beg your pardon, Woods, sir?'

'The fax.'

Slavko clearly didn't understand but, Eleanora saw, didn't want to trouble his father-in-law any more than necessary. They sipped the icy drink, not quite sweet but instantly warming. Slavko sipped twice more. 'Oh, yes, I see, of course, quite,' he said, glad of a pretext for issuing words. 'The original happy juice.'

'It's a Prohibition drink called a Side Car,' Palmer

volunteered. His glance crept sideways towards the sound of the fax, but he remained motionless.

The Puccini, an instrumental piece called 'Crisantemi', filled the room with longings never to be requited. Eleanora noted that its main theme was expressed by two melodic lines going in opposite directions. A bit like these two bears.

'I don't expect you know about our Prohibition,' Palmer said.

'From after the First World War,' Slavko recalled, 'until repeal by Roosevelt in 1933. Was it very onerous, sir?'

Palmer's smile was sardonic. 'I was ten when it was repealed. All I can remember is that in my father's house there was always hard liquor.'

'The lawless years,' Gerri quoted somewhat kiddingly.

A silence fell over them. They clearly heard the fax come to an end but Puccini continued to haunt them, his sorrow moving up and down at the same time. Eleanora broke the silence: 'Woods, you are dying to know about that fax.'

'It can wait.'

'But you can't.' She and Gerri exchanged looks. 'Sitting next to you is like sharing space with an electrical generator. You're giving off sparks.'

Palmer considered this for a moment. 'If it's for me,' he said then, 'it's Curtis, faxing the proofs of that article.'

'We'll just manage the cocktail hour till you return.'

He made his way into the office to find that three sheets had been printed. As he suspected, it was the *Klarion* article which seemed to cover facing pages of the magazine. The type was relieved by inset photographs of Radziwill, Palmer and the patio of the IUD building with its Hannah Kurd Christ. The caption did not miss the fact that Edith Palmer had commissioned the Christ.

Someone, in an almost illegible hand, had addressed a brief note to Eleanora and signed it illegibly. Palmer carried the sheets back to the other room. 'The nerve of these people,' he complained. 'Would you believe? It's all in German.'

Eleanora took it from him. 'Tanya sent this,' she deciphered. 'But what she says remains a secret. The headlines say: THE CASE OF THE MAFIA ARCHBISHOP. Banker Reveals How Eastern Europe Mortgages Its Future to Organized Crime.' She glanced up at Slavko. 'Oversimplified?'

His high, scholar's forehead creased horizontally. 'If I agree to that loan it is true. If I refuse, it is premature. But either way I like it.'

She was reading more thoroughly now. From time to time she glanced up. 'It's almost verbatim what you told Udo.'

'What's the third page?'

'Bits and pieces of other stuff. The headline for the cover of the magazine: HOLY MONEY: HOW THE VATICAN LAUNDERS MOB CASH. And some captions. "Heartbreakingly handsome Radziwill." Here's "Controversial Palmer".'

309

'Not heartbreaking?'

'And this last caption: "No wonder Christ weeps." They really go for the jugular, those boys.'

The Puccini rose in poignancy, as if to engulf them all. Eleanora folded the proofs in half and handed them to Palmer. 'You have your victory. Will it topple the mafia?'

Proofs in his lap, he sat by the big hearth, a huge version of the small stainless-steel one in the morning room. Three yard-long logs were laid with tinder, ready to be ignited after dinner when the mountain air grew chill.

'If it gets the bankers angry and off their collective arse. Otherwise it's a rerun of Basel two years ago.'

'How can they ignore it?' Slavko asked. 'It's a mortal blow.'

'Be surprised what bankers can pretend not to see. All during the seventies and eighties they were pretending to know what they were doing when all they knew was to cheat their customers, their government and each other.' He fell silent. Then: 'The one I feel sorry for is Teddy.' Puccini's strings sobbed and swayed in an ecstasy of melancholy.

'Woods, you are insane,' Eleanora told him.

'He has no inkling. It'll kill him.'

Palmer got a mulish look, as if playing Devil's Advocate was something unpleasant that still needed doing. 'He's only one of a dozen guilty parties, some of them with real blood on their hands. But he's the only one who will take the fall for this. He's the only one without protection. The rest will sneak out.'

'Woods, am I hearing you right?' she demanded. 'Mercy for the archbishop? Who is just a heartbreakingly high-class crook? Who did his absolute worst to ruin you at the open house last week? The way he lectured me. Curtis. You.'

'Those were words. This will be what you said, his jugular.'

'But that is what he deserves.'

Palmer was silent for a long moment. Then: 'You didn't hear me say to kill the article, did you?'

'That's better.'

'Controversial Palmer,' Gerri quoted. 'No quarter asked, none given.'

'It's just . . .' He shrugged and looked sheepish. 'Fifty years.'

His glance went from Gerri to Eleanora and found there not a shred of remorse. The music in the background might have been a death march. He turned to his son-in-law. 'In your country, since the death of the old regime, there has had to be a lot of forgiving and compromising.'

Slavko nodded. 'But there is still a very active underground, former secret police who want to overthrow us.'

'But millions who have to be forgiven if normal life is to resume.'

The younger man was silent for a long time. Then he gave Palmer a small, crooked smile, not of mirth. 'People as powerful as an archbishop,' Slavko said, 'have surrendered the right to mercy.'

The temperature in the cave, Eleanora realised,

had grown icy. She got up and switched the CD player to a different disc, up-tempo bossa nova. 'Woods, isn't it time to light the fire? So the happy drink starts to work?'

Chapter Thirty-Six

For stealth the archbishop directed the helicopter pilot to land at Linate, the smaller airport that served Milan. That would be as much as the pilot could testify to later, if asked. Instead of a taxi into town, the archbishop had joined a busload of travel-worn tourists, some wearing his style of leather jacket. More stealth. In the railroad terminus the archbishop bought a ticket for the diretto from Rome. Train 384 would bring him into Lugano early in the morning.

His Excellency's mind was not used to handling the details of stealth – much less the rigours of second class – but he coped much better than he'd expected. When the conductor, punching his ticket, gave him a studying look, he composed himself for sleep and shut his eyes.

No one was searching for a runaway archbishop. What would he look like? Short, paunchy, depraved? He had a six-seat compartment to himself. Most passengers had boarded in Rome and were asleep now in the pullmans.

He smiled, not with pleasure but with the resignation a bad fate receives. This, the smile points out, is what comes of hubris, lack of faith, of deals made in the name of the Church that would turn the most hardened cardinal pale. In short, the sins of worldliness.

Radziwill's mind wandered slowly into the region of half-sleep. He had no doubt what Palmer would do. He had been studying him for half a century. When he told Eleanora that Palmer was the last of his breed, he was being quite accurate. A son and grandson of bankers, Palmer loathed the crooked, greedy new breed, in league with politicians and organised crime. It was clear what publicity Palmer hoped to create at the bankers' convention. Starring the IUD's soiled linen, this scandal would expose an ambitious conspiracy to carve up the fledgling democracies of East Europe.

The young Germans at last week's open house were, thus, not simply friends of Eleanora's daughter. The fact that neither of them had spoken to him had been suspicious. When a journalist prepares a crucifixion the last person he needs to talk to is his victim. It now had become equally clear why Bradford Ames hadn't recovered the note. Palmer's daughter was genetically encoded to suspect and keep such bits of evidence. Damn paper! Damn Palmer!

Tranquillity, he ordered of himself. No open warfare. Carry old buddyism to its limits before drawing one's steel. With help from surprise, he would cool Palmer's damned, meddling head and leave him to Providence.

The archbishop's face relaxed into a mask of emotionless beauty. His mind tipped over the edge between waking and sleeping. He slid into the innocent slumber of those who are either guiltless or have pre-pardoned themselves.

Coming down the escalator, Radziwill glanced about him for taxis. Then prudence returned. If he hailed a cab here, he most certainly would be remembered and placed: handsome older man, very distinguished. Instead he struck off into the heart of old Lugano, its pace beginning to mount as Monday began.

Ahead huge palms shook their narrow leaves in an offshore breeze. Toward the edge of the lake an ornate fountain of marble produced a lush water display that dampened passers-by when the wind blew it sideways among its Rococco cherubs, nymphs and sea-gryphons.

He found a driver to take him to Paradiso. Sitting in the back of the long, cream-coloured Mercedes cab, His Excellency knew better than to strike up conversations. Good-looking gentleman, great sense of humour — Yes, it would have been a humorous chat, like the quick-draw vaudeville turns of his youth.

'Ever take an archbishop to paradise?'

'Above monsignore they go to the other place.'

'But, truly, why a suburb called Paradiso?'

'Ask the bosses and their secretaries who flock there on weekends.'

Et cetera. Radziwill got out in front of a lakeside hotel, many-storeyed, glittering with balconies. He sat on a bench and watched lake steamers puff past.

Then he hailed a different cab. 'Do you know Morcote?'

'Yes, sir. Where in Morcote?'

'It's the hill above,' His Excellency continued in idiomatic Italian. He had learned the language as a young seminarian in Rome. If anyone queried the cab driver, he would unerringly identify his passenger: mature, distinguished Roman.

'That's some rock,' the driver said.

My Gethsemane, Radziwill mused. Palmer's, too. Now was the time the element of surprise could be very helpful. Palmer had the kind of logical mind that could be derailed by an unplanned event. It only required a miracle.

As the cab rounded the Morcote spur, he glanced at a small café perched on the rim of the lake. 'Stop!' he called to the cabby.

'Here,' he said, pressing money — not too much to be memorable — into the man's hand. He hopped out of the cab and across the two-lane road.

The man in the track suit was sipping a glass of mineral water. At a nearby table his bartender, who made such good Martinis, was also sipping water. Not a big miracle, as these things went, but enough to lift His Excellency's heart.

'Fight to the finish,' he breathed in Palmer's ear. 'Never give in.'

Chapter Thirty-Seven

The Lugano airport is quite modest and located in a narrow valley west of the city between Agno and Muzzano. It can handle only small private jets and prop-driven aircraft on its short runways. Nevertheless, so scenic are the peaks and lakes nearby that a fairly bustling sightseeing service is available by STOL plane or helicopter.

Alex had booked the chopper for all of Monday, an expense over which he'd quarrelled with Bradford Ames, who had already done the aerial reconnaissance quite thoroughly a week or two before. 'Then it comes out of your fee.'

'It's my neck, please,' Alex pointed out. 'I risk it on my research, no one else's, please.'

The first part of his reconnaissance had been done earlier and on foot if, by that term, one includes wriggling through scrub and brush on one's belly, peeping at cyclone fencing and proximity sensors. Sacha had taken the trip with him and been seen, but this never fazed Sacha.

Alex was nearly over the peak at Morcote on which Palmer's eyrie was built. He had already spotted it from a distance, thanks to the photographs provided by Ames. This enabled Alex to avoid hovering over his target. But from what he could see this aroused no interest down below, especially on such a bright Monday morning. 'Dip down towards the lake, please,' Alex ordered.

He focused powerful binoculars ahead. A week-old growth of dark brown beard gave him a far more serious look. There had been a faintly clownish air to him, gotten up like a hairy-legged hayseed with a bunged-up wrist. Now, in pale grey-green combat trousers, pockets bulging with sinister equipment, he looked terribly serious. 'Hold steady. Hover.'

He bent forward against the concave inside of the plastic bubble that surrounded them. Down below a small snack bar glittered in the sunshine, people sitting at round tables. A Mercedes taxi stopped abruptly and a man in a leather jacket ran across the highway.

The binoculars showed very little. The vertical down-view made everyone into ovals of hair or bald spots. The man came up behind another in a track suit and clapped him on the back. The seated man got up so quickly his chair toppled over backwards. Another man, at an adjoining table, also jumped to his feet.

'Up,' Alex told the pilot. 'Come slowly across the peak in a northeast direction, please?'

This time he could not only see the guest house clearly, he could even make out the people sitting on its balcony. The man was speaking into a small radio-telephone. The woman had spread open suitcases in the sunshine. From time to time she held up something for the man to decide on packing or not packing.

Alex's broad face seemed to condense slightly, sniffing prey. 'Drop a hundred metres, please?'

'There's a danger of – '

'Just be careful.'

The helicopter swung slightly to one side as it began to sink lower in the air. Alex disguised his face by pressing binoculars to his eyes. The man on the balcony looked up.

Alex felt a pang of recognition, as keen as a stab wound. 'Up! Quick, please?' he watched Boluslav Krevic's high forehead wrinkle with alarm. With a fast sideways lift, the aircraft heeled aloft and was out of sight in a few seconds.

'Back to the airport, please?' Alex could feel his heart knocking against the inside of his ribs.

'I thought you wanted me for the whole – '

'You'll put in a full day. Fuel up and take me to Milan.'

Alex rubbed his right wrist, even though it didn't actually ache. Cursed bastard! Nemesis! Krevic had blighted Alex's entire career. But for bad luck, Alex could be sitting there like an American tycoon with his radiotelephone toy and long-legged whore. But for one unlucky choice. The turning point had been only five, six years ago. Life had handed Alex a choice of careers and he had picked the one that luck had doomed.

For the first time Alex contemplated the possibility that the mission might not go as he wished. Perhaps he missed Sacha's reassuring presence. Perhaps, too, he had finally realised what a treacherous man Ames was, sending him on instructions that misled as much as they explained. Ames had carefully hung back from being one of the attackers; he was not just treacherous, he was a coward. What had suddenly hinted to him that this mission might not turn out properly was the sight of Krevic's small, open face with its worried forehead. Worried but determined, wary, alert, ready to break wrists.

In the old regime that face had led a charmed life. A dozen times the police had tried to rearrange it, a tooth here, an eye there. Twice they had moved to liquidate him when he was in jail, once with the usual faked suicide by hanging, once with food poisoning in filthy grub. Twice his fellow prisoners had saved him. One cellmate died because he switched plates with Krevic. He had become part of the new regime's pantheon of heroes. No wonder Krevic stood very close to the premier.

If Alex had played his cards right, he could be as close. All three of them had graduated in the same class. It wouldn't have been too hard to worm his way into high favour. He had chosen not to go through the ordeal Krevic and the premier had, but neither had a lot of others clamouring for privilege in the new order. Don't worry, he told himself: soon enough the reformers will have need of a master of torture. Everything comes a circle. He smiled.

A wrong career choice, to join the ruling authorities, had put him on the opposite side from Krevic. Who knew his side would win? Sheer luck. Nothing to do with philosophy or ideology or democracy or any of the other bullshit words. Just damned bad luck. But squeezing information from prisoners is always needed.

Mountain passes, peaks and valleys wheeled slowly below them. What a married pair, Alex thought, packing to leave, as if on holiday. One whose every movement would be spied on, whose every conversation would be taped, whose itinerary would forever be the subject of charts and timetables kept up to date by not only the national police but the secret services of a great many other nations. But what power! Prestige! Respect! One lucky choice and all that could now be Alex's life. But that belonged to the world of pendulum swings. What was absolutely certain was this: Krevic must not be allowed to leave his eyrie-fortress for the cruel outside world. One way or another he had to remain inside the enclave until this business was completed.

Alex smiled. By then, it would be too late to escape. And the torture would be . . . sweet.

Chapter Thirty-Eight

At first the awkwardness was everything Archbishop Radziwill had hoped for. Surprise had, indeed, forced Palmer off his normal track. He had jumped up, stuffing papers in the inside breast pocket of his running-suit. His performance as a thoroughly surprised party was near-perfect. So was Ziggy's.

'Something I'm not supposed to read?' Radziwill asked, smiling, always smiling, as he leaned heavily on Palmer.

'A translation Eleanora made for me.'

The tall, handsome man in the leather jacket sat down opposite Palmer. 'From an original in German?' he asked, not lessening the pressure of surprise.

'Perhaps.'

'From that scandal-sheet *Die Klarion*.'

Palmer placed his hands on the table and folded them one into the other. The outward signs of surprise faded away. He produced an easy smile, steeped in confidence and supremacy, a true oh-I'm-sorry-but-you're-overdrawn banker's smile. 'Teddy, if you know that much you should know your days are numbered. Take the next Concorde to Brazil.'

His Excellency laughed, one of those really genuine sounds so few people know how to counterfeit. 'If I wanted to disappear, Rome's a far better place.'

'Inside Vatican City? No extradition?'

'But why should I disappear? Because you've arranged for them to print something damaging? Surely you don't think I've been spared libelous stories in the past? We're used to them, Woods. Especially from you, I might add, if you weren't my oldest friend.'

'You may be able to stand the heat. I've always considered you made of asbestos, anyway. But the people implicated with you are shyer flowers.'

Neither spoke for a moment. Mr Bartki gave Palmer an inquiring look. 'My friend would like a coffee.'

'Coffee and a cognac,' Radziwill amended.

'They're shy because they have blood on their hands,' Palmer went on conversationally, as if they were discussing whether to sip the brandy separately or add it to the coffee. 'Under the sunlamp of exposure, they will crisp to a burned husk.'

'There is a compliment hidden in there somewhere.'

'Yes. I can't quite see you as a murderer, Teddy. Especially my murderer. Just last night I – ' He stopped. Was it any business of this evil man that last night Palmer had had a belated attack of conscience about him?

'Just last night,' His Excellency finished, 'in the bosom of your family, you suggested I be put in nomination for a Nobel Prize. Right?'

Palmer chuckled. 'Right.'

The former classmates sat in silence until Mr Bartki

brought a coffee for the newcomer and two cognacs. 'You are drinking a toast?' he inquired.

Palmer started to shake his head, then paused. 'Yes, absolutely.' He lifted his glass to Radziwill. 'To you, Teddy. May they find a remote, lovely AIDS clinic to which you will be assigned as chaplain. Be sure I'll visit you there the day I get HIV-positive.'

They sipped their brandy. Mr Bartki nodded encouragingly and left them alone. 'Woods, tell me, who is they?'

'Your superiors, when they relieve you of power.'

'The Prefetura? His Holiness? Public opinion among rich lay Catholics? Who?'

'Perhaps all of them, if you're really unlucky.'

'Perhaps none of them,' Radziwill added. 'You have been many things in your time, Woods: conspirator, leader, prophet, fixer, philosopher. But this is the first time you've been downright naive.'

'And surely not the last,' Palmer responded.

The two men stopped watching each other and turned, as a respite, to watching the lovely Lake of Lugano beside them. A narrow mahogany speedboat of another era, both ends pointed, supercharger tubes exiting rakishly beside the cockpit, brass fittings gleaming hotly, shot past with a high spurt of wake, sat down hard as it veered left and sped across the heart of the lake towards the Italian enclave of Campione.

'They,' His Excellency said at last, 'are no longer what they used to be.'

'Meaning what?'

'Woods, I know you keep up with life in the US of

A, as I do. You read the incessant number of polls. You know that the American public has raised ignorance to the level of a philosophy. The concept of "don't know" has been elevated to the status of a political party. Poll after poll the liberals and the reactionaries jockey back and forth for any kind of majority. But the column labelled "Don't Know and Don't Vote" burgeons. And this isn't simple ignorance. It's dedicated, deliberate know-nothingism. Do you favour cleaning up the environment? Dear God, who doesn't? Eighteen per cent "don't know". Do you favour peace among nations? Who doesn't? 20.4 per cent "don't know". Do you – ?'

'Stai calma, bello. You'll pop an aorta.'

Excellency paused and sipped his coffee, then his cognac, then his coffee. He had the air of an elegant carrion bird, unruffled in his black leather skin, with all the feeding time in the world. 'In short, Woods, we're a nation of don't-knows who keep out of the voting booth. But when we do go in, we elect know-even-less types as our political leaders. Tell me I'm wrong?'

Palmer chuckled again. 'You know you're right.' He held his cognac up to the light and studied its warm amber colour. He never drank brandy. It made his heart skip beats and pound.

'But that's not a reason,' he went on in a stronger voice, 'to desist from rocking the boat. What I'm doing most people couldn't care less about, won't hear about and, if they do hear, will have no opinion? Hell, Teddy, that's the best reason to keep the boat rocking hard. A few don't-knows will begin to see that ignorance is the root of all their troubles.'

'No. Wrong.' Radziwill finished his brandy in one neat swig. He sighed as it burned its way down his throat. 'Most people won't bat an eyelid because they want to remain fast asleep. But some people never sleep, Woods. Them you will provoke to do something drastic. Soon. To you.'

'Possibly even more drastic than what they'll do to you?'

'That's – ' The archbishop stopped short. Palmer had the notion he hadn't considered before that such an exposé reduced his usefulness to the Honoured Society to zero, while broadcasting to the world how much confidential information he carried in his head. Dangerous position. 'That's just ludicrous,' Radziwill finished lamely. He picked up Palmer's cognac. 'That diretto from Milan had almost no amenities.'

Palmer got to his feet. 'Come on up the hill. We do a fair breakfast.'

'Walking, please, not running.' His Excellency got up, holding the stem of the brandy glass. 'Why does mid-life crisis get all the publicity? Here's a toast to end-life crisis. You don't get more final than that.'

Palmer grinned at him. 'You think the two of us will go down together?'

'Life is never that neat,' Radziwill cautioned him. He drank the cognac and stood there for a moment letting the soft shock radiate through his body. 'I imagine only one of us will fall. And I intend not to be the one.'

Thirty-Nine

What I like about you, diary, thanks to all-day parties and magazine exposés and sudden marriages, is that you've been neglected shamefully but you don't complain.

Several cognacs, breakfast, not getting much sleep on the train and general infirmity of age has sent Teddy napping. I've done something I hope I won't regret. I've talked B Krevic, boy finance minister, into delaying his departure another day. There is something very plain and straight about him that might get under Teddy's skin. His Infernal Excellency might see a way to clean up his act by lending directly to Slavko's country at a decent rate. Worth trying.

Teddy is probing for a compromise formula. He's beginning to realize he can't blast out of this with his usual bless-the-torpedoes-full-speed-ahead. He even went so far as to ask how late *Die Klarion* might take a kill order.

I phoned Curtis but he's left Berlin. Bert seemed

overjoyed at the possibility that the story might be killed. All along he's hated the idea. Too crass for his taste? Or, more likely, puts his beloved Udo too far out on a limb.

I do wish Curtis hadn't decamped. Yes, he has other jobs to do. But I grow more dependent on him the higher the anxiety rises. In any event, today being the ninth of June, Bert says we have till tomorrow to show cause for X'ing the article from *Die Klarion's* issue of fifteenth June.

Hole card. But my strongest is that Slavko respects what advice I give him. If I say a direct IUD loan is OK, he'll sign. A young man of great discernment, eh?

Hard to believe Gerri and he are going to disappear into the wilds of Eastern Europe. His parents are hollering for a look. His premier wants a face-to-face report. His country is wracked with strikes, demonstrations, the usual long lines at shops that have nothing to sell. The two ethnic groups out of which the Treaty of Versailles created his nation are back at their favourite sport, destroying each other.

And my one and only daughter is in the middle of it.

On the other hand, if Bradford Ames is planning something nasty, Gerri's far better off five hundred miles east of here. Maybe I should send Eleanora with her?

'Hullo.'

'Is this the Palmer residence?' a woman's voice asked.

Palmer's brow wrinkled. He knew that voice, but he was damned if he could put a name to it. 'Yes. Palmer here.'

'Woods, put Gerri on the line.'

'Edith!'

The realization sent both of them into a moment of shocked silence. Then: 'My God, Edith.'

'Is it true?'

'Is wh – Oh. Yes, I thought she phoned you last week with the news.'

'She phoned and left a message. I just got back today and played the message. I'm in shock. Who *is* this boy?'

'He's a nice boy.'

'Is that the best you can do? Put Gerri on.'

'She's off somewhere. She'll phone you at the apartment in an hour or two.'

'This is highly unsatisfactory.'

'He's a good kid. He's taking her home to his parents. That kind of kid.'

'Damn it, Woods. Home?'

'He's in the middle of a financial mess. All of Eastern Europe is.'

'I don't care if Eastern Europe slides into the Black Sea and is never seen again. Woods, how could you let her do this? Can't I count on you for anything?'

'When was the last time your thirty-year-old daughter asked for advice?'

His former wife was silent for a long moment. 'That's a cop-out,' she snapped then. 'She's in your part of the world. In your house. Don't you take any responsibility at all for your own daughter?'

'Would you believe, Edith? I've even stopped checking to see if she's washed her hands before dinner.'

'None of your gallows humour, Woods. I want – '

'What you'll get,' he cut in, 'is Gerri calling you when she returns. Good bye, Edith.' He hung up.

He sat there at the desk in his office, his mouth set in a grim line. Theirs had not been a bitterly contested divorce. The property settlements, the support payments, the irrevocable trusts, the alimony, all had been negotiated and handled quite smoothly by expensive lawyers. It had gone well because there was enough money on both sides. When Edith's next marriage had ended his alimony payments, that transaction, too, went smoothly and without rancour.

He'd seen her twice since, first at Woody's wedding, then at Tom's. Barely a dozen words exchanged, but civil ones. And now, suddenly, a great well of resentment seemed to have been uncovered, oozing recrimination. Until now her money and his had seemed more than enough cushioning.

He swung around to the battery of small TV monitors that showed him various points of view. The balcony and forecourt of the guest house were empty. He could make out, on another monitor, two people walking hand in hand up to the actual high point of the mountaintop, a grassy meadow choked with clover which, some years back when he commuted by helicopter, had served as a landing pad.

He watched his daughter and son-in-law, strolling slowly in deep conversation. The wind blew their hair this way and that. Palmer remembered what his helicopter pilot had told him: 'There's a permanent stiff breeze up here. It's bad for helicopters. But a hang glider pilot would love it.'

After all these years, twenty of them, it wasn't hard to let Edith's accusations fade away in his mind. As if this thought had been transmitted, Gerri, on the monitor, looked up and suddenly led them off the knoll in the direction of the house. Palmer caught another view of them as they strode past the wine cave. Then they went off his screens.

It would be nice to simplify my life. To end my dependency on electronic security devices. To find some always-sunny place by the sea where Eleanora's wardrobe and mine was reduced to two swimsuits and a towel. No phone, no fax, no mafia hit list. We would both go mad within a week.

This place, isolated behind TV cameras and proximity sensors, drives Eleanora crazy. She understands why I need the protection, but it bothers her nevertheless. Of course, this morning, with such a powerful celebrity snoozing under our roof, we can relax and breathe easy. The bishop is surrounded by our pawns again.

But I wasn't kidding when I said he was in danger of his life. The net effect of *Die Klarion's* exposé will be to brand him and Bradford Ames great bunglers. To a society that holds breach of loyalty to be a capital crime, gross incompetence runs a close second. Both are punishable by death.

In the guest house the telephone rang just as Gerri and Slavko returned from their walk. 'Krevic here.'

'It's Woods. Sorry to bother you. Can I speak to Gerri?'

'Dad? What's up?'

'Your mother called. Apparently she just now got your message about being married.'

'Blech! Say no more. I'll phone her.'

'At her apartment.' He hung up.

Gerri stuffed the phone under a sofa pillow and sat on it. 'Blech! I was premature, thinking she was too mad to phone me.'

'Your mother?'

'What I love about you is that you're on such good terms with your parents.'

'For this you love me?' He sat down on the pillow beside her, further muffling its presence. 'For nothing else?'

She blushed. 'A long list of reasons. That's one.'

'Any more?'

'Your hair.'

'Excellent. Who are you expecting to telephone you now? Or is it to them you must call?'

'Mother. She's daunting, like Dad, horrible overachiever. But I can handle him. Not her.' She stared hard at him. 'You get along *so well* with your family.'

'They do not have time for to daunt. Agenda is full of staying alive, making the government work. By the time we come to daunt I am too old and too married to daunt. I am . . . dauntless!'

Chapter Forty

The opening of EUR as a grandiose showcase for fascism was scheduled for 1942, delayed by Allied bombs. After the war a penniless Italy somewhere found the lire to finish the gross palazzi with their human-dwarfing Art Deco columns. These posthumous Il Duce gravestones were separated by a long reflecting pool from later constructions dedicated not to fascism but the 1960 Olympics. Today, thick with high-rent apartment buildings, EUR is a choice residential neighbourhood where domestics commute via four stations of the Metropolitana underground.

The stolen van arrived at sundown. After dark the jeep, repainted black from its original US Army olive drab, parked near the Enrico Fermi stop, across the street from the ministry of finance. The cringe-making ironies of the location were unknown to the two drivers, Grischka and Ivan, as they waited to load the jeep from the dirty beige panel van.

That they had chosen such a well-protected government street was the lesser of the ironies. Naming a subway station after the nuclear scientist who had fled for his life from fascist Italy was, perhaps, a stronger paradox.

Across the street, two armed guards protected the ministry of finance from assault. They had, of course, noted the jeep and the van, but both were parked *across* the street, an area beyond the guards' jurisdiction. With their elementary Italian and plethora of Marlboros, Grischka and Ivan became fast friends with the other two young men.

Still, it was better to wait until night had truly fallen. One guard, Rocco, explained that his shift ended at nine with dinner. The next shift shared a long, gossipy dinner with them before going on duty. Lounging along a grassy sward, having left most of their Marlboros with Rocco, Grischka and Ivan fell to arguing.

'Why Rome?' Explosives expert Ivan planned to cover the floor of the jeep with seven kilos of best Gladio Semtex. 'Why begin from here?' he went on, 'when Milan is only a few kilometres from the Swiss border?'

'Strategy,' Grischka said, tapping his forehead.

'I ask a civil question and get a joke answer.'

'Alex thinks these things out. You try it.'

Promptly at nine the two guards disappeared with smiles and friendly waves. Alex loaded the Semtex. He and Grischka then covered the explosive with flattish cartons that held two dismantled AK-47's and their double magazines, bound together with black friction tape, three .9 Brownings and a silenced Ingram M-10 with loaded magazines.

'What sort of strategy starts from a base five hundred kilometres south of Lugano?' Ivan asked in a churlish voice, as if being asked to walk the distance.

'People may see us here,' Grischka tried to explain.

'If interrogated, they remember the jeep. It is not the current HMV the Yanks use, what they call a Humvee. It is twenty years old, this jeep. Here it signifies nothing. If we were in Milan, the police would be that much closer to the . . . ah, scene of the crime. That much more likely to interrogate the populace.'

'Never call it a crime. Say we were chosen to liberate our nation.'

Having stowed all the weaponry, they added sacks of bubble-wrapped electronics. All that remained was a long object in a burlap sleeve. Out of one end peeped aluminium tubing and the corner of jet black canvas sailcloth.

'Careful,' Grischka muttered. 'One rip in this thing and we're done for.'

'Eh!' Rocco called out in the night. 'Eh, raggazzi!'

He was picking his teeth as he strolled over from the direction of the ministry of finance. As he got to the jeep he peered through the darkness and belched in a friendly way. Delicately, he waved away the expelled odours, mostly garlicky tomato sauce slightly broken down by hydrochloric acid. 'Ma, che fai, raggazzi?'

Grischka brought his forearm around Rocco's neck and lifted up in a choke-hold. It was identical to the one Alex had tried in Prague on Krevic.

Ivan, who was smaller, shoved three inches of blade into Rocco's friendly heart. There was almost no sound, certainly no cry and very little thump. They slid Rocco face down inside the rear gate of the jeep. They laid the burlap package over him like a shroud and strapped everything down. They drove off, abandoning the van. It had, in any event, been stolen in Naples, where auto thefts were commoner than pimping. When re-stolen in a day or two the van would go north to the wholesale used-car black market in Novara.

The jeep, however, like the ammo and weapons, had been bought with hard cash. Old, it still cost a lot of hundred-dollar bills. Like all Gladio merchandise, supervised by real NATO spooks, the real thing cost real cash.

Grischka drove right on the broad Via Laurentina. Near the Metropolitana stop of that name he backed the jeep inside a small garage and locked the doors.

'Do you think,' Ivan demanded, 'that in this upper bourgeois neighbourhood the jeep is safe?'

'Why not? We have left a guard with it.'

Chapter Forty-One

'I'm sorry,' Father Bernardin said. He held the telephone close to his ear. He looked sleepless, unshaven. 'I am out of touch with His Excellency.'

'That's hard to believe,' Bradford Ames snapped.

'If I hear from him, be assured I shall ask him to make contact with you.'

'That's highly uns – '

The young priest had not, until this post, had much to do with telephones. It would never have occurred to him to terminate a conversation someone else had begun. Nevertheless, he hung up on Ames.

But, dear God, this morning was like no other Monday. The young Swiss had been up most of the night, following tracks through the immense memory banks of the IUD mainframe. The fact was this: he still didn't know. He still could not say if his B-FLURD-directed fractal had gone underground or not. Would it keep its own characteristic form, but backwards? Or would the retrograde motion camouflage it? Obviously, in every sense of the word, it had to be considered hostile.

Bleary-eyed, he still clutched the telephone tightly as if glued to it by fear. Slowly he lifted the apparatus from its cradle and tapped in an internal Vatican number. It was not yet eight in the morning. He had no idea if Cardinal Huf was in his office. He might not even be in Rome.

On the ninth ring the old man answered himself. 'Your Eminence,' Bernardin said in a hushed tone.

'Speak up. Don't mumble. Who is it?'

Bernardin switched, without thinking, to the French dialect of their mutual homeland in the Vosges. 'Bernardin here, sir. I crave an audience.'

'An audience only His Holiness can give. To you I can offer a humble meeting. Encounter. Conversation.'

Bernardin could hear pages turning. Cardinal Huf had no faith in a paperless office. He used big, bound ledgers which remained implacable records of the mistakes and successes of life, long after life went on. To erase the past, one had to rip pages out of the binding.

'An hour from now? Is this good news or bad?' the old man asked.

'I . . . it's too . . . I hope not bad, sir.'

'Oh, dear.'

The cardinal hung up and Bernardin stared into the middle distance, rubbing his unshaven cheek and chin. To erase the past, at IUD, a touch of the button was enough. For the first time, Bernardin understood what a radical change archbishop Radziwill had made when he converted IUD to the new paperless faith. That was the future, was it not? Bernardin keyed in a command on his work terminal and saw that he had forty-five minutes before his appointment.

'Father?' One of the girls from Data Processing stood in the doorway, holding a small acrylic box of 3.5-inch floppy discs. A short, thin girl with a waif's eyes, she was regularly to be seen with a small glass vial collecting Christ's tears for friends and relatives of whom, to judge by appearances, she had thousands.

'Can you confirm these for backup and storage?'

'Covici's responsibility,' Berardin said.

'He's out today. We telephoned his home but there is no answer.'

'Put them on my desk.'

They left together, the girl going downstairs, Bernardin ascending to his room. He lathered an ancient shaving brush his father had given him years before. It carried a permanent, faint aroma of country herbs from the soap that had come with it.

He stared at himself in the mirror, plump cheeks fattened by a layer of soapsuds. No wonder the sleek, elegant archbishop didn't take him seriously. It was a wonder Cardinal Huf did. But they were Swiss and from the same village.

He had committed so many sins it was hard to know how Cardinal Huf would react. Beginning with stealing IUD mainframe time, Bernardin knew he had escalated sinning, with the help of the missing Covici, until he had triggered something so potentially unthinkable as to –

He finished shaving, still staring at his own face, in particular the bloodshot eyes with the small pockets of dissipation beneath them. Would you trust this priest? He winced.

Chapter Forty-Two

Bradford Ames rarely got angry. He had a temper; what Sicilian didn't? But one of the reasons he had risen high in the Honoured Society's managerial caste was that he could control that temper. He was now losing it.

The telephone call from Milan – coming minutes after being hung up on by that prize booby Bernardin – had finished off what control he was exerting. First the archbishop was out of reach, and now Alex had given him the unacceptable news that Krevic and his wife were leaving Palmer's mountain. What stung worst was when Alex, a nobody whose work on Ames' lower lip was not forgotten, issued this order: 'You have to keep him there,' Alex had shouted into the phone. 'He must not be allowed to leave! Tonight is the night.'

Ames slammed down the phone with a hint of paying back Bernardin in his gesture. 'When Alex calls back,' he yelled at Fiona, 'tell him to go to hell.'

'I don't und – ' The telephone rang.

'Tell him his message was received and to stop panicking.'

Brooding on his psychic hurts, Ames watched her handle the irate Alex. When she hung up, she said: 'He's coming down here anyway.'

'Plane or train?'

'He didn't say.'

'What in fuck's name do I pay you for? Get in the other room. I can't stand the sight of you.' He watched her rise, her great breasts surging up and down with emotion, and leave for the other office. 'Close the door!' he snarled.

Petty cruelties soothed him. Then he paged through his pocket diary until he found Palmer's Morcote telephone number. The telephone rang a long time before a woman answered it. 'I'll see if Mr Krevic is taking calls,' she said in almost unaccented English. 'Who's calling?'

'Taylor Wentworth of the World Bank.'

Bradford Ames sat back and lifted his long legs to his desk top. From the beginning, Krevic's regime had ruled out a normal IMF loan of the kind Poland was now smothered under. But perhaps he'd come to the phone just to say no again.

'Krevic here.'

'Ministair,' Ames enthused. 'It's Bradford Ames. I'm so glad I located you.'

'Mr Ames? You have with you a Mr Wentworth?'

'I have with me a completely revised loan proposal I think you'll find acceptable. We have sharpened our pencil, as the saying goes.' He took a breath and launched himself wildly, making it up as he went. 'How about no repayment for the first five years? Is that an opener?'

'Five-year moratorium?'

'We don't want to be parasites, feeding off your economic recovery. We want to be co-workers who have earned the right to share. If, after five years, you have not yet experienced an upturn, unlikely, I know, amortisation is delayed until you yourself are good and ready. Do I make myself clear?'

The salesman in Bradford Ames sensed it was time to stop talking. He gazed out his huge window at the dome of St Peter's. The bright June sunshine heated waves of air that made the dome shimmer with unbounded energy.

'For words,' Krevic said at last, 'I am at a loss, Mr Ames.'

'Think it over. No rush. I can meet you in Lugano tomorrow morning. If you have any questions, I can answer them then.' This, the delay at the heart of Ames' scheme to make sure Krevic was in Morcote when the hit squad attacked, was said almost negligently, with none of the dynamic force of his sales pitch.

'I . . . I must consult with . . . with my associates.'

'Certainly. May I have your fax number, sir.'

'Yes, certainly.' He repeated Palmer's fax number. Then, thoughtfully: 'Can soon come the fax?'

'It's being typed now. I'll transmit page by page, if you wish.'

'We are still discussing the sum of seven billion pounds sterling?'

'Any sum up to twelve billion. I'm afraid that's our limit.'

'During moratorium period, without interest being paid I understand. But will interest accrue?'

Ames smiled so broadly his pointed canines glistened. He had the fish hooked. 'As you will see when the proposal reaches you, the moratorium period is interest-free. Interest begins only when amortisation begins.'

'Most unusual. To tie up such a sum indefinitely could cost also you interest.' A long, thoughtful silence. Then, soberly: 'I am impressed, Mr Ames.'

'Most kind of you to reconsider us, ministair.'

'On such a basis, why not?'

'Good bye, ministair.'

Bradford Ames' feet crashed to the floor. He jumped up and strode to the closed door between offices. He slammed it open. 'Snap to, lass! Get your steno pad. I've got a lot of dictation for you.'

Fiona's face fell. 'You're not feeling mean any more?'

'Mean?'

'It fair turned me on before. I was expecting a whipping on the spot.'

'Work, lass. Work first, then pleasure.'

Chapter Forty-Three

Father Bernardin dashed down the front stairway of the IUD building, clean-shaven but dead tired. He paused for a moment and turned to look up at the tearful face of Christ. Lord, if You but knew. Then, pushing his tired body, he hurried doggedly along a tree-lined path through the Vatican gardens, fresh and green this Monday morning in early summer.

Propelled by anxiety and not a little fear, he made quick progress past the Radio Vaticano offices. There he swerved right in the direction of the small, intricately stuccoed Casina of Pius the Fourth, a favourite of strollers for its intimate charm and paintings dating back three centuries. Beyond it lies the Vatican's zecca, or mint.

Most people are aware that the Vatican prints its own postage stamps and that a letter mailed at the Vatican Post Office stands an excellent chance of being delivered. This is in sharp contrast to the rest of Italy where as much mail is burned as delivered. But the Holy See also mints its own coinage. It was Cardinal Huf's conceit to base his office at the mint. He had that Swiss no-nonsense approach to money that worried his fellow cardinals.

When Father Bernardin arrived at the stroke of nine he was winded, more by fatigue than exercise.

But he found he had plenty of time to catch his breath, as did the young priest waiting there.

'My appointment,' Bernardin murmured in the intense quiet of the waiting room, 'was for nine.'

'And mine for eight-thirty.'

They produced decent enough smiles and sank back into their thoughts. In any event, the other priest was soon ushered in by the cardinal himself, who opened an adjoining door and stood there, a small man whose true age was in part concealed by a short-cropped white beard.

Bernardin tried to contain his impatience. The cardinal bore more than a slight resemblance to photographs of Sigmund Freud, made sharper by the identical eyeglasses they both wore. But Huf's history tracked back to Freud's rebellious student, the cardinal's fellow Swiss, Jung.

Huf had begun as a doctor, training under Jung as a psychoanalyst. In his mid-twenties, Huf had abruptly left medicine for a seminary in Augst, near Basel. What he said then became so well known it was still being quoted: 'To help humanity some go through the head; I choose the heart.'

At nine-thirty the short man with the white beard opened his door to Bernardin. 'Your family?' he began at once. 'Are they well?'

'Quite well, sir.' Bernardin glanced around the plain room, its one window looking out on sun-drenched trees and shrubbery. It had the comforting constriction of a confessional booth. In the distance, a classical statue glowed a warm cream marble. 'I have a confession for your ears alone.'

'You do get to the point, don't you.' The cardinal was dressed in work clothes, a short-sleeved black shirt and clerical collar. He had removed his round-lensed spectacles, but instantly clipped them back on again, as if Bernardin would be shoving small print under his nose. Huf's slightly watery pale blue eyes looked closely at his visitor. 'Proceed, my son, not hastily but with all due speed. Begin.'

On his walk here, Bernardin had decided he lacked the art to tell any story but the one that had actually happened. When he finished, Huf frowned. 'Your co-worker should be here with you.'

'He's not at work today, sir. But Covici and all the rest are lay people.'

'Quite right. You bear the responsibility.' Huf's little body shifted around in his plain-backed chair as if seeking a more comfortable posture. 'Without pretending to understand computers, something inside the machine's memory could taint or destroy that memory?'

'Yes, Your Eminence. But I haven't described to you our regular Sunday afternoon forecast.'

'I'm familiar with it.'

'Yesterday afternoon, as it went out to its 100 subscribers, it may have been carrying this . . . this virus with it.'

Huf's eyes half closed. The bright glare of his blue irises dimmed. 'But, again, if you are not sure where this thing is, and if it remains hidden, you cannot be sure it has tainted the IUD memory . . . or anyone else's.'

'I must wait for empiric proof.'

'Like what? A complaint that something has gone wrong?'

Bernardin nodded. 'It may not be that obvious. Our subscribers may experience a degradation of accuracy that takes a long time to recognize.'

'A long time?' Huf almost shrieked.

'Weeks?'

The cardinal made a groaning sound as of having heard a bad joke. 'And your estimate of the danger? How sure are you that a virus has been transmitted?'

'I . . . perhaps . . . fifty-fifty, Your Eminence.'

Huf replaced the glasses and stared for a long time at the younger priest. 'Describe what the effect of this might be, assuming it was transmitted?'

'Eminence, a computer is like a sponge. You squeeze it in a puddle and it drinks up the water. Soon every airspace is full. In this form the sponge is very useful. You can clean with it. You can convey to dry areas – '

'Yes, yes.'

'Now the temperature drops below freezing and the sponge turns to a block of ice. Nothing can be done with it.'

An awkward silence ensued until Huf, frowning again, said: 'Your virus will freeze a computer into a block of ice?'

'Figuratively yes, Eminence.'

'Even the sophisticated computers of the central

banks, the brokerages, the insurance giants, the
international conglomerates who subscribe to the
forecast?'

'Yes.'

'Upon whose philanthropic largesse we have come
to depend?'

'Yes.'

'Whose confidential information enables Radziwill
to make profitable investments for the Holy See?'

'Yes.'

'Freeze them so that no business can any longer
be transacted?'

'Yes.'

'Nor old business referred to, terms of contracts
recalled, invoices prepared, registrations made, questions answered, funds shifted?'

'Yes.'

Behind his lenses, the cardinal's bright eyes flitted
this way and that as if seeking escape. To Bernardin
they seemed surgeon's eyes, the eyes of Doctor Huf,
deciding where to press the scalpel into the flesh.
Finally Huf gestured to his visitor to rise. 'You don't
bring me anything simple, do you? I must assess the
possibility of worldwide obloquy and disgrace. In
short, of IUD's good name having been destroyed. I
must consult some of my colleagues on the Prefetura.' He stared at Bernardin. 'Their first question to
me will be the obvious: how certain are we that this
virus has infected IUD subscribers? And I will have
to reply like a bookmaker presenting odds on a
racehorse: fifty-fifty.'

He darted back to his desk and opened a huge ledger bound in leather. He turned to a new page and scribbled something on it. 'Be back here tonight at five. You may have to wait, but you will be my last appointment of the day.'

'And, at that time . . .?'

'At that time I hope to tell you the degree of your error and the extent of your punishment.'

'Then, it is as bad as I feared.'

Cardinal Huf's bright glance swivelled across his face. 'Learn to live with the not-quiteness of life, Bernardin. Until tonight.'

'Of course,' Bernardin moaned, 'I have brought this on myself.'

'And your archbishop,' the cardinal added. 'Adieu.'

Chapter Forty-Four

His Excellency Archbishop Tadeusz Radziwill opened wide his great eyes and stared at the reinforced concrete of the ceiling. Typical of Palmer's fortress mentality. The graininess of the cement had been artistically exaggerated. If one rubbed against it, Radziwill thought, it would produce a raw bruise. Typical Palmer. But underneath the banker ran a streak of worried conscience.

'Teddy,' Palmer had kept insisting as they climbed the hill. 'You have to find a way out of this. Otherwise you're finished and I'm the guilty party.'

'Only you can cancel the *Klarion* article.'

'The moment I see some proof of your ... regeneration.'

'Dear me. I've never before had a lay confessor.'

He sat up and swung his legs off the bed. Time to get a few strong nooners down Palmer's gullet and let him listen to some groans about being forced into such a loan. In reality, Palmer was godfathering the first pilot move in the IUD's takeover of Eastern Europe, although on rotten terms.

His Excellency marched down the stairs and found Palmer out on his open-air terrace, sipping a tall, amber drink with minister of finance Boluslav Krevic. Both of them rose to their feet. 'How did you do it?' Palmer asked.

'Do what?'

'I know for a fact you were sacked out dead to the world. But somehow you worked the old ESP with that pet crocodile of yours.'

Masking bewilderment, Radziwill glanced from one face to the other, trying to scrape information from them. 'I did that, did I?'

Palmer held out sheets of fax paper. 'Here's Bradford Ames' revised tender.'

The archbishop glanced quickly through the new terms of the loan. 'Yes, quite,' he said then. 'He takes orders well, doesn't he?'

Palmer poured his guest a tall glass of the punch he and Krevic were sipping. 'It's a Side Car, Teddy, but charged with bubbly.'

His Excellency sipped and smiled. He turned to the younger man. 'How does the new proposal suit you, minister?'

'I have telephoned to make an interview with my premier, tomorrow.'

'What was his reaction to the terms?'

'I said only they were for the first time interesting. Face to face we will discuss it. Tomorrow.'

'But his decision will be influenced by your attitude. So, can you . . .?'

'Face to face. Tomorrow.'

Radziwill fell silent. Was he seeing in Krevic the genuine article or heavy coaching from Palmer. In either event, Ames had saved everyone's bacon by a bad joke. If he honoured any part of it, Ames would be terminated by Providence. But, meanwhile, as a stopgap to head off the *Klarion* exposé, it would do quite well.

Palmer lifted his glass. 'Thanks for your help, archbishop.'

'Do you feel you can call this magazine now and . . .?' His Excellency's voice trailed off suggestively.

'I've put them on kill-alert. We have till noon tomorrow, June tenth. I've said three things must happen before they kill it. First, the lending institution must change to a direct IUD tender, not some fogbound mafia-gremlin like Bradford Ames. Second, Krevic's government must agree to the terms. And, third, an IUD press release must move on AP and Reuters tomorrow.'

The archbishop pursed his lips, trying not to respond with a snap insult. He was being boxed into Ames' silly promises as only Palmer could engineer it. 'Fine,' he said at last, staring deeply into his punch. 'And me barefoot on broken glass in St Peter's Square, flagellating myself with barbed wire?'

Palmer thought a moment. 'Whatever turns you on, Teddy.'

'Woods, I must say – I mean this is sheer – '

'Sheer power of friendship,' Palmer cut in. 'You took your nap in total disgrace. You awake beloved by us all.' His attention was distracted for a moment by two hang gliders wheeling in the bright sunlight above them.

Radziwill's attention also shifted: when you're over a barrel, he thought, roll with it. Say yes. Betray all of them later. 'How lovely,' he murmured as the two triangular sails crisscrossed. How lovely to have Palmer thinking he'd won. Of course, on Ames' insane terms, he *had* won. Another reason to cut Ames loose.

Palmer turned to his old school chum. 'Teddy, I'm not doing this for you. I'm not even doing it for Slavko. I'm doing it because I want to restore a little dignity and a little public service to a profession that's sunk lower than pandery. I'm a banker, Teddy, and I don't want to be ashamed of the name.'

For a long moment the three men sat in silence, as if chewing at this remark. The younger was the first to speak. 'Woods, sir, I do not understand.'

'Your concept of banking,' his father-in-law observed, 'has been distorted by a philosophy one century old. Today's banks are so slime-bound as to make the grasping bankers of Marx's era look downright merciful.'

'Stop poisoning young minds,' His Excellency murmured.

'Think of how today's entrepreneurs make their fortunes,' Palmer continued. 'By looting established corporations, selling off the bleeding chunks and leaving the stockholders to pay the damage. The only way they can do this is through the treachery and greed of the banks that finance them. In Marx's era —'

'They were ever so benevolent,' Radziwill cut in.

'In Marx's era what he condemned was that the banks financed the construction of fledgling capitalism. Today they connive at its dismemberment. It's a cannibal feast.'

Slavko's small face looked pensive. 'In its original form, this loan would have dismembered my country.' His high forehead wrinkled with worry. 'The new proposal is . . . in this respect . . . better?'

Palmer refilled all their drinks. 'More open. These days publicity is everything. Most people see IUD as the Vatican bank. Willy-nilly, it sets a moral standard. For it to be caught in a criminal conspiracy diminishes all banking credibility. That's why it must be a pure, no-strings IUD loan, to make our friend here look like a benefactor, not a crook.'

Krevic fell silent, looking more worried than ever. 'But this is one instance. It cannot at a stroke undo the conspiracy. Next time, who knows?'

Palmer shrugged. 'Maybe I'm making a mistake, letting him off this easy. Maybe he's smarter than both of us put together and we've played into his hands. Blackmail is a complex art.' He turned to the archbishop.

Look at him, Palmer mused: smug. Pleased I'm running interference for his one-man catastrophes. He thinks he's got me. I think I've got him. Poor Slavko has to be a fast learner.

'Do we have a deal?'

'Do I have assurance the article is killed?'

'The second your release runs on the wire services.'

'Noon tomorrow?'

'Noon tomorrow.'

His Excellency's right hand shot out. 'Deal!'

Chapter Forty-Five

'I'll get you to the Milan airport,' Palmer promised His Excellency.

The archbishop didn't bother to look happy. There was no alternative. The idea was to get back to Rome so that he could issue the necessary press release.

They stood outside the garage that formed one of the underpinnings of the house. Ziggy had dry-polished the tiny white Peugeot 205 and was now working over the big VW combi minibus. The inside telephone rang. He put his polishing rags aside. 'Bun di.'

The archbishop's glance moved off into the distance where nearby mountain peaks seemed to form a granite open-air prison. It would take quite a while to rearrange the trap Palmer had sprung on him. And what of Ames' wild promises at Ciampino Airport? Tomorrow, wasn't it, the tenth of June, when he would strike?

Ziggy held the phone out to Palmer. 'I'm in Rome,' Curtis' voice announced. 'Listen closely.'

Father Bernardin reported at five sharp to the zecca. Cardinals came and went, consulting Huf. Finally, at half-past six, the small man with the close-cropped white beard opened the door and stared hard across the waiting room at Bernardin. 'What am I to do with you?' he asked.

'Eminence, you – '

'I addressed my question to God. At this point in your life, Bernardin, you are a non-person.' Huf's pale blue eyes watched the younger priest for a long time. Then: 'No decision has been made. My colleagues have convinced me ...' He stopped and sighed, an exhalation that seemed to come up from his boots. 'They have convinced me to consult with His Excellency Archbishop Radziwill. Unfortunately for you, Bernardin, His Excellency cannot be reached at the moment.'

'I know. I – '

'Silence.' Huf spoke the word with quiet calm. 'The moment he returns he is to call me. At any hour, day or night. Understand? Any hour!'

In Alex's native land there were hills like these he found around Lugano, sharp, acute angles, rarely over five hundred metres in height. There were dark, mysterious valleys, too, as acute as the surrounding peaks, no place for a farm, barely enough for a road that twisted and almost reversed itself. Darkness made it look all the more mysterious.

Alex glanced sideways at Grischka and Ivan, both tossing about on the heavy-laden jeep's hard seats, banging into each other. Their glances looked apprehensive as they stared out at the night. Alex smiled: a pair of clowns, these two. They had let him find the corpse of the guard Rocco for himself, as a joke.

Sacha, with her cat's diffidence, had not been amused, especially since the dead guard, lying wound down, had bled copiously over the weapons.

'His time would have been up soon enough,' Grischka explained. 'He was a heavy smoker.'

Alex had taken the journey from Rome at a prudent pace, never more than 100 kilometres an hour and using the jeep's two-wheel drive to conserve fuel. There had been no border search at Mendrisio. Now that all Europe was one market, border searches were a thing of the past. It was ten o'clock at night when they curved out of the Italian side of the lake across a well-lighted causeway to the Morcote side. The sky was bright with moonlight.

They would ignore Palmer's eyrie. They would now plunge into the tunnel beneath his peak and come out the other side. The moon had risen some time ago but clouds often obscured it. As they exited from the tunnel, before entering the city limits of Lugano, they would find a narrow road up the side of the peak of Agra Carona, next to Palmer's. The map showed endless hairpin curves and switchbacks.

Alex swung the wheel hard left on to the climbing road, braked and reached down for the lever to shift into four-wheel drive. 'When we get to the top, what do we do?' he asked.

Grischka cleared his throat. As the jeep slewed this way and that up the winding road, the cat on Alex's lap occasionally dug her front claws into his legs. He paid no attention to this, taking it as a sign of love.

'First we find you a nice takeoff brink,' Grischka began.

'Yes. Go on.'

'Then we load you. Will Rocco go with you?'

'Dump him where I take off from. Leave him a cigarette.'

'But when there is moonlight,' Ivan added. 'When we can be sure of moonlight, yes?'

'Exactly. Go on.'

'We don't wait,' Grischka picked up the catechism. 'We take the jeep down, back through the tunnel and up the road to Palmer's.'

'Slowly,' Ivan added. 'Without lights. Wary of passing traffic.'

'And no closer to the gate than fifty metres. He has that much of a range on his proximity sensors,' Grischka continued. 'A small copse of trees on the left will disguise our profile for the radar. We park and wait.'

'And watch,' Alex said. 'Watch the sky.'

The window that looked down from Fiona Campbell's apartment to the Via Sistina gave Bradford Ames only a cramped side glance at the world. 'I can as easily await the telephone call in my office,' he snapped.

'But I want to be with you.'

'Later. You've had your fuck.'

'You are so cruel.'

Ames stood, tall and naked, with the street lamp outside casting a yellowish sidelight on his elbow and ribs. He waggled his half-erect penis as if shaking off a last drop. 'Say guidbye to your maister,' he ordered her in his joke brogue.

Fiona, on her knees beside him, stroked the drooping member. It slowly responded. 'He's that sorry to say guidbye,' she murmured. 'Luik at him rise!'

He sank his fingers into her thick hair and yanked her to her feet. Then he tweaked her erect nipples, grinning at the sharp pain mirrored in her face. 'I'm not without a feeling heart, lass. If you've heard nothing by one in the morning, you have your master's permission to come to the office and help him wait.'

She watched him closely. 'This is an important night, is it?'

'The most. Could'y'nae tell?'

'It's to do with Switzerland, that I know.'

'And that's already too much.' With slow deliberation, he drew back his hand and struck her face once, twice. It shook her upper trunk and breasts.

She pressed her hand against the flaming skin of her cheek. 'Aye, maister, I've been naughty, have I?'

'When I have the time,' he said, his canines glittering in the streetlamp's yellow glare, 'my toothbrush will show you just how naughty you've been.'

The telephone rang. His eyes went wide. 'Too bloody soon,' he muttered, picking it up. 'Yes?'

The line went dead.

Curtis hung up the phone. He had made the call from a telephone off the lobby of the Hotel Eden.

Now he glanced around him to see if anyone were watching him. He got in the elevator. His best spot would be the penthouse bar, but it would close fairly soon, certainly by midnight.

When he reached the penthouse corridor it was, momentarily, empty of guests. He examined the lock on one of Ames' office doors, then disappeared around a corner to sort through his collection of lockpicks.

Every few minutes the clouds would drift enough to disclose the moon, three-quarters full. By its light, Alex had found the ideal brink. A fault in the underlying rock had split Agra Carona, leaving a sheer drop of several hundred metres on the side facing away from Palmer's eyrie.

As Grischka and Ivan finished assembling the hang glider, Alex checked his own kit, tools tucked in pockets, Grischka's electronic equipment belted in a small knapsack across his shoulder blades, weapons on inside holsters.

He had done a lot of gliding free of such added weight, always by day, when the sun created the strong updrafts necessary to launch and stay aloft. He knew that in summer any rockface that had heated during the day retained some heat at night. What he didn't know was whether now, near midnight, enough heat remained in the rock to sustain his takeoff.

Come to that, across these hills, did enough thermals exist at night to let him soar? It was not a question he could look up in a book. It required consultation with local glider pilots. But they were off limits. Too bad.

He knew he had the perfect mind for this job, not just the way he'd trained, but the way he was able, when leaping off into the unknown, not to let it bother him in advance. Just as, years ago, he had chosen the wrong career, the prospect could not be allowed to daunt him. Plenty of time to anguish over it if he dropped like a stone. No more assault, no more Alex. He would join Rocco. Too bad.

He frowned. 'Grischka,' he whispered. The breeze atop this peak was strong enough to ruffle his hair, a good sign. 'Grischka, take her.'

He handed over the small black cat. 'In her little nest in my backpack,' he said. 'Do it quickly before she understands what's happening.'

He watched Grischka stow the cat away and zip her safely inside her pocket faced with a net window. The cat began to mew soft complaints.

Alex consulted his wristwatch's phosphorescent dial. 'Ready?'

At the knife-sharp edge of the rock fault, Ivan and Grischka lifted the triangular black canvas sail, stretched on its aluminium poles. Alex fitted his body through webbing and grasped the crossbar brace with both hands. Together, the three young men back-tracked five or six yards from the cliff edge.

The moon came out. Alex took a deep breath. 'Release!'

They let the sail drop as he ran forward headlong

towards the edge. As he drove forward like a suicide, the sail picked up a vague puff of air. He catapulted over the edge into a breath-stopping drop down the side of Agra Carona, his body hanging from its taut webbing, forcing the sail to curve downward slightly at its farthest corners. Too bad.

For a moment he dropped. Then a lazy puff, warmer than the rest, buoyed him. He twisted the frame sharply into the thermal and glided off on a downward corkscrew around bleak rockface. He glanced ahead and saw the neighbouring peak where Palmer's house stood. He needed lift. Too bad. From this height he'd never rise high enough.

Alex hunched forward and sent the kite-like glider into a downward dive like a true suicide. Somewhere, soon, anywhere, but soon, there had to be an updraft.

The ground below, sharp boulders, was rushing up at him. In a few seconds it would be over. No more Alex. Too bad. He yanked the glider right, on instinct. He felt the beak-like front of his wing suddenly rise, lifting him in another graceful corkscrew, this time upwards. In a minute or two he had soared above both peaks. He could see the jeep, headlights switched off, making its way downhill.

Higher. Below him now Palmer's enclave seemed to wheel about, as if it were flying. Alex tried to spot the guest house he had seen so recently from the helicopter. Moonlight is always tricky. Behind that house lay the only open area where one might land without impaling oneself on small trees, bushes, or steel fenceposts. That area was far enough from fence-mounted sensors to avoid triggering them. Both the big house and the small one were dark at this late hour. Suddenly clouds obscured the moon.

Alex twisted into a wide downward spiral, stalling for time until he could see again. But he was dropping too quickly. He'd have to make a blind landing unless he could cheat another turn or two out of the thermals.

The clouds were leaving the face of the moon. He stared below him. The clearing was dead ahead. He warped his sail-like wing and dropped like a giant eagle, feet forward, legs braced to take the shock.

He hit the ground running and fell forward deliberately to collapse his wing. The impact snapped his chin shut on a mouthful of clover. Made it.

The bar at the Hotel Eden and the adjoining restaurant took their last orders. Curtis could delay matters no longer. He had already dawdled long enough. When Bradford Ames passed nearby and locked himself into his office, Curtis called for his bill. He paid cash to avoid leaving any kind of paper trail, and went to the bank of elevators. As he waited, he saw light under only one of the doors to Ames' offices.

He boarded an elevator and took it down one floor. He moved noiselessly until he found a back stairway. Earlier, after placing Ames at the apartment of Fiona Campbell, Curtis had let himself into Ames' office to place a mini-tap on the telephone.

He had spent a long, anxious wait wondering what was happening with Palmer and his party in Morcote. It was Palmer he should be in contact with, not Ames. Standing on the floor below, he wondered how easily he would be able to pick up the bug now that a thick masonry floor stood in the way. Curtis switched on his receiver and slowly dialled wavelengths.

'. . . Wouldn't even expect they've infiltrated yet,' Bradford Ames was saying. 'But their orders are to telephone the instant they take charge.'

Curtis moved back on to the stairway. It was a more secure place from which to eavesdrop. He heard Ames say: '. . . To phone me here. But in the excitement they may call you. Be sure to redirect them.'

'Aye, maister.'

Alex lay perfectly still, face down, covered by his sail-wing. The breeze had died to a faint whisper. The two Palmer houses were silent. For a moment he felt a wave of fatigue wash over him. He chewed at the clover between his teeth. It was not true tiredness, he realized, but only the relief of having done, successfully, what he had no idea would actually work.

Cautiously, he crawled backwards out of his loop-harness. This next business, he'd been assured, couldn't fail. The ten-year-old security system used EPROM chips specifically programmed for the job. As such, they had the weakness all EPROM chips were heir to: a static electrical overload burned them out instantly.

The security people had neglected to point out this weakness, of course. One day, to profit from an update, they might bring Palmer the bad news. But it would come tonight. Alex carried something very simple, a small fluorescent capacitor starter that shot a thousand volts across a gap.

Moving at a kind of infantry crawl that kept his head barely above ground level, and leaving the kite-glider behind him, he wriggled across expanses of grass and shrubbery. Inside the two houses, everyone slept.

Amazing how people fooled themselves. It was an easier life than constant vigilance. Bradford Ames had bought, from a corrupt employee of the security company, a wiring diagram. Once Alex found the inch-thick lead-in cable, he paused for a moment to calm his mind.

He stared at the open garage doors. Amazing how careless fools were. Inside stood the powerful white Peugeot 205. A perfect getaway car tonight. The pause steadied his nerves. He took a long breath.

He shoved the probes through the thick PVC coating until he felt them grate on braided copper wire inside. In the clear night air he heard the faint thrumming vibration of the jeep as it parked behind a copse of trees.

He pressed the capacitor button. The surge of power was soundless. But somewhere inside the house there was a muted snap, something very much like a slug from the great sleeve-silencer of an Ingram sub-machinegun, an instant of hornet-like vibration.

He pictured them all lying in bed, Palmer and his whore, Krevic and his whore. Ames had to be crazy if he thought Alex and his crew would kill off the women. Grischka and Ivan could have the older one. The tall, long-legged young one, Palmer's daughter, was reserved for Alex. It would be particularly sweet since he would have stolen her from Krevic, who would be tied up and forced to watch his whore do her tricks for Alex.

Alex stretched his taut leg muscles, easing tension. Tie up Krevic and Palmer as a captive audience for the mass rape of their women. Good opening, but better would be playing it reverse. Dripping, choking with semen, the two women would have to watch the killing of Palmer. A very good middle to the drama. There was no reason a capture and a killing had to be brute, silent acts of terror. They could also be choreographed artistically.

The nearest sensor sat atop a twelve-feet high cyclone fence post. Alex unlimbered his own Ingram M-10. If the sensor hadn't been blown, there would be an immediate need for rapid-fire agression.

Alex raised his hands over his head and gently clapped them, a small sound, no louder than the noise of an EPROM burnout. Nothing happened. No one awoke. Perhaps they stirred, Krevic feeling her long, slim body. A grin slowly split Alex's broad face.

Palmer slept. But his formidable ring of protection was breached. In a few moments, Alex would be inside, at the kitchen console that controlled the TV-posted entrance. From there he would swing open the gate and let in his tiny army of destruction.

And that would be that.

Chapter Forty-Six

Hunched forward on the concrete tread of the hotel stairway, Curtis held his interceptor radio to his ear, listening to crackle but no words from Bradford Ames' telephone. Then, a bit after midnight, he picked up an incoming call.

'Yes?' Ames said after a single ring.

'Inside,' a man's voice replied.

'Take care of P.'

'Of course.'

The line went dead. Curtis heard the elevator arrive at the floor above. He got to his feet, pocketing the small black instrument. Too bad he knew no prayers. Now was the time for one. And Rome was certainly not the place to say it.

As he started to leave he heard scuffling overhead. He raced up the stairs in time to see General Sforza and two of his men lead an elegant Bradford Ames, in handcuffs, to the elevator.

'See here! You know me, general!'

'Ah, my boy, so I do.'

'I've been ferrying all that cash. Ask Archbishop Radziwill.'

'Ah. A religious matter. In which we *never* interfere.'

*

With Fiona Campbell the general was more chivalrous. He sent two female officers to bring her in and prepare her as best as possible to identify some extremely nasty photographs of her father. Her obvious distress did not, however, prevent them from booking her on an open charge, as Ames had been. This meant they could be detained indefinitely. In Italy 'indefinitely' has no meaning whatsoever, since it covers anything from weeks to years. Or more.

Alex watched the jeep roll silently into the enclave and stop at the garage. Standing at the kitchen window, he beckoned Grischka and Ivan to enter the back way. As he let them in, he crossed his lips with an upraised forefinger. So far luck had been with them. But sleepers awake at the least opportune moments.

Did it matter? Whatever Palmer slept with, pistol, machinegun, he was outnumbered and outgunned. Even if the worst had happened and Krevic and his whore were in a bedroom here, not at the guest house, it still didn't matter.

These four bodies belong to me, Alex thought. I am their God. They live and die at my will. Prisoners awaiting torture, they no longer own themselves. All they have is the capacity to feel pain, humiliation and fear. And then die.

He hadn't felt such exhilaration for a long time, not since the new regime had outlawed his job. Someone had warned him once that such Godlike power was habit-forming, hardly a surprising discovery. But he had a more profound truth: why break the habit?

All these *special* people, these bankers and finance ministers and their dressed-up females, so special their fate had to be even more special: they lived simply to die for his pleasure.

Alex felt a flush of almost sexual pleasure heat his face. He led the other two to the foot of the stairs. With an upraised palm, he held them there while he mounted slowly, testing each step for a creak. At the top he turned right along the darkened corridor of bedroom doors. He summoned them up the stairs with a gesture of his hand.

He was breathing hard, as if a woman were playing with him. It had to be the end door beyond which lay his pleasure. The diagrams Ames had bought indicated that this master bedroom was the only one with a telephone.

Silence. Outside a wind had sprung up. A cat mewed. Alex spun around, finger on the Ingram M-10 trigger. Sacha produced one of those gravity-defying double leaps by which cats scale great heights. She leaped up on his belly, punched his chest with her forepaws, then sprang to his shoulder and snuggled down inside his vest. Alex stroked her head, then tucked it out of sight.

At the door to Palmer's bedroom he slipped off the Ingram's safety. The noise would be minimal, a few muffled hornet zaps, not enough to wake the others.

But enough to show Palmer his fate: torment and then death.

He brought out a small halogen flashlight. The rest of the moves were simple but fast. Open door, click on flash. He twisted the knob and eased the door open without a sound. He switched on the flash. Its hot yellow beams flared wildly on the huge king sized bed. Alex's trigger finger flexed.

The bed was empty.

He kicked open the door and snatched at the wall switch. The room flooded with light. No one. No prisoners waiting for torture.

He backed out of the room. 'Grischka! Ivan! That bastard Ames!' Alex shouted. 'Check the bedrooms. But I already know. The house is empty.'

The long corridor echoed with door slams as the three young men checked every bedroom and bath. 'The guest house,' Alex snapped. 'Be careful. They could be hiding there in wait.'

'The map shows also a wine cave,' Grischka reminded him.

'Yes, search there. No rush. We have been betrayed.'

At a quarter to one in the morning, the Via Veneto is quite deserted. If by this hour one hasn't made a contract for the night, there is no point in strolling. On the corner by one of the big newsstands Curtis waited. After a while, up the slight rise, the white VW combi appeared.

'Hop in,' Palmer said, swinging open the front

door. 'After six hours on the road, my bunch needs sleep.' He laughed slightly. 'If you hadn't tipped me off this afternoon, we'd be in much worse shape.'

'I tipped your pal, Colonel Staeli, too.'

Palmer grinned. 'Good old Swiss overkill.'

The archbishop, looking washed out, sat beside Eleanora on the bench behind the driver. Behind them Gerri snuggled up against her husband's shoulder. 'Where can I sleep all of you?' Curtis asked Palmer. 'Somewhere private.'

'Now that he's on the side of the angels,' Palmer said, 'His Excellency has remembered a secluded retreat house.'

'At the foot of the Janiculum,' His Excellency said in a tired voice. 'Just below the Regina Coeli prison.'

'Sounds terrific.'

'And it's shut up tight after eleven at night.'

Curtis turned back to face the archbishop. 'But one word from you . . .?'

'It's the Sisters of the Sanctitate. They run a Casa d'Ospitalitá'. He tapped Palmer's left shoulder. 'Get over to the Lungotevere. Then head south along the river to the Mazzini Bridge.'

Palmer swung out into the broad downward sweep of the Via Veneto. He glanced at Curtis. 'Well? What news?'

'You people alive. That's the news.'

Standing at the kitchen window, Alex tried to calm himself by brushing back Sacha's fur. He saw Grischka and Ivan leave the guest house, look at him

373

and pantomime their frustration. They were moving across the greensward toward the mouth of the wine cave.

Alex picked up the kitchen telephone and dialled the Rome number of Ames' office. He had a lot to unload on that nasty bungling traitor. On the first ring from the sky a monstrous voice bawled in Italian: 'Hands up! Drop your weapons!'

Alex dropped the phone and stared out the window at two Swiss Army helicopters hovering over them. Both carried blinding floodlights that bathed the knob of the hill in bluish-white glare.

Grischka made a run for it and dropped down into the declivity where the wine cave entrance stood. Ivan followed. Alex lost sight of them.

'Drop your weapons! Hands in the air!'

Two AK-47s opened fire on the helicopters in stuttering bursts of three. The army aircraft separated sideways like milkweed floss in a wind. One came in over the top of the cave spitting tracer bullets at an angle too obtuse.

Alex ducked down through the housekeeper's apartment. It had its own entrance around the corner from the garage, the only side of the house not baking in arc-like brilliance.

Someone, probably Grischka who was the better shot, managed to rip a volley of slugs through one of the floodlights. The noise was now deafening, helicopter rotors chopping and coughing, gear-whine rising in twin screams of anguish, AK-47 fire and the heavier .50 caliber machinegun barrage from the gunships.

Outside, Alex could smell the death stench of cordite. He edged his way around a corner and made a quick run for the tennis court hedges. Beyond, at the brink of Palmer's hill, was where he had first landed.

One of the gunships sent a rocket-propelled missile blast-roaring at the wine cave. It exploded somewhere near the door. For a moment all was silence. Goodbye Grischka, Alex thought, crawling along the base of the hedge, out of sight for the moment. Goodbye, Ivan. Clover brushed against his face. Too bad.

A feeble burst of AK-47 fire broke the silence and exploded the second floodlamp. In the abrupt darkness Alex snaked rapidly through the grass. He reached his hang glider, buttoned the Ingram inside his vest and grasped the main strut of his sail-wing.

One of the helicopters launched a brilliant white magnesium flare. The whole peak top stood out in stark relief like a stage set. Alex turned into the wind and began running. Feet still jigging, he lifted off and started a long series of swoops, sideways, spiralling downward. The technique was pure magic, starkly white in the magnesium flare. Then the helicopter gunships located him at the apex of two fiery flights of tracer bullets.

Chapter Forty-Seven

Father Bernardin had dozed off at midnight. But at two a.m. he could hear voices on the floor below. He pulled his battered robe around him and started down the stairs, determined to fend off burglars with his life.

The burglar in the leather jacket had opened the great vault set into the central ferro-concrete pillar of the building. The heavy, thick, round Diebold door, bristling with concentric vanadium steel and shiny bolts, hung open like a nightmare building of its own.

Deep inside the shelves were buried under bundles of money, more cash than any human should ever have seen. Bernardin almost cried out. Then he realized the burglar was Archbishop Radziwill. Two other men stood by the windows unable to peer inside the vault.

'Excuse my secrecy,' His Excellency called, swinging shut the vault door and bolting it. 'I had to be certain I could actually honour this surprise loan . . . forced on me.'

He sat at his keyboard. All this week, Bernardin thought, Guardia di Finanza trucks had delivered this vulgar glut of cash. How much of a surprise could such a loan be?

'Your Excellency?' he called out.

'How about ten billion? It's a sexier number for the press. Bernardin, make coffee.'

'But, sir, Cardinal Huf gave me orders.'

'Ah-ha!' Radziwill swung away from his monitor screen and glared at the young priest. 'Spit it out.'

'The moment you return, day or night, telephone him.'

The archbishop's pale, handsome face went dead for a moment, as if terminal fatigue had taken over. Then his eyes flashed. 'What've you been telling him?'

'Sir, his orders were to tell you to call him. Nothing more.'

'And you're nothing more than Huf's creature.' His Excellency sank back in his chair. 'Any hour day or night, is it?' He smiled maliciously. 'Let's see.'

He accessed a list on his computer screen and touched a key. In the silence they could hear the computer input the number to the telephone. The archbishop lifted the instrument to his ear. He glanced at Palmer and indicated a chair. 'Eminence,' he said at last. 'Radziwill a su disposizione.'

He sat in silence, listening. 'Now? I have people with me.' More silence. 'Relating to a loan matter in Eastern Europe? You are remarkably well informed. Bernardin has been working overtime.'

Hurt, as always, by his superior's taunts, Bernardin felt demeaned, held cheap. That had always been His Excellency's way. But for a computer person, Bernardin knew a lot about banking. He understood the perverse, paradoxical role of cash. Most Swiss, and

certainly Cardinal Huf, did. Cash was never to spend.
It was assets, held as a reserve. Against as much cash
as he had glimpsed in the vault, IUD could lend
eighty times more. Bernardin watched his superior
on the telephone with his sponsor, Cardinal Huf. The
new breed against the old. How sad Huf had to be
the antagonist.

The listening silence went on for a long time. 'Yes,
why not?' Radziwill hung up, his arm moving slowly
to replace the telephone, as if his mind had already
jumped far ahead to other, more engrossing matters.
Then, abruptly, he keyed another command to the
computer. Once again they could hear it transmit a
number to the telephone. 'Avanti, Carlo.' He hung
up. 'Bernardin?' He swung around in his chair. 'I
have always wondered exactly how you would try
to murder me. What is this business of a virus?'

'Sir, I beg of you. The cardinal has sealed my lips.'

His Excellency got to his feet. 'Woods, you and I
have a date.' He looked at his watch. 'It may be a
duel, so I need seconds.' He indicated Curtis and the
young priest. His slender body had taken on a sinister
kink, head thrust forward like a great bird facing an
attacker.

Palmer watched him. 'Huf is . . .?'

'One of the Prefetura. This man's protector.' His
glance raked past Bernardin. He drew himself up,
straightening his back. 'But I have my supporters
within the Prefetura. They have forced Huf to stay
his hand until he could speak with me. In the middle
of the night. Now.'

They seemed marooned in a sea of silence. A moment later the muffled purr of a limousine engine sounded. His Excellency looked out the window. 'Carlo.' His glance swung back to Palmer's face. 'Woods, are you with me?'

'Fight to the finish,' Palmer said, deadpan. 'Never give in.'

Westward from the centre of Rome the ancient thoroughfare called the Aurelia Antica leads straight, as old Roman roads do, an arrow-shot from the Trastevere through great green enclaves that surrounded the Villa Doria Pamphili.

The tall-sided black Rolls limousine surged swiftly along newer, more modern neighbourhoods, fast asleep, until it reached a rural landscape dotted with government short-wave aerials, country clubs and crumbling houses recently jerry-built of tufa, the soft sandstone that underlies much of the area. In some places these squatters' edifici abusivi, thrown together without permits on land of dubious ownership, shelter so many voters that local politicians lobby the government to grant squatters permanent residence. In other places great estates, like Cardinal Huf's Villa Vignona, remain untouched, hiding their Etruscan caves from tomb-robbers and insulating from the vulgar world dwellings of great charm.

Behind the chauffeur, the four men sat facing each other. In the hide-and-seek moonlight, Palmer's first glimpse of the Villa Vignona was brief. It stood atop a gentle slope overlooking groves of umbrella pines and needle-shaped cypresses. The Rolls juddered up an unpaved side road and stopped at the two white marble pillars of a gate.

A TV camera panned over to them as a lamp went on. The driveway was gravel, boxed by thick hedge-rows. The villa itself was invisible for five more minutes of driving. Then it reappeared in a sudden burst of moonlight, its great age betrayed by water reservoir, windmill and propane tanks behind it.

A little man who resembled Freud stood in a posture of expectation. 'Good morning,' Huf said in French-accented English. He ushered them into an entry hall about the size of half a tennis court. 'We'll be more private in the library,' he said, as if the villa were crowded with throngs.

Palmer could see portraits on the walls, great oil paintings in heavy gilt frames, gilded end tables against the green distemper of stucco, a bowl of dried flowers, a crucifix at the far end, endless shelves of old, well-kept books.

The library-proper had a fax machine in the corner and a computer station under a grey plastic cover. Curtis touched the plastic and examined the dust smear on his finger. The two Americans glanced at each other and traded meagre smiles.

Huf sat down behind a plain large desk with a black linoleum top. He waited, hands folded before him, glance lowered, for his congregation to find their pews. Only the archbishop seemed defiant, unwilling to acknowledge authority. Bernardin looked uneasy, almost guilty. Palmer and Curtis seemed more curious than anything else. But Radziwill tried his best to stare down his superior. Against lowered eyes, it just wasn't possible.

They seemed castaways on an island in the centre of a sea of utter silence, a trick perhaps of the night or, possibly, of the grave matter that had brought them together. Huf's bright blue eyes surveyed their faces one by one. Then he put on a pair of round-lensed glasses. 'I don't wish to make any mysteries, Radziwill. And I don't wish any mystification in return. Agreed?'

'Continue, Eminence.' The archbishop's voice sounded dry with fatigue and something else, close to contempt.

Huf's face froze at what was a clear rebuff. 'We have not been idle. It is possible – I stress possibility, not probability – that Sunday's forecast transmission was tainted with what is called a computer virus.'

'How could that be?' His Excellency demanded.

'All in good time. We have investigated, however superficially, the Eastern European loan proposal of a certain venture capital firm.' He stopped and pulled over to him a large, heavy, leather-bound ledger book. He paged through it. 'We have established this firm's connections with the underworld. We have examined its cooperation with IUD.' He paused, removed his glasses and closed the ledger with a hollow snap. 'We believe recent IUD activity to be tainted.'

'That word again.'

'We also,' Huf continued in his quiet voice, 'are

aware of a magazine article summarizing much of this, to which a contact in Berlin alerted us. It is timed to be issued when you address the bankers.'

Radziwill sat back slowly, cautiously in his chair. 'Father Bernardin?' Huf resumed. 'Explain the problem of the virus.'

The young priest stood up, as if in a classroom. 'It's a maze-solving fractal. It crossfiled into the IUD mainframe. I deleted it by reversal and can no longer find it anywhere in the mainframe memory. But it may have infected the Sunday forecast and been transmitted to subscriber databanks.'

'And what,' Radziwill demanded, 'has this to do with, as you put it, taint?'

Huf waved Bernardin back in his chair. 'They have all occurred under one roof, yours.' His mouth quirked in an odd half-smile, as if biting into a quince. 'We face a two-sided decision: that your supervision is slipshod or your judgement is tainted. But we do not have enough time. At any moment, if Bernardin is to be believed, we may face a disastrous decay of financial data worldwide.' He focused his pale, piercing glance on Radziwill. 'What the Prefetura requires is also two-fold. First, a solution to the virus problem. Second, your suggestions, archbishop, as to how to cleanse IUD.'

'This is quite monstrous.' His Excellency struck a note of fastidious concern, as if Huf had released a bucket of cockroaches on the floor. He avoided the cardinal's glance, gazing at the middle distance as if deep in sorrow. 'Quite beyond the norm of spiritual behaviour,' he went on, his tone growing surgically crisp. 'And quite destructive of the earning potential of IUD.'

Huf responded dryly: 'I hope I speak for the Prefetura when I say that the Holy See must try to do without tainted millions.'

Radziwill's laugh was dark and brief. 'Money has no smell,' he quoted. 'Has any Pontiff found fault with that motto?' When Huf didn't reply, he went on in that carefully emotionless, faintly disgusted tone: 'Has any Pontiff placed more demands on the Church? Has any Pontiff spent more, in this age of inflation?'

'It really isn't possible,' Huf said on a note of dry humour with that same sour half-smile, 'to transfer to His Holiness the guilt for your works.'

'You say this? When you of the Prefetura have an intimate knowledge of what has been going on since he took St Peter's throne?'

Palmer stirred in his chair. 'Cardinal Huf, Curtis and I are distinctly out of place here. Perhaps we can retire to another room till needed?'

'You are free to, of course. But as the source of this magazine article, Mr Palmer, we consider you central to the problem.' Huf turned back to the archbishop. 'A mobile Pontificate, an activist Pontiff expends funds more quickly, or perhaps I should say more openly, than one who shuns the world. Sometimes this appears from the outside to be unnecessary.'

'Naples,' Radziwill snapped. 'Nineteen-ninety.'

Huf nodded almost amicably. 'A perfect example, I grant you.'

'I beg your pardon?' Palmer asked.

Huf paced behind his desk and sat down. 'Italy's most troubled city, ravaged by earthquakes, disease, famine, drugs, squeezed under the heel of organised crime. To deny Naples a Papal visit would have been unacceptably cruel.'

Silence fell over them again. Huf stared at the closed ledger before him. When he spoke again, his voice had developed a slight edge to it, as if he could no longer speak with the judgement-free tones of an outside observer. 'Yes, prominent Neapolitans begged the Pontiff to use the visit's funds on medical care, food, clothing, shelter. Funds for a material lifeline, not a spiritual gesture.' The silence seemed to deepen. 'We were running at a deficit of thirty-three billion lire. His Holiness' five-day visit to Naples was budgeted very stringently at three billion. His Holiness had promised Naples a visit for many years. He intended to keep his promise.'

Radziwill's snicker was a shock. Everyone turned to him but his good-looking face was granite-still. Huf's reaction was to pull another leather-bound ledger on to his desk and begin paging through it. 'By the time the camorra had stolen thousands of benches and chairs along the parade routes, unleashed a wave of vandalism that wrecked altars, displays, arches, gardens, canopies and other way stations, forced us to use their contractors to clear the wreckage and build substitutes, the bill ended up as . . .' His finger went slowly down a neat book-keeper's list. 'Thirty billion lire, instead of three.' His pale blue eyes lifted to look at Palmer. 'Bad business, Mr Palmer, to double Vatican debt almost overnight?'

'But a promise is a promise,' Palmer said.

'Exactly.' Huf's penetrating glance shifted to the archbishop. 'That is why we demand so much of our more talented labourers in the vineyard of the Lord.' His tone iced the words with a rim of hoarfrost.

'But why not demand,' Radziwill snapped back, 'of His Holiness some moderation, some prudence in expenditure.'

Huf looked grave. 'Never.'

The library door creaked open and a small woman in a plain grey nightrobe, her hair hidden under a hastily wrapped turban, pushed a trolley inside. On it sat a steaming cast-aluminium coffee pot and five tiny espresso cups in their saucers, five spoons and an immense bowl of sugar with a hinged cover. The remarkable aroma of strong hot coffee pervaded the room.

'Grazie, Signora Frascá. Prende un caffé al Guidatore Carlo anche.'

Huf waited until she had closed the library door behind her. Then, as if passing among them with sacramental wine and wafers, he wheeled the cart to each man in turn, pouring a cup half full and waiting for him to add sugar. When he at last reached His Excellency the archbishop, Radziwill shook his head curtly. Huf took coffee. He sat back down behind his desk and his icy glance settled on the trolley, where a single unused cup remained. It had the effect of announcing a balloting in which the archbishop stood alone.

'We have discussed,' the cardinal said then, 'the, as it were, undiscussable subject of the Pontificate's budgetary limits. To sum up: there are none. Now,' he sipped his coffee and for the first time sat back in a relaxed posture, 'Archbishop Radziwill, let us hear your ideas for cleansing the IUD.'

Radziwill's voice went low. 'As to the virus, you would be better served to query its author, who sits here in this room. As for what you call the cleansing, it may take years. Most of the investments on our books are between five and ten years' duration. And one of our largest has just been made.'

Huf frowned, not at him but at Palmer. 'Is it not common practice, Mr Palmer, to sell investments from one financial institution to another?'

'Quite common.'

'Then would that not disinfect IUD's portfolio?'

Palmer glanced sideways at Radziwill. 'Not if the prospective buyer feels the deal is tainted. You would then have a problem unloading it to anyone.'

Huf snapped shut the heavy ledger before him. 'I must be frank,' he told the archbishop. 'I would have recommended to the Prefetura that you be granted leave in a retreat house. I would have recommended we, as Mr Palmer put it, unload your portfolio and start afresh. Now I see such an easy solution is impossible.' He finished his espresso and set the cup and saucer on top of the pile of ledgers. 'What I will now recommend is that you sell off every questionable investment without alarming the market. You will have no authority to make any new loans or investments. The Prefetura will supervise that work.'

His Excellency composed his face. 'I'm to be under house arrest, one hand tied behind my back. Is that it?'

Huf's white-fringed head shook from side to side as if in grudging admiration. 'I have seldom heard the matter put more accurately.'

Radziwill got to his feet, his slender frame kinked forward again. 'Eminence, under our common discipline I would, of course, obey. That doesn't prevent me from saying this will be the greatest mistake the Prefetura has ever made.'

Huf's white-bearded face looked both at ease and at peace. He turned to Palmer once again. 'An outside opinion?'

'Cardinal, I have known the archbishop half a century. He has one of the most experienced fiscal brains I have ever met. If he says this is a mistake, I would listen closely to his reasons.'

Radziwill flashed Palmer a sideways glance of gratitude. 'Eminence, ask him to describe the relationship of organised crime to the financial community.'

Huf's tart smile came and went. 'Can you, Mr Palmer?'

'What we call the mafia – it has other names like camorra, 'ndrangheta – is the high-risk, high-profit segment of the business establishment. It employs more people than any other multinational in the world. To get directly to the point, the mafia is also the largest source of cash flow on Earth.'

'And therefore we must deal with it,' Huf summarised in a dry voice. 'Several of my colleagues on the Prefetura hold similar opinions.'

'In fact,' Radziwill snapped, 'all of them but you.' His face grim until now, flared in a sardonic smile. 'When I report to the Prefetura an international financial victory that produces a geopolitical one, there will be hosannahs of joy. Eastern Europe, once more under the guidance and discipline of Mother Church. A major criminal network toppled into the dust.'

Huf looked numb. Bernardin crossed himself. 'Teddy,' Palmer groaned, 'you are *bad*. Is that a double or a triple cross?'

Huf looked wry. 'How unfortunate you are not a member of the Prefetura.'

'Is it too late for me?' Palmer joshed him.

Huf's eyes, sparkling with malice, swung sideways to Radziwill and went cold. 'Whereas, in His Excellency here, we have perfect credentials.' The remark seemed to echo in that great room of books.

'Eminence!' Bernardin cried out in a hollow echo of pain.

'Yes?'

'Please, Eminence, may I – ' He began to flounder. 'I ask to – '

'Yes?'

Face a shocked red, Bernardin seemed to get hold of himself. In a tight voice he blurted: 'May I beg the p-privilege of m-meeting with you afterwards?'

'Certainly.' Huf got to his feet. 'Gentlemen, we have had what the politicians call a frank exchange of views.'

Palmer chuckled. 'With the same results.' He stood up, too.

The cardinal turned to Radziwill. 'Be assured, archbishop, I do understand the importance of what you have promised. I trust you understand the importance of the Holy See being above suspicion.'

He rounded his desk, a small, grizzled man with a worried look. He shook Palmer's hand. Radziwill's he ignored. Outside the Villa Vignona the sky to the east had that nacreous shimmer of pearly grey that comes some time before dawn. The long black Rolls surged forward along the hedged driveway and back to Rome.

In the library Cardinal Huf grunted softly as he sat down in the chair Curtis had vacated. 'What do you have to tell me, my son?'

'Eminence, it is only perhaps a fantasy.'

'Tell me.'

'Eminence, they will kill you.'

'They?'

'The mafia,' he said. Then, a burst: 'The Prefetura!'

'Ah.' Huf settled back in the straight chair. 'I am seventy-seven years old, Bernardin. I lead a very secure life here at Villa Vignona. A driver and a guard take me to and from Vatican City each day. I am quite safe.'

'B-but – !'

'I saw how it struck you, a few moments ago, when you could hardly speak and hardly not speak. It does you credit. I believe you may even be right. I know Radziwill is correct when he says I alone on the Prefetura hold the views I do.'

'But that means yours is the only voice to be raised.'

'Possibly. Probably.'

'And must therefore be choked off.'

The great silence that lay around them like a vast inland sea now seemed to unfold in their midst. Bernardin almost reached out to touch him, shake him, warn him again. Seeing him so easy with the forecast of death filled the young priest's heart with terror.

'Eminence?'

'Bernardin, no one of us is entitled to any more of God's protection than any other. And even the mafia exists under God.'

'That's not the way I – '

'Because you're not seventy-seven.' The cardinal sighed. 'I have no idea whether it is better to know the death God has prepared, or to let it arrive as a surprise. Please ask Signora Frascá to call you a cab.' He sighed and settled himself against the hard-backed chair, easing the pain in his hips and lower back. 'I shall be fine. Oh, one thing.' His bright blue eyes opened wide. 'You were to do something about the virus?'

'Yes, Eminence?'

'I have made a decision. Do nothing.'

'But – '

'Sometimes, Bernardin, to do nothing . . .' For the first time his smile seemed absolutely pleased, '. . . is the greatest revenge.'

Epilogue September, 1994

On Morcote's heights the retreat of an autumnal night left a morning chill. Instead of getting up at once, Palmer lay there beside Eleanora and thought chill, autumnal thoughts. His youth and his prime had ended. As of last night he was now well into the life's third third, winter.

Gerri's excited telephone call had made all the difference. In February, she announced breathlessly, she would produce Palmer's first grandchild.

Lying in bed, Palmer made a curious face, wry and lopsided. He'd have to call old Huf this morning and give him the news, then get hold of Curtis in Paris. Of the two, only Huf was old enough to appreciate the Grampaw Syndrome. One trusted he had no grandchildren of his own, of course.

They had become great phone pals, he and the cardinal. The summer had been spent that way, Palmer reporting grapevine gleanings of IUD-virus disasters. His own UBCO had lost a fifth of its property department, mortgages and all. Half of Chase's securities division had evaporated. Both of the German insurance biggies found 14 per cent of their policies turned to gibberish. Britain's Inland Revenue had lost every scrap of tax file on 1.9 million Britons.

Palmer grinned at the sly, hit-and-run manner of

Father Bernardin's virus and the glee with which Cardinal Huf welcomed and documented each disaster. He told his colleagues he was preparing letters to each of the 100 IUD forecast subscribers, apologizing for the virus and hoping they would be charitable enough not to sue to recover damages. This, of course, would alert everyone to the source of their software disasters. The air would be thick with lawsuits, the end of IUD and its archbishop. But Huf would never send the letters. The mere mention of them would be his life insurance policy.

Still grinning, Palmer went to the bathroom. He stared at his unshaven face. It sort of went with his ratty seersucker Grampaw robe and his little black cat. Oh, yes, she'd come back and made herself right at home with the caged tiger.

Downstairs he switched on the coffee-maker as he tuned in a morning TV news round up from CNN by satellite. '. . . no further reports on the violence in Soweto, Johannesberg. Thirty-one reported dead, but . . .' The CNN announcer blandly watched an almost unseen hand lay a slip of paper on the desk before him. Glancing down, he read: 'This just in from Rome, where a disastrous fire has destroyed the suburban villa and priceless library of one of the inner circle of Vatican curia. The bodies of Cardinal Aloys Huf and his housekeeper, Signora Concetta Frascá, were recovered earlier this morning. In the world of sports, final games in all US baseball leagues got under way this week as top teams battled towards the World Series in – '

Palmer switched off the TV. His hearbeat had shot up alarmingly. Putting the almost full mug of coffee down, his hand shook hot brown liquid all over his fingers. Two felt scalded but he paid no attention. His hand went to his left breast, where with burned fingers he tried to cauterize Death. Slowly, mournfully, it eased. No, said Death: only Huf this time, not you, sinner.

But, Jesus, the nerve of those bastards! In his own villa! Burning the library! Those one hundred letters had to be real. And now ashes. Palmer arose, a tall, thin, angry figure in a robe now spotted with brownish stains.

And Teddy Radziwill lived on.

By eleven the shock had gone through rage and into grief. He watched Eleanora paint his fingers with egg-white she kept in the refrigerator for burns. As a coating dried, she painted on another coat. The pain of the burn went away.

The little black cat sat on his lap. She sniffed his fingers as they were bound with gauze. Eleanora had christened her Spot, because of her white bib, not knowing it was a dog's name. Palmer found this funny, but not this morning.

'I suppose,' Eleanora said, 'the funeral will be back in his home village?'

'Cardinal Huf?' He shrugged into his running jacket. 'I don't know. I'd call Father Bernardin but he's no longer at the Vatican.'

'Why not?'

He gave her a grim smile. 'They offered to let him

teach third-graders arithmetic in his home town, Huf's home town, and he jumped at the chance.' He held up his two fingers, bandaged into one. 'Nice work. Good as new.' He kissed her on the mouth and rubbed Spot's head. 'Back in an hour.'

The run down, with Ziggy plodding on ahead of him, brought them in fifteen minutes to the lakeside snack bar. Herr Bartki opened two small bottles of mineral water. 'You heard of Cardinal Huf's death?' Palmer asked, sipping his drink.

Both Ziggy and Bartki looked grave. 'We Swiss have always been so proud of the cardinal. One of our own,' Bartki said.

Ziggy growled: 'Not many Swiss in that gang of Vatican paisani.'

'Your hand?' Bartki asked.

'Nothing.' Palmer glanced at Ziggy, who nodded. 'Arrivederci.'

He started the dash back up the road as if to show how well he contrasted with dead Huf, bandaged hand or not. Half way up he passed the bench where he often rested. A white VW combi van beeped behind him. He almost panicked, but not quite. He knew Ziggy wasn't driving the van. Ziggy was, in fact, paused a few metres ahead of him, hand shoved inside his jacket for his automatic.

Then Palmer saw the orange-and-purple logo of SwisPres courier service on the side of the combi. 'Che c'é?' he demanded.

'Per il Dottore Palmer. Sopranotte da Roma.'

The driver got out and extended his clipboard and

a pencil. Once Palmer had signed the driver opened the rear of his van and brought out a corrugated SwisPres carton, resplendent in orange and purple. Palmer opened the carton top. There they stood, large envelopes bearing the Vatican's Prefetura seal in gold and black, each addressed to a different corporation, bank or governmental agency all over the world. Without counting, Palmer knew there were precisely 100 of them.

Curtis walked off the plane from Paris with a sense of *déjà vu*. Once again it was midnight. Once again it was Mulhouse, concealed airport for Basel. Once again he was meeting Palmer. But no one was waiting in the deserted terminal.

Curtis hefted his black overnight case and walked out past non-existent customs officers via the exit marked, 'SUISSE'. The Basel bus was waiting for other passengers. No private cars were parked nearby.

He wondered what had gone wrong. The plane was its usual half hour late. But Palmer had already warned him that might be the case. He'd telephoned him in Paris this noon, one of his usual do-or-die last-minute requests.

'It's something I can't do by myself,' he explained. 'And I don't want to involve Eleanora.'

'I thought you'd given up this stuff.'

'Yes or no?'

Well, hell, Curtis reminded himself now; it was always yes, wasn't it? He watched the bus pull away with its load of five tired-looking passengers. He was alone. The night sky was dark. He recalled the June sky of 1992 with its thousands of stars. September, two years later, was like standing at the bottom of a mine shaft.

In the distance, two non-French car headlights bore down on the terminal. Used to the normal amberish tint, Curtis watched the auto, hoping it would reveal itself as Eleanora's Lugano-registered small Peugeot 205 GTI 1.9. Instead Palmer's big white VW combi slowed for a U-turn and the passenger door swung open. 'Hop in. Fast!'

Palmer gunned the engine and the hefty vehicle shot off toward town again. 'What *is* it with you?' Curtis demanded. 'What happened to a full stop, hullo, how are you, please get in, you're looking well?'

'I'm in a sort of spot,' Palmer admitted. 'Good of you to come.'

'What kind of spot?' Curtis peered at the older man's face, vaguely lit by dashboard lamps. 'You look like home-made shit. What's with the bandage?'

Palmer kept glancing at his rear-view mirrors. 'I had a shock on the morning TV news. Cardinal Huf? You remember?'

'Nice old guy.'

'He and his housekeeper at the Villa Vignona. The propane tank in the rear of the house blew them sky-high. Both dead.'

'Those bastards never let up, do they?'

'He spent the summer preparing letters to each of the IUD forecast subscribers, explaining what had happened.'

'Too late now, huh?'

Palmer's eyes kept sweeping left and right to each outside rear-view mirror. There was no other car on the road. Far ahead the taillights of the bus moved ever closer to Basel along this fenced-in corridor. To the right, by a clump of oleander bushes, Curtis recognized the place where the 1992 takeout had been staged and then so sanitized that not even a spent shell remained.

'Not quite,' Palmer said then in a tone so crackling dry that he swallowed to relieve the tension. 'A lot's happened over the summer.' He glanced at the speedometer and slowed the van to a rattling 120 kilometres an hour. 'By the fateful fifteenth of June there'd been mass flight. You to Paris, Gerri to her in-laws, Teddy to some be-yachted widow to let the dust settle.'

'Nothing went wrong with that no-strings loan to Krevic?'

'It's holding firm. And he cancelled his speech to the bankers.' Palmer's glance kept flickering toward the mirrors. 'As for Huf, around lunchtime today SwisPres delivered one hundred signed, witnessed and fully addressed letters of confession.'

'Hey! Terrific!'

'I sent Ziggy into town in the Peugeot 205 with his fingers bandaged and dark glasses on his face. He was supposed to be mailing the stuff in Lugano.'

Palmer twitched his head sideways to indicate the rear of the combi. 'It's actually in the back of the van. Switzerland has always had a problem the further south it stretches. Lugano's too Italianate. The goddamned Post Office was staked out, half a dozen hard guys. Ziggy picked up a tail and as far as I know he's still leading it a merry chase all over southern Switzerland.' Palmer chuckled, but not with mirth. 'I got Colonel Staeli to promise that if I got the envelopes to the Basel Post Office, he'd guarantee they got mailed.' Ahead the bus's taillights began to widen.

Palmer slowed the van. He glared at the darkness. A traffic intersection showed. The bus stopped at a red light. 'There', Palmer muttered, indicating a short black 190 Mercedes sedan with three men in it.

'There what?' Curtis demanded.

'You carrying anything?'

'A gun? Of course not.'

'Swell. Hold tight.'

Palmer revved the van hard, shifted into second and shot around the side of the bus, using it as a shield. The van streaked off along the Flughafen-strasse toward the centre of Basel.

Curtis watched the right rear mirror. 'Nobody is following. Nobody at all, you paranoid person. Oh. Wait.' The black 190 surged past the bus and started gaining on them. 'Sorry.'

'Even paranoids get apologies,' Palmer observed.

'What do we do now, coach?'

Palmer tramped on the gas pedal. 'After Kannenfeld Park on the right there's a three-way split. You strapped in?'

The white van juddered wildly as it rammed over streetcar tracks half buried in pavement. Behind them the pursuing Mercedes switched on blinding brights.

'I'll feint left as if I'm crossing the Rhine.' Palmer's voice had taken on a hoarse note of excitement. 'As we hit the three-way, I'll do a sharp right. It's the ring road to the station. Tense up.'

Behind them, in second gear, the black car howled like a wild animal. The three-way crossing loomed ahead. Palmer let up on the accelerator enough to bring the black car almost on to his bumper. He veered left towards the Johanniter bridge. The Mercedes followed. Curtis clenched his teeth and hung on. Suddenly the van screamed in pain as Palmer jumped it sideways, skidding across steel tracks in a sharp right-hand screech. Rocking insanely, the VW combi shuddered as Palmer put it into a quick left-hand twist. Ahead the long road to the station led straight as a yardstick.

Behind them the Mercedes, wrong-footed, produced a series of high tyre whines as it moaned into a U-turn. A six-wheeled truck, bearing the emblem of a Basel papermaking company, hit its brakes. It's air-horns hooted loudly. It wasn't fast enough to keep the Mercedes from taking out its own left headlight as it swerved about and roared on.

Like a wounded, one-eyed beast of prey, it howled after the disappearing taillights of the white van.

Jamming down hard on the gas pedal, Palmer forced the combi to leap at crossings.

The neighbourhood began to blur. The dark night seemed to isolate the two vehicles. Around them Basel slept, giving its usual imitation of a sleepy college town.

Then an auto coming from a sidestreet, thinking it had the green, stuck with terror in their path.

'Why aren't you in bed?' Palmer snarled, racking the van sideways on two wheels to sideslip the stalled vehicle. His face had set in a kind of carved mask, the hollows under his cheekbones as sharp as if cut by a chisel. 'Reach behind you.' His voice had a deep tremor to it, as if he and not the engine were driving the car forward.

'SwisPres carton.' Curtis reached for it.

'This road we're on starts curving left as it reaches the Bahnhof.'

'The Amazing Curtis does the flying-leap-from-moving-car?'

Glancing in the mirrors, both of them saw the one-eyed car looming nearer. 'I'll slow down as much as I can. Run that carton to the Post Office at the east end of the railroad station. Staeli's there. Get all the envelopes registered and return-receipt tagged. I'll keep them chasing me as long as I can.'

'For this I left Paris, City of Light?'

'Get ready!'

The high van tilted dangerously as it swerved left. Curtis hit the faint patch of grass, carton tucked into his acrobat's gut, and rolled twice like a tumbler.

Then he flattened as the black, one-eyed Mercedes rounded the corner on Palmer's tail. He saw a man in the back seat. He seemed to have a walkie-talkie in his hand, its extended antenna glinting palely in the dark night.

Typical Palmer improvisation. A hundred letters to register and only French money to do it. Do they take American Express?

The ape with the walkie-talkie. He'll be in touch with others, Curtis reminded himself. There are always others. That, after all, was what walkie-talkies were for.

The Amazing Curtis: right place at the right time. He started running fast.

As it left the Bahnhof the white VW van swerved on to the normally busy St Alban Graben. This time the street held only the one-eyed Mercedes, engine moaning with blood-anxiousness, inching closer behind the van.

The two vehicles roared past the courtyard of the art museum where a Hannah Kurd sculpture of Palmer's three children stood. North towards the Rhine Palmer could see the empty span of the Wettstein bridge. He slowed.

At the intersection of Dufour, he slammed on his brakes with a horrid snarl of tormented rubber. The Mercedes plunged headlong into the rear of the combi, blinding itself.

Hot steam hissed out of the crumpled radiator. Palmer rammed down into low-gear and heard his tyres bite as he manhandled the white van loose and forward. The hefty vehicle jumped ahead towards the rise of the bridge. Behind him the stutter of machinegun fire sounded like a street jackhammer. Palmer could feel the heat rising inside him like lava.

'*Shoot* me?' Almost blind with rage he whipped the van in an insane U-turn that nearly toppled it. Ahead lay the museum courtyard and statue. 'Kill Huf and shoot *me*?' he screamed.

He hit the Merc face to face at thirty kilometres an hour. The smash was soul-satisfying. There seemed to be only two men, one with a pump-action riot gun, the other with an Uzi yammering bullets at him.

The recoil of the black car smashed them both face-first on to the pavement. Palmer paused for a moment, looking down at the wreckage which lay around him since the combi's engine sat further back inside the vehicle.

He reversed. This time he fed gas slowly, hoping everything was still intact. The VW van parted company reluctantly. By its tilt, Palmer realised he'd blown a front tyre. He hiphopped the van on one steel rim, shooting sparks. At the Bahnhof Post Office he saw two men running off with an orange and lavender carton. A dark brown station wagon hustled them away.

Staeli ran out, gesturing to a nearby police car. It started in pursuit, siren whining. Staeli paused, held his automatic in both hands and pumped bullets after the station wagon. Too late, too far. He saw

Palmer's van approaching, humping along like a man with a crutch that shot sparks.

'Dear old Basel,' the colonel shouted. 'More like Italy every day.'

Palmer wrenched open the buckled rear door of the combi. A moment later he was running inside the Post Office.

Curtis lay on the floor, a trickle of blood from scalp to mouth. Someone had folded a postal jacket under his head. Someone else was tilting a plastic glass of water to his lips.

Palmer bent over him. 'You OK?'

'Does it look like it? They got the goddamned envelopes.'

Palmer produced another orange and lavender carton. 'Dummy envelopes. Not these.' He handed them over the counter. 'Grüss Gott. Sprechen sie Englisch, bitte?'

'But,' Palmer told Staeli on the way home from Basel, 'each letter was slightly different. Only the gist was the same. The old fellow did a great job.'

'That's the end of Archbishop Radziwill. Guaranteed.'

Palmer saw Herr Bartki's little snack bar go past as Staeli's Porsche ate up the steep road to home. Palmer looked back at Curtis, stretched out sideways on the tiny seat. 'How y'doing?'

'Feeling puffed-up. Finally, at long last, we win.' Curtis' complexion, pale with shock, looked ghastly. 'Do you realize that? We win!'

'The evanescent flush of victory.'

'Will it keep you quiet?' Curtis demanded.

Palmer was silent for a while, examining Curtis' face. 'Kiddo, mailing those letters was my last act. No more fight to the finish. It's finished. I'm a spectator, honest.'

'Promise?'

'I'm gittin' old, sonny. Gonna set a spell n'pet'm'cat.'

Curtis laughed shakily. 'Hey, Grampaw. It's about time.'

A Selected List of Fiction Available from Mandarin

While every effort is made to keep prices low, it is sometimes necessary to increase prices at short notice. Mandarin Paperbacks reserves the right to show new retail prices on covers which may differ from those previously advertised in the text or elsewhere.

The prices shown below were correct at the time of going to press.

☐	7493 1352 8	**The Queen and I**	Sue Townsend	£4.99
☐	7493 0540 1	**The Liar**	Stephen Fry	£4.99
☐	7493 1132 0	**Arrivals and Departures**	Lesley Thomas	£4.99
☐	7493 0381 6	**Loves and Journeys of Revolving Jones**	Leslie Thomas	£4.99
☐	7493 0942 3	**Silence of the Lambs**	Thomas Harris	£4.99
☐	7493 0946 6	**The Godfather**	Mario Puzo	£4.99
☐	7493 1561 X	**Fear of Flying**	Erica Jong	£4.99
☐	7493 1221 1	**The Power of One**	Bryce Courtney	£4.99
☐	7493 0576 2	**Tandia**	Bryce Courtney	£5.99
☐	7493 0563 0	**Kill the Lights**	Simon Williams	£4.99
☐	7493 1319 6	**Air and Angels**	Susan Hill	£4.99
☐	7493 1477 X	**The Name of the Rose**	Umberto Eco	£4.99
☐	7493 0896 6	**The Stand-in**	Deborah Moggach	£4.99
☐	7493 0581 9	**Daddy's Girls**	Zoe Fairbairns	£4.99

All these books are available at your bookshop or newsagent, or can be ordered direct from the address below. Just tick the titles you want and fill in the form below.

Cash Sales Department, PO Box 5, Rushden, Northants NN10 6YX.
Fax: 0933 410321 : Phone 0933 410511.

Please send cheque, payable to 'Reed Book Services Ltd.', or postal order for purchase price quoted and allow the following for postage and packing:

£1.00 for the first book. 50p for the second; **FREE POSTAGE AND PACKING FOR THREE BOOKS OR MORE PER ORDER.**

NAME (Block letters) ....

ADDRESS ....

....

☐ I enclose my remittance for ....

☐ I wish to pay by Access/Visa Card Number ⬚⬚⬚⬚⬚⬚⬚⬚⬚⬚⬚⬚⬚⬚⬚⬚

Expiry Date ⬚⬚⬚⬚

Signature ....

Please quote our reference: MAND